Maureen Duffy published her f
1962. She is the author of a L
and *Londoners*, and has written
and Aphra Behn. Her most rece
was longlisted for the Booker Prize.

For automatic updates on Maureen Duffy visit
harperperennial.co.uk and register for AuthorTracker.

From the reviews of *Alchemy*:

'A hugely absorbing read . . . page-turning adventure. Jade's voice is wonderfully achieved and Duffy brilliantly charts a search for identity'
Independent

'Packed with wit and wisdom'
Daily Telegraph

'Erudite and entertaining. Jade's pacy narrative is cut with Amyntas's restrained, elegant prose, and Duffy deftly handles the movement between two worlds, four centuries apart. Her range of cultural reference is dazzling'
Literary Review

'Riveting . . . blending passion, wit, and witchcraft to sparkling effect'
Daily Mail

'A fascinating coda to the history of the twentieth-century politically engaged novel . . . a novel that bristles with ideas'
Sunday Times

'A novel of high emotion and devious stratagems . . . I read avidly to the (literally) incendiary close'
Spectator

'Duffy writes lyrically and convincingly'
Sunday Independent

By the same author

MAUREEN DUFFY

Alchemy

HARPER PERENNIAL

London, New York, Toronto and Sydney

Harper Perennial
An imprint of HarperCollins*Publishers*
77-85 Fulham Palace Road
Hammersmith
London W6 8JB

www.harperperennial.co.uk

This edition published by Harper Perennial 2005

2

First published in Great Britain in 2004 by Fourth Estate

A catalogue record for this book is available from the British Library

ISBN 0-00-714966-2

Set in Adobe Caslon by
Palimpsest Book Production Limited, Polmont, Stirlingshire

Printed and bound in Great Britain by
Clays Ltd, St Ives plc

I'm sitting with my feet up on the desk pretending to be Philip Marlowe when the phone rings. Marlowe's still the best when the phone hasn't rung for days and the overdraft's fast growing its fungoid web over the bank balance. Marlowe's cool. I know Warshawski's more my century. I ought to feel most at home with her but it's Marlowe when the going gets tough. There's just one problem though with my impersonation. By now I should have a tray full of dead butts. But I never learned how to inhale when we all tried it out in break at thirteen, behind the kitchen block where the smoke wouldn't notice. And he was older than my mid thirties too. Forty at least; that was how Bogey played him anyway and he was the definitive.

'Is that Lost Causes?' The voice is light, male, what used to be called 'cultured'.

'It is.'

'Do you do tribunals? Employment disputes?'

I do anything but I don't say so. 'Would you be applying for legal aid?'

'That won't be necessary. Will you represent me?'

'I need to see clients before I commit myself.'

'Who am I speaking to? Would it be you taking my case?'

'My name is Green, Jade Green. We'd better make an appointment Mr . . . ?'

'Dr Gilbert, Adrian Gilbert. I feel . . . if it could be as early as possible.'

'Is tomorrow too soon?' I try to keep any eagerness out of my voice.

'Not at all. That will suit me very well.'

'Ten o'clock then?'

'Excellent.'

'Just tell me who the plaintiff is?'

'Defendant. The defendant is the University of Wessex. Till tomorrow,' and he's gone.

While he was speaking I'd opened a case file under his name and then this second one. I keep two files: the first I let the client see and the other is for myself, encrypted so that, in theory, only I have access, except that any twelve-year-old hacker could probably be into it quick as a traditional cat burglar up a drainpipe.

Next I run a check on him. Nothing in criminal listings. Nothing in the medical file. Not that sort of a doctor then or at least not accredited. Idly I try a general search by name. And bingo. 'Adrian Gilbert. Died 1604.' Oh great, 'Uterine brother to Sir Walter Raleigh.' So my guy is either an impostor or a fantasist.

I try the University of Wessex. I've never heard of it but I see it has its own website, the minimum requirement for existence nowadays, as a validation, a sure sign that you're in business and up there with the big boys. Founded 1999. Not redbrick. Not even old poly. A private Thatcherite-style endowment, on the site of a former teacher training college. On the fringes of a London dormitory that might just qualify it for the Wessex brand. A 'uni' only in name. My intellectual snobbery is showing. We are the last generation who can afford it. Who am I to judge now, in these shapeshifting days?

Wessex campus is split between several sites. They show us a picture of the chapel. Nineteenth-century basilica style, a brick rotunda that must have been part of the original college, dedicated to St Walburgha. A fast train service to London every half hour: commutable. A global pharmaceutical giant has its base in the town and helps to fund the science faculty. Wessex offers the usual mishmash of courses, from artificial intelligence to sports tourism, boasting of its something for everyone policy. I wonder which of these Dr Adrian Gilbert fits into. I scroll through the list of subjects but it doesn't name the teaching staff. Just as I'm about to click off I spot theology almost at the end of the line, with only tourism and youth studies tagging along behind. It stands out in its long gown and Geneva bands like silk bloomers among the Knickerbox flimsies. Well, tomorrow I'll find out. It's time to change into my leathers, get my boots on, helmet, gloves and wheel out the bike for my evening delivery. If Dr Adrian Gilbert could see me now would he be impressed or would he want to withdraw his case?

The Chinese takeaway I deliver for is a small family business in a quiet suburb. When their only son decided to try his luck in Australia they lost their errand boy. 'Why,' I asked when I'd been there a couple of months, 'why me?' There must have been plenty of young immigrants, students even, from Hong Kong families applying for the job in *Loot*. Mr Gao's pale face with its delta of wrinkles had smiled fleetingly. 'You are not Chinese; you are girl. There are many bad people run Chinese takeaway delivery. Deliver drugs, demand money. They don't trouble you English girl.'

I found it hard to believe the triads had moved in on carriers of egg fried rice and bean curd but if Mr Gao thought so it was enough. They were a quiet close family, apart from Tommy who got away. Mr and Mrs Gao cook in the steaming, succulent kitchen behind, with a clashing of woks and metal pans. Mary takes the orders in the shop and over the phone. She's shy and plain. Probably she would have liked to marry and have children but who is there for her to meet in Streatham Hill, unless a visiting cousin? I flirt with her a little when I call for my orders but I don't think she understands. She ducks her head and smiles at me under her deep fringe, shadowing the liquorice pupils which are her only claim to attraction. As a young girl she must have had acne that's left her skin lumpy and pitted. Sometimes I imagine putting my lips to it and saying: 'It's okay; you're beautiful.' At the end of my stint she hands me my brown paper carrier with the little silver oblong dishes under their cardboard caps that hold my freebie supper. Every night there's something different so that I'm never sated. Mary always remembers what I've had the night before.

I didn't mean to put all this in, even for my eyes only. The program asks me if I want to save it when I try to shut down. The ghost in the machine prompts us all the time to consider our own motives, our needs, our desires. If you don't save, all will be lost. And yet it can always be found. Confiscated by the police, the computer gives up its secrets like any prisoner singing under the lash, rack, thumbscrew, electric prod, Chinese water torture. So why shouldn't I save it just for myself? What have I got to hide?

Dr Gilbert buzzes the intercom on the dot of ten, before I've even got my feet up. My office is home as well as workplace but he isn't to know that yet. Behind the desk is a partition with a door in it that leads to the kitchen, shower room and my student-style bedsit. Originally a warehouse, it was converted at the end of the nineties, leaving exposed minimalist steel girders and yellow London Brick walls. In its own way it's related to the Wessex campus. Gilbert should feel at home. I tell him to come up. As yet there's no lift, only stone steps and iron banisters.

When he puts his head round the door I see he's a youngish Dr Who, collar-length brown hair, bow tie and granny glasses. As I get up he comes forward putting out a hand of slim manicured fingers.

'I'm very grateful to you for seeing me so soon.'

'Have a chair. Would you like a coffee?'

'If it's not too much trouble.'

'Not at all.' I go over to the filter machine where the glass goldfish bowl is gently seething. 'Milk, sugar?'

'Just milk thank you.'

I turn back from my coffee maker with our steaming cups. I can see he's 'all of a twitch', as my mother would say. I'm afraid he might drop the cup and scald himself but he gets it safely down on my desk. 'Did you find me easily, the office I mean?' I'm trying to reassure him, to give him time to gather his wits. I guess he's not used to the paraphernalia of the law.

'I looked it up in the A–Z. I used to know London quite well but you get out of the habit . . .'

I open the top drawer of my desk and take out pad and pen. 'I'll need to make some notes.'

'Of course. Where shall I begin?'

'Tell me first about you. Date of birth, full name, address.'

The recitation of these simple facts steadies him. I could put them straight into my laptop of course but this sometimes frightens people, especially older people and Gilbert comes into that category though he's only forty-nine. It's more a cast of mind.

He takes me methodically through his degree and previous employment, before we get to Wessex and the immediate problem.

'I have been accused by a small group of students of trying to corrupt their minds by teaching Satanism and perversion.'

Long ago when I started in independent practice I wanted to put up a favourite cartoon of mine showing the inside of a confessional box, with a monk leaning forward to listen to the supplicant on the other side of the grille and a sign above the monk's head which reads: 'Do not sound too surprised.'

'Dangerous allegations.'

'Very dangerous. I was summoned before the dean and disciplinary council. It was the students' word against mine. They were believed. I was suspended and sacked.'

'Sacked?'

'I was on a short-term contract. When my first suspension ran out I expected to return to college, and my teaching, but a second suspension was slapped on, that took me to the end of my contract. I was told it would not be renewed.'

'Why should the dean and council have believed them rather than you? Couldn't you get other students to testify in your favour?'

'They were too frightened. Ms Green . . .' Gilbert hesitates, 'you may find this hard to believe. You may even think it is mere paranoia on my part, but the college has been taken over by a sect, a fundamentalist group.'

'What sort of sect?' Far from suspecting him of paranoia, I see shades of the Rushdie fatwa rushing towards me, and find myself less than enthralled at letting loose a whole farrago of death threats, riot and arson. Still, a job is a job.

'Extreme evangelical Christian.'

'Creationist, Happy-Clappy?' I'm showing off a bit.

'Neither. This is something new. From America. The mother church, as they call it, has put money into the University of Wessex. The dean is their appointee. Many of the students are American.'

'In these days of the internet, sects tend to be global. Didn't the last immolation take place in Switzerland?'

'There was a later one, in Zambia I seem to remember, but in both cases the cult originated in the States or had US links.'

'Those students who accused you, are they American?'

'Some of them. Not all. What would be their position in English law? Would it make a difference that they aren't British subjects?'

'The college must abide by UK employment law if it's within the UK.'

'So I can take them to an industrial tribunal?'

'Employment tribunal. Yes, at this preliminary stage, as far as I can see. But I should warn you, Dr Gilbert, that going to law is often at the very least a disappointment, if not a downright mistake. Think of Oscar Wilde, not to mention others in our own time. What exactly did the students allege?'

'There were many things, among them that I distributed pornographic material to them.'

'And did you?'

'One person's pornography is another's truth. For example there was a poem about an erotic relationship between a Roman soldier and Christ on the cross which was prosecuted as an "obscene libel". I think that was the term. You are too young to remember the case.'

'But not too young to have studied it, if only for its rarity. Did the material you distributed fall into that category?'

'Not quite.'

'You said you were accused of Satanism. What exactly is your subject, Dr Gilbert?'

'This particular course is on the history of science showing how it developed from earlier disciplines . . .'

'Like?'

'What some would call alchemy.'

'And you? What would you call it?'

'Proto-chemistry is a less emotive term. The great Liebig himself said that to him alchemy was merely the chemistry of the Middle Ages.'

I was remembering the big old Liebig condenser in a glass case in the school lab like some medieval retort.

'The alchemists have had a pretty bad press since Ben Jonson, as charlatans and cheats.'

'You are familiar with the work of Jonson, Ms Green? Somewhat unusual in a lawyer I should have thought.'

'I only switched to law halfway through my degree. I began with the humanities.'

'And why was that?' The tables have been suddenly and subtly turned. I'm now the one being questioned.

'I decided there was no money in teaching English literature at 'A' level until I qualify for a pension. I would find that life too . . .'

'Dull? Believe me, Ms Green, in my experience the academic life can be far from dull.'

'I need to see a copy of the material you distributed.' Perhaps he had been foolish, had thought young minds were more flexible, instead of less, often rigid with preconceptions, and fear of humiliation or exposure to the unknown. At thirty-six I'm a lot mellower, more tolerant than I was at sixteen.

'It wasn't just the material I distributed. That should have been harmless enough. After all I'm not a complete fool. I know about the duty of care and *in loco parentis*. I'll give you copies of course but the real damage, the evidence used against me, came from what I didn't circulate, that was stolen from my briefcase when I left it, carelessly I now realise, lying on a desk during a coffee break. Someone must have photocopied the lot and put the original back.'

'Then it wasn't stolen?'

'The theft of intellectual property by illegal copying is a crime.'

'Yes of course but one that's hard to prove. What exactly was copied?'

'Stolen. It's a manuscript.'

'By you?'

'No, no. It dates back to the early seventeenth century.'

'Then it's no longer in copyright.'

'But it's mine. I am the owner.'

'I think we would find it difficult to make much of a case out of that. I'm sorry, we'll need something better, stronger.'

'But the use to which it was put, to discredit me, blacken my reputation.'

'I shall need to see it before I can go any further, decide whether to take your case, whether I think you indeed have a case.' I see him wilt but I'm determined to get back the initiative in this interview.

'Surely I qualify as a lost cause.'

'Even with a cause that seems lost I have to see at least a chance of winning, otherwise I wouldn't make a living.' There's no need to tell him about the night job. 'I work on a no win no fee basis you see.'

'I'm willing to pay you a retainer, just for your advice and . . . and support. Since this began I've felt very isolated, alone.'

'You're not married?'

'No, and you?'

I hold up my ringless left hand. 'When can you let me have the material?'

He opens his briefcase and takes out a thick wad, bound in a blue plastic cover. 'I have a copy here.'

'How do I know it's the same as the original?'

'You'll have to trust me. The original is in cipher. This is a kind of translation.'

'You know the one thing you must never do is lie to your lawyer.'

'I'm well aware of that. And in any case where would be the point?'

'And this is the same document as was stolen from your brief-case, copied and returned?'

'Exactly.'

'Who do you believe stole it?'

'Oh I know. It was the secretary of the Temple of the Latent Christ.'

'The Temple of Christ?'

'The Latent Christ. That's what they call themselves.'

'The name of the secretary?'

'Mary-Ann Molders.' He spells it out for me.

'And she went to the dean and made the allegations against you that led to your being suspended? Were they of a sexual nature?'

'She alleged that I was encouraging students to take part in rituals that had a sexual element.'

'Did you?'

'I told them about allegations in which alchemists were lumped together with witches. Both were prepared to predict the future, like present-day newspaper astrologers. Both made their living by supplying potions, love philtres, the Viagra of the day. All substances were permissible in providing what we would now call pharmaceuticals. Poppy, mandragora, meadowsweet, St John's wort, sedatives, hallucinogens were all perfectly legal. Substances and procedures for affecting the minds and bodies of people and animals were sold all the time. Some of them were harmless, some to us would be disgusting, others are now outlawed.'

'Did Mary-Ann Molders accuse you of encouraging the use of illegal substances as well?'

'She did.'

'Do you yourself use drugs?'

'Like many people, I have used them. I've smoked some pot.'

'And did you advocate their use?'

'I might have been, shall we say, a little iconoclastic in my approach. I wanted my students to think, not just to accept what they were told.'

'Would you say your style inclines to the satirical? That you like to provoke? That perhaps you are anti-authority?'

'I believe a university education shouldn't be a matter of spoon-feeding material into students' heads. Life is more complex than that.'

I sense a certain arrogance in Dr Adrian Gilbert. 'At the moment I can't see that you have a legal leg to stand on to take an action to a tribunal.' I watch him sag a little. Why am I saying this? There's nothing in the in-tray. I need the money and I need to practise my profession, my craft. I pick up the plastic folder. 'I'll look at this and consider what you've told me and be in touch. I may make some enquiries of my own.'

'Thank you, Ms Green. I am most grateful. How much do I owe you so far?' He's taking out his cheque-book.

I hesitate. But the rent is due at the end of the month.

'The Law Society recommends standard minimum fees. I think we should stick to those.'

'Of course.'

I tell him the rate per hour for a practising solicitor of four years' standing. He writes the cheque without a quibble. Now he has me signed up, he thinks. We'll see.

As soon as he's out of the door, I open the typed document and read: *The Memorial of Amyntas Boston.*

This is the true memorial of Amyntas Boston now confined to Salisbury gaol for witchcraft, the which I deny, and writ in cipher as my father used for his own receipts, which is the common practice among those who call themselves the Sons of Hermes. Some would say that I am a witch by birth since they allege my father practised necromancy. He was a learned man, a magus and a chemist but no cheat or cozener or in league with the evil one. The countess would have had him live in her house as others did, the better to consult with him in her own laboratory, but he would not, for he valued his freedom too much and his pursuit of the philosopher's stone. So he brought me up to labour alongside him, not at the furnace or the bellows, for which he had his laborant Hugh Harnham, for he said the heat of it would blacken my skin and the fumes cause me to faint, but in wiping his brow and limbs, and bringing him food and drink as he sweat much. For in seeking the stone that is the *in principia* of transmutation, he said only heat would do the trick of turning base metal into gold, and all things into each other, according to the laws of mutability. As the poet Spenser has it that 'e'en the earth Great Mother of us all' does change in some sort even though she be not in thrall to mutability, and if the earth why not all things else. It wants only the key to unlock and enter the innermost mystery. For this work

I was clad only in my shirt and britches with wooden sandals to raise my feet above the hot cinders of the floor.

As there are those who keep watch for comets all night so my father laboured many hours together, for they who seek the stone, the adepts, are possessed by this search and nothing is for them beyond it, except that they must gain their bread as others do. And for this, which was the preparation of unguents, plaisters, syrups, and draughts to summon Morpheus, I took my full share to free him for the Great Work.

I therefore learned all that he could teach me of these mysteries so that when he died and the countess summoned me and demanded of me what skill I had, I could answer truthfully that, except for that art of transmutation which he kept secret even from me, aside from what I could see with my own eyes as he laboured at the furnace, I could do all those things she desired which was to assist her in her own concoctions. My father had been dead but a fortnight when she sent her servant to find me out and bid me come to Ivychurch, her house, where she then was in mourning, the earl himself being dead only three months.

I was led into her chamber where she was seated against the window so that when I looked at her I was dazzled by her beauty, for the light beaming through the lace of her ruff she was as it were haloed, and at every point winked sparklets of crystal from the pearls and precious stones that adorned it.

'Come here child,' she said. 'I could not have your father. Shall I have you instead?'

'As my lady pleases,' I answered.

'My lady does please then. I shall keep you here or Dr Gilbert may be jealous to have you underfoot at Wilton. Do you know Dr Gilbert child?'

'My father spoke of him madam. And sometimes they would meet at the Pheasant to talk of chemical matters.' I did not say my father had called him very sarcastic and a great buffoon but that his relation to Sir Walter Raleigh, he was his half-brother by the same mother, gave him the licence of speaking his mind to all, both great and little.

'What do they call you child Boston?' I hung my head and did not answer. 'Come now child, you must have a name. What did your father call you?'

'Sometimes one thing madam, sometimes another.'

'Shall I lose patience with you? What things?'

'Sometimes Amyntas madam and sometimes . . .'

'Yes?'

'Amaryllis.'

'He was not such a great philosopher as I supposed then, since he did not know the sex of his own child.'

'When he was engaged in the Great Work madam, he was forgetful of all else.'

'Come closer and let me look at you.'

I did as she commanded and as soon as I was near enough she took my chin in her white hand and turned my head first to the right and then to the left. I could smell her scent which I recognised as a distillation of roses with some other sweetness such as jasmine admixed. 'How old are you?'

'Near sixteen madam.'

'And yet there is no sign of hair upon your lip or chin. What is the mystery of these names? What did your mother call you?'

'Nothing madam. She died in giving birth to me, and my twin brother who died with her.' I paused.

'Go on.'

'He was christened Amyntas.'

'And you are Amaryllis? Yet you dress as your brother were he alive. Do you always so?'

'No madam. When visitors came to see my father's house I dressed in female attire to attend my father.'

'But were not the neighbours and his friends puzzled?'

'He had no family madam. And the neighbours believed there were still two of us.'

'And you, what do you believe?'

'Sometimes when I look in the glass I do not know who looks back at me. Whichever I am carries the other inside.'

'Such confusion we find in dreams or in the fancies of the play, where boy plays girl playing boy. Which would you choose?'

'I cannot say madam.'

'One day the choice will be forced on you. For now we will continue with the game. Do you bleed child?'

'No my lady.'

'Strange. I bled at thirteen. Well you shall be Amyntas, my page and assistant, when we are alone here at Ivychurch, or even in Ramsbury, but at Wilton, the great house, or in London if we should go there, you shall put on your woman's clothes and not be noticed among the press of other maids. Shall you like this game child Boston?'

'If my lady pleases.'

'As she does. Can you read aloud child?'

'Yes madam. I read often to my father, both in our own tongue and from the Latin works of the chemical masters as Paracelsus and Nicholas Flammel.'

'Then you shall read to me. I have a humour to hear my brother, Sir Philip Sidney's *Arcadia*. Do you know his book? It is many years since I have opened it, when last I closed it for the printer, at the end of my labours to restore his work to the world in full. I have a mind to visit it again now that I am alone and my time is my own.'

'My lady is still young. She may marry again.'

'I am the age now the earl was when he married me but it is not the same for women. A ripe man may marry a young maid who will give him children as I did. And you are the age I was when I was espoused to him after two years at court in her majesty's service. Sir Philip, my brother, wrote of passion between young lovers but I have never known it. Only duty. Yet a woman must marry, and not be too picky in her choice, for without marriage she has no domain, no power. When he was away the earl left all things in my hands. I have had, you could say, my own little court far removed from London. All this will change now, changes already, and will change more when I am just the dowager and mother of the earl and my son takes a wife to be his countess. Enough of sighing, come my young Amyntas-Amaryllis let me hear you read to judge whether your voice and your understanding be good enough for my brother's words.'

So began my new life in the lady's household as it moved here and there between her domains, now in London, at Barnard's Castle or at her three country estates in Wiltshire or in Wales at Cardiff Castle. The young earl was still in disgrace with the queen for he had got her lady-in-waiting, Mistress Fitton, with child yet would not marry her. It was said Mrs Fitton had tucked up her clothes and gone out from the court disguised as a man in a white cloak to meet her lover. The child was born dead and Earl William, after a stay in the Fleet, banished to Wilton, where he moped about the house. His mother could not forgive him and kept herself apart while he wrote begging letters to Sir Robert Cecil to be taken back into her majesty's favour and given some small posts which his father had held, and be freed of the royal wardship he suffered rather than enjoyed. I was glad not to go to Wilton in my maid's clothes at this time, for the young earl was said to be immoderately given up to women.

In the mornings my lady prayed privately and read from her own book of psalms which she and her noble brother had made together. Then when we had breakfasted on milk, white bread and honey we went to our work in the laboratory where we made medicines from all kind of herbs, seeds and minerals, both salves, cordials and other potions.

I would chop and grind the ingredients with pestle and mortar, then transfer them according to her instructions to the limbec for distilling into the liquors that gleamed bright as gemstones, sapphire, emerald, ruby or the garnet yellow of sulphurous emetics from her own receipt 'The Countess of Pembroke's Vomit' for purging.

There were many little drawers with clay boxes of substances such as I knew from my father, already powdered: saltpetre and opiates, poppy and St John's wort, saffron, and spices from the East, sandalwood, spikenard or our own meadowsweet that brings a merry heart.

After, her patients would come to her with all manner of complaints and sicknesses: ulcers, wounds, bruises, ills of every member and part of the body and we would apply the salves, plaisters and dressings or mix up fresh remedies to cleanse the insides, or wash the skin or eyes, and to dispel melancholy. When she had attended to her own family there would come those from the town and the villages round about because of her reputation for skill and kindness.

All this I helped her in and also was at her side when she wrought at the business of the household and her estates, writing letters and paying bills and keeping her diurnal of instructions and accounts for food and drink, bed-linen and clothing, tutors' and stewards' reports, for her hand was in everything, great and small. Sometimes she would sigh and regret the days of her youth when she, her noble brother and her ladies would laugh and read together, lolling on the grass under the trees, or be pleasantly busy at their writings.

Other times though we were all merry enough: the ladies at their cushions and tapestries according to her pattern, for she is the finest needlewoman in England at making hangings of her own devising to adorn the walls and beds of Wilton, and other her houses. As they worked I would read aloud or Signor Ferrabosco, the younger, as he was known still even though his father had long returned to his native Italy, would play upon his lute and sing of his own composing. But best of all I came to like those times when we were alone together and I read to her from the *Arcadia* or she opened her heart to me and talked of past, present or future cares. Then some about her began to be envious that she should spend so much time on her page and labourant who was not of noble birth. I thought I heard whisperings, words that broke off at my appearance, small acts of spite, as drink spilled by my elbow jogged when I had fresh clothes on, the toughest cuts of meat and smallest portions, and sometimes rough teasing from her ladies when she was absent. Once I heard one say that she had loved her brother too well and was like to make the same mistake again.

Then one day she sent two of her ladies to fetch me from the laboratory when I was alone, Mistress Marchmont an old duenna, and the young Mistress Griffiths, the countess had fetched from Cardiff at her mother's request that she might be polished for marriage and found a husband.

'Why Master Boston,' the old one said, 'you must leave your potions and devil's cookery and come to our lady the countess.'

'Can you make love philtres Master Boston?' the young one asked, 'for they say you have bewitched our lady. Make me a potion that will do the same for the young earl and when I am married I will reward you handsomely.'

I saw that I must be cautious. 'Alas madam, there is no such thing or all physicians would be rich men.'

'They say your father was a great necromancer seeking the philosopher's stone and the elixir of life. Is that what you and my lady do here together?' She began to open the many little drawers of the cabinet and put in a delicate finger.

'Be careful madam for many of those substances, tasted by those who do not know their properties, are strong poisons that will harm you.'

'But they are safe in your hands Master Boston. You understand them. They say that when your father's house was cleared after his death there was found a great quantity of eggshells used in transmutation.'

'I have never seen my father use such.'

'What is this transmutation you all seek? Is it not against God's will that things should become what he has not made them, as gold from base metal, or that men should live for ever?'

'Nothing can be done without it is God's will. He has made all things, even the earth itself as the poet Spenser has it, subject to mutability in some degree. We must therefore call it a divine principle.'

'Unless it be of the devil and witchcraft. Are you a priest, Master Boston, to decide such matters? When were you at the university? Or perhaps you learnt such supernatural counsels from your father's divinations.'

'My father was a physician and chymist madam, and no magician.'

'And have you never seen things change their nature or spirits arise?'

'Both those things are possible, but by the workings of nature not the charms of magicians. Look I will show you.' I placed a little heap of salts of mercury in a clay dish and put it over a small fire we kept always burning to heat water for cordials. 'Now watch.'

They both drew near. 'It is liquefying.' The duenna, who had not spoken since her first words summoning me to my lady, stared into the dish. 'It is becoming silver.'

'No madam, only quicksilver by the agency of the fire. Think how cold changes water to solid ice that men may walk upon or snow that drops from the sky and when it melts there is just a little, little water on the ground from a whole hill of snow, which is bound together into crystals and thence into ice rocks, only from a drift of cloud feathers.'

'You are poet as well as chymist, Master Boston, or rather magician truly for there is witchcraft in words which can steal into the heart and head just as potently as poppy closes the eyes. Our lady will wonder that we stay so long. Come. Can you arise spirits in a bottle as Master Forman does? He is a great distiller of love philtres and the ladies flock to him now he is gone to London.'

I had heard my father speak of this Simon Forman who was born at Quidhampton in our own country, but a half mile from Wilton. 'He grows rich then at the expense of the credulous. There is nothing to love philtres but the longing, and the belief of them that take them. So my father taught me. Love comes from the heart not the stomach.'

'Some say it springs rather from the loins.'

'Lust is of the loins.'

'And some young men would say the better for it. Ask Mistress Fitton where love and lust are joined. You must be still a virgin Master Boston.'

I felt my cheeks redden under this assault so that I feared for my disguise and answered rashly, 'As I trust you are and as your husband will surely discover on your wedding night.'

'You are impertinent. You at least shan't have the discovery. Others should hear of your speaking above your station.'

Then I remembered that she claimed to come from a some-time line of Welsh princes and knew she would complain of me to my lady. But she would do it privately, behind my back.

The duenna laughed at our jousting. 'Green children you spit like cats in autumn. We have kept our mistress waiting too long.' And she led the way out of the laboratory.

As the days passed I came to understand that Mistress Griffiths was half inclined to make trial of me herself and when I read to them from Sir Philip's *Arcadia* of the beauties of the naked and shipwrecked youth, Musidorus, then I found her eyes upon me in speculation if I should raise mine from the page. But I did so only to look upon my mistress, the countess, her face.

Last night, under the spell of Amyntas Boston's memorial I suppose, or the weird case I might be embarking on, I dreamt I was that gladiator girl they dug up in Southwark in Great Dover Street. Outside the city wall, beside the highway and about my age. They think she was a rich pagan buried with eight lamps to light her on her way. Anubis lamps, that may just mean she was a devotee of Isis some academics claim, wanting to take away her status as gladiator, to deny the existence of fighting women. When they first dug her up there was a fierce battle of words, articles, letters, interviews flying back and forth, 'She was: she wasn't. They did, they didn't.' The archaeologists found a piece of pelvic bone in the grave, female, and then lost it. Was it really lost, suppressed, stolen? Talisman or uncomfortable evidence? Someone said Petronius had written of women gladiators so I looked up his *Satyricon* and there it was: a girl at the games fighting in a chariot like Boadicea. But weren't most of the male gladiators criminals, who'd been given a last chance to fight to their deaths? Where did the women come from? Were they criminals too or just captives from some war, offered the choice of slavery and prostitution or the sword? I can't find out. Those are the kind of references the early Christian copyists would have silently let drop, along with most of Sappho.

How much truth was there in the stories of the Amazons, cutting off a breast so they could swing their swords more easily, exposing their boy babies to death in the jaws of wild beasts on the rocky hillsides of Turkey? They don't put that in the tourist brochures. At Halicarnassus they're still fighting in stone on the wall, brave as lionesses behind their shields. Queen Penthesilea fell at Troy after leading her troops successfully against the Greeks. The brute Achilles killed her and then fell for her corpse.

I start up the bike and head off for the China Kitchen. Tonight I have Gilbert's money and don't need to work but I can't let the Gaos down. I find them anxious and depressed. A shop next to theirs that has been empty for months has suddenly been let. Rumour has it it's to be a rival Chinese takeaway but bigger. Already workmen are hacking the heart out of it, and Mr Gao has seen stoves and hobs being ferried into the newly plastered shell.

I try to reassure them. No one can compete with Mrs Gao's chicken chow mein, her sweet and sour pork, her crispy aromatic duck, her sauced king prawns. They have their regulars for home delivery, some as I know from a longish way off, and the locals who've come there since the seventies when the Gaos first opened up. I wonder silently whether Mary herself sees a little light in this sudden darkness, that life might be different, Streatham Hill left behind at last and Bruce Lee's successor kicking down first the door and then the counter to carry her off. If she does she doesn't voice any such rebellion but shares her parents' worried expressions.

Tonight my saddlebox is packed full for a dinner party in Clapham Old Town's elegant heart where the tele presenter and his architect wife will boast over the steaming dishes, transferred daintily to the blue and white bowls and salvers, of 'this little place we always go to, so authentic'.

'Hi, Jade,' Diana Bosco says as she opens the door. 'How's it going?' She takes the thick brown paper carrier bags I hand her, without waiting for an answer. The first time she saw me helmeted in the dazzling burst of security light, she stepped back quickly, half closing the door on its chain. I took off my helmet.

'Oh my God, I was really afraid back there but you're a girl. I get so nervous opening up after dark. Will you always bring our order? I'll feel much safer if you do. In future I'm going to ask if you're on that night before I get in the food.'

'I don't work at weekends unless there's an emergency.'

'What about Friday?' She flashes out the question.

'I'm there on Fridays as a rule.'

'Then that's when we'll have our dinner parties.'

So I bring her comfort food and she makes the gesture of concern that salves her conscience, and doesn't ask whether I like to ride around in the dark and cold, and often wet, or skidding on the mush of fallen plane leaves big as saucers, like the dog's eyes in the fairy tale, with rain slashing at my face through the visor and the other traffic trying to crush or shoulder me into the gutter.

Tonight it's clear and moonlit. The rest of my drops are in a tight radius from the kitchen, out and back, out and back, out and back. This is the boring bit when you begin to lose concentration, cut familiar corners. At last I drop off the final order and am free to head home with my own supper in the box behind. Coming out I had to weave through cars, buses and vans fleeing the city. Now the road's almost deserted. I ride by the lit pub windows of Brixton with their customers aswim inside like koi or darker mullet, and jostling queues for clubs held back by brawny bouncers: thin-clothed kids shivering in the damp air. I zoom on past the drowsing Oval and into the theatreland of Old and New Vics where the Thai and Italian restaurants are still packed and noisy. Their doors open to let in the post-play crowd and let out the wafts of garlic, olive oil, wine and coffee to sting the palates of passers-by. Then it's into the grim underpass beside the glass canopy and grandiose steps of Waterloo Station, the automatic gunfire of my engine bouncing back off walls and roof, and down to my own train-shaken pad. I haul the bike into its ground-floor garage and climb up to my familiar shell, wondering again what was warehoused inside these walls to be trained down to Dover or what exotics could have waited here to be carried off. One day I mean to look it all up and know for sure. I peel off my leathers and run my hand through my hair flattened by the helmet.

In the back kitchen I get an open bottle of Pinot Grigio out of the fridge, pour myself a big glass while a plate is warming, lay out my silvery dishes, spoon and chopsticks, and switch on the late review to watch while I eat. The interviewer is nagging and prodding, pulling on a hangnail of dispute in the hope of drawing blood. With half my mind I'm turning over Gilbert's case and what I've had time to read of Amyntas Boston's memorial. So far it's hard to see the harm in it. But then it's all a matter of viewpoint and selection. What exactly did Gilbert distribute to his students and what commentary did he give them on the material? I pull a sheet of paper towards me and start to put down questions I should ask him. And suddenly I realise that I'm already hooked. In my head I've taken on this case I don't really understand or see the shape of. I want more background.

I'll run another check on the website for Wessex Uni but I think I need more than they may decide to tell me, more than the acceptable face of the college in competition with all its rivals. I need to go there, see for myself, get the feel. I finish my plateful, put the cardboard lids over the remains to be heated up for lunch tomorrow, pressing down the frilled soft metal rims, and stack the little dishes in the fridge. Then I go through to my office to surf for Wessex and input my thinking so far.

Is it Amyntas Boston's memorial that's turning this, that ought to be just case notes, into a diary, a commonplace book of my own? I must watch myself. I'm in danger of becoming one of those dreary, pitiful loners whose only relationships are on screen, pseudonymous trawlings. "Is there anybody there?" said the Traveller.' That was in our GCE set-book anthology. The last lines had a bleakness I still remember in moments when they might be best forgotten.

> And how the silence surged softly backward
> When the plunging hoofs were gone.

There were ghostly listeners in that otherwise empty house, like the silent observers of messages we send out into cyberspace, that can log on to you, track you down and even offer you stuff you haven't asked for, porn sites and cheap fags, enticements to fly away or join a cult.

Tomorrow I'll pay Wessex a visit. It can't take more than an hour from London. What excuse can I give to get on to the campus if they're very security minded? I could be considering enrolling for a course, needing application forms and a full brochure, more than I can download from their website. Or I could be delivering something. A letter to the principal. Make a note of his name: the Revd Luther Bishop. Or I could just ring for an interview with him. Tell the truth. Say I've been asked to represent Dr Gilbert and I want to hear his, the college's, side of the case. Tell the truth until you're forced to lie.

He might refuse to see me or it might take time to get an appointment. I need to be doing something. After all this is potentially the most interesting case I've had since I set up on my own. True it's only a tribunal not a full court or even magistrates' but compared with the messy divorce settlements, hedge and right of way claims, conveyancing and inheritance squabbles that have come my way it is High Court stuff. I can see me as a legal Lara Croft slaying ghostly monsters or Buffy slapping down vampires, except that I'm not sure Gilbert isn't himself some kind of shapechanger or at least charlatan.

Already I'm empathising with that dead girl, Amyntas Boston. If she was tried for witchcraft who did she have to defend her? What would I plead if I could go back to her time and her trial? I wouldn't be allowed of course. In spite of Portia, who anyway had to dress up as a young man, not many women would have had the knowledge, let alone the chance, to stand up in court except as witnesses or defendants.

'A Daniel come to judgement. O wise young judge.' What was Shakespeare getting at with his boy, girl, boy impersonations, especially there in *The Merchant*? That it was all right to pretend, to lie, to turn nature and society upside down in the interest of justice? Or was it just about what women will do for love? None of the guys in the play are worthy of her. Won't she get bored with Bassanio after a few years of marriage and children? So many of the plays call out for a sequel, a what happens next to his Olivia, Rosalind, Kate, Beatrice. Maybe they'll be widowed and take over the running of vast estates like Amyntas Boston's countess. It's the soft ones he provides an endstop to with death: Cordelia, Ophelia, Desdemona.

Then there's the female physician in what's it called, who cures the king and gets her man as reward. Maybe he based cool women like that on the Mistress Fittons he saw around the court, flouting convention in a flurry of cloak and feathered bonnet.

Amyntas Boston's final sentences I read last night sound as if s/he was falling in love with the countess, a Cherubino or Rose Cavalier situation, the kind of admission you'd pounce on in court. 'Please turn to File E, item 29. Have you got it? Please read it carefully. Do you recognise those words? Do you remember writing them? What precisely did you mean by them?' Is this the witchcraft Amyntas was accused of, where the beloved becomes pure gold and everything else is dross? Until you find only food's gold and a heart turned to stone.

I shut down the file. Tomorrow, I'll have an expedition to Wessex. There's a bus from the station and to the campus if I don't want to bike it and risk frightening the horses in my helmet and leathers. On the other hand it would be good to roar up like Nemesis or the US cavalry. Or a witch on a motorised broomstick if that's what they want to see.

In the end I've decided for the full frontal and I'm on my way this morning, a dark wedge parting the air, at one with my bike, like any centaur, except that I have to feel she's both metal and flesh. On a bike you ride astride. With a scooter you've got your legs together. Next stop sidesaddle. Did witches straddle or sidesit on their broomsticks? I'm in danger of falling into verse, a kind of incantation, as I zoom down the M3 leaving the saloons almost standing still. On past, zip between and away. 'Poop-poop, poop-poop,' translated into modernish as 'zoom zoom, zoom zoom'. We're the incarnate sound the rap car drivers try to conjure from their stereos: 'boom boom, boom boom,' while they wait in traffic snarls. We divide the airwaves, the bike and me. If we could go fast enough we'd hear the sound barrier crash open behind us. As it is we hardly dare hit a ton in case the fuzz is lurking somewhere behind a camera. Still it's great hacking and yawing between the dawdling cars, the dinosaur container lorries, and their pot-bellied liquid carrier cousins. In no time there's the junction six sliproad and I must sidle across the lanes and settle down to a respectable thirty. I pull in to a layby and study the map I downloaded from the Wessex website. Then I'm off again, weaving a leisurely route round the outskirts of the town that boasts on a hoarding that it's home to the international pharmaceutical making pills for ills, and on the hit list I remember, of animal rights activists.

Down Wessex Road now towards the campus. Which came first, the name of the road or the uni? It was St Walburgha before, so someone must have taken inspiration from the location or nobbled the council to change the name. I cruise towards the first cluster of buildings and I'm stopped dead by a high gated iron fence. Fuck! No storming arrival then with a spectacular purring of the engine in low gear, and skirl of tyres to wake the dead. Drifting right up to the gate I cut the juice and prop the old girl up on her stand. I swing my leg over, take off my helmet and go up to the gate.

It's the right place. A neat brass plate says so. There's an entry phone and a numeric pad to open the side panel of the gate to let pedestrians in. But you have to know the code. That's very clear. I stare at it, willing it to open, for someone to come through and hold it conveniently ajar for me. Beyond I can see grounds with grass, shrubs and winding gravel paths. Way back are buildings, some old brick, others new, glass, steel and what must be concrete under the pale recon stone cladding. I can just make out the octagonal chapel of St Walburgha almost hidden by dark azaleas, where Anglican nuns once taught aspirant scholarship girls to teach.

I go back to the bike and get out my mobile. Gilbert must give me the entry code.

'Where are you?'

'I'm outside the fence like *Love Locked Out*.'

'In my day the gate was always open.'

'Well it isn't now. And no one seems to be going in and out. No students I mean.'

'They wouldn't be.'

'Why not?'

'Term hasn't begun. Not until next week.'

I feel a complete Wally. Why didn't I check my facts, instead of zooming off into the sunrise?

'Maybe I'll just ring the bell and see what happens.'

'There won't be anyone there, except maintenance staff, porters and so on.'

I've just put myself at a disadvantage with Gilbert, given him the chance to feel superior. Somehow I have to reclaim the high ground.

'Can't you think of anyone who supported you, who might help? I need to get inside, to get the feel of things, when the place is back in business of course. I need to see someone, talk to them, sniff out the background. You're going to want help. There must be someone who at least knows the entry code.'

'You must realise they would be putting their own job at risk. These new security arrangements aren't for general safety purposes, keeping out voyeurs or even would-be rapists. They are designed to keep me out and the students in. Their comings and goings will be monitored by closed-circuit video.'

'Then we have to find someone now, before term begins, before they're banged up inside.'

He's gone. I peer through the bars again and think I see a blue-overalled figure moving about among the far trees with a wheelbarrow. Is Gilbert telling the truth or lying to me in spite of my warning? Did he know about the new security? Suddenly all the excitement that rode behind me on the way down like a following wind has gone out of the case and I'm stranded, gasping for air, with only an empty ride back ahead of me.

That Christmas was the first that I went to the great house but still in my guise of Amyntas, for my lady said that I was too known already in that form to pass now as another. She must have her ladies about her at Wilton which should include Mistress Griffiths who could not be sworn to secrecy. To tell truth I was glad of this for I had become so used to see myself as Amyntas as green summer turned to autumn and thence to foul winter, when all the ways were muddied to the axle and fever ran through our company at Ramsbury and the ladies took to their beds with streaming eyes and noses, and vomiting. The countess and I were kept busy with cordials and balms, boiling pimpernel in wine for healing draughts, hot and cold, and then mixing onion and honey mustard hot for unguents against sores and blains, and for purging the head. I felt a little jealousy stir in me to see how our lady tended them, holding their heads while they drew up the smell of the honey mustard to cleanse the rheum or sitting them up with an arm about their shoulders to drink down the vinum pimpernel.

For ourselves as a prophylactic, the countess and I drank every morning a draught of rosemary-flower wine. Whether that strengthened our bodies to resist the infection or drove it out once in I cannot say, only that we ourselves stayed free of rheum and fever. Then she commended me for this was a receipt of my father's that I learned of him, and served him well for many years until that death that no man can escape.

In December came a week of sharp frosts. Suddenly all were well again and busy with preparations to remove to the great house. There was laughter and bustle and talk of who might come to Wilton. Mistress Griffiths was disappointed that the young earl would not come, being still in disgrace, but would keep the feast with his uncle Sidney, if her majesty would let my lady's brother home to Penshurst from his employment in Flushing as governor there, or if not Earl William would pass the season with other friends, for the countess would not receive him, he showing no sign of remorse now that his lover had been delivered of a dead child, but was gone to London to attend at the Parliament and petition her majesty to let him travel abroad to wipe out his disgrace in her service.

'Perhaps,' I said, 'the other young lord, Mr Philip, will come.' But she would have none of that saying he was but a schoolboy still.

'Many are married younger than seventeen,' said the duenna, and she began to sing in a low cracked voice:

O daughter, o daughter I've done to you no wrong,
I've married you to a bonny boy, his age it is but young,
And a lady he will make you, that's if you will be made
Saying your bonny boy is young but a-growing.

So we took our journey from Ramsbury to Wilton, my lady in her coach with Mistress Griffiths and the duenna, and the other ladies following in their coach, and the rest of the household train behind them. I rode with the steward and other gentlemen through Marlborough where we stayed only for dinner at the Bear Inn and thence to Upavon, a pretty village by the river where we were received for the night at the manor house to lie there as the countess was accustomed to do to break her journey, though some of the household were obliged to lie at the Antelope, it being but a small house for such a company. Often my lady would rest there two or more nights but this time she was eager to be at Wilton. So we resumed our way early in the morning as soon as it was light which being December and St Lucy's Day was late enough if we were to reach the great house before nightfall.

'Dearest Wilton, where I first came as a bride, how soon shall we be sundered,' the countess said as the great gateway and the lofty walls came towards us out of the down-setting sun that turned all the sky behind to a furnace of red and gold where the clouds were puffs of pink smoke as from a giant bellows. Beside its walls runs the river whose name of 'Nadder' signified in the British language 'birds', as my father told me, and to this day the waterfowl swim there in great numbers, in especial the painted mallards in blue and green livery with their dun wives and the silver swans who sing only at their dying.

When the gate was flung open we saw the whole household assembled in the courtyard to greet their lady, all bowing deep, with music playing and the children from the cathedral to sing one of her own psalms in greeting.

> When long absent from lovely Zion
> By the lord's conduct home we returned
> We our senses scarcely believing
> Thought mere visions moved our fancy.
>
> Then in our merry mouths laughter abounded
> Tongues with gladness loudly resounded
> While thus wond'ring nations whispered,
> 'God with them most royally dealeth.'

My lady took up her own chamber again where she used always to lie. The steward would have had me lie with one of the grooms of the late earl's chamber but I said I was accustomed to lie near my lady to fetch and carry, and he let me put a pallet in an alcove of the passage that led from her anteroom, where Mistress Griffiths lay, to the great staircase. Then I saw that my sex might be the more hard of concealing among such a press of people for we were like a little town in ourselves or a country echo of the queen her court.

Every day more company resorted to us, as all the nobility and gentry of the county bringing rich presents and petitions for my lady's word in high places, for the earl being but a minor, and besides out of favour, the world still made suit to the countess though but the dowager. There came too some of her people out of Wales from her castle of Cardiff and other her properties so that Mistress Griffiths spoke with many in her own tongue which seemed to me truly like the language of the adepts or necromancers.

She made great play to tease me with my ignorance of it, laughing and nodding towards me as the words poured from her to one of her kinswomen. 'Ah,' she said in English, 'if you had been bred up by the old earl you would understand us for our language came easier to his tongue than the English.' And indeed I have heard it said that the old earl writ English but poorly.

At her other houses as Ramsbury and Ivychurch the countess ate modestly but at the great house we dined and supped in state with many dishes of meat of birds, and beasts, as beef and mutton, coney pies, herons, larks baked, bitterns, plovers and teals with chickens, pheasant and partridge. Cheat and manchet, both coarse and fine wheaten bread we had with butter and eggs and sallets in season, for drink ale and beer and Rhenish wine, and for sweetness tarts, fritters, custards and doucets. The ladies' skins glistened and plumped, and there was much laughter behind hands and whispering in dark passages when there was no dancing or the play to be had.

All this time the duenna became more kindly to me, telling me many things of my lady's childhood, she having been with her since her birth when her mother was my lady's wet nurse. 'Which if I should lean upon it would give me the right to call her foster sister but I would not. Yet I am privy to many things known to none else.' And here she looked at me straightly as if some of them might pertain to me so that I kept very still.

'My mother brought me into her service when I was a girl and charged me to watch over her and keep her from harm. And this I do as best I may. I think there is no harm in you, child Boston, but as for the others I do not trust them. They use her to gain their own ends and not out of love. But any that harm her I will find ways to bring down. There is more than one power that may be called on and the angels, as the old ways say, have care for the innocent.'

From this I understood that she had been brought up a papist and might be one still but this she would keep from my lady, being with her brother, Sir Philip, and my Lord of Leicester their uncle among the foremost in the work of reformation, and the preservation of the Protestant faith, as her psalms do attest.

One thing in especial I was glad of in our stay at Wilton in that I might find occasion to visit our old home in Salisbury and that churchyard of St Edmund's where my father is buried. And now I think as I sit here writing this memorial, that if they should hang me as a witch I shall not lie beside him, my mother and brother in consecrated ground but be flung into a limepit to dissolve without hope of resurrection when the dead shall rise in the flesh. And yet I am innocent of any malicious practice which, if this is not made manifest, then I shall doubt of God himself as the atheists do since he has no power to protect the innocent.

The first night of our coming to the great house we did not sup in state for my lady was tired from the journey, the ways being very foul and rutted so that she and her ladies were bruised from riding in the coaches which swayed and jolted extremely. The countess went at once to her bedchamber and said that she would receive only the chief steward until the next day. Then came in Mr Davys her steward to report, with gifts newly come from her brother Sir Robert in Flushing where there is much trade with the Indies. Among them, with some French wines, was a parcel of tobacco which she had requested from him, of the finest high Trinidad which my lady became accustomed to during the sickness of the late earl, her husband. 'For nothing,' she said, 'would give him any ease but to take tobacco and I trying it found likewise and for the headache it is the only thing.'

She called at once for her pipe which Mistress Griffiths filled with a little of the leaf and laid a wax taper to it. My lady drew in the smoke very daintily and her face which before had been warped with fatigue softened at once. 'Come Amyntas and try what it will do for you,' she said. So I took my first breath of tobacco to the envy of her ladies who would try it for themselves but she would not let them suck on the pipe for she said their teeth were rotten and their tongues like goats. When I coughed a little from the smoke they laughed very much together and I saw that her speech which was sweet to me would do me harm with the other servants. The taste of it was of herbs blended together as rosemary and sorrel. It seemed to suffuse through my veins like a draught of spiced wine on a winter morning.

Mr Davys then handed my lady letters from several parts which she bade me open and read. Two were of little account but when I opened the third from Sir Philip her brother's friend Sir Edward Wotton I found two sheets of paper folded small that seemed to have slipped between the pages by chance. First I read her the letter which was but a report of the queen's health and the court's progress towards London. There was no mention of the enclosures which raised my suspicion that they were not intended for the countess.

'What more have you there?' she asked. I unfolded the papers which were written in a different hand.

'My lady some verses which I think have got in by chance.'

'How so? What verses?'

'They are inscribed "to my dear brother Edward".'

'Go on child.'

'From his loving brother Henry. Some lines sent me in a letter by my friend the wit J. Donne, secretary to the Lord Keeper. Since he asked that no copies be made of them I send you the originals.'

'This is done to raise his brother's interest. Let us hear them.'

'My lady, the first is titled "On his Mistress Going to Bed".'

'Young man's bawdy. And the second?'

'An heroical epistle. "Sappho to Philaenis."'

'Begin the first.'

So I read her:

> Come madam come all rest my powers defy
> Until I labour I in labour lie . . .

'Enough,' she said laughing, 'it is as I supposed. Not to be read in company. Leave us.' She waved her hand in dismissal to her ladies and Mr Davys and moved from the tapestried chair she had been sitting in to her daily couch, where she reclined in a smoky cloud like to some goddess on an altar wreathed with the haze of sacrifice.

'The tobacco has made me easier. Go on. Begin the second. Let us see if that is meant for women's ears and eyes.

'Where is that holy fire that verse is said to have . . .' I began not seeing as I read what lay in wait for me.

> Plays some soft boy with thee, oh there wants yet
> A mutual feeling that should sweeten it
> His chin a thorny hairy unevenness
> Doth threaten, and some daily change possess.
> Thy body is a natural Paradise,
> In whose self, unmanur'd, all pleasure lies

> Nor needs perfection; why shouldst thou then
> Admit the tillage of a rough harsh man?
> Men leave behind them that which their sin shows,
> And are as thieves trac'd, which rob when it snows,
> But of our dalliance no more signs there are,
> Than fishes leave in streams or birds in air,
> And between us all sweetness may be had;
> All, all that Nature yields, or Art can add.

'What is this Philaenis: man or woman?'

'I do not know my lady. The name suggests a man Philo, the teacher of Cicero.'

'Read on and let us see. There were the brothers, the Philaeni who were buried alive to save their country.'

My eye had travelled down the page while she was speaking. I did not know how to continue but did not dare refuse.

'Must I read it myself?' she said, suddenly assuming the mistress who must be obeyed.

> My two lips, eyes, thighs differ from thy two,
> But so as thine from one another do;
> And oh no more; the likeness being such,
> Why should they not alike in all parts touch?
> Hand to strange hand, lip to lip none denies;
> Why should they breast to breast or thighs to thighs?
> Likeness begets such strange self flattery,
> That touching myself, all seems done to thee.

I faltered, feeling a throb begin in my loins and pass up through my stomach and thighs in a hot wave that I attributed to the tobacco I had smoked that now I thought reached down to those parts and caused this fever as if a hot poultice had been laid to them.

'This is a woman to a woman. Give me the paper. It is

something near some words of my brother's. Fetch me my *Arcadia*.'

I went to the bag which contained the most precious things she carried always with her, that held her jewels and gloves, and those two books, the other being of the psalms, which she was never parted from.

'It is in Book Two where he wrote of the love of Philoclea for Zelmane believing her to be an Amazon and not knowing yet it was the Prince Pyrocles in disguise,' the countess said turning the pages. 'Here it is. "First she would wish that they two might live all their lives together like two of Diana's nymphs . . . Then grown bolder she would wish either herself or Zelmane a man."' She read on silently for a little and then continued aloud. '"It is the impossibility that doth torment me: for unlawful desires are punished after the effect of enjoying but unpossible desires are punished in the desire itself . . . thou lovest me excellent Zelmane and I love thee. And if she can love poor me shall I think scorn to love such a woman as Zelmane."'

I'm reading slowly so as not to miss anything. What was Gilbert up to with this text? It seems harmless enough so far but then I'm not reading it as the Wessex people might. When I got back from my abortive trip today I rang the Gaos to see if they needed me and was glad to find they could manage with just Charlie, a young cousin from Hong Kong, studying English. He's probably a would-be illegal and one day I may find myself defending him in some immigration tribunal but at the moment he's safely enrolled in some language school or college. The Gaos have bought him a crap second-hand scooter he can't go too fast on, and that isn't worth stealing. I think he sleeps on a camp bed in the front part of the shop that becomes a hot house of green pads like bladderwrack, under the flashy canopy of my namesake the jade plant and the rubber plants that thrive to fifteen feet in the steam of a Chinese kitchen. Two of them arch from pots inside the doorway making it like the entrance to some temple hung with scarlet fringed lanterns. It must be good for my stomach to have an occasional night off Mary's tofu and egg fried rice. I munch on crisp cos lettuce and Fribourg Camembert I picked up from the stall in the Waterloo Road on my way home as the commuters scurried like a disturbed antheap into the open maw of the station.

Amyntas' memorial hypnotises me. I'm the rabbit caught in headlights or stunned by the snake's stare as I watch her falling for her countess and remember my own plunge into passion, the crazy roller coaster of it, a ride on the out-of-control merry-go-round at the end of Hitchcock's *Strangers on a Train*. To take liberties with the bard: my mistress' eyes were nothing like the sun, coral was far more red than her lips' red. If snow is white why then her breasts were dun; if hairs are wires, gold wires grew on her head. I'm slipping into hindsight. At the time of course nothing was more shining than those gold wires.

How naff to fall in love at the office party even if it was on a boat, a shipboard romance of three hours up the river to Greenwich with its baroque enticements in stone a fine backdrop for corporate lust. My first outing with the comrades of Settle and Fixit. Somehow I hadn't expected legal minds and loins to be as susceptible to booze and bonking as any works outing or accounts department communal thrash. And I expected nothing on board to be to my special taste. So when she beckoned me over and patted the padded bench beside her I went unsuspecting, careful not to let the boat's movement make too rough seas in my glass of wine.

'You look a bit out of things over there. As if you don't know too many of these renegades.'

'I've only been in the firm a couple of months.' I heard myself sounding almost tremulous. Pity poor me. Not my usual style at all.

'Helen Chalmers,' she said putting out a hand tipped with

iridescent green fingernails. Her name was on the list of partners just before a James Chalmers.

'Jade Green.'

'Your parents must have had a sense of humour.'

'My mother believed no one could forget it or shorten it.'

'You could be Jay or even J.G. She could be wrong. Mothers
often are. My daughter tells me I'm wrong most of the time. I
wonder where the wine's got to? I don't feel like tottering up
that gangway for a refill.'

'I'll get us both one.' I stood up.

She held out her glass and looked up at me, smiling. 'Don't
forget to come back.'

That was when I fell overboard and went down for the first
time. My heart began to thud and I seemed to be holding my
breath without knowing it. No wonder we invented the image
of Cupid's arrow, plugging in tipped with adrenaline. The buzzing
in my ears was like a flight of feathers. I hauled myself up to
the next deck, the mess deck it soon would be if it wasn't already,
cupped my fingers round the neck of a bottle of claret and hurried
back.

'Someone tried to steal your seat but I shooed them away.
Great that you brought the bottle.'

Later when we first made love I asked you how you knew.

'Hadn't I been looking for you all my life?'

It was a tease, a lying tease but it was true too. Many women
turn over in their minds what it would be like to try it, just
once, with another woman. Not seriously perhaps. Just for a
laugh maybe and then back to the real thing. That's what the
researchers say anyway. All those articles in mags like *Cosmo*
that no doubt once seemed so daring are run-of-the-mill soft
porn now, offered on the internet every time you open your
email or in the personal columns of respectable newspapers:
'Women seeking women.'

The noise was growing all round us as the booze took hold

but we were in our own pocket of stillness, at least I was. You never told me. 'How was it for you?' But there aren't any words; not reliable words in spite of all the poets have written trying to pin down that moment, to catch the butterfly in their net without breaking its wings.

The boat was turning at the smooth concrete sickles of the flood barrier. We were riding into the west into a dazzling sun that threw up sparkles from the water and drenched us in the luminous haze of a Turner. The river pushed against us as we turned, swaying little ship of fools that had become for me a voyage to Cythera, Venus' island of loves. We were swayed against each other by our rocking horse as it rode the wake of another passing pleasure boat. You were trying to stand up, bracing yourself against the varnished ribs of the hull. I stood up too.

'I suppose I should go and find Jim.' The smile was almost apologetic. You looked directly at me still smiling. I held on to your look with my own eyes. 'Let's have lunch. I like to get to know new members. Where can I find you?'

'I'm in Drew's office.'

'Drew?'

'Drewpad Singh.'

'I've no memory for anyone's name. You're Jay. I can just about hang on to that.'

I don't know how I got home. In those days home was a studio flat in Earl's Court among the last wave of nostalgic Aussies, and the new wave of Arabs who come over for treatment in the Cromwell Hospital. I walked a bit along the Embankment after we docked and then the wine hit me. I was looking for Embankment Station. The rest is a blank. The next morning when I woke I tried to put it all back together in sequence but it seemed something I'd dreamt, unreal. My clothes were hung over a chair. There was a half empty glass of red wine on the draining board in my slip of a kitchen. Had any of it happened? What had happened? I was rough with myself.

Don't expect her to call. That was it. Just chatting up one of the juniors. Being kind. It meant nothing. If you bumped into her in the corridor she'd be embarrassed if she remembered at all.

I was ripe for disaster after an unhappy attempt to conform with a guy in Humanities at Sussex, a switch to law and aching after Zena who thought we were just mates, protecting each other from the sweaty socks and stewy underpants, when they wore them at all, of those colleagues we didn't fancy, whose youthful necks were still aflame with fiery volcanic zits. At weekends I'd drift up to the Phoenix in Cavendish Square, rave the night away, sometimes ending up in a strange bed, learning new tricks, a rite of passage I felt entitled to. Chastity wasn't an option as we neared the gay nineties. But heart and cunt stayed resolutely apart and one Saturday night the serpent scales came off my eyes and I saw the club scene for the frenetic search it was that could only end in tears after bedtime. When I moved to Settle and Fixit I'd been back just twice in seven years since I left Sussex and found myself a job and the studio flat. Grew up. Except that you never do, not inside. Zena had finally lost it to an ex-public schoolboy who already had his place booked as PPA to a rising Tory politician. He was too clever a lawyer to make the mistake of date rape but then he didn't need to. By then she was tired of saying no and at least he bathed and washed his thin pale hair.

Instead of clubbing I took to going home at the weekends, hanging out with the parents, the black labrador, the ginger cat and my brother's family, the other members of our extending clan if they happened to be visiting. I knew Mam was worried about me, that she and Dad lay in bed in the morning talking around what I was or wasn't doing. I said I was studying for my Bar exams, which was true, and that didn't leave much time or energy for anything else.

In true English style nothing was said of course. But there

was no mention of Mr Right coming along either. Only once Roger my brother looked at me straight and said, 'I don't suppose you'll be getting married.'

I looked straight back at him. 'I shouldn't think so.'

'So I'll have to provide the grandchildren.' Two years later he did, marrying Jenny, a schoolfriend's sister who got conveniently pregnant on their Barcelona honeymoon. It left me free and gave my parents a new topic of concern. I began to think about moving up and into chambers, becoming a real lawyer instead of just a legal adviser to a small firm, drawing up contracts and leases, and keeping them the right side of company law.

'So you'll be able to get us out of trouble,' Dad said when I told them I'd been called to the Bar.

'What did you have in mind?'

'I fancy one of those anti-capitalism demos myself. What about you, Linda?' I knew he was only half joking. After taking early retirement when British Rail was privatised Dad was helping out at the local union branch office.

'I might have a go at that Leylandii hedge they've planted next door if it grows any higher.'

They were proud of having put me and Roger through university and we were both careful not to let a distance come between us as we moved away from Acton, further into London, Roger to the trendy Notting Hill semi his accountancy fees could afford, and me to the anonymity of Earl's Court.

Why am I dredging all this stuff up? Because, I suppose, it's been lying there at the bottom of the pit that's my stomach, a lumpy mess of potage, part birthright, part the indigestible experience I've swallowed whole over my thirty-odd years. Maybe it's time to spew it all up and start again if you ever can. Marlowe was a dedicated melancholic for all his wisecracks so perhaps he isn't the best role model for me after all. I've got to put all this aside and get back to Adrian Gilbert: I have to get into Wessex. Why don't I just pick up the phone tomorrow morning, get the number off their website, and see what happens. I pour myself another glass of wine. Decision time.

I dream I'm in somewhere cold and dark, lying on straw. I know my clothes are filthy and my hair matted. Then I'm talking to someone I can't see. 'I can help you,' I say. 'I can defend you.' There's a shrill buzzing noise. It's the alarm going off. My heart is thudding somewhere up in my throat and I'm slippery with the acid sweat of nightmare or the killer night fevers of consumption and Aids.

As I butter my toast and drink my coffee I bone up on tribunal procedure which isn't something I've had to do before, and rehearse what I'm going to say when I get through to Wessex. Then I think I'll try to see if the Temple of the Latent Christ has its own website. I log on and search via the ridiculously named Google. Bingo.

They have indeed and it tells me there are branches of the Temple in Switzerland, Peru, Swaziland and the UK. It even invites punters to sign on for courses at Wessex. The fees seem astronomical but maybe things have changed since I left Sussex and these aren't as bad as I think. Now I can listen, and watch, an address by a bishop. The site also offers me almost instant ordination if I will subscribe to their beliefs, become a member of their church, as I suppose I have to call it. 'Unlike other sites offering immediate ordination we offer only to the committed who have subscribed to the tenets of our faith. You may choose to be a lay member or one of the chosen, the elect who may perform certain ceremonies as prescribed by the council of bishops and elders under the guidance of our Father in Christ, Apostle Joachim after a period of probation.'

I wait for the address. First comes some unidentified but unmistakably numinous music, tonal religious candy floss. Then the bishop, or should I say the Apostle, against a desert background like that in pictures of St Jerome in the wilderness, except that there're no friendly lion and lamb lying down together.

The Temple of the Latent Christ it seems is every one of us. So far not too far from certain wings of traditional Christian theology. But it's also all the committed wherever they may be. Shots of smiling faces and uplifted hands, brown and pink and black. We are all bound together once we have dedicated ourselves. No going back.

Most religions have an opt out clause, except I've read somewhere, the Parsees' Zoroastrians where you can't get in and you can't get out. I've frozen the frame on 'His Charisma'. Now we go on. The Temple rejects the later Christian accretions of the Synoptic Gospels and bases its teachings on the scriptures of the Dead Sea Scrolls and those writings, the Apostle would not call them apocrypha, rejected by those who have perverted the true faith, together with Revelation. I begin to smell Gnosticism, usually somewhere at the heart of DIY Christian sects, the new evangelicals of our corporatist culture.

Joachim is clean-shaven and smiling gravely. He gestures with shapely hands; expanding and contracting his meaning, pushing out into the world leaving his vulnerable heart unguarded and then drawing his audience back into it. He isn't a passionate orator like Paisley or Martin Luther King. This is new style, low key, almost murmured. Nevertheless I can see that it could be hypnotic. In case we miss anything, bullet points are texted across the wilderness behind his head, in a verbal nimbus. Christ is latent in all of us individually, only asking to be found. He is to be 'accessed', he smiles a little at the term, 'by identification with the suffering servant, by giving yourself up to sacrifice. There are places, temples where the committed and the elect have all things in common and live in chastity until the coming of the kingdom. These places are temples because of those who live there, not because of brick or concrete.

'Now through the internet anyone can join in, in spirit. Virtual reality is God's gift of the latter day. Anyone, anywhere in the world, who wishes can enter into the new kingdom of

God, the new covenant, by becoming a member of the Temple which will ensure them the password, the key to the kingdom.

'And there's no time to lose. Apocalypse, in the shape of global warming and finally a meteorite strike that sends the remnants of earth spinning into the sun's gravity field for our last baptism of fire, can happen at any moment. What after all is time? As the old hymn had it: "A thousand ages in thy sight are like an evening gone."

'Unlike the creationists who interpret those parts of the received scriptures literally, and refuse the promised revelations, the Temple with the knowledge given us by modern science, under God's eye knows this now to be literally true. I don't say it will come tomorrow, only that it will come, that we are living in the latter days of John's Revelation and then the children of darkness shall perish and only the children of light be saved to enter another, some scientists claim, the eleventh, dimension, the heavenly kingdom of a more radiant universe, where we shall find the promised mansions.'

I hear him winding up for the crunch. 'The scrolls from the Dead Sea give us the rule of the covenant by which we should live. There are those who live in the world following the rule as best they can but susceptible to many temptations. Then there are those, the elect as they are called, who live together in a community. It was out of such a community in the desert that John the Baptist and Jesus of Nazareth came. But the time wasn't right. The children of darkness overcame the children of light through God's will, for nothing happens without his will. Now the time has come again for those who will listen and act. It is your choice: obliteration or eternal life beyond this finite universe. To know more, to take the first step towards salvation fill in the form that will appear on the screen and email it to: temple@latentchrist.org.'

Wait. The mesmeric voice has got to me. I'm almost about to click on to the first box that comes up asking me if I want to continue. If I do I'll be traceable. Maybe I am already. I click on the close window and exit, pursued by what? A tracking system, a virus that will eat up all my data, the following click of a mouse more potent than the bear that ate up Antigonus in *The Winter's Tale*? Let me out.

Is Wessex a temple as Joachim defined it? And what does the bit about identifying with the suffering servant and preparing for sacrifice mean? Then there's the idea of having all things in common like the early Christians. The Temple seems to be harking back to the Essenes, though Joachim didn't use that word, the desert sect that was said to be the origin of John the Baptist preaching his doom message in the wilderness. But Jesus didn't go for all that rule stuff. They hated him for breaking the rules, drinking wine, allowing his disciples to pick ears of corn on the Sabbath and eat the grains when they were hungry. Let's look up Essenes in the on-line encyclopedia. See if anything fits.

'Sect (Second century BC to First century AD) which together with the Sadducees and Pharisees made up late Jewish political and religious life before the Diaspora. Rejected temple sacrifice. Referred to in Dead Sea Scrolls. Practised an early communism and strict adherence to their religious rule, including celibacy for the elect. Massacred by the Romans. Their centre at Qumran deserted in AD 68 after the destruction of the temple at Jerusalem.

Well, there's the property in common. A beautiful concept but very dangerous in the wrong hands. Who keeps the purse strings? Joachim and his cronies? Is the principal of Wessex one of the elect? Or is it a perfectly ordinary college being used as a cover? Did they plan to get rid of Gilbert because he wouldn't join their club?

Strange that he doesn't seem too worried by all this, except insofar as it's lost him his job. Maybe I'm making too much of the Temple lot. Maybe they just see Wessex as a way of getting a bit of money out of overseas students. Where's their centre, their home base then? Here in this country or somewhere else? The States, Switzerland, Africa? Or perhaps you don't need a centre. If you have the internet your organisation can be as amorphous as the universe itself. The terrorists who hole up in caves or on mountain tops in real locations have got it all wrong. They should be fluid. They're still too physical. Real horror will be virtual, in a cloud of unknowing. As fantastical as a James Bond movie or a Playstation game. The Great Dictator will flood all our screens with images of violence and horror, brain-washing us until we give in. Orwell saw it all over half a century ago. How we could be duped by a semblance of reality, by shots in a war that may not exist at all. Mam and Dad have told me about the Cold War and what that did to their young lives and maybe it was just another con.

What a strange blend of pseudo science and history whoever started it has dreamt up with the Temple of the Latent Christ. And do they believe it themselves, or is it just a money-spinning scam? I want to know more but I'm scared of being identified if I simply pretend to join, though I can see I might have to if I can't get at them any other way. What must your needs be to make you want to sign up to such a group?

I can understand about young men who feel themselves outside the society they were born into on some grotty estate in the Midlands, looking for dignity and conviction in belief and action, seeing the white male ceiling above them they can never climb through, much as it's been for women. And still is. That's partly why I'm sitting here with Lost Causes on my nameplate. To get anywhere those boys have to start from some sort of middle class, even if that may be just up from the corner shop, if they aspire to accountancy, law, business management.

Like my sometime boss Drewpad Singh who steered me through my first weeks at Settle and Fixit. I should have got to know him better, asked him more but I was too obsessed with Helen once the lightning struck. And if you're unemployed because the mills and sweatshops your parents came to this cold country to work in have closed, the rackety machines are all stitching away busily in some corner of an old empire, the bright clothes tumbling to the ground at half the UK minimum wage in Indonesia, Morocco, Quanjiao, then what do you do? How do you make yourself a place in this world where we can all see how the other half lives? Maybe Mr Goa's nephew will end up joining the Triad boys on their bikes running the protection racket in the takeaway trade. Or do his law degree and find himself defending them. Maybe I should offer him a job, except that I can't even make enough to keep myself.

I had awaited the return of Dr Adrian Gilbert, who had been on a visit to his friends and estate in Devon, on our arrival at the Great House with some flutterings of fear because of my father's talk of his choleric temper and my lady's own apprehension that he would not be pleased at finding a new young physician at her side. And so it proved.

The second day of our stay at Wilton she took me to view her laboratory there which was in size and variety of vessels and means for performing all kinds of experiments so far superior to our little room at Ramsbury, as I now saw it, where before I had thought it spacious and equipped with everything needful for our work. There were many delicate glass retorts and cups as well as of clay, and polished lenses for magnification. There were lodestones and a set of sailors' needles pointing north. One wall was of cupboards whereof each drawer was neatly labelled with the name of the herb or mineral within. There were two furnaces, great and small, scales for weighing greater quantities and a fine balance for the littlest. There were also glass boxes with curiosities inside them as snake skins, a monkey's skull, a dried bat pinned to a board and many fine big crystals that glinted rose pink, opal, sapphire and emerald in the light from the long windows.

'That quadrant was given to the late earl by Sir Walter Raleigh on his return from his voyage of discovery to the Caribees,' my lady said pointing to a fine instrument lying beside a pair of globes. 'Should you like to make experiments here?'

I picked up the box with the monkey's skull.

'If my lady will allow me. How like this is to a man's skull in little.'

At that the door was thrust violently open and an old stout man strode in. At once he came up to me and seized the glass box from my hand. He turned and bowed to the countess.

'Forgive me madam but this clumsy boy might have let it drop.'

'This is my new page Amyntas Boston, Dr Gilbert, who helps me with my work at Ramsbury.'

'Where are you from boy?'

'From Salisbury sir.'

'I knew a Boston in Salisbury, he that was sometime mayor of St Edmunds and thought himself a great laborant in the chemical arts.'

'He was my father sir.'

'Many times I have bid him come to my service,' the countess said, 'and he would not but now I have his child.'

'He was a puffer madam and not worthy of your service, a mere mechanical.'

'My father was not a mere puffer sir as you are pleased to say but a physician and philosopher.' Something more of what my father had told me concerning this Gilbert had returned to me, that he had dabbled in necromancy with Dr John Dee and been the instrument of his own brother, Sir Humphrey his death on his return voyage from Atlantis which was as my father told me two years before my birth. And had my father been with them, as well he might have as physician to the fleet, I had never entered this world.

'I say again madam this insolent boy's father was a mere mechanical and he is unfit for your service. I will try him with some questions and then you shall see.'

'Will you be tried Amyntas?' my lady asked, seating herself in the chair from which she was used to oversee the work.

'I will do my best to answer to anything madam, as long as you do not take my answers for mere impertinence.'

'Have at you both then,' she said and let fall her fine lawn handkerchief as at a joust, a sign that we should begin.

'Under what sign should *Amara dulcis* be gathered and against what diseases is it sovereign?'

'There are those who say that it is a mercurial plant and should therefore be gathered under that sign on Tuesday in the month of July, and that it is a remedy against witchcraft if hung about the neck. But the true use of woody nightshade, as it is known to the country people in these parts, is as an infusion in white wine to open obstructions of the liver and spleen and therefore against yellow or black jaundice and the dropsy.'

'Do you not believe then that diseases vary by the operation of the stars and are to be cured by herbs whose planet is contrary to that of the disease or in some cases in sympathy with it, as the herbs of Venus cure diseases of the loins and generation?'

'Sir my father taught me that the efficacy of which herbs are sovereign against which diseases is a matter of experience and experiment.'

'So that if my lady, the countess, were sick you would not seek out the cause but only apply some remedy of your own approving?'

'I would seek out the cause in nature and the body sir, not in the stars.'

'Then you have no guiding principle but would make the body of your lady a laboratory for experiment, trying first this remedy, then that? You reject the wisdom of the great Paracelsus or perhaps you do not know it in your rustic learning.'

'My father and I often read together in Paracelsus, his writing. But there was much that my father did not accept.'

'As . . . ?'

'As that doctrine that sees man as the microcosmos of the whole world, and his *tria prima*. But of his saying that some minerals may be efficacious as remedies or of the value of experiment then my father held that these might be followed but always with extreme care.'

'And for the cure of witchcraft?'

'My father believed that witchcraft lies in the minds of those that hold themselves bewitched as a delusion or fancy, and so too in the minds of those that deem themselves to have power as witches.'

'Do you not believe in the power of Satan?'

'My father said that such questions were the domain of priests not physicians.'

'And angels and demons that they may be conjured up and converse with men?'

My father had indeed told me of this conjuring by means of a crystal ball or polished mirror in which some men called skryers professed to descry such visions which for reward they would describe to others who saw nothing of themselves, and that the famous Dr Dee was so cozened for many years by divers rogues until men thought he was mad or a necromancer, who was in truth merely deceived.

'I do not see sir why angels and demons who may have the freedom of the heavens should allow themselves to be confined in a glass or sphere for the benefit of one person.'

'Do you not believe in good and evil?'

'I believe in good men and evil men.'

'Are you then an atheist Master Boston?'

'My lady knows otherwise for I join her in the reading of her psalms and in her daily prayers in chapel, in private or in public devotion.'

'But it may be that at such times your thoughts stray else-where.'

'As all men's do at times but that is not a hanging matter or who should escape the gallows.'

'Then perhaps you are a papist in disguise.'

'My allegiance is to the queen's majesty and the church she is head of.'

'And God and his son.'

'He is the creator of heaven and earth and his son our teacher of the way we should follow.'

'Is this what your father taught you?'

'These are my own thoughts sir from reading in the scriptures.'

'And does it not speak there of angels and devils and of the witch of Endor?'

'Indeed. But many things in the scriptures are to be understood not word for word but as an image or symbol as Our Lord used his parables for instruction.'

'And divination, the foretelling of future matters? Our fate in the stars?'

'Our fate may indeed be there sir but it is not to be found out by divination for then we might seek to change it and no man can change the courses of the stars.'

'Then you are a traitor to her majesty for did she not ask Dr Dee to cast her horoscope and that of the Queen of Scots when first she came to the throne and he foretold the fate of them both exactly as it came about. Was her majesty then deceived?'

'Her majesty in her wisdom left nothing undone that might be judged by some to be efficacious. But had Dr Dee foreseen the opposite fates for her majesty and the Queen of Scots would he have dared to name them? Therefore I think he spoke as a courtier not as one who can see truly into the future.'

'And your father, the puffer, did he not foretell the future and seek the tincture of immortality and of transformation in the soot and smoke of the furnace? Did you blow the bellows for him boy?'

Here I had to pause before I could answer for it was indeed true that my father sought the philosopher's stone and the tincture of immortality but not for riches or that he and I might live for ever, flouting God's commandment that all things and men must die, but to understand better the nature of creation, for he saw transmutation as a natural effect not of alchemy or magic. And although he rejected Paracelsus, his idea of the microcosmos that man is a world in little but saw him as closer to the beasts, of the same blood and breath and appetites with them, yet he laboured to find cures for body and mind wherever he could, that sickness might be trans-muted into health.

'I did not,' I was able to answer truthfully, 'for my father thought me too tender for any such work even if he undertook it himself, which I never saw, although certainly he used fire to make the white star of antimony which is a sovereign cure for many ills if taken with care and according to instruction.'

'Come Dr Gilbert,' the countess said then, 'you have run through your whole armoury of shots and Amyntas has suffered them all and turned them back.'

'I have others madam he shall not find so easy.'

'Then you must try them another day. The game no longer amuses me.'

Gilbert bowed and left us.

'Did your father not seek after those things Amyntas? Tell me truly,' she asked when he had gone.

'He did madam but not in my presence and not for gain but for knowledge. He laboured ceaselessly and it brought him early to his death as I see it but he never allowed me to observe him at that work.'

'A pity. We might have continued with it. I should like to be first to find that which so many have lusted after. Did your father believe with Copernicus that the earth and the planets circle the sun?'

'He did madam. He said that it was only pride that had led us into that error that the sun revolved about the earth and made man the centre of all things, and that Copernicus his theory was not contrary to scripture, for the Bible says only that God created the sun, stars and moon and set them in the sky as lights to divide day from night, and to govern the length of days and years and the seasons, but nothing of which should circle the other. And that all is to be understood as in a picture which shows on a small flat plane that which in life has depth and magnitude so that a whole landscape of trees and meadows may fit into a work by Hilliard or Oliver less than the size of a child's palm.'

'Some say that the matter cannot be resolved, for the same calculations in astronomy are agreeable to both theories and satisfy the same phenomena. Therefore it is wise to accept both indifferently until the philosophers agree with each other or some astronomer finds a way to settle the question. Now how shall we amuse ourselves in these twelve days of Christmas? Shall we make an actor of you Master Boston?'

'I cannot say madam.'

'Bring me the new little book of pieces, Mr Davison's *Poetical Rapsodie* my son has sent, hoping to soften my heart. It is beside my bed. And call my ladies.'

I went on my errand through the long dark passages of the house and up the stairs, taking a lantern with me whose flame leapt and flickered in the draught, for the short day had closed on us already.

'Your mistress bids you attend her in the great hall.' They had been gossiping of lovers past, present or to come, I thought, for their chatter had stilled as soon as I entered the room. Some were playing cards while one picked out a new song by Dowland brought over from Flushing by my lady's brother Sir Robert.

The lutenist was a papist forced to seek employment overseas in Denmark since the queen would not let him come home although she kept the papist Byrd as her organist in the Chapel Royal.

'I saw my lady weep,' the girl sang.

The duenna clapped her hands. 'You will all weep, if you do not put by your cards and attend her at once.'

Going through into the bedchamber I picked up the book. Her bed was still tousled as if she had just risen from it and I put my hand between the sheets almost expecting them to be warm. I thought I could smell the now familiar fragrance of her perfume. Picking up her nightshift of fine white linen embroidered with black silk and with panels of delicate lace as also at the neck and wrists, I held it to my cheek and drew in her scent. Then I was forced to hurry behind the ladies as they clattered down the stairs.

In the great hall the sconces had all been lit, the fire burned bright and the countess had caused a little dais to be brought in with a Turkey carpet over it on which she sat in a great chair as if enthroned. I thought no queen could have looked more regal and that truly this was a court in little so that I bowed as I presented her the book.

'This is the dialogue of *Astrea* I wrote for the visit of the queen's majesty that was suddenly cancelled. But she need not be present for it to be played in her honour and the country invited to see it. You Amyntas shall play Piers. Now I need someone for Thenot who be old.'

'Not I my lady,' said the duenna. 'I am too old to keep words in my head. And besides it is not womanly. I could not dress myself in breeches at my age.'

'Then we shall have to try you Mistress Griffiths how you shall look in a grey beard. You may hide your legs under a long gown like an alderman or beneath a shepherd's smock.'

'I do not care about the legs madam but the grey beard I hate.'

'Then Secretary Samford must do it. He will need no addition to his grey hairs. One of you fetch him.'

'He has been confined to his chamber with a rheum madam ever since we arrived here.'

'See if he is well enough to attend us.' When he came, for of course he darst not refuse, she said, 'We shall have an entertainment for twelfth night that shall be my dialogue of "Astrea" made for the queen's majesty.'

'Why did her majesty not come madam when all was prepared for her?' I asked.

'It was a bad year, rain fell all through August, and her advisers thought it might injure her health. They said of course that it would be injurious to her people to wait on her in such weather which they knew was the argument she would best heed.'

'Madam I have never acted before,' Secretary Samford said.

I myself had never yet even seen a play except for the Salisbury street mummers at festival time enacting some old story of Robin Hood.

'You remember Mr Samford,' the countess went on, 'that in my husband the late earl's time we had our own troupe of players when four years after the coming of the Spanish ships the plague closed the London theatres and sent them out on the road where they were forced to sell their very play books and attire. Yet my lord had them to play in Shrewsbury and Ludlow and other places of his patronage. My brother Sidney writes that the lords are every day at plays in London when they are not at court, and even there the players come to perform after at the queen's bidding. Now take the book between you and read the verses to us.'

So we began with our theatricals and although we stumbled at first because the words were new to us, the countess was pleased to say that we should do very well with practice and that we should quickly get our lines by heart.

'We shall need rustic music to bring you in,' she said, 'and after it is over there shall be country dances. Then there must be shepherds' weeds for the actors, and for my ladies they shall be dressed as shepherdesses and dance a hey. That should make us some sport.'

That night as I lay on my pallet outside my lady's door I thought that the actor's life was strange personating others, for I felt a confusion in my own mind that Amyntas-Amaryllis must now be Piers. Yet when I thought on the words that I must say which the countess had written, it was not Astrea I praised not even the great queen she personified but my own queen.

Naught like to her the earth enfolds.

And as I lay there I saw in the half-light from a lantern far off, a shape glide into the passage and towards her door. It stayed beside me and I could hear its breathing in the gloom and smell the pomander that hung on its belt. I judged it to be a man for there was no rustle as from lady's skirts. I let my hand creep towards the little dagger I had bound about my leg under my nightshirt, for I distrusted the great house since we had come there and the many unknown persons about me. Feigning sleep I was yet ready to leap up and defend myself. The shape stood a minute or two beside me as if deliberating and truly a quick thrust of a rapier and I would have been dead. Whether that was in his mind I have never known but at last while I breathed heavily as deep in slumber he turned silently away, leaving me sick with fear either for my life or for my sex.

For I had begun at last to see those changes in my body that might unmask me and show me up as an imposture. When I had held my lady's nightshift against my face and smelled her perfume, as when I put my hand between her sheets, I was aware of my heart keep intemperate time and a sweet tingling in my secrets, then a little gush between my thighs. After when I examined myself I was still moist as with a thick milky dew that I was afraid might appear as a stain on my slops if I should be seated so I took care to remain standing. I determined to wear some rag of linen always about my loins.

Also I felt a little ache and swelling in my breasts though not such as would appear beneath my doublet and shirt but only if I should be surprised naked without my nightshirt which I made sure never to be. Nevertheless I determined to bind my breasts for greater safety. I did not yet wish to lose my life as Amyntas for Amaryllis, to be confined by skirts and forced to consider marriage but would serve my lady as long as I could.

And while I lay there on my pallet I felt for the first time a fear of what would become of me, how I should make my living. Cast out by my countess I could only practise as a wise woman or a midwife and I had no mind to marry, to become subject to a husband and bear children. Perhaps I could continue in disguise in some place where no man knew me but that was to lose sight of my lady and daily intercourse with her. Suddenly my life which seemed so sweet and easy had been darkened by that shadow standing over me and all seemed at risk that before had been secure.

'Secrets': what a sweet word for it. Or them. Like bees thrusting into the trumpet bodies of newly opened flowers. And not like cunt that rhymes with grunt, hunt, runt, stunt and National Front. All hard rude masculine monosyllables. The female organ as devourer, a mouth with teeth that would chop a prick down to size. Not petalled softness. Just an excuse for violence and rape. A word to be shouted back in defiance or orgasm, that can be used for men as well as women. 'You fucking cunt!' I suppose the American equivalent is motherfucker. The ultimate insult. Coney, cunni was gentler. And pussy. Each with a slightly different feel to it.

My delight is a coney in the night
When she turns up her furry tail.

A fun bunny. Whereas pussy is more dangerous, with claws, naughty and a bit spiteful. Twat is just contemptuous, taken over by schoolboys and shouted on the bus going home.

After the boat docked at Westminster I walked back along the Embankment elated with booze and lust, not wanting to go tamely home to my studio flat. The city was afloat on the river, the floodlit Shell building, Somerset House and on the opposite bank, the County and Royal Festival Halls were moored ships that seemed to rise and fall with the dark waters as they leaned over their own reflections. Other drunks came towards me out of the night but I was too exultant and pissed to care. I was fireproof, more alive than for years. Would she seek me out? Would I ever hear from Helen Chalmers, my charmer, again?

The bridges were slung across the Thames on ropes of stars. I turned up Beaufort Street, crossed over King's Road where London was still swinging its Friday night away. Then memory goes blank. I must have gone on up Dovehouse Street over Fulham Road and up into Earl's Court, got out my keys, unlocked the house door and climbed up to my first-floor flat but in the morning I remembered nothing after I left the river and my vision of the floating city.

My clothes were hung up neatly. There was an untouched glass of water by the bed.

Saturday morning. Nothing could happen for two days. How to pass this time? I could call up Joel and we'd go to Heaven. I felt like dancing. I was still high.

'You wouldn't like it,' he said when I told him my great idea.

'Why not? I haven't had a dance since for ever.'

'That's the point. We're too old. It's strictly for kids now.'

'How do you know?'

'I thought the same as you. You know: haven't been for a long time. Check it out. It took me half an hour queuing to get in. I thought the bouncers on the door gave me a funny look. I left after another half hour. It was embarrassing. Nobody over twenty. Thirty you might as well be on crutches.'

'Where do all the thirty-year-olds go then?'

'Serial partnerships. "Going steady" it used to be called. They stay home or visit each other's pads and cook what they've seen on the tele. There were some really dishy young guys there though and everyone was on something: pot, pills, speed. Who knows? You have to be to rave on like that all night.'

'Where can we go then?'

'The pub and a pizza, and then the pub.'

It was our usual routine. Only I'd fancied something different.

Joel is one of the most stable things in my life. We met when he was being cautious over boy-shags-boy encounters at the height of the Aids scare, when people had just found out that what they'd been doing in fun was killing them. For some it was already too late. Joel and I found ourselves going to too many hospitals followed by too many funerals. That was before they found the drugs to put it on hold. Sometimes I didn't even know the guy but I'd go along so Joel didn't have to face it alone, wondering what was happening in his own bloodstream and when the trodden-on rake would jump up and smack him in the face, a favourite image of Dad's for disaster lying in wait.

What first brought us together was his accent. 'You come from Gateshead?' I said.

'How do you know?'

'My parents sound just like you.'

'So what happened to you?'

'I was born here. Corrupted from birth.'

I can do it of course, talk like Mam and Dad, but it's fake, imitation, acting. Like assuming a foreign language that you know well. Sometimes my parents make the duty trip to see ageing relatives. 'Gateshead Revisited,' Dad cracks. I've gone with them when I was still at school, seeing the streets where they were born, touring the homes of great-aunts and cousins. Feeling just that: a tourist. Roger always managed to slide out of it somehow with exams or football: a game he couldn't miss.

'It's the Sunday dinners I can't face,' he once admitted to me. 'As if time had stood still up there with meat and two veg, Yorkshire pudding swimming in gravy, tinned fruit and ersatz topping.' His corners are smoother or rounder than mine and he can trade on being a man and the indulgent smiles that still brings to excuse him. At home with Jenny it's watercress soup and pasta with pears belle Hélène, or whatever manifestation of the latest nouvelle cuisine, the fashionable foodie common- place for a time until the next chic chef woks it out.

'What's all the excitement?' Joel asked after we'd sat down with our pints, his Guinness, mine bitter. It was a bit of old Gateshead I'd learned from Dad and still stuck to. It will all change now with the opening of the Baltic Museum and the gentrification of the Northeast.

I wasn't ready to tell Joel I'd fallen for someone at the office party. After all nothing might come of it. She might not seek me out and if she bumped into me, or more likely sidled past in the corridor, she'd avoid eye contact, perhaps pretend we hadn't met at all. No it was too soon for confession. There would have to be something to confess first. So I stalled with: 'I was afraid we might be getting set in our ways, stale, that's all.'

My passion for the older woman had begun after uni though it didn't extend to Margaret Thatcher who was still reigning at the time. I found myself speculating about other members of staff, wondering if they saw through me or if I was as opaque to them as they were to me. Not that I was hiding anything. They could infer what they liked from my not taking part in the girl chat of the staff ladies' loo. Susie Jubal was one, power dressing CEO whose smooth black suiting, elegant sheer tights and high heels gave me a frisson whenever I was called in to draft a new contract. Not that I had much time for dalliance with the hard evening graft of Bar studies. Even my visits to another sort of bar with Joel had to become rare treats or necessary diversions.

Joel worked for the NHS as an accountant and taught an evening course at his local uni upgraded from an old poly. Now there are so many of those about you'd wonder why anyone would think it worthwhile to start something like Wessex. There has to be an ulterior motive in its founding, as a front for the Temple of the Latent Christ or some kind of fundraising scam. I pick up the phone and dial their number. Maybe a more oblique approach than rattling the bars of the gates will get me further.

Listening to the recorded voice on the other end I make notes. At the end I press hash and leave Joel's name and address, an arrangement we have for when I want to stay anonymous. He'll ring me when a message or packet comes. I've asked for the full kit of courses and application forms. The anonymous but faintly North American and female voice tells me: 'Wessex University is closed right now. We shall reopen on 3 May. Meanwhile you can visit our website . . .' I think it's time I saw Dr Adrian Gilbert again.

'Can you come to my office? The college is still closed but now I've read more of the Boston memorial there are questions, issues I think we should discuss.'

I arrange for him to come the next day. It doesn't seem a problem. He has plenty of time on his hands. I can spend the intervening hours carrying on with Amyntas, as I think of him/her, and reading up on tribunal procedure. Meanwhile I search for traces of Amyntas Boston on the internet, surfing the International Genealogical Index, that useful tool set up by the curious theology of the Mormons of Salt Lake City. There are only births and marriages. Deaths don't interest them since the purpose of the Index is to retrospectively initiate your ancestor into the true church and thereby guarantee them immortality. Briefly I wonder where the dead have been hanging out all this time waiting for their resurrection on screen. Still, out of strange acorns useful oak trees grow.

But there's no mention of Amyntas or Amaryllis being born in Salisbury at the right sort of time or at all. There is a Robert Boston nearby at Broad Chalke who married Margaret Brown on 26 September 1588, the year of the Armada, and they had two daughters in the following two years, Joan and Mary. And that's all.

Where else to go? I try the surname Boston and am sent to a *History of Wiltshire* by John Aubrey. The index says just: 'Boston, Salisbury physician.' But it's enough to get me out of my chair and pacing the room. I print out the reference. I need a library. At last somebody knows, knew about a Salisbury Boston and a physician at that. Is it her dad or Amyntas herself? I have to find out. I try underline bracket booksearch.com.

Well at least they've heard of John Aubrey but they can only offer me a second-hand classic reprint of his *Brief Lives*, though it does look as if it's the same guy. So I need a library and not any old library. I need the best. I need to get on my bike and head for Euston and the Inca courts of the British Library itself. Though now I think it might be asking for my darling to be nicked to abandon it in the backstreets of Euston. I lock up the office and pick my way past the morning drunks under their newspaper wrappers through the stinking gloom of the underpass up into the airy station concourse with its Eurostar promise of not-too-distant foreign parts of wine and women if not song, and into the gullet of the tube, almost running down the escalator steps while the halt and old hang on to the right-hand rail.

An hour later I've filled in the form with family history, seventeenth century as my area of study, got my pass, and am climbing up to the reading room, hushed, packed with seekers and the acolytes who serve them. There's more than one copy of my book. Which shall I go for? Not the earliest because it's in a special category, hedged around with access barriers no doubt to stop it being stolen. I wonder what it would fetch on the antiquarian market.

I decide on an edition of 1848 as a compromise and sit back to wait for it. Then I think I could use the time seeing what I can find on the open shelves and I'm just about to get up and browse when, hey presto, here's my book. It's a bigger size than books today, with thick cardboardy yellowed pages. It's been mended at some time and when I open the dried-blood cover it lies very flat as if exhausted, worn out. A faint memory comes to me. Is it the smell or the feel of the thick paper? The memory is of being about six and walking in crocodile through the Acton streets, always it seemed shrouded in winter, from our primary school to the redbrick Gothic of the public library where we were allowed to choose our books in the children's section with its low, brightly painted chairs, posters and smell of damp wool. Outside in the streets we passed among people who must have been young but seemed old to us, walking about in clothes as bright as our kiddy furniture, young men like the dandies in history books with cavalier hair. Fluid, always on the run, they seemed to dance along the muddy streets. Their pastel flairs were stained six inches up the leg with the puddle water thrown up by passing cars. Yet I remember they appeared cheerful and trusting, unlike my parents, Rob and Linda, born in that unimaginable, except to them, before-the-war time and tarred with its sobering brush.

I turn to the index. There's no mention of Boston. I try Gilbert. And there he is: Adrian; I look up his entry. It's in a section where the writer says: 'I shall now pass to the illustrious Lady Mary, Countess of Pembroke' under the heading: 'Of Learned Men that had Pensions Granted to them by the Earls of

Pembroke'. First comes the bit about Gilbert, confirming Amyntas' story in the memorial, and then pay dirt.

> There lived in Wilton, in those days, one Mr Boston, a Salisbury man (his father was a brewer there) who was a great chymist, and did great cures by his art. The Lady Mary, Countess of Pembroke did much esteem him for his skill, and would have had him to be her operator, and live with her, but he would not accept of her Ladyship's kind offer. But after long search after the philosopher's stone, he died at Wilton, having spent his estate. After his death they found in his laboratory two or three baskets of egg shells, which I remember Geber saith, is a principal ingredient of that stone.

I head for the photocopying department. My find lies like the philosopher's stone itself faintly glowing in my briefcase as I make my way home again.

Geber, Geber, who was Geber? Google tracks him down: 'Jabir ibn Hayyan, known to the Western world as Geber, Muslim alchemist of the eighth century. Put forward the Sulphur Mercury theory of the origin of metals based on abstraction from experiments with naturally occurring red ore or cinnabar, a form of mercury oxide which when heated produces quicksilver and sulphurous fumes. According to this theory fire was sulphur or brimstone; mercury was water. Not however the substances themselves but the abstractions: combustibility and fusibility.' Wow!

That's Amyntas' experiment before the countess' ladies. You can see how those old alchemists were trying to feel their way to some universal theory that would explain everything. Wasn't that what Einstein was after towards the end of his life? Every so often along comes someone with a discovery or a theory that seems to have the answer: particle physics, relativity, static state cosmology, DNA and the genome. But there's always another question unanswered beyond it, even if the theory itself stands up. A new dimension, a micro universe we can't see into or space we can't penetrate. Will we ever? Or will we destroy ourselves or be smashed into our elements by an asteroid before we can find out? Every new thing we discover only seems to make the universe bigger and us smaller. Shrinking man. There ought to be pride in what we know but mostly there's only fear. Is that why so many attempts at an alternative answer are popular now? Because we can't face it. It's too big for us. Like the Temple of the Latent Christ offers its believers. Do what we tell you and you'll be all right, saved when the universe blows apart.

Maybe I'm wrong to be digging into all this. What seemed a simple case to make some bread is leading me into a cross between *Star Wars* and *The Moral Maze*. Heavy bananas, Jade. Cool it. Get back to the kitchen and cook up something solid. Get real.

An evening with the Gaos pushing out the noodles and chop suey will bring me down to earth.

'Mary,' I say as she hands me the small brown carrier bags to pack into my vacuum box, 'I hope your cousin is careful to have all his papers in order. The police are very hard on illegals these days.'

Mary often interprets for her parents when a precise meaning is important. That's why I'm telling this to her. 'Oh he is very careful, Jade. He has his attendance sheet signed regularly at the college to show he is real student.'

'Well if there's ever anything I can do to help . . .'

'That is kind of you, Jade.'

I realise she doesn't know what I do when I'm not riding delivery for them. 'It's just that I studied law . . .' I trail off, not wanting to put myself forward, not wanting them to think they've been deceived and I'm not what I've seemed these past few months.

'I will remember, Jade, if there is any trouble, thank you.'

In the morning I'm up betimes as old Pepys had it, determined to get some answers out of Gilbert. His cheque has been lying in my desk drawer since he gave it to me while I make up my mind whether I'm taking his case or not. Now I think I'll have a look at his writing and see if I can tell anything from it. I take out the cheque, still folded neatly in half as he passed it across the desk. I never look at clients' cheques in front of them, out of some deep-seated embarrassment about money learnt from Linda and Rob. First it would be rude, as if you doubted their honesty. Second, it would infringe one of the sacred tenets such as: never flash your cash in public or even count it; never inspect cheques or query bills. The financial delicacies of a vanished age when a gentleman's word was his bond and to show an interest in lucre, your own or someone else's, was vulgar and bourgeois. Now we reel from fraud to scandal with our creative accounting and ethos of grab-all-you-can in this free-market free-for-all where the Darwinian survival of the fittest is jungle law.

I flatten the cheque and study the writing. Very small and neat like a monastic script. The date, my own name, the amount. Hang about. It isn't Gilbert's signature. The name on the cheque is Alastair Galton. I can't wait for his buzz on the entry phone to confront him. I'm trying out opening questions in my head such as 'Who the fuck are you? What the fuck are you playing at?' But while I'm waiting I run a quick search on this new name and get a complete blank. At least Adrian Gilbert existed, once upon a time. This guy is totally unknown. The buzzer sounds; punctual as usual. I let him in. I say good morning, shake hands and sit him down. I'm careful not to address him by name.

'You haven't paid in my cheque, Ms Green.'

The breath is almost knocked out of me by his audacity. 'That's because I didn't recognise the name on the cheque,' I lie.

'I rather expected you to query it on the telephone.'

'You told me when we first met that you were Dr Adrian Gilbert.'

'The "Dr" is correct.'

'Why did you give me a false name? I warned you about trying to deceive your own lawyer.'

'Yes, you did. Quite properly. But you see when I first came to you, you weren't my lawyer. I knew nothing about you. I wanted to see how suitable you were before I entrusted my case to you. You are, after all, very young and . . .'

'And a woman?'

'Well, yes.'

'Dr Galton, if that is your name, there's enough gender discrimination in the legal profession already without you adding to it.'

'Have you decided to represent me?'

'Have you decided you really want me to with my obvious disabilities?'

'I haven't cancelled the cheque.'

'And I haven't paid it in. So we have reached some kind of stalemate.'

'Stasis equilibrium, you could say.'

What the fuck am I doing with this guy? Do I need all this? 'I think we should begin again. Your name is really Alastair Galton?'

'Yes.'

'Why did you pick the name of Adrian Gilbert?'

'I regard him as some sort of spiritual ancestor.'

'Why are you anxious to identify with a long dead necromancer, the friend of John Dee who was both self-deceiving and deceived others and was conned in his turn?'

'I see you have been doing your homework, Ms Green. That's good. Gilbert was in many ways a brilliant man. He lived at a time still deficient in information whereas, we're told, we live in the information society although I'm not ever quite sure what that means, and perhaps we too are deceiving ourselves. You know as well as being a respected physician he was involved in navigation and the quest for the Northwest Passage. He was a fine mathematician, a would-be discoverer who never put to sea.'

'An astrologer?'

'So was Sir Isaac Newton, a scientific genius comparable in his own field to Shakespeare, in a time when astrology and true astronomy shaded into each other.'

'Still, why pick his name?'

'Because he is part of the story. And also I wanted to give you a clue, an Ariadne's thread to follow to see whether you could find your way out.'

'It may indeed be my way out. You were testing me.'

'And you have come through splendidly if I may say so.'

'Dr Galton, there's something you should understand now before we go any further, if we are to go further. I may be younger than you and female but I will not be patronised. It wouldn't be the first time either that I turned something down because I refused to be patronised.'

Suddenly I see the counsel room at Settle and Fixit and the senior partner, Henry Radipole, saying to James Chalmers, and only half joking: 'Can't you keep your wife under control?' when she had tried to intervene in the discussion of a case they'd both been working on.

'It's difficult for a man of my generation . . .'

'I know you are in your late forties. Young enough to know better. Who is Dr Alastair Galton?'

There's a pause while he decides what to tell me. I stare him out across the desk.

'Very well then. I am nobody. I tell you to save you the trouble of looking because you will find nothing on me in any reference book. I once published a monograph on white witches, long out of print. You, I imagine, will have looked me up on that thing,' he waves a hand at my desktop PC, 'and the internet where they will know nothing of me either. I still prefer books myself of course. I see that electric gadget not as an instrument for greater knowledge and freedom but as an instrument for censorship, as a spoon-feeder which supplies you with what other people think you should know. You will find my doctorate in the records of the University of London at Senate House, together with a copy of my thesis.'

'What was it on?'

'Oh, witchcraft of course.' He smiles.

'They gave you a doctorate for that?'

'It was presented as a revisitation of Margaret Murray's *The Witch Cult in Western Europe* which a number of people, academics that is, in the seventies had tried to discredit.'

I'm lost. I don't know where this conversation is going. 'To get back to your CV.'

'I followed the usual course, a BA in history, and my doctorate. Then I found a nice little post in a teacher training college.'

'The original before Wessex, St Walburgha?'

'Exactly so.'

'Presumably you weren't engaged to teach young ladies witchcraft.'

Galton, as I now have to think of him, even gives another little smile. 'That was my private research. I taught them just the conventional history they would need to pass on to their pupils.'

'So you stayed when Wessex took over?'

'I had to apply for the new job in the normal way. When St Walburgha's amalgamated with the BEd course at the local university I could have applied for a post there. In fact I did but the competition was very fierce. Status you see. And then I saw that Wessex was recruiting.'

'Can anyone set up as a university? Don't there have to be standards, regulations?'

'You have to be registered of course with the appropriate examining authority and inspected. Your qualifications have to be validated. They've jumped through all the right hoops. On the surface and for about a foot below they're bona fide. It's what lies beneath and behind . . '

'And the Boston memorial? Where did that come from?'

'I found it in a bookshop specialising in incunabula and early manuscripts. I have quite a collection.'

'What interested you particularly in this book?'

'It was leafing through and realising that it was all in cipher, except that on the last blank page someone had written a key to the names represented by numbers in the text and Adrian Gilbert's name caught my eye.'

'You knew about him already?'

'His name had cropped up from time to time.'

'Dr Galton, what exactly did you give your students to read?'

'I would prefer you to finish the whole book, or no, not perhaps that, but at least to have decided to represent me before we pursue that any further.'

I let that pass. 'Were you able to decipher the book yourself?' I think I know the answer to this from Amyntas' own words that she had used a cipher of her father's but two can play this game of testing.

'I could read it myself. It uses a fairly common, common to the alchemists that is, set of symbols, combined with a simple alphabetical displacement code.'

'No need for a Ventris then.' There's something about Galton that makes me show off in this childish way, as if we're in some schoolboy competition. 'I've sent for an information pack from Wessex to get more background on them. Maybe I'll register for a course just to get inside. Would you be willing to pay the fee if I decide it's the only way in?'

'Then you'll take my case?'

'I still don't know if you have one. This is just preparatory investigation.'

For the first time the irritating smugness drops away and he looks really gutted. I mustn't start feeling sorry for the guy and give more than I'm ready to out of pity.

'When will you make up your mind?'

'I'll call you,' I say, 'when I've come to some decision.'

'Please at least pay in my cheque for what you've already done. Expenses must have been incurred . . .'

'As long as it isn't regarded by you as a contract.' I type out a receipt with disclaimer and print it off. Galton signs it meekly. We shake hands. And yet I know I'll take the case and not just because I need the bread. I'm hooked, like falling in love. You don't feel the gaff go in that flips you gasping on to the bank, however much you twist and turn. You ignore the stab of the knives you're suddenly walking on like the Little Mermaid, out of your rational element, in thin air that's heady with the ecstasy of lust or power or the thrill of the chase.

I think those words of my lady's contriving will never leave me that I learned the next day and rehearsed with Secretary Samford in the forenoon. They are here with me now in my cell and I repeat them like some old receipt against the madness that threatens, for if I should lose my reason I should indeed lose all.

The secretary began with the words of old Thenot:

> I sing divine Astrea's praise,
> O Muses! Help my wittes to raise
> And heave my verses higher.

Then I was to answer as Piers:

> Thou needst the truth but plainly tell,
> Which much I doubt thou canst not well,
> Thou art so oft a liar.

And so we jousted through the verses in our litany of praise.

He:

> Astrea is our chiefest joy,
> Our chiefest guard against annoy,
> Our chiefest wealth, our treasure.

I:

> Where chiefest are, there others be
> To us none else but only she.
> When wilt thou speak in measure?

He:

> Astrea may be justly sayd,
> A field in flowry robe arrayed,
> In season freshly springing.

I:

> That spring endures but shortest time,
> This never leaves Astrea's clime,
> Thou liest instead of singing.

Thenot:

> As heavenly light that guides the day
> Right so doth shine each lovely ray
> That from Astrea flyeth.

Piers:

> Nay darkness oft that light enclouds
> Astrea's beams no darkness shrouds.
> How loudly Thenot lyeth.

Coming all too soon as it seemed to me to the last verse he began:

> Then Piers of friendship tell me why,
> My meaning true, my words should lie
> And strive in vain to raise her.

I answered:

> Words from conceit do only rise,
> Above conceit her honour flies;
> But silence, naught can praise her.

As we ended we both fell upon our knees before the countess, for we spoke in homage to her who was our queen indeed however she might have writ for another and greater. I was aware of the richness of her dress of her favourite white silk sewn all over with pearls and the intricacy of her lace at throat and wrists, floating gossamer against the darkness of the hall as the winter day passed, lit only by sconces and the leaping flames from the hearth. There was much applause and our lady rising to her feet clapped her hands too and cried out, 'Excellently done. I would that her majesty herself had seen it. Let more candles be brought and the music play now for dancing. Come, Piers who would praise by silence, and lead me out. I would not have you dumb for ever.'

'Madam, as I have never acted before so too I have never danced.'

'It is only to put one foot before the other in time to the music. Give me your hand. You will soon learn. Was there no dancing in your father's house?'

'His only visitors were old grey physicians like himself.'

'Dancing is good for body and mind. You will see you have only to observe what others do and all is easy.'

So I learned to lead my lady by her soft hand, to turn her about and gaze into her face and bow, and all the while my heart felt caged in my chest like some animal that would break forth. When the music stopped I bowed deeply and handed her to her chair where she sat fanning herself while she watched the other dancers. 'We must have back the dancing master who taught my children so that you may learn new steps to please me, Amyntas.'

'As my lady pleases.'

'Your lady does please. There is no one else here I care to dance with.'

Though my head swam with pleasure at this, nevertheless I saw that such a liking was dangerous if perceived by others, for now Mistress Griffiths approached and asked if she might borrow my lady's dancing partner and on permission being given she said as we took our place: 'Do not count on my lady's favour to last for ever, boy, pretty as you are. Great ones are ever fickle and you will find yourself soon cast aside when your beard begins to grow and pustules come on that pretty cheek.'

I quickly learned that where it had been my lady's pleasure to encourage me, it was Mistress Griffiths' to cause me to stumble. My lady had put out her hand to guide me even as she made it seem that the taking was mine. Mistress Griffiths held back so that I did not know which way to move until I got the trick of watching my neighbour from the corner of my eye.

'You have much to learn of women as well as dancing,' Mistress Griffiths said as we bowed to each other at the end of the coranto.

'You must dance with the other my ladies Amyntas, or they will be jealous. But you must return to me again.'

So I took out each one in turn and whether it was the music, the motion or the touching of hands and meeting of eyes, I felt myself lifted up in an eager body, proud and full of a new quick spirit that found an answer in my partners. Then I thought of Thenot's words in praise of Astrea that she was both a 'manly palm and a maiden boy' and that I was myself indeed the two in one. And I found that I could cause the maidens I danced with, apart from Mistress Griffiths, to raise their eyes to mine and then to cast them down again simply by my own gaze upon their faces.

My lady too observed all this which was a kind of play acting, and whispered laughing. 'Have a care, Amyntas, or you will have all the ladies in love with you and what does the player say: "that they had better love a dream".' Then she sighed. 'How my brother would have smiled to see his *Arcadia* played out in this sport of ours. But you must beware Mistress Griffiths who is not as enamoured of you as the rest or inclined to fall under your spell. Her eye is on marriage for wealth and position not an idle dalliance with one of neither. She may yet unmask you and then I cannot save you.'

I should have taken warning from this but I was too dazzled and besides she said it laughing as a thing of no importance and as if she jested merely.

The next day I took a quiet horse and rode into Salisbury, pausing on the brow of the hill before the city to look down at the spires of its churches rising above the huddle of roofs, and, taller than all, the great needle of the cathedral piercing the winter sky. I rode down to the market where stalls were set up for the goose fair with all manner of birds, fishes and sweet-meats for the Christmas feast.

I was afraid the noise would alarm the horse so I dismounted to lead it. Suddenly a young pig that had been tethered by a leg to a post bit through the thong that bound it and set off through the market square with a hue and cry after it. A young boy was nimblest and at last contrived to throw himself upon the piglet and pin it to the ground and was given a groat for his pains. Away from the market, and in the din of birds clucking in their baskets, wheels over cobbles and the bawling of the hucksters I mounted again and turned right through Green Croft, past the Pheasant and up towards our house beside St Edmund's church where I had lived in what seemed a whole life ago. Now the house must be another's. I stared at its dark windows and felt in a sudden rush the loss of my father as I had not done before then, so that tears came into my eyes. I had not wept till now.

As I sat there on the patient animal whose flanks were wreathed in the mist of its own breath in the frosty air, a door was opened to the house of our former neighbour, Dame Milburn.

'Why is that you Master Boston? I came out to see who had stopped at our door on such a fine horse. I am glad to see you for I have a packet that was come for your father and I not knowing where to send have kept it these three months.' And she was gone back into the house before I could speak but soon to return with what I perceived from the shape must be a book. I got down from the horse to take it from her.

'Why,' she began again, 'how you have grown and in such fine clothes too. Where may I find you if another such should come?'

'I am in the Countess of Pembroke's service and go with her wherever she goes to any of her houses but you may send for me at the great house at Wilton for her people there will know where she lies.'

'And what news of your sister? Is she not married?'

'She goes where I go, and is not yet married nor like to be. I thank you for this. I shall go into the church and say a prayer for my father.'

'He was always a kind man to me and gave me physick freely whenever I was sick.'

'And you would give us some of your baking in return.'

'You shall have some now, Master Boston, for your father's

sake. I was all day baking yesterday against Christmas when my daughter will come visiting with her husband and little ones. But there is enough and to spare.' And she was gone back into the house to return a moment later with an apple turnover in a napkin which she pressed upon me.

'Thank you mistress. I will eat it on my journey back to Wilton.'

I tethered my horse to the lychgate of St Edmund's and went inside. I knelt above where I knew my father lay in the side aisle. Yet I could neither feel his presence nor find words to pray. Instead I vowed that one day he should have a monument upon the wall close by that all should know a great physician lay there who might have found out all the secrets of the world, one who was not proud but healed the poor and sick, that would not become a great lady's lapdog. Then I began to question myself that I should be her amusement and be played with for her sport. But I was like a linnet straining at a silken leash who fears lest she indeed break it and be let fly away into hunger and dark.

Soon I too grew cold and got to my feet again. It was as if a portcullis had come down between me and my old life so that I could only look through the bars but not touch what lay beyond. And how would it be if the gate were drawn up and I were thrust out, with the gate fallen to behind me and no way back? How could I enter again that former world?

When I got back to Wilton it was nearly dark, the day being so short. 'My lady is calling for you,' the secretary said in a great fluster and wringing of hands. 'You must go to her at once in her chamber.'

'May I not shift my clothes a little?' for they were greasy and stained from riding.

'No you must come at once.'

So I entered where my lady was pacing the floor and fell on my knee before her.

'Where have you been? How dare you be absent when I need you.'

'Madam I went to visit my old home and pray in the church where my father lies.'

'Yes, yes. Well I suppose we must excuse filial piety. What have you there?'

I was still holding the little packet. 'It was something that came for my father. Our old neighbour gave it to me.'

'Let us see what is in it. We are in need of some diversion. Bring it here.'

And when I had given it to her: 'I cannot read the marks on the seal.' Her soft white fingers broke the red wax on the covering. 'It must be undone fully to reveal its secret.' Again her hands moved to press back the wrapping. 'I believe it is a book.' She took it out and opened the front cover. A letter was tucked inside it. 'What is this? A book of love poems? *De Magnete*. The work of William Gilbert, physician to the queen's majesty. The letter is addressed to your father. What does it say Amyntas?'

She handed it to me. I unfolded it and began to read. 'He does not know that my father is no longer living. It says madam, that he would value my father's opinion on the book, whether his idea be right or no. He hopes that my father is well and continuing with his experiments. That they are both old men with little time before them and must do what they can while they may.' I felt the tears begin to start in my eyes again.

'You weep for your father child, as I weep still for my brother,' the countess said putting out a hand to take mine. 'That is becoming in you.' The tears still flowed but at her touch I felt again the rush of heat in my secrets and my heart rise up in my chest as if to burst. 'Ah Amyntas, you are too soft-hearted. The world is a harsh place,' and she drew me to her, pressing me to her bosom where with the scent of her and its touch I felt myself near to swooning.

'Go and shift yourself child,' she said pushing me from her.

'You stink of horseflesh. Come back to me when you smell more sweet.'

'That will be never then madam,' Mistress Griffiths said for she had stood by all this time in the hope to hear my lady chide me or even to see me put out of her service.

I hurried then to shift myself as the countess bid lest Mistress Griffiths should do me an injury in my absence. Taking a sconce I made my way along the dark passages to the armoire by my pallet where I was used to hang my clothes, and rinsed my hands and face in a basin of rosewater for sweetness. But when I returned to my lady's chamber I found her mood altogether changed. Signor Ferrabosco had been sent for to sing to her a song of her brother Sir Philip.

> What have I thus betrayed my liberty?
> Can those black beams such burning marks engrave
> In my free side? Or am I born a slave
> Whose neck becomes such yoke of tyranny?
>
> Virtue awake, beauty but beauty is.
> I may, I must, I can, I will do
> Leave following that, which it is gain to miss.
>
> Let her go: soft, but here she comes go to,
> Unkind, I love you not: O me, that eye
> Doth make my heart give to my tongue the lie.

The last sighings of the lute strings died away. 'Are my dear brother's verses not beyond compare? When will there be some such another again? Bring me my purse Mr Samford.' And she took from it a gold piece and gave it to the musician. 'You have earned this not just by the composing of the music but by the singing and playing of it. Even Tom Morley could not have set it better. But it has made me melancholy. What sport have we?'

'Madam,' the duenna said, 'the mummers await you in the great hall with their play of Christemas as is your custom to see and hear at this season, if it please you now. Or they may come again another time.'

'No let us go in to them. Their antics will lift this blackness from me.'

So we took our places with the whole household gathered together and the mummers began on their play of St George and the Turkish Knight that was such a piece of flummery, with its quack physician, Dame Betty, and mock fights between the two knights, that my lady was soon laughing. Then they fell to a morris with pipe and tabor, with fool and hobby horse and finally to the wassail: 'God bless the mistress of the house', which pleased my lady so much she clapped her hands to it and rose up to dance herself with me.

After, Mr Samford led them away to be feasted and given their Christmas box and we too went to our supper. That night it began to snow and in the morning it lay a carpet six inches deep. Nevertheless we took coaches and with my lady's chaplain rode into Salisbury to be there for public prayer for the Nativity with great solemnity and excellent singing of the cathedral choristers. Then we returned to dine in great state off many dishes of fish, meat and fowl brought in with a flourish by the servingmen accompanied on the fiddles. Many healths were drunk to her majesty, the countess, the country of Wiltshire, Wilton and the gentry present, for there had come several from roundabout with their wives to celebrate with my lady. There we drank also to absent friends, the young earl and other of the countess' children as Master Philip who stayed with his tutor in Oxford and the Lady Anne who lay with her aunt at Penshurst so that my brains swam, for as a man I dare not refuse to drink as the ladies might.

At last feeling my head begin to sink towards the trestle I staggered to my feet, bowed to my lady and left the hall as if going to piss. Unsure of finding my way to the jakes, I went out into the frosty night under the Great Bear hanging above, and hid myself behind a bush to lower my slops, hoping that no other would come out with the same intention and find me half squatting with my slops around my ankles. I had thought the cold air would clear my head but it had an effect quite otherwise. I feared but longed to lie down in the snow and sleep, yet forced myself back into the house where I found my own straw pallet, lay down and at once fell into a kind of swoon.

The next morning I found myself suited as I had lain down with much relief that none had tried to undress me. My head still swam, but after a manchet of bread and some ale I was able to go to my lady who was still in her bed. I was afraid that she would be angry with me but instead she laughed and held out her hand for me to kiss.

'Well child, there were those who wished to wake you for some sport but I saved you from them, for I thought you slept so sweetly with your mouth open. They would have thrown you into the horse trough.'

'My lady is very kind.' I had put on a clean shirt and hose and was relieved that I had not soiled my slops while I slept or rather lay in my drunken swoon.

I had seen no more of Dr Gilbert since our first meeting. He was gone again to Devon to lie with his friends there, being of those parts. Now however when the feast was over he returned to the countess. I had determined not to quarrel with him but to keep my counsel if he should ask me anything. Only in matters touching my father I knew I could not be silent so I heard of his return with some trepidation.

My lady had let it be known that the next day she would take up her care of the sick again that morning. There came a great press of poor persons to be cured, the weather being foul and winter sickness about. Some had fallen in the snow and gashed themselves. Others wanted for potions and medicines to take back to those too sick to go abroad themselves.

All morning we were viewing and anointing and binding up, and after they were sent by my lady to the kitchen for bread, ale, broth and broken meats from her own table for many ailed more from hunger than any other sickness. My head cleared as I was kept running, fetching and carrying, grinding and mixing for the poor wretches who sought our help.

At length when we had but one man more to cure that had slipped and broken his head, to which my lady laid self-heal as an unguent and bound it with a clean rag, came in Dr Gilbert to us.

'You are too good madam in treating these wastrels. No doubt the man was drunk when he fell and came here in search of more ale to mend his head.'

'I do not doubt it Dr Gilbert. Yet it must be mended or he cannot work and he and his family will fall as a charge upon the parish which we must all bear.'

He had no answer to this except to bow his head in acceptance of her reasoning.

'Amyntas,' she went on, 'fetch here the book that was sent to your father. I would have Dr Gilbert's opinion on it.'

Most unwillingly I went for it but yet I dare not disobey her.

'This is scarcely new,' he said when he had opened it. 'This was out a year almost before your lord's death.'

'Yes, yes,' she answered. 'Matters do not reach us here so swiftly as in London. And it has lain in a neighbour's house for some months, she not knowing where to send it. But this William Gilbert is he not of your family?'

'Indeed no madam for he comes from the eastern parts, Suffolk or Essex as I believe though I have seen him often at court.'

'But the matter of the book?'

'I have spoken of it with Mr Francis Bacon. He believes there may be some use in it to find out latitude in navigation but he thinks little of such theories when they do not tend to the practical. He believes that only experiment or chance can discover useful truths, not idle speculation upon causes.'

'What do you think Amyntas?'

I saw that I trod on dangerous ground. 'I have not yet had the chance to read it madam so can have no opinion.'

'Come you must do better than that.'

'If the world is a magnet madam and as some say, and my father believed, in perpetual motion about the sun, would we not be flung off among the other planets if there were not some force to bind us to the earth, as a lodestone draws and holds metal? And since knowledge gives rise to more and we can sometimes build as an arch from one part of knowledge to another by taking thought, then I think theory may be of good use when purified in the fire of practice.'

'Ingenious boy. What do you to that Dr Gilbert?'

'I think I may stick upon the wisdom of her majesty's counsel rather than a mere boy. When were you at the university Master Boston?'

'Never sir. My tutoring was all from my father. He too believed in the virtues of experiment, like Mr Bacon, as you say sir.'

'And how came he to know her majesty's physician?'

'I believe they met sir at the Royal College of Physicians when my father had gone there about some business while Dr Gilbard, as he often writ his name, was treasurer. And he was often also wont to seek my father's opinion, saying that he was uncorrupted by the court or the quest for money or position.'

'Yet he looked to turn base metal into gold.'

'He looked only for the truth sir not for private gain. He would have made his knowledge available to all the world had he come by it, and not hoarded it like a miser.'

'So he may have said but we do not know how his resolution would have kept.'

I was silent then for I knew from my father that Dr Gilbert's pursuit of truth had been often directed towards gain and the filling of his own pockets as in his brother's settling of Newfoundland and quest for the Northwest Passage, in which

Dr Gilbert was a mover but not to the hazarding his own person.

When he had left us the countess said: 'Now child I must to Cardiff to see to my affairs there and I shall take my ladies with me, and in special Mistress Griffiths to visit her friends but you will return to Ramsbury where you will be safe until my return. Meanwhile you will not be idle for I shall give all my works in the laboratory and the curing the sick into your hands.'

Joel rings to say he has post for me and he will drop it in on his way to see a client. I offer him a cup of coffee but he declines 'your instant filth'. The traffic's all snarled up and he's running late. We make a date to meet in Finch's, one of the last unmade-over pubs in London. I settle back when he's gone and open the info pack for Wessex: glossy brochures, application forms, CD-ROM, courses, credentials, fees, minimum qualifications for enrolment in the various subjects. I see that whereas they're obviously keen to attract as many students as possible with all kinds of subjects including Open University home study-type options, the theology department is a closed shop. You have to be studying for acceptance into the Temple for an ordinary diploma course and be already received for the full-blown degree. It looks as if they're teaching a very selective kind of theology here.

How do I get in without revealing something of my hand? Assume a completely false identity? A birth certificate would do. And some fake academic documents. By the time they got round to checking them, if they did, it should be all over. University exam verification offices are notoriously slow. Now I come to think of it I've already got an alternative birth certificate from a previous job. An Aussie girl about my age who needed to prove her nationality, or at least her parents', for a work permit. I had two copies made in case one went astray.

The second should still be in my file. Her name, let's see, was Lucinda Jane Cowell, Lucy to her mates. I could become her. Her parents had emigrated when she was one year old and had become naturalised Roos but none of that showed on her birth certificate.

Suppose they tracked her down wherever she is now? But that was eighteen months ago. She's probably long gone backpacking round the world, enjoying Thailand on her way home. 'Nothing venture, Jade,' Mam would say. It's strange that Wessex doesn't encourage its would-be students to go through UCAS. Is that another sign that we're dealing with something different here?

I can't see myself signing up to the Temple just to get on the theology course. Who knows what you might be letting yourself in for? Maybe though I can show an interest enough to suss it out. Or rather Lucy Cowell can show an interest. Nobody is what they seem. Dr Adrian Gilbert turns out to be Dr Alastair Galton, if that really is his name, Amyntas is Amaryllis and I'm becoming Lucy. It's a kind of virtual shapechanging. These days everything is ephemeral, smoke drifting into different forms, gone in a minute while we long for stability, certainty and look back to what seems a more solid world of truly visceral pain and passion, Mam and Dad's world. But who'd really go back if they could? No. Yet if only we could carry the best on with us. Some sense of belonging, even of being. Maybe that's what the Temple of the Latent Christ offers believers: the passion we've lost. Or is it just you, Jade, who's fallen into limbo?

Even my love for Helen Chalmers that seemed so searing at the time became, after that first flood of anger, betrayal and absence, a dull ache, a long drawn-out mourning. 'Men have died and worms have eaten them but not for love.' You don't die, not as a rule, but something dies in you. 'I die daily,' as the man said. The body goes on, the cells rejuvenate until even they get tired of it and only mad cancer cells go on and on, endlessly multiplying until they consume their host like a parasitic wasp.

Gloomy thoughts, Jade. Click on delete. They'll still be there though, the spectral texts that a clever anorak can always flush out again. Nothing need ever die that we create now except the creators. But then that's not new. Our best has outlived us for thousands of years. Now the worst can outlive us too. Only the means to get at it may be lost with the built-in obsolescence of our technologies. Secrets, works of genius even, locked up on hard disks in landfill sites all over the world. What would Marlowe have done with email and the internet? Sat in his office like me or pulled on his hat and raincoat and gone out into the mist?

I make myself get up and go to the filing cabinet. Find Lucy Cowell's file neatly under 'C'. Something a bit anal in the way you keep your files, Jade. Still it works, so don't knock it. Now a little desktop publishing to produce some convincing qualifications. 'A' levels and a BA so that Lucy can get into an MA or PHD course. She needs a subject and a title for a thesis. The psychology of cross-dressing in Elizabethan theatre. Amyntas should come in handy there. Back to my first love before I decided to make a living out of the law's delays.

I make perfect digital copies of my own certificates, white out my name, recopy. Fill in with Lucinda Jane Cowell. There: Jade Green's deleted. 'Do you really want to delete Jade Green?' Only for now. 'If you select "Yes" this file will be deleted.' Death by a thousand clicks. Death by a mouse byte. But I have the original. I am the original. 'Prick us. Do we not bleed?' Fill in the forms. Joel's address. My mobile phone number. My second email address, the one that's only a number I use for anonymity. Availability for interview. 'When do you wish your course to start?' As soon as possible. A handy US-style summer school where you can knock up some points. Only Lucy Cowell will never finish her thesis; never kneel down for her master's hood to be draped around her shoulders. I pin the false evidence to the application form with a paper clip, fold the documents in three and put them into a self-sealing envelope I've already addressed, go down my iron and concrete staircase and open the door.

I stand there blinking like a bat that's got up too early, struck a blow by the sunlight and the din and stink of the city. Astronauts must feel like this, stepping out of their space capsule after wheeling in silence through time above the earth, with the stars for company and the moon rising and setting its several cycles a day. The escalator carries me up into the station where I can do or buy everything I want or don't, post my letter, get a *Guardian* and egg salad baguette in a paper sleeve for my lunch, queue for the cash point, pick up a bottle of wine, a pack of new floppies for the computer, drink a cup of cappuccino. The only thing I don't do is buy a ticket and travel. Get away from it all. Instead I turn back, squirrelling away with my hoard to my silent lair. That's enough of the world for now.

Living and working alone you become a hermit: Simeon Stylites on the top of his pillar in the desert; Diogenes in his tub, or follow the rule for anchoresses. 'The nuns may keep no beast but a cat. They may make pleasing gestures from the window but not speak.' You could say I chose this solitude out of pique.

After that first meeting my charmer let two days pass before she rang me on the internal phone. Just when I'd reconciled myself to her having been a bit pissed and saying things she either regretted or didn't remember, alternating with wondering whether it would be totally uncool to ring her, there was her voice, slightly husky and posh, as I remembered it, saying, 'So you do exist. I didn't invent you. Was I going to call you or you me? I couldn't remember what we'd said.'

'I couldn't either,' I lied, feeling myself flush like Pavlov's dogs at the sound of the dinner bell. Don't be too laid-back, Jade, or she might ring off. 'I think we said something about lunch but maybe you're too busy lunching with clients.'

'I'm sure I've got one free day. What about you? Do they let you out for a civilised eat sometimes?'

'We could always say you wanted to brief me about something. That should be good for an extra hour.'

'Actually you could do some research for me. I'll speak to Drewpad. Would Tuesday suit?'

'Fine by me.'

'Do you have wheels? We could go out somewhere.'

'Only two I'm afraid.' Then I added quickly in case she thought I was a pedal pusher, 'A motor bike. You could cling on behind but that would be very undignified and you'd need the space suit.'

'How exotic. Maybe when we know each other better. I'll book a table at the Garden. It's usually fairly empty at lunchtime. I'll buzz you when I'm ready to leave.'

'The bosses have blown for you.' Drew had called me into his office. 'Mrs Boss wants you to do some work for her. Have you got the time?'

'I'd better find it, hadn't I?' I always joined in his conspiracy that we were both living out the last days of the Raj where the partners were concerned.

'Anyway you'll get a decent lunch out of it. Helen always lunches the juniors when they first arrive, to suss them out.' This was to let me know that I wasn't the first, so not to let it go to my head. 'She asked if you were free on Tuesday. I said I'd ask you and let her know. I refuse to take umbrage at being used as a go-between.'

'You should charge commission.'

'Your lunch with the boss-lady is all fixed,' he told me later when we were leaving the building together. 'She'll let you know when she's ready to leave.'

'My, we're smart today,' he said when I appeared on Tuesday morning.

'Got to make a good impression on the Begum. She wouldn't want to be seen with anything manky.'

That unmistakable voice called me at twelve-thirty. She would meet me in the foyer. My legs were trembling too much for the stairs. I took the lift, trying not to tweak my hair in its mirror wall.

She looked me up and down as I stepped out towards her, forcing a smile. 'Nice,' she said. 'We'll take a taxi. Can you get one?'

We stepped out into Fetter Lane. I would find a cab or perish in the attempt. I would be efficient, authoritative. I lost the first to another lawyer, judging by his dark suit, but the next came along behind and I stepped off the pavement determined he should stop.

'Where to?'

'The Garden,' I said as if I knew where it was.

'Which one?'

'Portugal Wharf,' she said, her elegant high heels stepping up into the darkness of the cab. I caught a draught of her scent as I sank down beside her, careful not to let any part of our bodies connect by accident. I just hoped that when the time came I should be able to swallow whatever I'd chosen to try to eat, something I couldn't choke on for preference. Careful, Jade, I was warning myself, don't assume she knows, or that this is anything more than curiosity about a junior. After all she can't have it off with them all, of both sexes. Or does she? I hadn't been able to ask Drew without seeming to show an uncommon interest and losing my reputation for cool.

The Garden, Portugal Wharf, was an evening place, Helen explained, which was why it was quiet at lunchtime. You could sit out under a glass awning and look across the river where each passing pleasure boat set up a sparkling wash, to the green and silver ziggurats of new riverside apartments beached beside the Thames.

'It was where the Portuguese wines came ashore,' she said as we studied our menus with their riverine design of fishtailed

Nereides and Tritons on sea horses blowing horns, 'in this part of Vintry Ward. Most of the port houses were owned by the British, like Blandy's you know.'

I didn't know but wasn't going to say so. I simply nodded in agreement.

'I thought we should continue our association with water.'

Was I wrong or was she flirting with me? Had I been wrong before? Perhaps it was just her style. 'Now what will you have? A starter? The goat's cheese and rocket isn't bad as that goes. Or the fritto misto.'

I opted for the insalata tricolore and a poached sea bass steak to follow. Helen took her own advice on the fritto misto and a filet mignon. 'What would you like to drink?'

We agreed on a white wine as less likely to send us into an afternoon coma, and she ordered up a bottle of chablis and some fizzy water. 'I refuse to be bound by those old ideas of red wine with red meat. Anyway white's lighter at lunchtime. Convention is there to be broken, don't you think?'

'I don't think I ever had any to break.'

'A gypsy life?'

'Something like that.'

'You're very lucky. No baggage.'

'Oh, everyone has baggage, don't they? Whole attics full of stuff you can't look at but can't throw out. A childhood, parents.'

'Of course. But for some it doesn't stay there, up in the attic. It comes downstairs and clutters up the living space. Conventions, other people's expectations. Biology, gender, becoming a parent yourself.'

I thought of Roger and how easily he had managed to slide himself sideways out of all this, letting his wife take the strain for our family as well as her own. It was still easier for men to get someone else to carry the can and free them up. His example had made me hold out for independence. Even more so when he married and I saw Jenny falling into the role of wife, mother, carer, social secretary, writing the letters, keeping in touch, remembering birthdays, taking up the white woman's burden.

'So tell me the story of your life.'

'Not much to it. School, Sussex Uni, in-house lawyer to a property company. Ate my dinners, took my Bar exams.'

'I hadn't realised you're a barrister. Not just a pretty face. We must look after you. How much time have you spent in court?'

I had to admit to my court virginity. 'We must see you lose it soon. I'll suggest you go along with James next time he's appearing, get the feel of it.'

'I wouldn't want to put Drew's nose out. He's been very kind and supportive.'

'If you're to get on you'll have to get rid of that sort of senti-ment. He's an able solicitor but essentially an office boy. I have other things in mind for you. We need to see if you can perform. Forget all the stuff about truth and justice, that's for the tabloids or Perry Mason. You need to be able to act like Olivier and interrogate like the KGB, while flattering the judge and jury. I'll bet they didn't teach you that at Sussex.'

Was I disappointed? My breath was taken away by her sophis-tication. The combination of power and control came off her like a flash of static, sexy, heady, a gush of irresistible energy that lit up her whole face as she held my gaze with the inten-sity of her own, iron drawn to a magnet, Amyntas' lodestone.

'Do you like music, real music not pop? James doesn't. I miss a lot through having to go on my own which means I don't go, of course. Do you?'

At that moment I would have sworn to enjoying baked toad if I'd been asked. 'I'm better on early.'

'Meaning what?'

'Mozart backwards.'

'Not too many chanting monks and nuns or nannygoat-counter-tenors, I hope. I can always smell unwashed hair and damp stone.'

'And then I pick up later. Tchaikovsky, Elgar, Britten.'

'Strauss? There's a good production of *Der Rosenkavalier* by Opera Bauhaus at Sadler's Wells. I'll tell my secretary to get us some tickets. She can ring you for some dates.'

Was my new lifestyle going to be all as whirlwind as this? I felt like young Kay in 'The Snow Queen', lifted up on wings above the earth. But there was no ice splinter in my heart, rather a glowing lump of charcoal that threatened to barbecue me from the inside. The wine was having an effect after only a couple of glasses, that and my heightened awareness of her every look and gesture. They would have made me drunk just on the deep gulps of San Pellegrino I was taking to try to stay sober. I was glad that at least the spotlight was off me and my past and the conversation had switched to music. I sensed that too much knowledge might make me less interesting to her. I couldn't see Gateshead or Acton as high on her list of places to visit. She certainly wouldn't have found my evening job now as a Chinese takeaway courier an amusing occupation.

It must be Amyntas who's led me into this memorial maze but maybe that's what I've needed to bring to the surface stuff that's been lying below in the silt and murk, things I haven't faced, that I was brought up to not to face, Mam and Dad belonging to the old school of so much best left unsaid and 'what the head doesn't know the heart doesn't grieve over' or 'no good crying over spilt milk', a horror of navel gazing or letting go.

Back in the office I was pretty useless for the rest of the afternoon. 'Well?' Drew asked as I sat down at my desk.

'Hard to say really. She seems to want me to get some court experience, shadow the boss to learn how it's done.'

'He's not Marcus Lately. You'd do better sitting in the public gallery.'

'Can't argue with the Begum. Theirs to command; ours to obey.' I got out a file and tried to look busy.

'Let's have a quick one when we leave before I go home to the family.'

Drew still lived with his mother and sister. I had been to his home to dinner where we had eaten so many delicious south Indian dishes that the finest curry restaurant in town would have been put to shame. Tonight I didn't want to join a bevy of lawyers in the Globe downing pints. I wanted to go home and try to make sense of it all but I knew I couldn't say 'no' to Drew.

Later in the pub half listening to his account of a complex piracy case he was working on, I found myself watching a girl, probably in her first job, being sent up by a posse of young suits, becoming flushed and a bit shrill as she tried to hold her own against a barrage of heavy teasing. That's what you had to deal with if you were straight and pretty. The disproportion in numbers of male and female lawyers makes any girl, especially in her first job, irresistible prey to a gang of young men vying for her attention. If she's cool and tough enough she can handle it, even enjoy the experience and give as good back. But if she gets flustered then the pack will goad her into unwitting double entendres, to be pounced on and held up to braying laughter until she's close to tears or takes refuge in a shouting match that only eggs them on. It wasn't just a broken heart that made me duck out of Settle and Fixit.

Now the days passed for me on leaden feet, alone except for the servants, and the sick people I was charged by my lady to tend at Ramsbury. When Twelfth Night had come and gone and all our sports were over, the wagons and carriages were laden with beds and coverings, clothes and necessaries of every kind, both for the long journey and to furnish the castles fit for my lady to lie there while she attended to her affairs.

First we returned all together to Ramsbury from where my

lady might most conveniently set out for her journey west. Two nights she lay there. Then in the morning they set off again after breakfast, muffled in mantles and rugs against the cold, the wheels and the horses' hooves skittering on the hard ground glinting with frost, as they strained to set the countess' progress, almost as great as her majesty's own, on its slow way towards Wales. They would lie first at Marlborough, then Chippenham, where they would turn north to Malmesbury, Stroud and Gloucester to take the bridge over the head of the river, thence south to Chepstow and Cardiff, her domain still by her late lord's will.

When she had settled affairs there she intended to visit her other castle of Ludlow where she was happy as a child among her brothers and sister when her noble father's duties took him there as Lord President of the Council of the Marches of Wales. I was sad not to be able to go with her to see this beloved place but the length of the journey and the necessity often for many to lie together for want of beds, and the great size of her household made it too likely that I might be discovered. There was rumour also that some in their drunken sleep cared not who they lay with, whether man or woman, so long as they were young and fair. It was therefore a kindness and wisdom in my lady that I should remain at Ramsbury.

Nevertheless when they were gone I moped about the house, thinking myself abandoned and alone until I came upon the duenna working at a tapestry in my lady's chamber where I had strayed to feel some nearness to her in absence.

'So,' said the duenna, 'you and I both are left behind Master Boston, I out of the kindness of her heart that would not force me upon such a journey at my age. And you, why do you stay behind?'

'I am to take on the cure of her patients that when she returns it shall not be to a string of sick people needing her attentions at once.'

'And will they trust you to cure them Master Boston, being still green?'

'They have seen me with my lady on many occasions and if I indeed cure some then by word of mouth they will come to me. And I am to replenish all our stock of medicines, cordials, pills and unguents against her return.'

'Where did you get the knowledge to step into my lady's shoes?'

'From my father who was a physician in Salisbury, and often my lady would have had him to live with her but he would not be persuaded.'

'This is the first time I have heard of anyone that refused to come under her roof. So many of them there have been that were like sponges to sop up her goodness, in special the poets and physicians who thought by their dedications and experiments to have her favour or her lord's.'

'I do not care for favours if I have her love.'

'Indeed, that I see. But what love is it Master Boston? Is it like mine that asks nothing but to serve, with enough food to maintain my old body and somewhere to lie?'

'I have never asked for more mistress.'

'Perhaps not. But I think there is something more you crave. I feel the hunger in you. Be careful. It is witchcraft to incline another to unlawful love.'

'I have no practice in witchcraft madam. Indeed my father taught me that all such were mere deceptions of weak minds.'

'There is the witch of Endor in the Holy Book that had dealings with Saul and brought up Samuel from the dead. Will you go against scripture and deny the possibility?'

'Those were other times and countries. Who knows how Saul might be deceived when he had gone against God's will in opposing David, his kingship.'

'So you are priest as well as physician.'

'My father taught me to study the Bible and I have continued to read in it, especially since my lady gave me a copy of her psalms. This witch of Endor was but a cozening woman, for she professed to call up Samuel as our skryers do yet Saul saw nothing. Only he asked her what she saw. To which she replied "an old man in a mantle" and then Saul prostrated himself to the ground so that he still saw nothing but only heard a voice, until he fell into a swoon for he had not eaten that day.'

'You know this story very well Master Boston. As if you had made a special study of it.'

'As I have madam, for my father commended it to me as showing the folly of even great kings, who believe those who say they can call up the dead or angels and demons, for who else might they be that the witch said she saw in the form of gods ascending out of the earth?'

'Some might say that such as you should not presume to teach. You will be preaching next.'

I thought then that she suspected my sex and that I must do everything in my power to win her over or she might cause me great harm, not least with my lady.

'I am content to be my lady's servant and follow her example of service to the sick as our religion teaches through the pattern of Our Lord who commended his followers for tending the sick as she does.'

'You know how to win my heart Master Boston by praising my lady but my head is not swayed, and my eyes will keep watch to see you do her no harm, even though you may not believe in the power of your own witchcraft.'

I bowed and left her to her tapestry. Returning to the laboratory I thought how I might best occupy my time so that I would stand well in the countess' sight on her return. I determined to embark on some experiments that might yield something of interest.

First noticing that we had little opiate left in any form, and it being a time of fevers and restlessness because of the sharp cold, I set about converting the plants that had been gathered in the summer and stored in jars, in their most efficacious forms. These were of the garden poppy which self-seeding grows wild among the vegetables. Its leaves are of a whitish green, much cut about the edges, and it has a pretty pale violet flower. It has many white threads at its heart about the seed box, which at the last hardens with a little stiff lace ruff at its crown through which the seeds scatter. All parts of it are gathered at their different seasons from June to September and all may be used.

There are some physicians who pretend that all opium comes from the East and that the juice of those poppies is the tears of the moon, yet we see them grow freely in English gardens and even the wild crimson poppies of the field, or corn roses, may make a syrup good against pleurisy and the falling sickness. Therefore I ground the heads in a mortar and mixed them with treacle and boiling water to form a syrup which would bring rest and sleep to the sick and weak and abate the cough caused by catarrhs and defluxions, which may often be the forerunner of a consumption.

Some heads with their seed I boiled and mixed with sweet wine to make a cordial that would dry the flux of the belly and women's courses. This I put aside in stone bottles to cool. For an unguent I pounded the seeds very fine until they gave up their oil, and this I mixed with hog's grease. I stored this in jars, labelling it carefully as being precious, the quantities small and laborious to make since many seeds are needed even for a teaspoon of oil.

All these, and other receipts we lacked took me many hours spread over several days but at last I had an array of medicines stored and labelled in the different shapes of bottle and jar. They gave me much pleasure when I looked on them and thought that they were all the work of my own hands, more pleasing to me than if they had been the finest jewels. And indeed they shared with jewels the clearest colours as amethyst, emerald, ruby, the yellow of topaz, the milk of opals. Only sapphires were missing. They not occurring easily in nature, for blue flowers turn blackish in preparation except they be candied. You must have some powdered mineral mixed for a true blue as lapis lazuli or sapphire.

When all our dispensary was set in order against my lady's return I turned my mind to what new thing I might do that would entice her admiration. Then I remembered Dr Gilbard, his book, which I had not studied since it came into my hands through want of occasion while attending on the countess, there being so much to do towards the feast of Christmas. Now I took it up and set myself to study its two hundred and forty pages.

For those who have not read in it I will describe what is writ therein so that if ever any read these memorials of mine in time to come they may know its nature and that it is far from any practice of witchcraft and indeed as I found in several places Dr Gilbard makes scorn of such as profess these artifices and especially of Paracelsus with his poultices of powdered lodestones. The book is called in our mother tongue, *Of the magnet, magnetism of bodies and of the great magnet of the earth. A new natural philosophy demonstrated by many arguments and experiments.*

First he shows how necessary it is to ascend from simple experiments to the more difficult arguments. To this end he has gathered instruments from many nations and constructed lodestones of many shapes and magnitudes to use in his experiments. That of most novel application is a sphere modelled upon that of our mother the earth, and for this reason called a terrella, behaving in all ways like to our mother herself so as seaman's needles placed alongside the terrella do turn just as they do in the differing latitudes of the globe.

Many observations were sent him by the great mariner Sir Francis Drake and other famous seamen. More, he found his terrella to be enclosed by an *orbis virtutis* or sphere of influence and if this is true of the model may it not be true of the earth? But this we might only know if we could fly above it as the birds do.

All this was set forth with many woodcuts showing his experiments with great clearness, but I wanted a lapidary to grind the lodestones to their different shapes so that I might accomplish the like. One thing I was able to do was to magnetise an iron rod by laying it out in a north and south position, according to the compass, and beating it with a hammer. The picture which depicted this experiment enabling me to fulfil it perfectly, was like those in books of alchemy where the magus is shown at work. It made me think upon my father's labours though I understood that Dr Gilbard might not have looked kindly on his search for the philosopher's stone as a thing impractical.

But what I might do and carry further than the doctor came in the second book where he discoursed on his discovery of the electrics, called by him after electrum or, vulgarly, amber, wherein the property was first noted. For both amber itself and jet being rubbed upon will attract light objects as straw, paper, feathers, as had been known since antiquity, and such powers attributed to magic in the gems themselves. Dr Gilbard by making trial of many substances shows that this is a property of them and of a natural origin. Yet there were some still which I might examine and note whether they were electrics or anelectrics, as he has called these: not having this property.

I determined to pursue this and to let him know of my intention, yet not as myself but as if my father still lived and was forced to use his son as his secretary and assistant through failing sight, for I feared such a great man would not accept the work of one still so young. Much of the next part of the book was concerned with matters of moment to seamen as the variation and dip of the needle and his hope to produce a new table of latitude for the aid of navigation.

In Book 5 he wrote of the animate nature of the whole universe as a thing living, while in Book 6 he embraced Copernicus his theory of the central position of the sun, and said more that there was no eighth sphere above us where the stars were fixed but that every one had its station at greater or lesser distance from the earth. That night I went out into the garden, it being fine and frosty to look up at the heavens and gauge whether he were right or no, a thing hard to do. Yet I thought that those that were of a greater brightness as the Plough or Orion, that their brighter shining might denote them as nearer to us, and those very faint and small might be further away since all things diminish with distance. If this be so then where are those mansions where God is to dwell, the thrones and angels sitting upon them? They must lie at the very edge of the heavens where the stars go out.

That day had come a present for my lady from her noble brother Sir Robert Sidney in Flushing where he was governor. It was long and encased in a box for safety. The box was marked for the laboratory at Ramsbury. I was to open anything that was so labelled in case it should contain any substance that might decay or suffer from being kept too long enclosed. The box contained a long wooden funnel with what seemed ground glasses as from spectacles set at either end. A note said:

Dearest sister,
    I send of you here a Dutch trunk which be all the fashion in Flanders since one invented it. It makes small things at a distance come bigger and closer and may be most useful in hunting to espy the game before it espy you or at sea to watch for land, or other ships as Spanish privateers or treasure ships from the Indies. Perhaps you may have the good fortune of being the first to make it known to Her Majesty who

will surely find it of sovereign use and will reward you in return.

Your loving bro.

Taking up this novelty I went back into the garden with it questioning whether, if it indeed had the properties Sir Robert had written of, it might answer the doctor's doubting of the position of the fixed stars. I leant it upon the trellis of an arbour pointing towards the sky and put my eyes to the larger end of the funnel. At first I saw nothing but blackness. Then I turned back towards the house and saw the door into it with the candle burning inside shrunk to faerie size as if I must bend down and crawl to go back in. Even then I would be too big and could only put my eye to the door as if it were the window into another country of pygmy people and dwarves.

Next I reversed the trunk so that one eye only was at the smaller end and held it steady against the trellis again to look at the heavens, this time in that quarter where the moon sat, letting fall her light upon the garden. I moved the trunk slowly from east to west and north to south to try whether I could catch the moon in my glass. Of a sudden she swam before me like as a great bladder of light, and her face which we see smiling down upon us as a sign of God's goodness, though some say to sleep with the full light of the moon upon you brings madness, was no longer the features of a man in the moon, as my lady's brother Sir Philip has writ in his poem of the moon but like the shadows of mountains where men might live and walk as he yet also writ.

> Are beauties there as proud as here they be?
> Do they above love to be lov'd, and yet
> Those lovers scorn whom that love do possess?

I had heard my father speak of one Tycho Brahe who had

caused to be built upon an island near the Danish capital a laboratory, called Uranienborg, where he worked at discoveries for the King of Denmark and in particular helped by his sister, my father said, though he could not remember her name, at mapping the stars on a brass globe of the heavens as an aid to mariners. Now I made bold to look at the fiery planet Mars that seemed to jump at me out of the darkness, and then again at a star nearby. And it seemed to me that if Dr Gilbard was right then Brahe plotted the stars in vain upon a fixed sphere and that the whole universe might be in motion and unimaginable distances lie before us where the stars swam, as we see in a prospective painting by a skilled hand that on a flat board there seem to be men walking afar off in a fair landscape beyond where the eye may reach.

And I was caught up on a sudden in a vision, a great spiral of light made of many stars that turned slowly above me like to a wheel as I looked up into the night and that seemed as if it might draw the earth and me with it into an ever deeper ocean of sky. I determined therefore to look no more on the heavens lest I should be made mad as punishment for staring too hard into the face of God and his mysteries.

They must be very short on applications: they've actually rung my mobile while I'm getting kitted up to go to the Gaos. I'm taken off guard and don't recognise myself at first, especially since I'm standing in front of a full-length mirror in my leathers.

'Ms Cowell?'

'Ms Lucinda Cowell?'

'Hello. Yes?'

'You applied to Wessex University to do a short summer course as part of an MA.'

'Yes, that's right.'

'Unfortunately our short courses are only accredited for US further degrees.'

'Oh I see.' Think, Jade. Something convincing now. Where's your imagination? My mind's gone blank.

'I'm not sure if that matters. I mean a US master's is recognised here, for some purposes at least.'

'Well of course if it's all right with you, we would be happy to consider your application.'

'There's also the value of being in an academic ambience, the motivation factor. I think I need the stimulus of a learning culture.'

'Oh I think we can lay claim to provide you with that. When would you be available for interview? An interview would clearly provide the best opportunity to assess our mutual expectations.'

'When are you offering?'

It's a date close enough so that I don't lose interest but far enough away not to give the impression of overeagerness. We fix on it. The voice gives me instructions on how to get there. I don't let on that I already know. I'll take the staid train they suggest from Waterloo rather than roaring up on the bike.

'What are you up to, Jade?' Joel asks as we swig our pints the next evening.

I'm in a difficulty. I need to keep him on side but in the dark. I need his help. But I also have a sense that this whole enterprise could go horribly wrong in some way I can't foresee and if I'm going down I don't want to drag him down with me. Someone has to stay outside to bake the cake with a file in it and provide the getaway car.

'I can't tell you much. Client confidentiality. And also I don't really understand much of what's going on myself. But I'm very grateful for the postbox. I don't want to be tracked down.'

'Who's looking for you?'

'Maybe nobody. I just don't know.'

'Sounds dodgy to me.' And later as we give each other the

fraternal kiss goodbye he says: 'Take care. If you need any help ring me.'

I feel a sense of relief. Joel's not your expected pasty office worker. He's into the gay gym culture of body building, not just for fashion and pretty pecs but with a helping of judo on the side to dish out to anyone who thinks they can rough him up, who thinks a queen's easy meat to mess with.

As the interview day looms I'm increasingly anxious. What do I wear as a mature student working on a thesis? Somehow jeans and a T-shirt don't seem right. But then my court blacks are too severe. I might find myself addressing him as your honour. I settle for something in between. Black of course. I'm into black whether on the bike or off it. It gives me a persona, a mask. A touch of the intellectual, the sophisticate, the gothick.

I've had my usual stand-off dialogue with Dr Alastair Galton, whom I still want to call Adrian Gilbert, especially since I've read Amyntas' account of his original. Not that Galton's stout. It's the manner; the inner man. The feeling that he waits to see if I will fall into some trap he's set so that he can put me down, exercise the petty tyrant's power over the weak. He makes me paranoid but that doesn't mean, as the old psychiatrist's joke has it, that he isn't trying to trip me. Only that part of the game is that I must know he is.

I tell him that any fees for Wessex I have to sign up to will be put on his bill.

'I'll be interested to hear who's taken my place.' I can imagine the little supercilious moue he's making as he speaks. Who needs videophones? 'Someone must be teaching the history of religion. It's written into the syllabus. What did you say was the subject of your thesis?'

'I didn't.'

'I feel I should know what I'm paying for.'

'I don't see that you really need to know, since in any case I shan't be doing it.'

'Won't you have to present a synopsis, for instance to the tutor overseeing it?'

'I shall tell them this course is only a preliminary to identify whether there's a real topic there.'

'I still think I should know. I might be able to give you some advice on presentation.'

'The social significance of cross-dressing in Elizabethan theatre. Or some variation on that.'

'I wonder who they'll offer you as overseer.'

'I may not get that far.'

'You will. I shall be all agog to hear how you get on.'

Why do I always feel such pressure from him? His final comment could be a perfectly friendly statement of interest but something in me reads it as a threat. 'Report back to me at once or else . . .' Or else what? Galton has no hold over me, except my being half hooked on the case. Somehow he knows he's got me, as if he could look inside my head, lift the top off and watch me thinking as they do with wretched laboratory animals.

'Listen,' I say to Joel the night before my Wessex interview. 'I think someone other than the client ought to know where I'm going tomorrow, in case anything happens. I mean if I don't come back.' Put like that it sounds so melodramatic. Oates going out into the blizzard. I may be gone some time.

'Are you certain you want to get into this, Jade?'

'It's just a precaution. I'm probably being overcautious, hearing things that go bump in the night. I'll phone you tomorrow evening just to let you know you can stand down. Here's the address.'

'Hang on while I switch to record.' Joel always has everything that opens and shuts in the new technology. 'Sounds innocent enough,' he says at the end.

'Who knows what lurks behind the closed doors of academe?' I joke, more to keep up my own spirits than his.

I knock back a bottle of wine and fall asleep in front of

University Challenge, not even trying to beat the buzzer, to wake with a start and stagger to bed. Remember, Jade, you're still a lawyer not a lapsed gumshoe. You're going on a recce that's all, to get the feel of the place.

This morning the sky's the familiar London grey of too-often washed blankets, pre-duvet, with a dismal rain not fine enough to be called soft, insidious, soaking. I phone rail enquiries for train times. Pick one that'll get me there at the appointed hour with enough leeway for contingencies, signal failure, breakdown, off the rails, suicide, that could be a catalogue of the ills modern flesh is heir to. I swathe myself in a black plastic shortie mac, put up my umbrella and dare the rush-hour traffic across to the station, climbing the main steps against the almost irresistible lava flow of those on the way in, commuting from urban villages with their executive estates of Barratt Homes, pony clubs and bridge nights, enlivened by an occasional partner-swapping evening if the broadsheets are to be believed.

I get a seat among those wise enough to be going the other way, to drop salary for the luxury of being able to breathe en route to and from the office while still keeping a toehold in the capital. We sit, not touching or speaking, hunched into our newspapers or paperbacks, wired up to earplug headphones or dozing through the fractured south London suburbs down to the leaf-fringed lawns of Hampshire.

The rain is stopping as I leave the station, and a sudden break in the clouds lights up the wet surfaces, bead-droplets and tran-sient bubbles, with refracted sunshine, giving that spurious lift to the spirits our fickle weather generates in its better moments, and that people in more stable climates don't understand, the switchback of mood that comes from living a perpetual pathetic fallacy. I find the promised bus and climb in among the frail, clinging on grimly for a taste of freedom, and young mothers, probably single, distraught with toddlers' buggies and hung round with plastic bags of shopping. I decide it must be character rebuilding for me to sometimes see how the other half travels, not to be always riding jackboot past them.

Wessex has its own bus stop outside the remembered iron gate. This time I buzz the intercom and state my business to the voice from within. 'I've an appointment with the dean, Revd Luther Bishop.' Surely it's a false name.

'Do come in. Dr Bishop is expecting you.'

So at last I get to go through the gate, like Alice shrunk to the right size by the magic bottle. Or was it the mushroom? I'm in a new reception area tacked on to the older building in conventionally cheerful laminates and glass to impress with an immediate apprehension of sweetness and light. There's nothing murky about our courses and staff, it says. We're the first rung of the ladder to success. Well, don't knock it, Jade. You and Roger both had to climb up this way out of Acton Primary School. Galton's route was different I suspect. Prep school, very minor independent. Nothing too fancy but still an easier route, especially back then, with his thirteen years previous on me.

The receptionist directs me to a spindly tube of plastic chair, chic minimalist. There's a display of tidy magazines and supplements to the educational trade. I'd like to pick one out to give myself something to do but I don't want to disturb their neat arrangement or risk dropping any on the gleaming straw coloured parquet, followed by an undignified, bum-in-the-air, scramble to pick them up. Am I observed? There were closed-circuit cameras beyond the gate but I can't see anything here. At least not without craning my neck and showing my hand.

A door marked 'Secretariat' opens to the right and a youngish woman in neat grey slacks and a white polo neck, nipped in waist, full breasts, 'like two white hills all covered in snow', clacks across the parquet in elegant sandals. I know at once that she's Mary-Ann Molders and feel a lift of confidence at my advantage. 'You don't know me, baby, but I know all about you.'

'Ms Cowell?' She's extending a hand. Glasses hang round her neck on a cord. She's brought her pen out with her as if she can only pause a moment to attend to me and then I must stop cluttering up her day.

I put out my hand. 'That's right.'

Her grip is just right. The palm slightly cold to the touch. Sweat, sticky would be inefficient.

'Dr Bishop can see you now.' Does she think the name sounds fake?

'Aren't the students back yet? It seems very quiet.'

'We're not in full spate, that's true. Just mainly staff, and some students who've been called in, specially to run by some problems before term begins.'

I'm following her through a swing glass-panelled fire door into a bright corridor with one windowed length looking out on a quadrangle as if we're in some mediaeval cloister. She knocks briskly but not too loudly on a light oak door marked 'Dean'.

'Come,' a voice calls.

Molders opens the door and holds it back for me. I murmur a thankyou and slip inside. She closes it behind us. A man is rising from a desk in front of me and leaning forward to stretch out a hand. He's tall, heavily built, a little flushed, with crinkly gingerish hair. For a moment I'm stunned. I'd expected him to be black. The name, the gospel style setup of the Temple, the physical website presence of Apostle Joachim with his honeyed sincerity, had all led me down a steep path of misconception. You'd better stick to conveyancing, Jade. Marlowe would be ashamed of you.

'Ms Cowell. We're pleased you want to join us.' The voice has a hint of post-colonial. South African maybe. Then it clicks. Not post-colonial. Old colonial. What I'm getting is the last traces of Northern Ireland Protestant, a much overlain whiff of polemic and intolerance. I reach out for the hand which bristles with stiff gingery hairs.

'Well, thank you for seeing me so quickly,' I say. 'Of course we don't know yet if what I want to do can fit into your curriculum.'

'I'm sure something to our mutual advantage can be worked out. I see you have a degree in law from Sussex. Yet your subject for the proposed thesis seems to lie in a very different direction.'

'It's a return to my first love.' Always stick as much to the truth as possible when lying. 'I began in English studies but then I became disillusioned with the career prospects. It was that time in the eighties when we were all urged to get on, to pursue our own success and that meant making money in a high-powered job.'

'And did you?'

'Certainly more than I would have as a new teacher.'

'And now?'

'Now I want something different.' Here's where the truth and I have to part. 'I've managed to save enough to study for a further degree while I reconsider what to do with my life, what I really want. Maybe in the end I'll decide to go back to the law after all. I always have that option in our increasingly litigious society. But at least I'll have given myself the time to reconsider.'

'And what made you choose Wessex, Ms Cowell?'

I've rehearsed for this one. It's such a standard. 'I wanted a small campus where I could have time to think. Big campuses can suck you into too much activity. I need the quiet and space to get my head straight. I see your short course, very informal, unstructured as a chance to explore.'

'You would of course have to have a supervisor, just to make sure you weren't wasting your time. We expect our further degree students to keep in contact via bi-monthly meetings, seminars with a tutor, in your case presumably the head of English.'

'Or history,' I offer.

'Yes indeed. I'll see who is willing to take you on. After all it will be more work for one of them.'

And more money for you I think.

'Perhaps you would like to see round the campus while you're here. I'll ask Ms Molders to give you the guided tour. Then perhaps we can speak about your impressions before you go.'

'Do you have an open day for potential students?'

'Many institutions do of course. But I prefer to see people on a one-to-one basis. Our intake is quite small and selective.' We both stand and he presses some kind of intercom I haven't noticed before.

'Ms Molders, do you have a few moments to show Ms Cowell around?'

Of course she does. It must be all set up beforehand. This is their usual drill and she's been painting her nails or cleaning her ears while she waits for the buzz. She holds the door open for me but I wave her on.

'You lead the way. You know where we're going.' We pass through corridors, pausing to peer into classrooms assembled from a child's plastic bricks until suddenly we're in the older part, what must have been St Walburgha's.

'This is our pride,' Mary-Ann Molders says, 'our chapel.'

She opens the door on an array of columns, between painted walls imitating mosaic, nineteenth-century repro Verona but in black, dried blood and gilding without the light and grace of the original frescos of the Emperor Justinian and his entourage. These are nineteenth-century saints with long cloudy beards and hair, barefoot patriarchs bearing the torture trappings of their martyrdoms. Surprisingly there's no altar and no furnishings apart from stacking chairs and what must be the original pulpit but set where the altar would have been.

'Do you have services in here?'

'We call them "Gatherings". They are mainly for theology

students. They live together in hall, unlike students of other faculties who tend to have lodgings in the town.'

'But other people, students, can attend the Gatherings.'

'We have a couple each term that are open to all.'

'And for a quiet moment of meditation?'

'Oh the chapel is always open as you see, as long as nothing else is going on.'

'So interesting that you've kept what must be the original decoration.'

'Well, there's a preservation order but anyway we wouldn't want to change it. The students find it a real inspiration.'

I turn away as if anxious to move on, hoping I haven't awakened any suspicions with my interest.

'Your theology students seem to follow an almost monastic lifestyle.'

'They prefer it that way. It makes it easier for them to concentrate on their development. And they have to be protected.'

'Protected?'

'From distracting external influences, although we did have one case recently on campus of a tutor encouraging them to experiment with illegal substances. He was suspended of course.'

Amyntas' recipe for opiates. I resist an impulse to joke about heightened perceptions. Instead I bring out an anodyne, 'I should think so,' as we pass through the refectory, hall, and more classrooms, stopping to look into the gym and admire the Olympic-length swimming pool, not yet filled for the beginning of term.

'And this is the library.'

It's a miniature version of the round dome of the old reading room at the British Library that I've seen in early photographs. Spot Karl Marx in the lower right-hand corner. Here there are the same galleries with fireproof metal stairs, floors and shelves. The original readers' seats in red leather with individual lamps and solid chairs. Like the chapel it gives this foundation of a few years a feeling of permanence and reliability.

'Splendid,' I hear myself saying. 'I really look forward to working in here.'

'You have to book. But those doing MAs and doctorates like you get priority. There's more space behind for the ordinary students.' She leads me into a modern extension with a wall of desktop PCs and long central tables and chairs. Light floods in from tall plate-glass windows with a view over another quadrangle, bordered at the back by an urban shrubbery of japonica, forsythia and azalea with tall poplars beyond.

'I suppose this is better for the eyes,' I say, 'but it doesn't have the atmosphere of the old library.' I feel myself running out of platitudes.

Mary-Ann, I suspect, feels much the same. 'I think the dean will be ready to see you now.'

'Well, Ms Cowell, how do you like us?'

'Very much indeed. Very impressive.'

'And do you think you could work well here?'

'After what I've seen I'm sure I could.'

'Then we would be very pleased to have you among us. I've spoken to the heads of English and history and either would be happy to be your supervisor. Perhaps when you start you could see both of them and come to a mutually satisfactory arrangement. We shall of course be putting all this in writing to you with details of fees and so on. And we will need your formal acceptance of the terms and conditions.'

'Of course.'

He stands up. We shake hands. Apple-pie Mary-Ann shows me out, back to reception, presses the white security switch opening the door to the outside world, shakes hands too. And I'm on the other side again. Why do I feel such a sense of relief, and like walking away very fast, even running? There's a timetable at the college bus stop. The next bus isn't for half an hour but I can't wait here at the gates. I feel as if I might be watched by the CCTV cameras pointing through the railings. I start off down the road to the town, striding out like some twentieth-century hiker with stick, rucksack and boots, heading for the uplands where the air's clean and fresh.

At the beginning of March of the new year a messenger arrived, sent ahead by the countess, to say that she would be with us within the week. How gladly my heart beat now. I gave myself to pay particular attention to her patients so that all should give a good report of me and of my cure of them. Next I combed through our dispensary to see if anything were lacking that I had missed before, and remedied it. Meanwhile the house was made ready to receive her with clean bed linen, fresh supplies of meats, ale and wine and candles. The steward sent abroad for the tenants to come in with birds, fish and flesh of every sort and the kitchens were full of flying down, bowls of blood and entrails to feast the dogs.

Carters rolled into the courtyard with loads of logs and kindling. Fires were lit in every room to chase away the winter damp. All was as merry as if Christmas had never ceased and we fallen into foul winter. Then after three days, in an afternoon of bitter wind but high clouds and a thin sunlight, the cry went up from the boy posted in a fork of a tree beside the road. 'She comes, she comes.' All we her servants crowded out to meet her as the first of the carriages came into view. The horses were snorting great clouds in the cold air and their sides were flecked with foam.

We fell on our knees as the carriage doors opened, the riders dismounted and the chamberlain stepped down from my lady's coach with the arms of Pembroke and Sidney emblazoned on the door, the colours still bright in spite of their coating of mire and dust of travel. But my lady herself came not out as was her custom to greet us all. The chamberlain called for a litter to be brought. Then I ran with two of the serving men to fetch the one that we kept always in the dispensary for the feeble sick, laid a clean silk cover upon it and cushions, and returned to the courtyard. Three of her ladies helped her from the coach into it and she was borne away to her bedchamber. 'Attend me Amyntas,' she said. 'I have need of your aid and physic.'

Letting a few minutes pass that her ladies might settle her, I entered and fell on my knees at her bedside. She put out a hand that trembled a little and touched my hair. 'What can you prescribe my little physician, for weariness and melancholy?'

'I have some fresh poppy syrup my lady that will bring you rest and sleep.'

'I do not want to sleep; there is too much to be done. I must write letters to friends at court, to Sir Robert Cecil and Cousin Wotton, even to her majesty herself. Bring me some brandy.'

When she had sipped a little, and the colour had returned somewhat to her cheeks which had been like to a yellowed parchment at first upon her arrival, I begged my lady to tell me what had so disordered her.

'You see that Mistress Griffiths is not with me. That is because her friends are among those who defy my authority in the city, mine by my husband's will in trust for our son until he will come of age, and then his. Some turbulent people, among them the town recorder and my own bailiff of the town, have set up their own court in rival to that Council of the Marches which is the only true court of which my husband was president and my father before him. Some others of them of the meaner sort have torn down the walls fast under my castle and my private walks there which they have cast away. And all this which was begun in my lord's time is carried on now with the greater insolence because I am a weak woman alone.'

I saw that all this speech much agitated her and urged her to a little more brandy, hoping that that, the heat of the fire, and the fatigue of the journey would cause her to fall into a restful slumber. 'My cares deny all rest Amyntas. Only perhaps if you should sing me some words of my brother's, I might find a little quiet.'

Get hence foule grief, the canker of the mind:
Farewell complaint, the miser's only pleasure:
Away vain cares, by which few men do find
Their sought-for treasure.

Ye helpless sighs, blow out your breath to nought,
Tears, drown your selves, for woe (your cause) is wasted.
Thought, think to end, too long the fruit of thought
My mind hath tasted.

But thou sure hope, tickle my leaping heart,
Comfort, step thou in place of wonted sadness.
Fore-felt desire, begin to savour parts
Of coming gladness.

Let voice of sighs into clear music run,
Eyes, let your tears with gazing now be mended,
In stead of thought, true pleasure be begun,
And never ended.

She had dismissed her ladies, who indeed were also weary from the journey and glad to be gone from their duties. Therefore I sat on alone beside her on a red and gold footstool, bearing the countess' own symbol of a phoenix, so that when she waked I should be there to serve her.

At length she began to stir about in the bed and suddenly sitting up looked around wildly as if not knowing where she lay. 'Do not fear madam. You are safe at Ramsbury.'

'I am in my own chamber again. I dreamt I was still on the road and surrounded by murderers in the forest. My throat is like parchment. Bring me some beer, child.'

So I brought it to her and held the cup for her to drink. 'I am afraid to sleep lest the nightmare should ride me again. Come here and lie with me to keep the hobgoblins away. Take off your clothes. We will be together like Diana and her nymphs.'

Now my hands trembled so much I could scarcely undo the fastenings of my doublet and shirt. At last I dropped my slops, having slipped off my shoes and stood only in my hose and the binding about my breasts.

'Make haste with the rest child. Such slim white legs. Come.' She threw back her bedclothes and patted the place beside her with her ringed hand. 'You bind your breasts. Are they then growing? Let me see.'

My lady pulled at the linen. 'So small still.' Her fingers traced their shape. 'And the little mouse between your thighs. If only that might be pricked out for my pleasure.' Her hand moved down to touch my secrets and it was if a sheet of flame enfolded me so that I cried out and trembled under her touch. 'There child do not cry. That cannot hurt you. You must suffer more when you come to a man. What does the poem say: "no more signs there are / Than fishes leave in streams or birds in air." Perhaps my body disgusts you, is no longer young.'

'Madam is still beautiful.' And indeed so I thought her, for aside from those necessary marks of childbearing her flesh was firm and rosy, her breasts, freed by the wet nurse from giving suck, were as a maid's still, of whitest yet warm marble, blue veined and coral tipped. Yet I found it hard to look upon her for I had never seen either woman or man full naked before.

'Therefore since there can be no sin in impossibility, hold me child and let me sleep in your arms.' So I put mine about her and soon she slept indeed. Then was I able to withdraw my arms from about her for the flame I had not understood seared me again when our breasts touched and kept me from sleep myself, as also the fear that she might wake and wonder what she did or that one coming in early might surprise us as we lay, with me in all my nakedness.

In the darkness of the winter night I could not tell how long we lay together but at the first touch of russet grey in the sky I rose softly and dressed myself. The countess lay still sleeping while exhausted nature replenished herself. I crept from her room and regained my own pallet where I lay trembling full dressed under the coverlet until I heard others stirring. Then I took myself to the kitchen for bread and half a pint of wine and to stop the chattering of my teeth by warming myself at the fire.

Only Joan the cook and a scullery maid were up and busy about the breakfasts, laying out chines of beef, mutton and coneys for boiling with gruel of chickens for the weaker stomachs.

'You are betimes Master Boston.'

'I could not sleep for the cold.'

'You should have hot young blood to keep you from that, unless you have a cold heart or too many sharp thoughts in your head.'

When my shivering had ceased I made my way towards my lady's bedchamber, staying my steps in the passage where I slept when I heard her call out for her ladies. 'Bring me rags. I bleed.'

Swiftly I turned and made my way back to the kitchen. 'A hot posset for my lady and the finest mancheate with a clean napkin.' I placed all on a silver tray and returned to her chamber.

She lay back in her bed with her ladies about her, making no attempt to rise. 'What have you brought me Amyntas?'

'A little breakfast madam that shall gently soothe the stomach.'

'I can scarce open my eyes, even though I slept like a child after the draught you gave me. Give me some bread and wine and then I feel I shall sleep again.'

'Nature commends such rest madam after so much travelling by the way. It is the best physick.'

'And for the pain in my belly what will you prescribe?'

'Syrup of comfrey madam.'

'Does my lady well to have such faith in one so young?' the duenna asked. 'Let me send to Wilton for one of your other physicians, more experienced in the healing arts.'

'Let Master Boston try what he can do. When he has failed then is the time to send for others. Besides it is only a little ache that I have not felt these last three months. Perhaps I shall get with child again by a cloud or a shower of gold.'

'You will need a man hid therein then my lady,' said the duenna, and all the women laughed together.

'Bring me your draught child and then all of you let me sleep. When I wake I have much to do.'

As I walked to the dispensary for the syrup I thought that my lady's melancholy with which she had returned was much eased and that as yet she had no memory of what had passed that night. Nor would I dare to remind her of it. Perhaps she had thought it but a dream brought on by the brandy into which I had managed to slip a spoonful of poppy syrup at the bottom of her last cup, and now believed I saw the beneficial results of this in her greater ease.

When I returned she had raised herself against her pillows so that I could see through the disorder of her bedgown some of what had pleasured me the night before.

'Shall I trust you truly, Amyntas?' she asked, 'for I believe you gave me poppy even though I forbade it. I had such dreams.'

'Madam, I cannot deceive you. There was a very little in the brandy but only to give you rest as it has done. You know I would serve and preserve you with my life, and would die rather than any harm should come to you, in especial from my hand.'

The letter from Wessex has come by the next morning, this morning. Briefly I wonder why they're so keen to sign me up, and decide it must be the hefty fee they charge postgraduates just for a short summer course. The dean makes it clear that if all goes well I can stay on if I want, maybe for ever, at a price, gathering points towards an eventual elevation. I study the names of the heads of department to try to penetrate through to their owners.

Ranee Raval. English.

Daniel Davidson. History.

'I'm in. But at a price.'

'Well done. I think the expression is spare no expense. As I hope I made clear, Ms Green, I fully expected to have to pay. Tell me what you thought of the setup.' Galton's on a high because he knows that now he's truly hooked me. I have to remind myself I can back away at any time. Or can I? We haven't signed a contract yet. And I'm supposed to be the lawyer. I choose my words carefully.

'It's hard to say. Some things struck me as weird. The way they keep their theologs as if in a monastery. And the chapel without any altar and almost out of bounds to the ordinary students who're expected to lodge in the town.'

'Along with most of the staff, apart from a privileged few.'

Galton's own address must be somewhere in the town I realise. I might even have passed it on the bus from the station. The thought makes me uneasy though I don't know why. It adds to my feeling of having been watched while I was there.

'Perhaps you could express an interest in their temple and get yourself into a service.'

'I thought of that.' I mustn't lose the initiative in this conversation with Galton as so often happens. 'They call them Gatherings.'

'Ah yes, of course. How quickly one forgets. And the Revd Bishop, what did you think of him?'

'Esau? Very hairy.'

'And did you meet the secretary?'

'Of course. The Molders was given the job of showing me round. Very apple pie and efficient. I imagine she lives in.'

'Certainly. You mustn't be deceived by that wholesomely efficient manner.'

'If you think that then perhaps we should call it all off.' Cue
for a song.

'No, no, of course not. It's only that I feel so powerless, so
unable to influence things.' I realise it's the closest Galton can
get to an apology.

Later when he's rung off I consider the power-freak side of
Galton. He's used to being in control, his every word hung on
by eager, open-mouthed students. That's how he got himself
into this mess. Exercising power; believing he could say and do
what he liked and get away with it. Did he give some of Amyntas'
steamier confessions to his students? Or are they only in the
full part of the manuscript he says was stolen? Why don't I want
to ask him? Because he might lie in spite of my warnings, and
I couldn't trust his answer.

The students are all over the age of consent so exposing them
to adult material shouldn't be a sackable offence. That's the
ground he stands on. But is it an abuse of trust? Only if it can
be seen as truly pornographic, obscene. But nothing has really
happened in the memoirs, not as far as I've read anyway. Surely
no one could accuse such a sad love story of being obscene in
these days? No court would support such a judgement.

Suppose I wrote my own memoirs and published them:
Confessions of a legal loner. Briefs and tarts. Inns and outs of
the wig trade. How I played Cherubino to my countess. More
like Bottom to Titania.

Once again I'd been left dangling, wondering if the call would
ever come. Then Helen Chalmers' secretary rang me with a
couple of dates. I said either was fine. When she rang again it
was the later one. I turned this over, wondering how to read it.
Sometimes in hope, often in doubt as the week passed, expecting
all along that her secretary would ring to say it was all off. Then
it was the day. We would meet in the foyer at six-thirty for a

pre-drink. Helen was there first. I walked towards her on traditionally jellied legs hoping she couldn't see them tremble under
black velvet pants.

'Very smart,' she said. 'What would you like to drink? There's
the stalls bar through there.'

'I'll get them. What will you have?'

'Gin and tonic would be great.'

It was the usual theatre crush bar with nowhere to sit. I left
her leaning against a mahogany shelf and fought my way through,
got the drinks, ordered a repeat for the interval and struggled
back. She had lit a cigarette and was looking about her.

'Jim would hate this but not as much as the performance
itself.'

'I ordered the same for the interval. Is that OK?'

'Perfect. It's more civilised to drink wine but I find it makes
me sleepy.'

'I got a couple of programmes.'

'Do you know the plot? If not you'd better read up on the
first act.'

Doing as I was told I opened the glossy pages. It was sung
in German with a famous Czech mezzo as the Marschallin, the
older woman, to a young Austrian as Octavian, her lover. I just
about got the first act under my belt before the bell rang to call
us to our seats. Sitting next to Helen in the dark, my nostrils
filled with her scent, the lines of her profile within my sideways
glance against the darkened theatre and her arm touching mine,
I couldn't hear the overture for the singing in my ears. I didn't
want the distraction of the stage, simply to savour being so close
beside her, but as the plot unfolded and the rich dark music
poured into me with all the passionate yet creamy sweetness of
an Austrian pineapple cake, I was sucked in, absorbed as an
amoeba metamorphoses its prey. And I hadn't realised from the
programme and the unfamiliar names of the cast, that the
Marschallin's young lover, Octavian, was played by a woman,

not a drag role for lack of a castrato as in Handel but a delib-
erate choice of the composer or his librettist.

By the time of the first interval I had completely transposed
myself and Helen into Octavian and the Marschallin and could
no longer draw any distinction between the fiction of the stage
and the reality of its two watchers. For there were only the two
of us in the half light. The rest emerged chattering, laughing,
comparing notes as we made our way to the bar.

'Well, what do you think?'

'It's fantastic. The music. The voices.'

'Even Baron Ochs?'

'Even him. He's not my favourite of course but maybe you
need that element of lumbering danger to threaten the lovers.
It's very well sung. But the Marschallin, she's brilliant.' I heard
myself trying to impress.

'You haven't seen any Strauss before?'

'I told you I'm not well up on later stuff.'

'It was carefully chosen. I thought this would appeal to you,
more than some of his other pieces.'

Yet even as she was speaking I was hearing something else
in my head, that variation Dryden and Purcell made on
Shakespeare's if music be the food of love, in Deller's high pure
counter-tenor.

Sure I must perish by your charms.
Unless you save me in your arms.

Then the bell was calling us back. I hadn't had time to read
the summary of the next act. We swallowed our drinks and
fought our way back to our seats.

Suddenly the plot had taken a turn for the worse. Octavian,
splendid in silver as the Rosenkavalier, was presenting a rose to
a young girl and obviously falling for her and she for him.

At this moment Helen leant sideways towards me and whispered, 'This is how you will leave me.' At least I thought that was what she said but I was trying too hard to penetrate the German text as it soared on passionate cadences from the new lovers. I understood that Octavian was leaving the Marschellin for the vapid Sophie but I wanted, longed to understand every syllable of the change. By the final trio I was drowning in the Straussian melodies.

'How can he?' I asked in the next interval. 'There's no comparison between the two.'

'Wait and see.'

I found myself impatient with the farce that opened the third act, with Baron Ochs' pursuit of Octavian dressed as a maid. It was Viola and Olivia in reverse and I wasn't in the mood for it. I longed for the Marschallin's return but it was only to a dignified renunciation. Octavian hesitates. Surely he can't leave her. For a few seconds when the music finally ceased and the lights went up, I couldn't clap. I was like a child at its first pantomime, my disbelief not just suspended but sunk fathoms down.

I stumbled up the steps after Helen still blinking, unable to believe it was over and life would pick up where it had left off and go on again.

'I've got the car round the corner,' Helen said as we came out on to the pavement. 'I'll drop you home. Where do you live?'

'Earl's Court. But it's out of your way isn't it? I don't want to . . .'

'Not much. We live in Camden Hill. Only ten minutes or so away. I'll go through Hyde Park.'

And because I didn't want the evening to end, was still under the spell of the music, I found myself walking beside her round to the street where she'd parked, getting into what I saw was a smallish BMW and directing her, after we had passed under the shadowy trees of Hyde Park and over the Serpentine luminous under a cold full moon, down Earl's Court Road and into the side street of handsome square houses chopped into flats or harbouring grimly cheap hotels.

Helen stopped her car in a lone space at the kerb.

'Thank you,' I said knowing it sounded flat and lame. 'It's been terrific. And for the lift.'

'Aren't you going to ask me in? I could do with a drink. I take it you've got something drinkable in there.'

How could I refuse? Yet I dreaded her seeing what must be the comparative squalor of how I lived. My breakfast bowl and mug were still unwashed in the sink. Had I made the bed? I couldn't remember.

'It's not very big or tidy. We could look for a pub or a wine bar if you want a drink.'

'I want to see where you live, silly.'

I gave in. 'OK. I think I've got a bottle of red. Only plonk I'm afraid. But you mustn't look at anything too closely. I'm not a great one for housework.'

'I never supposed you were.' She was getting out of the car. I had no choice but to do the same. When had I last cleaned the place? Would there be whorls of fluff behind the bathroom door and in the corners of the studio that would dance like dervishes in the draught?

Deliberately forgetting my manners I opened the door and went in first. At a quick glance it didn't look too bad. For once I'd chucked my clothes on the bed instead of on the floor. 'Have a seat.' I tried to sound cool as I pointed to the only armchair. 'I'll get the wine.'

I uncorked the bottle and found two glasses.

'Cheers!'

'Salut. Tell me more about what you thought of this evening. Have you ever been chased by a Baron Ochs?'

'There was a lecturer at Sussex, typical groper. Thought I was gamine or game. I wasn't sure which. What about you?'

'Oh, all the time. That's what dinner parties are for. Footsie under the table and a hand up your skirt. And for getting on, making deals, networking of course. It's all part of the game.'

'Doesn't anyone complain or say no?'

'What would be the point? And who to when everyone's doing it? You'll have to learn some of the tricks yourself if you want to get on. Maybe I should teach you, take you in hand as they say.'

I felt like someone brought up in the forest by gentle wolves who now had to learn to talk, and the bitter ways of humankind. Helen took a packet of cigarettes and a gold lighter out of her bag and lit up. The little bright eye in the middle of the lighter, diamond or glass, winked at me. 'I'll need an ashtray if you don't want me to flick ash all over your floor.'

'I'll find you something.'

'You don't smoke, I take it?'

'Only an occasional cigar.' I rummaged in the cupboard under the sink and came back with a saucer. Somewhere the temperature had dropped. Was she bored? Had I blown it?

'So what did you think of Sophie?'

'She's an old-fashioned ingénue. He's had his mistress but she has to be sweetness and light. At least that's changed. There was only one girl I was at uni with who was a virgin, my best friend actually, and even she got it off in the end with a boring fellow student.'

'And you?'

'That's a long story.'

'OK. Another time then. I'd better go. Jim doesn't worry about me but I had to borrow his car. Mine was being serviced and they hadn't finished with it. So he'll be twitchy until I bring his home safely.' She stubbed out her cigarette and tilted back her glass. 'By the way, I've fixed for you to join him the next time he's in court. His secretary will send you down the brief. He's very good. You can learn a lot from watching and listening to him.'

She stood up and brushed at her skirt where some flakes of ash had settled. I put down my glass and stood too. 'Thanks for the drink.'

'My pleasure.' I turned towards the door.

'Aren't you going to kiss me?'

'Are you sure you want me to?'

'That's what it's all about, isn't it?'

I moved towards her. Helen was wearing high heels that meant I had to reach up a little with my lips to find hers. It began as a chaste kiss, friends might almost have exchanged but then I heard her gasp a little, her mouth opened and our arms went out as if we had to hold each other up from falling in a tangle on the bed.

Helen drew back. 'I think we'd better stop this or Jim will really have to worry about his car.' She walked away from me to the door. Should I ask when I could see her again? We were out in the hall, the quaintly named 'common parts'. Then I was standing on the pavement as she opened the car door and got in. There must be something I could say. She switched on the engine and wound down the window.

'I'll ring you. Soon.'

'I'll get a more decent bottle for next time.'

'Some gin would be great.' With a wave she drove off.

'How are you?' It was Helen's voice next day on the internal phone. Was that risky? She hadn't said her name or: 'It's me.' She knew she didn't need to.

'Lonely,' I risked. 'What about you?'

'A bit dazed I think. My mind doesn't seem to be working properly. Someone's at my door. I'll call you again.' She put down the receiver. It was weird knowing she was there in the building, that I only had to walk out into the corridor and I might bump into her heading for the loo, that I could climb the stairs or take the lift and knock on her door. I wouldn't, of course. This was a delicate moment when she was maybe regretting last night, wondering what she was getting into and where it could go.

Which of us was seducing the other or were we both the hunter and the hunted, the willing Leda in the swan's clasp, the Venus trap for her many eager lovers whose goings-on adorn the walls of palaces and galleries and still have power to bring a blush or a flush, especially to those falling in love?

My head was full of half-remembered lines, rags of verse, unsatisfying scraps from the feast I'd left when I switched to the law.

> Helen, thy beauty is to me
> Like those Nicean barques of yore . . .

> I wish I were where Helen lies
> Night and day on me she cries . . .

And most potently:

> Sweet Helen, make me immortal with a kiss.
> Thy lips suck up my soul . . .

It was as if my memory had been storing them up with some terrifying foresight by a kind of osmosis, against the time when they would leap out at me like a tune that unspools again and again in your head no matter how much you try to press the stop button or chase it away with another. Except that I wasn't trying. I was happy to sink into the repetition of her name, to wade out into its clear green waters and drown.

At lunchtime I walked to Covent Garden and bought a CD of *Der Rosenkavalier* in the Royal Opera House shop: highlights with Elisabeth Schwarzkopf as the Marschallin and Christa Ludwig as Octavian. That night, alone in my flat where I could still see her sitting in my armchair, the smoke rising from her cigarette in an incense prayer to some goddess, could still taste her mouth with its tang of wine and that same smoke, I played it endlessly, obsessively, cutting out the bits that said nothing to me, until I could sing along in my head with the bits that did. I finished the bottle of wine and fell asleep on my bed, to wake shakily seeing it was three o'clock, and undress, drink a glass of water and fall asleep again to the Marschallin's aria near the end of the first act, her outpouring of melancholy and the anticipation of love lost.

Helen didn't call the next day. I played it cool and didn't ring her but by the evening I was desperate, prey to the *plus ça change* of Shakespeare's sonnet:

> Being your slave, what should I do but tend
> Upon the hours and times of your desire?
> I have no precious time at all to spend,
> Nor services to do, till you require.

I rang Joel and signed him up for an evening in the local pub so that I shouldn't be left drinking at home alone. I didn't feel like a club where there'd be dancing. We sat over our pints revisiting the Gateshead we'd neither of us seen in a decade, wondering if we could keep up the payments on our flats. Joel's in Norbury was much cheaper than mine in Earl's Court and as an accountant he was already earning more but I'd had a little nest egg from Nana I'd been able to put down as deposit. We talked about the property boom and should we sell now.

'You'd only have to buy somewhere for just as much unless you got out of London. But then you'd never get back.' It was the scene that was the great draw for Joel only equalled by Manchester, but the attraction of the northern Piccadilly set was offset by the thought of starting again, finding a job, somewhere to live, without friends. I didn't tell him why I specially needed his company tonight. Tomorrow was Friday. If Helen didn't ring then there was the whole weekend to get through not knowing how she was feeling, whether she was regretting the whole thing.

Joel went off to catch the last bus to Norbury while I wandered back along the Old Brompton Road, under the lamplit silhouettes of the plane trees, their branches heavy with the broad palmed leaves of August, coated in a thin film of carbon from the constant flow of traffic beneath them, their bark starting its annual peel of fibrous scabbed patches, a scurf of dead cells. If she didn't ring I would have to look for another job. It would be impossible to inhabit the same building day after day with all the likelihood of a chance encounter: the eyes cast down, a brief hallo as our bodies brushed past each other. Or worse, nothing, her eyes looking straight ahead without acknowledgement.

There was a stack of files on my desk in the morning, neat, fat dark-blue ring-binders with the firm's name across each. Inside the first was a small yellow sticker. 'What are you doing on Monday evening? I'll ring. H.'

I shut the cover again quickly in case Drew should spot the bright yellow slip. Only when he left the room to go to the loo did I open it again and make sure I'd read it all right. I studied the writing but couldn't make anything much of it, except that it was fluent, middle sized with no obvious quirks. Before Drew came back I detached the sticker and reapplied it to that day's page in my diary. Dimly I remembered something about Queen Elizabeth I putting away Leicester's final note, sent as he was dying, with 'His last letter' written on it. But maybe I'd made that up. Anyway this was Helen's first and perhaps last too. It was already a relic to be preserved.

James Chalmers' secretary was on the line. 'Did you get the brief and the witness statements? Could you study them over the weekend? The case starts on Tuesday but Mr Chalmers would like you to attend a short conference at two this afternoon and then a fuller one on Monday when you're more familiar with the details.'

That took care of my weekend. I'd have to work like hell to get my head round the stuff, not to let Helen down, after all she'd recommended me so her head was on the line too. I'd dazzle everyone with my brilliance, especially the boss, her husband. While we discussed the case I'd be thinking: I kissed her.

'I see you've got the call to higher things,' Drewpad picked up the first of the files. 'When does the trial open?'

'Tuesday I think, but the boss wants me for a conference this afternoon.'

'You'd better get used to it Drew; you're on your own from now on.' He was only half joking.

'No boss can come between me and my buddy. Let's have a drink tonight to start the weekend. It's the last one I'll get until I've got a grip on this lot.'

Dutifully I presented myself at Chalmers' office, joining a group of three others, apart from himself, eager young suits who'd been taking the witness statements. All I could do was listen while they sparred above my head, flashing their findings and opinions and probably wondering why the hell I'd been brought in. At the end Chalmers said: 'Is there anything you want to add, Jade?'

'I think I'd rather listen today. Maybe by Monday I'll have had some thoughts.' I couldn't wait to get back to Drew, realising suddenly as I made my way along the anonymous corridors that neither of us would get on unless we became as thrusting as the rest, that as Helen had said, rising up the hierarchy depended as much on performance as knowledge, and maybe it was already too late for Drew.

'I'm thinking of moving on,' he confided as we sat in a corner of the Mitre, leaving the pavement outside and the standing room by the bar to the noisy crew of overgrown kids let out of school but not ready to go home yet. 'I can't see any future for me with S & F. You're going to be okay. Someone up there obviously loves you.'

'I haven't done anything to earn it.'

'I'm not blaming you. These things have their own mysterious dynamic. I just haven't connected. I've been there four years. It's time to move on.'

'Have you put out any feelers?'

'A few.' He looked down at his pint of lager.

'I think you should.'

'Nobody may want me. That's why I'd rather you didn't say anything at S & F.'

'As if I would. But of course there'll be firms wanting to snap you up, with your qualifications and experience.'

'I might go back into company practice where I can make something of my own. How did it go with the boss man today?'

'I tried not to show my complete ignorance of the case, the procedure, you name it. I just hope I'm better briefed by Monday.'

'Lucky you. I wish I could spend a quiet weekend with work instead of having to entertain the cousins from Bangalore, looking for a nice girl for their son and expecting me to be the marriage broker when I haven't been able to find one for myself.'

Drew's life was a succession of visiting family from all over the world, all believing succour could be had in Maida Vale for their diverse needs: education, employment, finance, marriage. After a couple of drinks we set off for the nearest tube where a handwritten notice warned us of a signal failure that meant the line wasn't going further than Marble Arch. I left him staring at the criss-cross coloured lines of the underground map, trying to figure out a way home.

There had been no call from Helen as promised in the note. Maybe after my inarticulate performance at the conference, James had convinced her I wasn't worth bothering with. I did myself a fry-up of egg, tomatoes, mushrooms on toast, decided I'd better stay off the booze for at least an hour and opened the first file.

It was one of our media cases: the division and stripping of assets after an independent TV company had succumbed to the tentacular embrace of a corporate. Jobs and contracts had been scrapped and now those who'd gone down in the rationalisation were trying to claw something back. We were representing the corporate Goliath. Not a pretty sight since he also had the sling. I set to with my magic marker on the statement of case.

The phone rang about eight. It was Helen.

'I didn't know you had my number.'

'Oh I have my ways. Are you on for Monday?'

'Sure.'

'James is out at a Silks' dinner. He thought you were very cool.'

'Just plain ignorance I'm afraid.'

'Anyway you went down OK. What are you doing now?'

'Sitting here boning up on the paperwork. And you?'

'I've had some people in for drinks. They've just gone. I'm going to have a long soak. We're off to the country tomorrow; a wedding in Berkshire.'

'I'll be stuck with more of this.' I didn't want to tell her this weekend was also Sunday lunch with Linda and Rob, Roger, Jenny and the children, the dog and cat, in the suburbs.

'I thought we'd go to the movies on Monday. Jim's out and there's nothing I particularly want to hear. Is that OK with you?'

'Absolutely fine.'

'I'll ring you on Monday to fix it.'

'We've got another conference on Monday.'

'I know. But that's in the afternoon.'

I knew as well as studying the brief this weekend I'd be cleaning the flat, getting some gin and the dressing to go with it, tonic, lemons, filling the ice cube tray with fresh water and lastly changing the sheets, just in case.

On Monday afternoon we all gathered again in James' room but this time there were two representatives of the clients,

Mediatex. Looking round at the rest I felt more confidence. After all I'm a barrister and as far as I knew they weren't, not then.

'It looks pretty open and shut to me, sir,' young, still slightly acned, Jason offered when James asked if we'd had any further thoughts.

'You don't think we need to bring in counsel, then? Judges can be very eccentric. Jade, what do you think now you've had a proper look at the stuff?'

This was my moment. If I bogged it he would despise me and so would Helen. The pack of young suits would fall on me and tear me to pieces.

'I think we have to be rather careful in our presentation. After all the other party can be said to have a moral right on their side.'

'Oh come on, the law's quite clear,' someone to the left of me said.

'The law may be, but we could find ourselves in trouble, our client paying compensation to dozens of claimants, if we appear too greedy and hardline. We don't want any suggestion of abuse of a dominant position. Apart from anything else think of the bad publicity if the media suddenly woke up to a nice bit of juicy corporate bashing.'

'That's to be avoided at all cost.' The older representative of the client, small and balding, spoke for the first time. 'We don't need any more column inches on starving artists and corporate fat cats.'

I thought there was another way to avoid it, by a negotiated settlement, but now wasn't the time to say so.

'So you would recommend the softly, softly, more in sorrow than in anger approach?' James was asking me.

'The erosion of sales by piracy leading to a need to cut titles, much regretted. Making a Calderbank offer quite early in the proceedings to show willingness to cooperate.'

'That's not really the purpose of a Calderbank,' James said.

'I like it,' the little man said. 'I'll talk to my board about an offer. That's the way to play it. At first anyway. We've always got the iron fist to fall back on.'

I left the meeting elated. I could do it. I'd done it. I'd talked and they'd listened and in the end I'd swung them my way. It was my first taste of power, the power of persuasion, and it was as heady as booze or maybe even sex. I could meet Helen more as an equal. I could have her if I wanted. And I did.

I had continued my experiments with the electrics while my lady was absent and when my duties as physician allowed, and now I determined to write to Dr William Gilbard and tell him what further substances beyond those he had himself discovered showed this property. Following the instructions in his book, which included many cuts for greater understanding, I constructed a versorium after his model, a light needle like to a sailor's compass, upon a pin which should swing when the electrics were rubbed and electricitas was present. Writing to him as the amanuensis of my father lest he should discountenance such practices of a mere girl, or even of the youth Amyntas, I questioned whether this presence in things might be the same or akin to that magnetism he had also explored, begging him of his kindness to vouchsafe his opinion on these matters.

My lady still did not know of this work for I felt in my bones that she would not approve unless I could show it to have more purpose than mere experiment, for it was held by some that no man ever found out a truth by experiment but that all knowledge came by chance, and the countess might indeed be of this opinion. Also that no knowledge came by speculation, as I believed Dr Adrian Gilbert held, but that it might be by revelation of the angels as some scryers claimed. But my father said that all such were but deceivers of the gullible and that truth would only be sweated out by labour and experiment. Yet he himself, as I now saw, had profited little by all his toil and therefore I was inclined to observation and then taking thought thereon as the likeliest way to proceed.

So I writ to Dr Gilbard with my trials and the results thereof but there came no answer and one day my lady made it clear why I had heard nothing. Her majesty was sick and Dr Gilbard had been appointed one of her physicians, and must therefore be always ready to attend her wherever she might go for she still determined to keep up her visits whenever her body allowed although she had passed her climacteric and was now in her sixty-ninth year which some believed, though they dare not say so openly, was the mark of the beast, and was eager to go on progress as far as Bristol when summer came. Whether she would make a stay at Wilton the countess much doubted for she was still angry at the young earl and as yet would give him no favour.

I had laid aside the Dutch trunk sent to my lady by her brother from Flushing after my attempt to turn it on the moon which had so frightened me but now I brought it forth for her amusement lest her brother should ask how she did with it.

'Let us see what it will show us,' she said when I had explained its purpose and use. Then she made great sport to look through it at different objects but most it gave her much amusement when she spied upon her favourite stallion as it mounted the mares in season, to see its great prick unfold as a snake to climb up the mares' bellies and pierce their secrets. This she could do without alarming them for the trunk allowed her to watch from such a distance and yet she saw every particular of their mating even to when some of the seed ran back out again.

Then she would take it hunting to prove how serviceable it might be in that sport. So in a March morning when the ground was still hard and slippery with ice and snow, and the horses' hooves broke the cart ruts into slivers of shattered glass with every step, we rode out from Ramsbury towards the forest of

Savernake, my lady the very likeness of Diana herself in full hunting dress of Spanish farthingale and little round hat with sprightly curling plumes, and slung about her a bow and quiver of silver-tipped arrows, attended by her ladies, themselves glittering on horseback and the servants afoot to act as beaters. Before us had gone the head forester to spy where the most game might be hiding.

We passed under leafless trees where the beech mast crackled underfoot and an occasional small bird sang among the branches for St Valentine's was already past. 'Will you be my Valentine, Amyntas?' my lady had asked me on the eve.

'If it would please my lady.'

'And do I have your heart?'

'Oh madam for ever.'

'For ever is too long. No man keeps faith for ever. Will you outdo all man else?'

'For ever and a day madam.'

'You will find a little year is a long time. We shall see how you bear up when summer comes again. Come to my window or rather my door as soon as day dawns.'

So I was there in the morning as bid, with sweetmeats and wine which I presented on my knee and she throwing back the bedcovers showed me herself again in her loose gown and had me into her bed.

'There is no sin, in impossibility,' she said, putting my hand on her breast, 'you but feel how my heart beats.'

Then I remembered some words of that poet knight Sir Thomas Wyatt, one that nearly lost his head over her majesty, her mother, Queen Anne Bullen.

> Thanked be fortune, it hath been otherwise
> Twenty times better; but once, in special,
> In thin array, after a pleasant guise,
> When her loose gown from her shoulders did fall,

And she caught me in her arms long and small,
Therewith all sweetly did me kiss,
And softly said, 'Dear heart, how like you this?'

So we had dallied there in the warmth of her bed like fishes in the crystal flood of our own sweat or in the pure tears gathered in a limbec.

That day we had found nothing to spy on and soon returned. On another day of our hunting we rode out early as soon as it was light, taking only such of her ladies as would ride and a groom in case of mishap, who carried the bows and quivers. Here and there the birds of spring now fluttered and sang among the branches green with fresh leaf and the grass was soft under the horses' hooves.

'Stop,' she said, 'we shall see if we have the advantage of the deer with my brother's gift.' She took a bow from the groom and slung it about her. Now indeed she seemed like Venus, indeed arrayed in her favourite hat with the green feather and velvet cloak for the chase upon a milk white horse, or the Fairy Queen herself gone a-maying so that I remembered the poet Jonson's words from his masque of Cynthia which my father had in a little book printed: 'Queen and Huntress chaste and fair.'

At last we drew up in a clearing so that the countess might try the Dutch trunk and putting it to her eye she began a slow sweep of what lay before us, down a long ride between the trunks of ancient beeches and oaks. 'See,' she said, 'there are the horns of deer as if we had come upon Herne the Hunter in his hide among his people of the forest.'

We had brought no dogs with us in order to our experiment with the trunk, for their noise would have alarmed the prey for miles around unless we had surrounded the woods with beaters. 'It is as if I could take part with them in their sylvan lives. I see the very breath from their nostrils and the twitch as they scent the air for danger. They have no heed of us, poor silly beasts whose lives are forfeit to arrow or dog. Let us return. Now that I perceive them stand so quiet I no longer wish to hunt. This is the strange power of this instrument that seeing so clearly, and so close as if they stood but a yard before me, I cannot shoot. What other wonders will it show us that will unmake our thoughts, even unman the hunter? And what then should we eat but farm cattle and sheep? Every hair of their bodies is distinct as if drawn by Holbein.'

Then I told her how I had frightened myself with turning the trunk upon the heavens and in special the moon. 'And you found no man in the moon nor any goddess there?'

'Venus has left the moon and dwells now among us here, my lady.'

'You have learned to flatter like a courtier. I would my son can do as well in her majesty's presence if he is ever to prosper. Now I am grown melancholy. Let us go back. We will have some music to lighten our spirits.'

And indeed the day which had been so bright was now overcast and a cold wind had driven even those few birds from the branches.

'Stop,' the countess said and we all reined in our horses. 'Give me the trunk again. I think I see a hare on that hillside.' For we had left the forest and were in open country now. So I gave her the instrument and we waited while she put it to her eye, the horses stamping and snorting their breathy clouds into the frosty air. 'It is two hares and they fight like men. Now one has the mastery and the other slinks away. Such gentle creatures yet even they are seized with the madness of love. They rear up like stallions and strike against each other with their forelegs even as cocks or dogs set on one another. So the whole earth is in thrall to passion as men are. Yet only we can look for redemption and know when we sin. Sir Thomas Wyatt who gave not all for love but saved his own neck the while he condemned the queen's to the headsman's blade, saw his own lust as nothing but the chase when he writ: "Whoso list to hunt I know where is an hind . . ." Are not all women hinds for the hunting? No matter how hard we struggle or fast we run, like Daphne when she fled Apollo, we are brought down at last.'

I saw that my lady had indeed fallen into a melancholy fit. 'You are growing cold madam. We should return home at once and I will make you a hot posset to drive out this black humour and the chill,' and I took the trunk from her and rode on to set an example.

At Ramsbury when we arrived she sat close to the fire in her chamber and allowed me to chafe her hands and feet while she sipped at a cup of spiced wine. Then she took up a letter from her younger son Philip still at his studies in Oxford. 'Read it to me Amyntas. I foresee that he writes because he wants money as all Oxford scholars do.'

So I read and indeed she was right and the young nobleman did write for his mother's help towards his debts though I do not remember all the details of that letter. But some gossip of the court I do remember as that Master John Donne that was secretary to the Lord Egerton, was sent to prison for marrying without the consent of the bride's guardian in whose employ he was.

'It is as I said: this loving is a madness. Young people should avoid it and marry as their friends direct. Yet I would not have them do as my own son, to father a child and not marry with the mother. You are fortunate Amyntas that passion does not move you and you are safe in your boy's clothes. I dread to hear any day that my own daughter has fallen prey to some young courtier and lost her chance of a good marriage, and therefore I continually beseech my sister Sidney at Penshurst to keep her close until we can find a good match, since she would not affect the old Earl Hertford who desired her before my lord's death. Yet for all our care it may be in vain as in the case of Mistress

More who has eloped with Master Donne. Was it not some verses of his that were once sent to me in error? It touches me more nearly for that her father, Sir George, was guardian to my cousin Edward Herbert, and indeed perhaps the verses came from him who also aspires to be a poet.'

Then I lied and feigned that I did not remember for I feared that if she recalled them distinctly the countess might turn against me and bar me from her chamber. So I took myself to the kitchen about her supper and afterwards mixed a little poppy with her wine so that she would sleep deeply and not ask for me till morning. And this I did, I swear to God, out of my care of her, though since they have made it seem otherwise.

Yet it caused me again to look many times upon those verses of which I had made a secret copy, until they were committed to memory and would leap unbidden to my mind as potent as any cabbala of the alchemists.

Pressing concerns now called my lady again to her castle of Cardiff where the people had grown ever more mutinous without the old earl's strong hand to govern them. Yet she lingered at Ramsbury, unwilling, she said, to go on her journey leaving our peaceful lives for the turmoil of the city with its lawless people who would be free of the Herbert yoke, free of their lord, the countess, and her Council of the Marches wherein she stood as for the queen's majesty herself.

Now came summer on and there was much famine throughout the land so that my lady was driven to take pity on the poor who gathered at the gates of Wilton, for all their stocks of flour were used up and the salt meats they had put down in the autumn all gone. There was no more grain for the mills to grind except that in my lady's barns. Then we removed to Wilton so that she might more easily give orders for their relief and for money to be given to the parish also to that end, so that when she rode out into the town the people knelt by the roadside to bless her.

Yet in spite of all we could do many were sick, as she said, not of fevers, chills and impostumes but of hunger and even cold for the weather itself seemed determined to punish us, raining daily until the very corn sickened in the fields. The dry wood stacked up for winter was all burnt and the new too green and gave off thick smoke that made the poor to cough up a green phlegm. Many came to the great house with children whose bellies were swollen and whose scant limbs would not bear them. These we gave bread and gruel as much as we might yet there were always more.

Then some blamed the queen for the long wars against the Spaniards that had wasted the land, even though they had been soundly beaten in Ireland by the Lord Mountjoy at the end of the last year. Only the news of the taking of a rich prize, a Portugal carrack, by Sir Richard Leveson under the very guns of their fort brought us some joy in June and men said that Sir Francis Drake was risen and come again.

'Can you cast horoscopes Amyntas?' my lady asked me one day. 'They say at the beginning of her majesty's reign Dr Dee foretold that she would govern long, while Mary of Scots would die first a violent death. So it turned out. Can you tell what the future holds?'

'Is Dr Dee not exiled to Manchester since his return from Bohemia? I think he was lucky in his predictions or perhaps he understood the nature of those two queens and so judged of their fates.'

'Are our fates not written in the stars then for the wise to read?'

'Madam if the stars are not fixed in their stations but move about the heavens, as Mr Digges his discovery of an unknown celestial body does suggest, and Copernicus has written, then how can they influence the lives of men? And indeed even our Great Bear if we watch it on several nights and at several seasons will change its station.'

'But when the planets come near the earth, if we are to believe this theory of their mutability, do they not shed an influence over us as Mars to stir up war or Venus to make the world amorous with her shining as morning and evening star?'

'The poets may say so madam, when they write in parables, but the natural philosopher must reason otherwise or pretend to things to cozen money out of the credulous.'

'Are you a stargazer Master Boston?' asked the duenna who was privy to our discourse.

'I observe the stars when I have occasion to do so as on a journey at night.'

'Be careful or the moon may turn your brains into a lunacy or men say you are a necromancer yourself with your looking into the secrets of God's heaven.'

'Such stories are akin to the Romish superstition that forbade us to enquire into God's ways except as they were interpreted by their priests or to read His words in our own tongue,' the countess said.

'My lady and her noble brother have made the scriptures open to all who can read English as far as David's psalms.'

'I was raised under the old queen Mary, her present majesty's sister,' the Duenna said, 'when we did not question as they do in these times but accepted God's will and our fate, and could be shriven of our sins. But now we must shrive ourselves with looking into our consciences or risk the fires of hell. The old way was easier for simple men and the unlearned to get to heaven.'

I saw that this angered the countess. 'You presume on your long service to me if you question our religion. Would you indeed return to those old ways? Be careful how you answer. Remember that our family which has given you to eat and lodge for fifty years has always supported the Protestant cause and the truth of our religion.'

The duenna sank to her knees. 'I meant only madam that

the way seemed easier then for silly folk. The easy way is not always the right way but as I grow old and perhaps silly myself I find it hard to be always at prayer and examining my conscience. Old age asks ease.'

'We would lie now under the yoke of the Spaniard, a subject people, if God had not protected us.'

'As he did madam in driving them out of Ireland,' I said, anxious to end this dangerous dispute that had so agitated my lady, for I knew that her wrath might not fall on the duenna alone but that she might strike out at anyone near at hand.

> 'O sing Jehovah, He hath wonders wrought,
> A song of praise that newness may command.'

The countess began.

And I answered again with her own words:

> 'His hand, His holy arm alone hath brought
> Conquest on all that durst with Him contend.'

'Thank you Master Boston,' the duenna said when we were alone later. 'My tongue had lost me my place, if not my head for treason, if you had not deflected madam's anger. I see you will be a courtier as well as physician. Is she not fine in her choler? Do her eyes not flash fire and her cheeks flame like a maid's blush? Such passions we must expect from great ones and still love them for it for they are as children in these matters. And truly I have seen her majesty herself stamp her foot and toss away her glove in a rage though I have never known how much this was simulate to her will.'

Such words seemed to me almost treasonable themselves so I did not answer but bowed and turned away.

'I must attend in the stillroom. There will be patients waiting.'

After the rains that summer came days of extreme heat that sucked up the moisture from the earth and brought a sickly miasma that foretold fevers and plagues. Within doors we gasped for air and the sweat dried salt on our skins as if we were being pickled in brine. The ladies went about with pomanders and nosegays and even the gentlemen carried sprigs of herbs, rosemary, thyme and lavender in their hats or brooches against the stink and the fear of sickness. These bunches I made continually to distribute to the household to keep us all refreshed. Distilled rose and jasmine water was also sprinkled on the bedlinen and on kerchiefs for both men and women.

The countess found these days most oppressive and walked often in her garden where the air was fresher and scented with summer flowers. Even so, one day of great heat this would not suffice. She commanded her horse and mine to be saddled, and two others for a groom and one of her ladies. She would ride into the forest in search of a cooler shade under its canopy. So we rode out, with me beside her and the others behind. After we had ridden for half an hour through the glades she drew up.

'Are we not near that deserted estate of Sir Henry Stilman, he that was arraigned for treason, and now none will rent or live in it? Yet I remember it had a fountain and a most rare pool that I should like to see again,' and she set off at a canter through the trees until we came to the edge of a park where sheep were grazing and beyond what seemed from a distance a fine house but with no sign of life about it apart from the sheep. My lady reined in her horse.

'Here one might retire from the world and live a shepherd's life as in my brother his *Arcadia*.'

'Yet there were princes too in Arcadia madam and all the distractions of a court.'

'I spoke of a thing to be desired but not attained. The fountain as I remember lies behind the house beyond a garden.'

We rode on towards the house which was set upon a green

knoll so that from its windows there must be a fine view over the countryside around and I marvelled that such a rare seat should stand empty out of a superstition that it was in some way accursed.

The great panelled front door, which was approached by a double staircase leading to a stone dais, seemed barred from within. We rode around to the back where the groom dismounted and knocked. There was no sound from inside the house.

'Look under that stone beside the door,' the countess directed as if she knew what lay there, and indeed when the groom turned it over there was revealed a little brick cistern with a heavy iron key inside it which fitted the lock in the door and turned, though but stiffly. Still the door held until the groom put his shoulder against it, and it yielded slowly at last as if unwilling to give up the secrets of the house. Inside was cold and dark, smelling of damp and decay.

'Open the shutters,' the countess ordered. The light streamed in on empty rooms inhabited only by dust and cobwebs that laced the corners of the windows and hung here and there, sad banners, from the beams.

'Stay here with the horses,' she said to the other two. 'Amyntas come with me. I have a wish to find if the fountain still runs.'

Leaving the others in the house and the horses to crop the overgrown lawn we set off down a path through an arch in a yew hedge grown straggly with neglect. The day was hot and still. The scent from the yews almost came near to overpower the senses as they sweated under the sun. We passed through a knot garden, rank with weeds, where rue and thyme still struggled to sustain life, and into a dense maze.

'I had forgot the maze,' the countess said, from which I understood that she had indeed been here many years before. 'You will wonder how I know this place Amyntas. When my brother was in retirement here and out of favour with her majesty we often rode out to this place to discourse alone even when I was heavy with my first child and some said I should not ride. Here in this garden he would take out his tablets and write a little in his *Arcadia* then read it to me, sitting beside the same fountain, for even then the house was inhabited only by servants, Sir Harry being on the queen's employ in Ireland.'

I knew then that it was the memory of her beloved brother that had brought her this far. We passed by a little summer lodge and at last came upon the fountain, a great stone conch shell held by a giant Triton, spewing water into a basin so large a group of Diana's nymphs or Nereides bathed in its crystal waters, life-size and seeming to laugh with the splash of the spray against their stone bodies.

'Come Amyntas let us bathe with them.' My lady began to unlock her bodice, for she had ridden out lightly clothed because of the heat.

'Madam I may not. Suppose we should be surprised.'

'They will not dare to come after us when I have ordered them to stay with the horses. Must I play the goddess and bathe alone with only these stone companions?'

I could see that my lady was becoming angry. 'Madam remember when Philoclea and her companion bathed in the river and Zelmane was forced to watch from the bank, guarding them from jealous eyes. Let me be your watchdog.'

'A little spaniel came and stole Philoclea's glove and book and took it to his master who overlooked them from some bushes. Perhaps you are right. Even now my brother watches over me with his words. At least help me off with my apparel.'

Then indeed I felt like Zelmane who quivered when she would have put out a helping hand to her princess until at last the countess stood, her smock fallen to the ground, as her brother wrote, like a diamond taken out of a rock or rather like the sun getting from under a cloud and showing his naked beams to the full view, and as I guided her to the edge of the basin and she stepped down into the water resting the other hand on the cold stone breast of one of the nymphs, the same 'pretty kind of shrugging came over her body like the twinkling of the fairest among the fixed stars' as overtook the princess Philoclea, and I saw that her noble brother's imaginings were but a mirror of nature herself.

The sun threw up sparklets from the waters where she stood. Then she reclined herself among the nymphs, her skin white and gleaming against their dull chill flesh and striking the water with her hands set up a watery firework of spray and bubbles as a child will play with no thought of being observed. Indeed I had never seen her so carefree.

A little cloud obscured the sun. The countess stood up from among the motionless Nereides. 'Phoebus warns me to return to dry land. Give me your hand. What shall I dry myself on?' she asked as she stepped out on to the grass.

'My shirt madam,' I said and unbuttoning my doublet I took the shirt of fine white lawn off and gave it to her.

'You must rub me dry Amyntas.'

So I was fain to steel my senses and tenderly dry her body with trembling hands, feeling the blushes mount in my own cheeks as I worked my way round.

'Is my old woman's body not disgusting to you Amyntas? Do you not flinch at it?'

'My lady has borne three children yet her form is as young still as a maid.' I knelt down before her and taking her hand kissed it, almost overcome with the desire to go further and print my lips everywhere upon her person.

'Now help me to dress. Our English air is not so soft as that of Arcadia. I am greatly refreshed and even grow hungry as I have not been these several days of heat. We will ride back to Wilton. Will you remember this place?'

'I shall remember it as one of the most charming on earth,' I answered as I refastened my doublet over my damp shirt, happy to feel it take warmth from my own body and absorb the moisture that had clung to hers like a crystal dew.

'Jim said you were quite brilliant today. Clients were frightfully impressed.'

We had bought our tickets and were whiling away the time with big goblets of red wine and a fag for Helen in the nearest pub to the plush King's Road cinema where the steamy French movie she'd elected to see was showing.

'Good. I'm glad he thought I got it right.' Already I was having trouble saying her husband's name. It seemed to stick somewhere in my chest like a piece of cold potato that won't go down or rather in this case wouldn't come up.

'He said when you pointed out to them the adverse publicity they might attract they backed off into sweet reasonableness. Suppose you weren't right? Suppose they could have got away with it without any media attention?'

'It was a risk they weren't willing to take. And anyway the opposition had nothing to lose by keeping it quiet. As it is Mediatex will try not to use them again. They'll find that hard of course. Their sales depend on those artists' names. They can't afford to drop them all.'

'You're not really on the clients' side are you, Jade?'

'As a lawyer I'm trained to advise my client and do the best for them. Aren't we?'

'Of course we are. But I was asking what you really think.'

'What do you think? Really.'

'Oh it's the old chestnut: investment versus talent. I'm on whichever side pays me.'

'As we have to be.' I realised I'd just dodged a twenty-ton artic. A bit of Helen liked living dangerously. I was the legal equivalent of rough trade. A few lawyers develop the art of the maverick, take on the hard cases, the underdogs and get famous in the process. You see them on TV giving interviews outside the Law Courts while passers-by pause to eavesdrop and get their own mugshots on camera. They become TV personalities, always ready with a soundbite. Tolerated as pinpricks of colourful rebellion in a system geared still to pinstripe conformity. Tolerated because they're few enough not to disturb the even process of law and, I sometimes think, to give an acceptable face to the heavy hand of repression that fills up our jails to bursting and comes down hard on the dispossessed and desperate. But although she, Mrs Helen Chalmers, my charmer, might dally with the maverick, find a touch of it a turn on, she would always draw back from the edge of the platform as the fast train thundered through the station. Prudent, of course.

Did I know this then, sitting there in the bar with the world going by outside the plate-glass window, able to peer in at us and wonder perhaps? Or is it just hindsight, the backward look clouded by the present and its distancing perspective? I did realise that without James Chalmers' approval I wasn't going anywhere in the firm or with Helen and that I'd have to keep on my toes, sharp as a tack and no slouching if I was to stay in the game.

'How do you feel about Catherine Deneuve?'

'I think she's sexier now she's older.'

'A weakness for the older woman, Jay?'

'You'll be asking me about my mother next.'

We were playing a game of cat and mouse again, hunter and hunted with role-swapping thrown in to raise the temperature so that as soon as I seemed to get close, to have her in my sights, she would turn to run me down like Actaeon's hounds. I wasn't used to such heavy calculated flirting. But later in the dark of the cinema as the lovers' lips came together above the tangle of sheets she took my hand and that's all I remember of the movie and its simulated passion.

'Can you get a cab from your place? I didn't bring the car.

Have you got something drinkable there?' Wine, I think, at this witching hour. Red.'

Inside my flat I quickly poured her a glass. And then when I'd filled it again, 'Aren't you going to take me to bed?'

'If you're sure you want to.'

'I shan't know till I've tried, shall I?'

So I took her hand and led her to my bed.

Even now, years later, I sweat and tremble like Sappho and though I know I don't look it I can still feel paler than grass, the bleached summer grass of Greece, that she must have had in her mind's eye. It had been a long time since I'd had a fuck except with myself. I wonder if that's what Sappho did in the end, poor cow, lying in her bed alone.

I have to get back on the case again, stop this retrospective show filling my head with its private view of old horny, porny images. I have to answer Wessex's offer of a place. Galton will pay, he says, so nothing should hold me back apart from this lethargy of ancient lust. To work, Jade. Decide where you're going to put yourself, in English or in history. Ranee or Daniel. Maybe Daniel would be safer. Remember you're looking – for what? Something to strengthen Galton's case if he insists on going to tribunal. He wants revenge, his name cleared, damages I suppose, not, surely, reinstatement.

I email my acceptance and put myself down for the history department. Only a week to go and I'm legitimate. I can swan up to the gates any time and flash my credentials. The phone rings suddenly. Someone's offering me a surprise job, rescuing their house sale from nasty hidden conditions, rights of way they'd forgotten about, a whiff of subsidence that will keep me out of mischief for a few days until Galton's little problem claims me back. Then there are the Gaos I've been neglecting shamefully and the Crusader gathering dust on the ground floor, her engine oil coagulating until she seizes up on me. I get into my leather gear and go downstairs. As I kick her into life I feel that old pathetic fallacy: the promise of spring even in the Waterloo Cut, growing stronger as I head south where forsythia and almond are beginning to make the best of suburban gardens.

'– If Winter comes, can Spring be far behind?' as the man said.

Two days later an instruction pack thuds through my letter box with more details of courses, staff, a plan of the buildings, an acknowledgement of the fee, the registration procedure, rules, no smoking, no games, no jogging, circumspect clothing, no sunbathing or even semi-nudity, and finally the pass code to the gates. 'We have suffered in the past from unauthorised intruders who have particularly alarmed female students and staff to the point where we have been forced to install security systems and identity cards. Never lend your card to anyone else or allow it to be copied. The system will recognise not only your identity number but the photograph which we have asked you to supply three copies of.' And Galton thought it was all because of him. The nearer I get to Wessex the thinner his case seems. Maybe they had reason to see him as a real threat to their legal duty of care with his flaky ideas and weird arrogance.

I pick out student parking on the plan. How long will it take me to find out all I need? A month? More? I'll have to accept Galton's retainer if I'm to keep the bread on the table. That'll make him happy. He'll think again that he's got me. Then he'll be so surprised if I just turn and walk away, saying what I've seen of the background isn't enough to justify a demanding letter, let alone go to tribunal with.

Riding the M3 on the first morning I feel a kind of apprehension as if I'm really a student again, a green fresher who doesn't know the drill, as if I'm up for inspection, not Wessex. And then, when I swipe my card, I've keyed in the number, and I hear a click of recognition from the gates that give to my push against them, apprehension is replaced with a kind of exhilaration. I've done it. I'm in. I consult the map again and push the

Crusader towards the parking bay for cycles and motorcycles. 'No cycling in the grounds.'

Arrowed signs direct me to registration. I chain up the Crusader and padlock my helmet in the pannier, smelling faintly of chicken noodles and spring rolls, along with my leathers and boots. I don't want to frighten the horses. Not yet. I join a stream of carefully dishevelled yet somehow fresh-skinned young women and men, suddenly feeling old. What did we call mature students in my day: the wrinklies?

At registration my credentials are all checked again and under the heading: History on the notice board I find a timetable for interviews by the head of department and the name that's now mine, L. J. Cowell, Lucy, down for 10.30. So I shall soon meet Daniel, who was so keen to have me as you might say. I consult the plan in the registration pack and head off to the history department.

I both see and hear at once that Daniel Davidson is a handsome café-au-lait Afro-American as he gets up from his chair behind his desk, stretches out his hand to shake mine and says the ritual, 'Welcome to Wessex, Ms Cowell. We hope you'll be very happy among us and be able to take full advantage of all we have to offer.'

I shake his hand which is dry and slightly scaly to the touch. 'I'm sure I shall, Dr Davidson.'

'Now tell me more about your project. Are you sure it would not sit better in an English discipline?'

'To be honest with you I'm not sure. But then, presumably I can switch if we both feel it would be better environed elsewhere, from the point of view of the research of course.' I smile, in what I hope is a disarming way, though I may just look like a crocodile about to snap shut.

'So.' He puts the tips of his fingers together and leans back in his chair like a professional, imperturbable psychiatrist about to hear some startling revelation. 'Your subject "cross-dressing and the Jacobean stage" isn't new. Do you not think the ground has been well gone over in the past? There's Spinks for instance. You will realise I felt I had to do a little research on my own account, get up to speed if I am to mindfully oversee your thesis.'

'Yes but Spinks writes from an exclusively male viewpoint. I feel that the female perspective has been both overshadowed and neglected.'

'As is so often sadly the case. As too with any black perspective.'

'Of course. The two so often go side by side if not quite hand in hand.'

'That would be good to see would it not? Eve and the Hamitic people in union. It brings us of course to the vexed question: 'Of what colour was Adam?'

I don't quite get the 'of course' but decide to play along with his train of thought even though we seem in one short leap to have got a long way from Shakespeare's boy-girls. Maybe this is some trick question that determines whether you're in or out.

'Well the latest theory says that Eve came out of Africa so presumably Adam did too.' I'd like to add 'otherwise we'd have to wonder what Mrs Noah had been up to,' but bite my tongue. Something tells me this bit of flippancy wouldn't go down well, and the next minute I'm sure.

'Ah, but we don't have truck with the latest theories at Wessex. We rely on The Word. Such pseudo-scientific theorising can be very dangerous, especially to young minds.'

I hear the capital letters round The Word. Tread very softly, Jade.

'Unless,' Davidson goes on, 'you locate the Garden of Eden and therefore the act of creation in Africa. After all The Word is not specific about its location and the old land of the chosen people may be seen as the extreme north of Africa rather than the south of Asia. Egypt where the people were enslaved was, is, Africa.'

Count the angels on the point of a pin. My heart which had been quite cold towards Dr Alastair Galton and his supposed woes, is warming up fast. If this is history as taught at Wessex I can see why he would have been unable to resist sticking a needle into this hot-air balloon and watching the whole thing collapse. And if this is history as taught at Wessex what must the theology department be like?

'Indeed,' I nod. 'Then there is no necessary contradiction between the two.'

'When in doubt go back to The Word. You will always find the correct answer. It may take a little teasing out by our finite human minds but it is surely there. However we seem to have strayed somewhat from your thesis into deeper waters. I think we have arrived at the point of a mutual trial. I like what I hear of your thinking, Ms Cowell. We must talk some more soon.'

I am being dismissed. I stand up. 'Thank you so much for your time, Dr Davidson. I'm sure we shall get on just fine together.' I reach for the hand again that now seems to have a distinct feel of the mummy about it.

Maybe I've made the wrong choice of supervisor. The dean had suggested that I saw both Davidson and Raval when I arrived and I've jumped the gun and gone for the prophet Daniel. But I can always change my mind though Davidson with his promisingly whacky, yet at the same time potentially frightening, ideas seems just where I need to be. Why do I feel this gulp of apprehension? As if I wasn't going home at the end of the day. As if something stifling might settle on me and hug me to death.

The students are milling about the corridors like any other kids of their age, even those who seem slightly older than usual, like me. Hard to tell in the ubiquitous jeans, trainers and baggy or fitting tops who's meant to be 'mature'. It's a warm spring day and I can see through the long windows, students sitting on the grass in groups, gossiping and swigging from water or soft-drink bottles. Don't let your imagination run wild, Jade. All may indeed be as nice as Apple-pie Molders who is presumably shut in familiarly with her boss, the dean, or juggling with the computer in her office, not mingling with the plebs.

My wanderings have brought me to the octagonal chapel. I try the door but it's locked. No question then of popping in for a quiet word with whomever. Then I realise there's a CCTV monitor above the door and wonder what holy gesture I can make for its benefit. Somehow I feel genuflexion or crossing myself would be a bad mistake. I settle my face into an expression of disappointment and turn away sighing.

Mary-Ann Molders told me the chapel was always open. Why should she lie about that? I've nearly reached the end of the corridor when I hear voices behind me: faint voices. A group of students streams past, nodding and smiling at each other. 'Brother! Sister!' are all the words I can make out. Perhaps that's all they're saying. I don't need to look behind me to know they've come from the chapel and now I remember Molders telling me that it's locked during, what was the word she used? Not services. Gatherings. That's what they call them.

I remember my nana, Linda's mother, singing a hymn from her childhood at the Band of Hope on Sunday afternoons in Gateshead: 'Let's all gather at the river.' Then there was the miracle of the loaves and fishes in the Bible, that I studied in RI, a soft option for GCE as it was then, the fragments gathered up into baskets enough to feed another multitude. Then there was something about two or three gathered together in my name. There are plenty of precedents even I can think of for 'Gatherings'.

The theologs, for that's what they must be, are ahead of me now as I deliberately dawdle. They said a polite 'excuse me' as they went past with lowered eyes like nuns are supposed to do. Inseparable from the other students in their uniform clothes; mixed colours, shapes and heights.

The chapel doors must be soundproofed since I hadn't heard

a murmur from inside. Or perhaps the entire service, if you could use the word at all, was conducted in silence, just meditation like Quakers and Buddhists.

Suddenly I've had enough of my own pretence and the subtly oppressive atmosphere of the place, as if the very buildings are waiting for something only they can foresee. Was it always like this when the well-behaved Anglican girl teachers in training were here, I wonder, as I make my way out to the parking lot, get into my kit, release the Crusader and wheel her towards the gates. Then I'm astride, kicking her into life, feeling her throb under me. I gun the engine and roar off up the road, not caring if the CCTV picks me up as I feel the power of what, I'm sure, the denizens of Wessex would see as my devil's machine. I laugh out loud inside the mask of my helmet at the access of freedom and the simple joy of speed.

My phone is ringing as I climb the stairs. It's Galton of course, wanting to know how I got on.

'I signed up with Daniel Davidson, history.'

'I hope you weren't swayed by any notions of political correctness.'

'You mean because he's brownish?' The guy is irritating me already.

'Exactly.'

I resist the impulse to point out that the alternative is probably brownish too.

'If you have so little faith in my judgement, Dr Galton I suggest I abandon your case.' I'm tired of having to use this kind of blackmail on him but there comes a point where however much he's paying me it can't compensate for his smug interference or faintly veiled suggestions that I'm incompetent. I smell the misogynist in him. I want to ask if he's married but I'm pretty sure what the answer is. What woman would put up with his patronising manner unless she was desperate for a home and children and didn't care what price she had to pay. She could always divorce him later.

'So what comes next, Ms Green?'

'I spend some days there. Suss the place out. See what I can dig up. Whether anyone's prepared to be a witness for you. Meanwhile I'm preparing a brief and looking into the exact procedure for bringing a case before the relevant tribunal.' I want to add: 'Is that enough for you? Do you feel you're getting your money's worth?' but I don't. I'm mindful of the quarter's looming rent day and the interest on the bank loan. The way we live now, hand to mouth as my parents would see it, with the kind of debts and insecurity that would have terrified them.

'That all sounds excellent. So I can take it we have a contract?'

I can't hold out any longer. It would be unrealistic since I'm taking so much of the guy's dosh. 'I'll draw up a letter of agreement for us both to sign.' This is how girls must have felt in Amyntas' time when they were married off by contract to boost the family fortunes, to men they had to learn to love or rub along with, at least.

Suddenly I'm tired, too tired to turn out for the Gaos. I ring. Mary says the nephew will be glad of the money. I slip down to the corner for a mushroom pizza, open a bottle of red and settle myself with the memorial. I feel I've lost sight of Amyntas in the excitement of Wessex. Maybe he's got something to tell me, a clue I can tease out, that will lift my spirits and set me back on the scent.

That Christmas we were merry again as we had been my first year in my lady's service. All was as before. The country gentry came to pay their respects. There was feasting and dancing in which I led out my lady. The peasants came again with their play of St George and the Turkish Knight and sang us wassail. Dr Gilbert went as before to his own people in Devon so there was none to disturb my peace, and now I knew the customs of the great house I was able to avoid those occasions which might bring danger. Besides I sat so easily now in my role as Amyntas that I could scarcely believe I had been born Amaryllis. The young lords and the Lady Anne were away, the earl being still in disgrace at Sir John Harington his house in Exton with his uncle Sidney, back for the while from his duties in Flushing. All seemed as if such a simple life might last for ever as my lady and I tended the sick, I continued with the electricals and with stocking of the dispensary and laboratory with all remedies we might need.

From time to time I sent my results of electrical experiments to Dr Gilbard, still on my father's behalf and he wrote back when his duties allowed him, glad that my father was eager to pursue those matters he no longer had time for as one of her majesty's physicians.

If my lady was weary of this life she did not show it but seemed entirely content. Little did I know that the hourglass was almost run out and such days would never come again. Then came more evil news from her castle of Cardiff that had us hurrying to furnish horses and carriages for the long journey on foul ways and in foul weather. No sooner had she set out than the wind changed to the northeast bringing such bitter frost and snow as none remembered before. I had no time to grieve for my lady's absence for I was kept busy ministering to the whole house where almost everyone was sick, with none but a boy, Robin, to help me, for Dr Gilbert could not stir from Devon. Robin was willing enough yet he knew little more than to stir the fire or the pot when bidden.

When the weather grew kinder I rode into Salisbury for the ingredients to make antimony which in small doses may be efficacious against rheum and flux. In the market I bought a broadsheet with an account of the splendid audience at court which her majesty had granted to the new ambassador from Venice, the first that had come to our country in all the queen's reign, she being then at Richmond and dressed for the occasion as rich as any empress in the history of the world for, as the paper told it, she was arrayed in silver and white taffeta trimmed with gold, an imperial crown on her head and her person studded all with gems, as rubies, diamonds and great pearls the size and smoothness of small birds' eggs, which jewels threw back the light from a thousand candles. The paper also told how she had reproached their ambassador for his tardiness in paying his respects, saying that it could not be her sex that had fathered this discourtesy: 'For my sex cannot diminish my prestige, nor offend those who treat me as other princes are treated.' And by this I understood her to say that it was not the sex that made a prince but the prince who might honour her sex and that we might all be what we will if we have the skill and strength to command the world.

This I sent on also in my next packet of letters to Cardiff as I waited for news of how the countess did in this bleak weather and if her spirits held up as well as her majesty's. Yet the next news that came to me told a different story in a letter from my lady's sister at Richmond. The queen's cousin, the Countess of Nottingham, had been struck down by the continuing bad weather and the queen who had loved her and leant upon her, could not be consoled. Ill humours let in sickness in their turn. Had I been present in such a case I would have tried to lift the spirits with physic, as syrup of fumitory or viper's bugloss yet it was said that her majesty would take none. She was feverish and could not sleep but lay upon her cushions in deepest melancholy. Her heart, she said, was sad and heavy.

Now she began to refuse food, yet even so her coronation ring by which she held herself wedded to her people had to be sawn off for it had grown into the flesh, betokening perhaps a dropsy as her father King Harry died of, some said. My lady's sister wrote that all at court were in fear that she could not live and some were eagerly making court to King James of Scotland as if she were already cold, and hastening north. When I took myself again to an alehouse in Salisbury city I saw nothing but long faces, men sitting silent or speaking in whispers of what might come upon us if the queen did not rally. Yet we knew she was mortal and must die like all mankind since the world began. Then I wrote quickly to my lady and sent word with a groom on our fastest horse in case the news of the queen's decline had not come to Cardiff.

Every day I rode into the city for news. Rumour was everywhere. The queen was already dead but none would say so while men jostled for the throne. The queen had rallied and danced a coranto. The archbishop, 'her black husband' as she was said by those at court to call him, had told her she was dying and must turn her thought to God. Still she would not eat and refused all physic as if eager herself to hasten her going.

Then at last about noon on the 24th of March I heard the cathedral bell begin to toll the dead knoll as I rode towards the city and knew all was indeed over. The next day came a messenger from my lady saying she was already on her way to London to her house of Baynard's Castle and that mourning weeds should be sent in haste to her there. The duenna who had stayed behind in Ramsbury, saying she was too old and infirm for a journey to Wales in rough weather, helped me to pack up those clothes my lady had last worn for the late earl, her husband, and send them off in a coach while I rode beside in much sorrow for the queen her death but eager for this chance to see the great city where I had never been in all my life.

It were tedious to rehearse our journey, only that at every place where we lay to change horse, King James was proclaimed, bells rang and bonfires were lit as men rejoiced at they knew not what, as it seemed to me, but only for the newness of a king when they had known just a great queen for forty-five years. So after three days of hard riding we came to the city of Westminster, passing through Richmond but not staying. We rode along Tothill Street by many fair houses of the nobility some still in building, past the great Abbey of Westminster and the Palace of Whitehall where the queen now lay in state, having been brought hither by horse, up the Strand, past several mansions where lawyers in their gowns were coming and going, which I supposed to be the Inns of Court, and into Fleet Street where we were stopped at Temple Bar to pay our toll for entering the City of London. At once we were surrounded by a myriad of people all shouting and thrusting, and a myriad more poured out of every narrow alley like emmets from their holes. Then we rode up Ludgate Hill and into Castle Baynard Ward where I first smelt the stink of the river, for the castle was situate beside the Thames which I thought must be dangerous to the health of all that lay there for the noxious effluvia rising up therefrom as one might perceive simply by the nose. Also the house was old and damp from the same cause of nearness to the river so that even as we entered I longed for the sweet airs of Ramsbury and that my lady should not linger there long for the health of her body and mind both their sakes. The streets round about stank too with such a press of people, trades of every kind, smoke of fires and furnace, horse piss and dung and the rancid stink from cookshops and ale houses.

Her majesty's funeral was to be soon for the new king was already on his journey south, divers having gone to meet him along the way hoping thereby to be first in his favour, and at Burleigh House the young Earl William himself, the countess her son, freed from disgrace and the queen's disfavour by her death, paid his court, and was said to be well used by his majesty before hastening south again to London. Some said that a multitude of rude Scots would descend upon the court and that all the English would be put out. Others that the king liked young men about him that were handsome and did not care where they might come from. Others that the new queen loved masques and jousting and that the court would be merry now as it had not in the old queen's time, so quick were men to forget the debt they owed to her who had kept the country safe for so long.

My lady had told me more of the queen's dying as it had been told to her, how some of the foolish women about her in the palace of Richmond had cried that she was bewitched and that one had claimed to see an apparition of her majesty in several rooms distant from where she lay in her bed in the privy chamber. Once she rose and sat upon a stool for three days. Once she would be pulled up and stood upon her feet for fifteen hours but then being put to bed again she had said that she did not wish to live longer but desired to die. At this the council was called and she signified by putting her hand to her head when he was named, that King James of Scotland was to succeed her. Then, after she had heard the prayers of the archbishop, all left her except her women and she, turning her face to the wall, fell into a deep sleep, drifting away until she came at last into the land of continual brightness, of the sun shining clearly upon the huge and mighty sea.

'Women are very apt to see witchcraft Amyntas, where there is none', my lady said, 'especially when they have watched many hours without sleep. And there is a sacredness about a prince that conjures up strange fancies in the death of a sovereign as if there must be more cause thereof than age and infirmity.'

Her majesty lay in state for many days with ladies watching over her as if we could not bear to let her go. Then at last on the 28th of April was the day of the funeral that she should be carried to her rest in the cathedral church of Westminster. I was got up in a window in Whitehall to see the procession pass through so great a throng as had never been seen before, all sighing, weeping and groaning at windows and doors, on the very roofs and clinging to the gutters. When her painted image laid upon the coffin, borne on a chariot, passed, showing her in all her robes with the crown, orb and sceptre, a great groan went up.

First came the knight marshal's men to make room through the press of people, then fifteen poor men and two hundred and sixty poor women, four by four. Then followed her household in order: grooms, yeomen, children, clerks, sergeants and between them banners, heralds, trumpeters, horses caparisoned in black, the gentlemen and children of the chapel singing all the way.

At last came the guard, five by five, their halberds pointing down, and the twelve banderols of her ancestors carried by twelve barons. My lady with other countesses marched with the Lady Countess of Northampton, as chief mourner, while the Lady Anne, her daughter, came further back in the procession with other earls' daughters. The young earl himself assisted Lord Howard to carry the great embroidered banner of England while his younger brother, Sir Philip, carried the standard of the greyhound.

My lady was saddened that she could not wear all her jewels to walk in the procession for her steward, Hugh Davys, coming after her from Cardiff with them, had been attacked, his head broken in several places and robbed of his precious cargo. 'Yet it was no ordinary theft,' my lady said, 'but malice by those who oppose my authority in the city and tore down my walls and walks. I know who is to blame and will prosecute them through the courts and in the court itself to defend my rights and those of my son which I hold in trust.'

I was sorry for the injuries done to Hugh Davys who had always been my friend in the household with none of that envy I perceived in others who thought the countess put too much trust in me. He was never to recover from his injuries and so I lost one who might have aided me in my own affliction. Also my lady dwelt too much upon the evil done to her and I could find no means to distract her from it, either with diversions or physic. She saw that the death of the queen had changed our world for ever and could not be reconciled to the new order that should come about.

'I am become an old woman, tedious and of no account, while power and position are given to youth and new favourites.'

This she said when she learned she was not to be one of those ladies summoned to escort the new queen, Anne, from Scotland, although her daughter, the Lady Anne, being among them was some consolation. I found the countess at the end of April gazing from her window down at the river below busy with barges and skiffs though we were too high to hear the shouts of the watermen.

'Ah Amyntas to be fourteen again and being rowed up river with all the Sidney flags fluttering about me, to some great occasion of state or pleasure. I find no comfort in my own psalms in these times when all my world is turned upside down. My faith deserts me when there is none to share it. What will happen to the Protestant cause now that the great men, as my uncle Leicester and my noble brother, are dead? Rumour says her majesty inclines towards the pope. They say, too, the king will make peace with Spain and if they live may marry one of the little princes to a papist. Then perhaps we shall have a papist prince again in time.'

Nine days later, His Majesty King James having lain four days at Sir Robert Cecil his house of Theobalds, entered the city by the charterhouse where he was entertained for three nights by Sir Thomas Howard before making his way to Whitehall and then by barge to the Tower. There he was received with a great cannonade of the whole ordnance of two hundred and fifty guns. Two days after, the king having visited the several rooms of the Tower and baited the lions with dogs, before dinner he made many new lords and knights, among the first being my lady's brother, Sir Robert Sidney, as Lord Sidney of Penshurst.

Now we began to have many alarms of the spread of the plague in London and elsewhere so that men wondered if the king and queen would be crowned at all. Her majesty was long in coming, being entertained at houses and towns along the way as Althorp with a lavish masque and the city of York with a civic feast. On the 27th of June she reached Sir George Farmer his house near Northampton where the king rode out from London to meet her and escort her back with a great train.

The king was eager to bind men to him and to this end created a great many knights. For the ceremony the royal couple resided at Windsor and there my lady went to greet her daughter who had accompanied the queen south, and to perform her own homage to her majesty among the other countesses and ladies, leaving me behind in Baynard's Castle, that gloomy pile beside the Thames. There at Windsor too the king created the young earl a Knight of the Garter and his brother Philip a Knight of the Bath.

The following week the court removed to Westminster at last for the coronation but by reason of the plague increasing so that near a thousand died in those days, all were forbidden to come near except they who had a part to bear as my lady who attended upon the queen.

The countess returned, weary with the weight of her robes and jewels, saying that all were leaving London that could and that we should make haste to Wilton where the court intended to come, her two sons being high in his majesty's favour, and she herself appointed with her brother, Lord Robert and her daughter Anne, to be of the queen's court whenever the two should separate while her sons were to follow the king.

And now I understood that our quiet country pastimes were no more and indeed that my lady had matters of state to occupy her, as well as the loss of her jewellery and the murder of her steward for he had never recovered from his wounds and died three months later in great pain. I felt too that there began a coldness towards me. She no longer asked my advice or cared to be read to while we sat close together. She began to call for unguents as that would keep her skin youthful, and richer perfumes than the jasmine and rose water she had been used to use. She no longer came to the dispensary or laboratory and indeed was so busy ordering the house against the court's arrival that all else must be neglected. One day she scolded me for being underfoot and would banish me to Ramsbury with the duenna, saying their majesties liked only young faces about them and merry ones at that. Yet I knew that in heart she too was sad for I often heard her sigh. But then she would tell me upon my enquiring that she did very well, and lacked nothing I could prescribe.

My supervisor Dr Davidson thought I should elaborate my synopsis before we met again. Presumably with my new status I can turn up any time with the excuse that I need to use the library. This has the added bonus of being true because I do need to do some research if I'm to present him with a more credible take on my notional thesis. I have to crank up my rusty writing skills, unused except for legal briefs since uni. At first I think I'll do just that: turn up at Wessex and work there. But then I begin to wonder what monitoring technology their library computers might have programmed into them. Taking a book off a shelf is safer than searching the internet, unless their CCTV records every action, every title consulted. It's a mad world my mistresses. Orwell didn't predict the half of it. The brothers are watching you and you're watching everyone else. Spies and eyes everywhere. Just as in Amyntas' time with Walsingham's police network, carefully undercutting the seals on letters, sending reports in invisible ink, infiltrating his *agents provocateurs* until men and women ended up broken, hanged, cut down alive and disembowelled, put to the flames.

We're more subtle now of course, in some countries anyway. Our forms of torture are mostly threats, blackmail, confusion, the dark, the hood, uncertainty, assassination. And endless surveillance. Yet still people revolt, plot, duck and weave to escape. Where did I read that we're the most overseen people in Europe, our streets and highways sown with all-seeing eyes that we accept because their blurry images might also show us a child being led away to murder, a student stabbed by a gang, a woman dragged into the bushes beside the unlit car park?

Coming from the North where people left their doors on the latch when they were kids, Linda and Rob still shake their heads over our lack of trust. 'But Mam,' I said once, 'Nana didn't have anything worth stealing. You've said so. Now everyone's got something other people want. We're the top nation for burglary in Europe.'

'And why's that?'

'It's because we've always been more interested in our own homes and turning them into little castles or palaces. That's what we like to spend our money on and now we've got more to spend we still eat cheap junk food but the kids all have mobiles and Playstations, and the house has new everything and the garden's decked in, with a water feature and perpetual solar lighting.'

'That's progress, that is.'

Yet when Christmas comes round they'll give Roger's children expensive toys so as not to appear mean and because they know about the peer pressure of the playground for all the gaudy ephemera with built-in obsolescence. How did I get to Christmas toys from Wessex library? Anyway it's not worth the risk. I'll do what I need to on my own computer and then chance the books on the shelves. After all I can pretend they're what I want to consult without really giving anything away.

I need to look into that Spinks Davidson mentioned and his study of Tudor cross-dressing. I had to flannel my way through that because I'd never heard of the guy. So I type him in and hey presto there he is, expensively published by a top US university press. I order a copy, fumble for my credit card and are assured the book will be delivered in a week. Which means I have to be inventive and stall a bit longer.

Galton implied there was a US presence behind Wessex but it isn't too obvious at first inspection. True Davidson himself is a damned Yankee, like Molders, but then so was Marlowe, though Chandler started off in old England and it was never a problem for me before. How we loved Tracy and Hepburn, Ginger and Fred: benign images that beguiled Linda and Rob in the forties: glancing repartee, witty feet tapping out a message of hope. But back then we thought we had a place in the world. Now we're not sure we can control even our own lives, let alone what's happening elsewhere. Decisions are made for us while we're being fed the sugar sops to keep the baby happy. You're old and cynical, Jade. Settle and Fixit took away your adolescent illusion that the law was an honourable trade and Helen Chalmers taught you that love was a commodity.

Briefly I wondered whether the firm was really pleased that I'd encouraged the client to settle and avoid any bad publicity. After all they lost a potentially fatter fee if the case had dragged on through a week or so in court. But on the other hand it isn't good to lose a case. It soon gets about as I quickly discovered when I joined Settle and Fixit. Gossip among lawyers is as potent and juicily enjoyed as in any other sphere or profession. I remembered the phrase 'a Pyrrhic victory' and tried it out on James Chalmers when we gathered for a debriefing. The negotiation over the settlement had needed all his suavity and skill not to let the other side know we wanted out and to get a good face-saving price for withdrawing.

'I'm sure you're right, Jade. That's exactly what it would have been if we'd stood out for a million and been splashed all over the tabloids as greedy Goliaths who'd taken the little guy's sling away. As it is the client's seen the sense of it and is pleased with us and their half a million. Especially pleased with you. They'll come to us again. Why don't you take Helen out for the day. I'm sure she's longing for a ride on your bike.'

What did he mean? Was it all some kind of fit-up? Was he innocent or complicit? Maybe this was how they ran their marriage and she went home from me with the titillating details. I'd read that some people, lovers whose passion has staled, long-marrieds, turn each other on in this way. I had no personal experience of it though a couple I'd been drinking with in my local pub had once suggested a threesome. I had a hard time wriggling out of that one, without giving offence or seeming a prude. Loveless sex isn't really my scene though I tried it at uni, clubbing, hopelessly in love with Zena who only saw me as a friend, tried it, scared of not seeming hip, of not being cool, regretting it next day, in the morning-after hangover of a one – night stand, *triste omne animal.*

I couldn't, wouldn't, believe Helen would kiss and tell. Hadn't she chased me as much as I had her? But even then I could see that didn't mean she felt as I did. What had Drewpad said that suggested she liked to pull the newcomers to the firm? I tried to remember his exact words but they wouldn't come right. Anyway where was his evidence? If I asked him he probably wouldn't tell me. There would be more innuendo but no substance. His suspicion of 'the bosses' had grown as he became more convinced that he was given more than his fair share of the rough, searches, lengthy witness statements to prepare along with essential back-up documents, but none of the front line where the real action and the glamour were.

Perhaps I should warn Helen that he was increasingly disaffected, suspecting that he was the wrong colour, had studied at the wrong place, was there only as window dressing to give the firm a liberal face. I was a bit of the decoration too, not Oxbridge but Sussex. Probably the Chalmerses joked about us both over the breakfast table if not in bed. It was a bad moment. I was back at my desk. Drew had gone to Bread, Love and Dreams to queue for sandwiches for us both. Surely she wouldn't betray me, join in some jokey conspiracy of what I'd said or we'd done. Suddenly I was glad I'd never admitted I was in so deep, had never mentioned love.

Some moments you never forget, like sitting for an exam, waiting for a result and opening the envelope, passing the driving test, your first taste of death. If anyone asks me what I was doing when such and such an earth-shaking event took place, the assassination of a world leader, the outbreak of a war, an earthquake, a terror attack, like most people I can't remember and I always suspect that those who seem to are inventing to get their moment of limelight, in front of the microphone or camera. The remembered moments are those of personal expectation or fear when the adrenaline flooded through you. So I can recall perfectly the feel of the wooden desktop under my hands, how a spotlight bounced back off the computer screen so that when I wanted to use it I would have to adjust its position to cut out the highlight. It was a moment of black doubt. I should have turned back then, got out from under. But it was already too late. I had fallen in love with the boss-lady. The rose in my hand was for her and its thorn was already causing my blood to flow.

And then the phone rang. 'Hallo. How are you?'

'Fine.' But already at the sound of her voice my heart seemed to be truly in my mouth, a live thing that had leapt up in my throat and cut off the oxygen supply, making my ears buzz as if I was strung on a stretched humming wire.

'Jim says you've earned a day off and could take me out somewhere.'

'Where would you like to go?'

'Somewhere quiet. How far could we get? To the sea?'

'Your wheels or mine?'

'I think it's time I gave yours a try.'

'We could probably get down to Brighton in a couple of hours.'

'Too populated. The Downs. A village with a pub for lunch.'

'You'll have to wear something warm. I'll lend you some weatherproof or rather windproof gear to go over the top and a helmet. You're sure you're on for this? It isn't very comfortable.'

'You only live once as the man said. But don't go too fast.'

'Would I take risks with you? When would you like to go?'

'Tomorrow? If it's fine.'

'OK.'

'I'll come round to your flat about ten o'clock and leave my car. It's handy that we live in the same borough and my parking permit will cover it.'

I can't remember eating the sandwiches Drew brought back: tuna and salad for him, egg mayonnaise for me, tasting of sick, or how I managed to work or got home. I washed my hair: I must have cleaned the bike, checked out some gear for Helen and, too edgy to stay home, went out to the Trebovir, with its mix of boozy eccentrics, a jazz pianist who sometimes had a gig at Ronnie Scott's, a retired airline pilot who'd been in bombers in the last war and still sounded and looked the part in cravat and moustache, a home help who'd danced in a chorus line-up, and the usual bag of petty crims, fences, conmen who set up their business in their office local. No one questioned me or knew what I did. 'Ask no questions be told no lies,' was the basis of the pub etiquette, and if anyone broke the unwritten rules I simply said I worked in an office which was true enough.

In the morning Helen kept me waiting but only enough to put an edge on the expedition, to make it more desirable because anticipated in the fear that she might have changed her mind or suddenly not feel up for it or Jim could have gone off the whole idea. I tried not to think of what she might be doing when she was away from me. Shakespeare gave his usual ambiguous comfort:

> Nor dare I question with my jealous thought
> Where you might be or your affairs suppose,
> But like a sad slave stay and think of nought
> Save where you are, how happy you make those . . .

Then the entry phone buzzed and she was coming through the hallway on a cloud of scent I didn't recognise, presenting her cheek for a peck.

'Can't I kiss you properly?'

'Too early in the morning and I'd have to redo my face. Besides if we started on that we might never get to our expedition. Where are these clothes you promised me?'

She was in designer jeans and top that made me long to put out a hand to the smooth mounds of her breasts, below the green silk scarf at her throat. I'd never seen her out of skirt and high heels before but the effect was the same. Powerful, sexy in a mature way, hypnotic. I showed her the biker kit lying over the back of a chair.

'Coffee?'

'Maybe we should get going. I'd like a pee before I climb into that gear. It looks as if it might be hard to get out again.' The intimacy of her remark with its bluntness surprised me. It wasn't Gateshead or even Acton. It smacked of boarding school and all girls together.

'I feel like a deep-sea diver.' She pulled on the gloves and we went out into the road where the Crusader was chained up.

'Just a couple of things before we go. You have to hold on to me rather tight, both arms round, and try to lean as I do, especially when I'm cornering.' We put our helmets on. I undid the security chain and got astride. I felt her climbing on behind me as I held the bike steady, then her arms go round my waist. I kicked off.

I'd never had the knightly fantasy before, Lancelot with Guinevere up front or back, held in his arms or clinging on, galloping off into the night, abduction or rescue. But I did now although instead of over the hills and far away it was into the traffic miasma of south London, past the turning for the Gaos though I didn't know that then, and down to the sea like Tom in *The Water Babies* with my own mermaid for company, weaving between the white sharks of unmarked vans, through shoals of silvery cars and grey tanker whales. Soon we were past Norbury and heading for the redbrick suburbs of Reigate on to the Brighton Road where the traffic was lighter, the two currents flowing up and down the double motorway canal.

After nearly an hour on the road it was time to check on Helen. I could feel her arms around me so I knew she was still there but how was she surviving? I signalled a left turn and pulled gently into a roadhouse car park, brought the bike to a standstill, put my foot down, kicked the stand into place and took off my helmet.

'How are you doing?'

She took hers off too and shook her dark hair loose. 'Wow!'

'What about a stop for coffee now?'

'That sounds great.'

'Do you find it very uncomfortable? I've never ridden in back myself.' We were sitting in a repro bow window with our cups of coffee that tasted as if it had been stewing in a glass jug ever since the bar had opened. I half expected her to have something tart to say about it. I was pretty sure she wasn't used to roadhouse or service station fare.

'It's too exciting. I keep expecting either to fall off or be crushed to death. You get the full experience of speed that you don't get shut in a car. I feel as if I'm living dangerously, as if I'm more in touch, more alive. I can see why you like it, love it maybe?'

No I don't love it, I wanted to say. It's part of me and I don't love myself. I love you. I can't love myself because I'm my own subject. OK you need a bit of self-love to get up every morning but you need an object for love, like Pygmalion making himself a living, breathing statue or Cliff's walking, talking living doll.

'Where does this road go to?'

'Brighton. But you said you wanted something less touristy so we'll turn off at the A272 and go east towards Bateman's and then south towards Herstmonceux. They're quieter lanes and little villages round there. Of course it won't be as exciting as bombing down the motorway. I looked up some places to eat in the *Good Pub Guide*.'

Then we were riding away again through Hayward's Heath and Maresfield, built-up lengths of suburbia snipped off south London and stitched over the fields and downs of Sussex. We left the main roads behind at Broad Oak and took to forested lanes. By the time I pulled up beside my chosen pub we were in another world, a secret green place that couldn't have been guessed at from the sprawl of boxy houses we had left behind.

'Let's have lunch and walk up that hill,' Helen said, pointing towards a green mound behind the Blacksmith's Hammer. 'Can we get out of the Superman outfits for a bit?'

'You can. I can lock yours in the pannier.'

'I'll tidy myself up in the loo.'

I waited for her to bring back her discarded gear. I would have to carry my helmet. There wasn't room for two in the carrier.

'You made a good choice, Jay.' We had eaten smooth green watercress soup with an ice floe of cream in the middle, followed by a lemon sole for Helen and aubergine au gratin for me, with a glass of wine each.

'Do we want a bottle?' she'd asked, 'or would that make you a danger to ride behind?'

'Better not if you want to be sure of getting back safely.' For a moment I saw us buried together tangled up in the bike and I didn't seem to be afraid of that dying.

I clipped my helmet to my belt and we set off up the little hill that could have been a burial mound itself. From the top we could look down into a wooded valley with a handsome house in the distance. We sank down in the lee of the mound out of sight of the pub. I took off my jacket and spread it under Helen.

'Thank God it isn't raining. It's so rare to be able to do this in England.' She lay back closing her eyes. I picked a long grass stem with a feathery brush at its tip and gently moved it across her throat. After a few tickling passes she opened her eyes.

'Isn't that a bit naff?'

'Only if you don't see the symbolism.'

She reached up and took my hand guiding it to undo the fastening and then the zip on her jeans.

'Make love to me.'

'Here?'

'Why not.' It wasn't a question but a command and I didn't need to be told twice.

We slept a little and then woke to wander down into the wooded valley so moist underfoot that when we made love again it was against the smooth bark of a beech. The world had fallen away as if we had strayed into another Blakean dimension of innocence and pleasure outside time.

After that we made love whenever and wherever we could. I drowned in her, was saturated with her but never sated.

Now the great house was made ready for the visit of their majesties, they being retired first to Purford because of the great pestilence which approaching nearer from the city forced them to flee further into the more healthful air of the country. At first they had purposed to hold their court at Oxford but hearing that the colleges were all closed up on account of the sickness the king took ship for the Isle of Wight. Yet because this might seem a going into exile and abandonment of the kingdom in its time of need, and provoke panic among the people, his majesty returned and at the entreaty of the young earl and Sir Philip who were foremost among the new knights and favoured greatly by his majesty, he had determined to retire further from the pestilence to Wilton. Then first came my lady's sons to prepare the way and they being still unmarried the countess must play the hostess for the young earl which was no stranger to her for she had entertained her late majesty Queen Elizabeth at both the great house and Ramsbury. There would come also my lady's brother, now Lord Sidney of Penshurst, and the Lady Anne her daughter in the train of Queen Anne. Indeed so many with their servants that the duenna and I were instructed to return to Ramsbury the day before the arrival of their majesties as the month of August was ending, the summer giving greater and greater encouragement to the spread of the plague.

Word came to us at Ramsbury that their majesties had not rested long at Wilton but had divided again, the queen going to the palace at Greenwich taking my lady, Lord Sidney and the Lady Anne, with her. Yet they could not stay long so close to the city, and in danger of the sickness being carried down river towards them so that at the beginning of October my lady sent word that I was to join her at Wilton where the whole court was returned, for the great number of people and the winter coming on brought a need for as many physicians to attend as might be had, even though their majesties had their own skilled doctors with them. So I set out again for the great house which was now become a town in itself and all the surrounding inns and cottages, every barn and shed, were filled to overflowing with a great multitude of every kind of servant, grooms, clerks, stewards, maids and men of all degrees. My lady's own servants were forced to scour the countryside to feed both men and beasts for there were also horses enough to carry an army.

The duenna had been jealous of my summons to Wilton.

'There are some say it is an ill omen that this sickness has come to us at the beginning of a new reign, that the dog star causes it to rain down upon us because King James has forsaken his mother's old religion for which she was martyred.'

'The infection is the work of nature and man. It leaps from one to the other by contagion and not by descent from the stars.'

'You should have more care of religion Master Boston. Those who mock or set themselves above it will be struck down by God's hand in their pride when they least expect it.'

'I do not mock God or religion, only the cheats of the astrologers who pretend to a knowledge of what is in the stars and of their influence on all things.'

'Fate and the stars may show God's hand too, for all your learning.'

Two days after I had reached Wilton the wagons of the players rumbled up and pitched outside the wall. His majesty, tiring of the country sports, had summoned his own troupe of the king's men from Mortlake where they were quartered away from the sickness, to divert him with a play. Now the house was indeed filled to overflowing and there came carpenters to set up a stage in the hall. The noise of their hammers and saws was added to the din of so many people.

The players themselves were quartered in the biggest of the barns, those already lying there being forced to find a corner elsewhere or lie under the stars. On the second day after their coming I was sent for to dress a wound to the head one of them had sustained in a fight. I filled a little bag with tincture of arnica to cleanse the wound, soft cloth, bandages and healing unguents and went out to the barn. I pushed open the door and it was as if I entered another world where men went about their business unmindful of any sphere beyond them.

Some sat and played at cards, others lay on their straw pallets smoking so that the air was sweet with the smell of tobacco, while others tried over their words together. Two were painting shields as for a joust. Another was casting up accounts in a ledger. Two women sat sewing in a corner with a pot of ale between them. I could not see where the wounded man might be. I stood in the doorway and peered about.

At length one of the players noticed me and approached. 'Who have we here?'

'Where is he with the wounded head?'

'Who wants to know?'

I decided to exercise my patience. This boy was, I thought, about my own age or younger but with a pretty face and a bold look that dared challenge anyone. 'I have been sent to tend the wounded man.'

'Hollo Nick, they have sent a child to physick you.'

One who had been lying still under a cloak unnoticed by me now sat up with a groan, revealing a sword cut to his head that instead of going in deep and clean had gashed his scalp, leaving a bloody mash. 'What kind of physician are you boy? What college taught you your skill, if you indeed have any?'

'I am physician to the Countess of Pembroke.'

'Does she trust to the wisdom of a child?'

'My lady employs several doctors of physick.'

'And where did you learn your healing arts?'

'In my father's house where he practised for many years with, many said, uncommon efficacy.'

Some others among the players now took an interest in our discourse. 'Shall I let the child treat me?' the wounded one asked them.

Now the boy who had first spoken to me took a hand again. 'He is no physician. His skin is soft as a girl's. This is some ruse to be admitted sharer in our company.'

Another took my wrist as if he would feel my pulse. 'Tell the truth now. Are you seeking employment among us as some lovely boy in Diana's shape? We have enough mincing maids already, and to spare.'

'I look for no such sir. Indeed I have no skill in those ways. My little skill is in making of medicines and their use.' And here I opened my bag and showed my wares. 'These are all the tools of my trade. And if the gentleman will not let me tend him he must go untreated for there is none other, all being occupied with other sick persons among so many. But if his wound is not cleansed and anointed daily it will fester and grow rank and may endanger his very life.'

'Come Nick,' another joined in, 'he says you will die if he does not treat you. Is it not worth the try?'

'Already sir,' I said taking the wounded man by his wrist, 'your pulse is quick and shallow. The wound has brought on a fever. Your head throbs and you cannot sleep.'

He groaned a little and leant back against the saddle that was serving him as a pillow. 'How did you know? Are you a necromancer as well?'

'It is my occupation to know sir. I need no magic to divine the symptoms of your case. Inflammation attends such a wound. The body is weakened. Poison is engendered by the wound and flows through the veins.'

'Should I be let blood then?'

'My father believed in the quick letting of blood only if other means could not prevail. I follow his example.'

'Come then. If there is no other, try your skill. Will it hurt? I am a player not a soldier hardened to pain.'

I thought then that he had done better to avoid the cause of it if he feared to suffer.

'It must hurt as I cleanse it for the blood has dried and must be removed. But after I will give you a sleeping draught and when you wake you will begin to feel better. Some one of you hold his hands and press tightly while I work.'

Two of them came forward and took him on either side. I pulled out the bottle of arnica water and began to sponge the gash. He cried out when I first touched him until one of them gave him a wooden spoon to bite on. I worked as gently and swiftly as I could and when the flesh was clean I put ointment of burnet on a pad and laid it to his head, bandaging it firmly in place. Then I mixed opiate in wine and gave him to drink.

One of those who had held his hand now took mine and gazed at it. 'So soft. It is indeed like a maid's hand.'

'My father said a physician should be known for gentle hands since in sickness the lightest touch may be as a blow to one in health. And indeed women may make cunning enough physicians if they are let, as witness many midwives. My lady herself helps in the healing of her house and the many poor who come to her.'

'Midwives and witches too,' another said. 'I would not put myself under the hands of a cunning woman.'

'Then you should not travel abroad to foreign lands,' the first said, 'for women there may play the physician if Boccaccio is to be believed. Meanwhile if you should lack employment in your father's trade, master physician, you may repair to us and we will soon teach you to play a maid. Then you can physick us while we are on the road.'

I thought that his words were too close to the truth. A player who dealt in dreams and things imagined might see deeper into the heart and mind than other men and put me at risk of discovery. Therefore I bowed to them all and said that now I had other business I must attend to, that they should let the wounded man sleep and I would come again to dress his wound. I urged them to give him only broth with a little white bread when he awoke and to call for me if he should seem to grow weaker or the fever grow hotter.

The new steward who had succeeded the murdered Davys met me in the hall where the stage was now set up and the players would perform next day. 'You must go at once to the countess who has been calling for you.'

'I was sent for to attend one of the players and was hard put to leave their company.' I found my lady distracted with all the confusion and their majesties' demands.

'I have none to help me. My sons are constantly riding or hunting and I do not trust the new steward as I did Hugh Davys to smooth our path so that all things are in order as I like. My head throbs. Where have you been Amyntas? Dr Gilbert was here to tend me but his ways are too harsh. I do not need either to be purged or let blood now but only some soothing draught. Where were you?' she asked again.

'Madam I was sent for to tend a wounded man among the players and as they are the king's servants I could not refuse. Then after I had treated his wound, the others would have discourse with me trying to bend me to be of their company and play the maid.'

I had hoped that this would cause her to smile and lighten her humour for I saw she was on the edge of a black melancholy which would serve her badly with a court that looked always for amusement and diversion, and where only princes or their favourites are suffered to indulge damp or dark humours.

'And do you intend to leave me to become a mere player?'

'My lady knows I will never leave while she has need of me. Let me bring you some special wine to calm your agitation.' So I went to our laboratory and mixed a decoction of that plant called the melancholy thistle that grows in moist places, in wine, which together will expel superfluous melancholy which causes care and despair and agitation, and will leave the patient merry after a time.

When I returned with the cup I had prepared, my lady asked me to bring her commonplace book in which she was used to note all such things as it amused her to keep to look on again.

'I remember,' she said, 'when the young earl my son was first

at Oxford he sent me some sonnets that were passed from hand
to hand among his friends, asking me to compare them with
the incomparable *Astrophel and Stella* of my dear brother. Some
I copied into this book, not that they came near his in beauty,
but that I might have to hand what passes for poetry in these
degenerate days, being more sugared than my brother's verses
or those near to him in time as Mr Spenser his *Amoretti* or even
my son's tutor Daniel his *Delia*. Read this one to me.'

She handed me her book, all in her own delicate hand, open
at the page.

> A woman's face, with Nature's own hand painted,
> Hast thou the Master Mistress of my passion.
> A woman's gentle heart, but not acquainted
> With shifting change as is false woman's fashion.

'They are hard on us women, the male poets, when I think
it is not we who are fickle. Go on.'

> An eye more bright than theirs, less false in rolling,
> Gilding the object whereupon it gazeth . . .

My lady sighed, 'yet more of our inconstancy. Even my dear
brother might write so sometimes.'

> A man in hue all hues in his controlling
> Which steals men's eyes and women's souls amazeth.
> And for a woman wert thou first created
> Till nature as she wrought thee fell adoting,
> And by addition me of thee defeated
> By adding one thing to my purpose nothing.
> But since she pricked thee out for women's pleasure,
> Mine be thy love, and thy love's use their treasure.

'There Amyntas you may hear the coarseness that my brother

was never guilty of in that "pricked", an effect of young men's idle wit that seeks praise for itself above that it would seem to praise. Yet are not you in the opposite case to this, Amyntas, being indeed not pricked out for women's pleasure?'

'Madam, I often forget in what form I was made and then I remember and wish to be other than I am.'

'But then I could not take you into my bed and pass the time with you in innocent games.'

I could not answer my lady.

The play was to be given the next day. In the afternoon while there was still a little grey light lingering outside the house I crossed to the barn where the sick player lay to tend his wound. This time when I entered a few looked up to salute me but none challenged my presence. I saw at once why this was, for the wounded man was sitting up on his straw pallet, his face cheerful and not flushed with fever, his eye bright but not extremely so.

'Here is my little physician. Truly I must speak as I find and I find you the very master of physick. If I had had the king's physician himself I could not have been cured more quickly. If they could find a part for me as a wounded soldier coming from the wars in this bandage I would strut my part on stage tomorrow.'

Going close to him I took his wrist. 'Sir you must be quiet a little yet or you may cause the fever to return by overheating of the blood. Your pulse is still too quick and shallow for all your wound is recovering. I will dress it again and then prescribe you a draught to make you sleepy for fear you should excite a hot vapour in the brain or should stumble and inflict a new contusion on your broken head.'

'If you promise me such a sweet drink as yesterday I will be good and lie still.'

I unwrapped his head and found the wound clean, with just a little weeping I could wipe away without causing him such pain that he had to be held down by his fellows. Then I applied fresh burnet ointment and bound him up again. Although I was as gentle as I could be, by the time I had finished he was content to lie back while I mixed his potion and raised his head to drink. The smell of his breath was rank in my face as I bent over him so that I was hard put not to turn away until he had emptied the cup, and the stench from his body and clothing almost caused me to let his head drop.

'Tomorrow you should wash a little and shift your shirt and slops.'

'Will you not come and do it for me master physician? Those hands of yours would be kinder to my flesh than my own.'

'Now Nick,' one of the players said, 'he is not for you. Let one of the hirelings wash you. They will do well enough. But not they that are to play the maids tomorrow. Keep them fresh for their parts. You should be gone master physician, unless you want the work. He stinks because he has pissed himself in sleep.'

'He will sleep again soon,' I said returning my things to my bag. 'It is an effect of the draught that it gives some men imaginings.'

'He needs a potion for excess heat in the loins and privities, master physician. But he would not thank you for it.'

I had never been at a play apart from seeing the mummers in the inn yards at the fair and at Easter and Christmas feasts in the great house. I was therefore determined to find a place where I might hear and see all. This was not easy for everyone was of the same mind so that there was a great press of people behind the seats provided for their majesties, my lady herself and the first among the courtiers. Her two sons lay on either side of their majesties propped upon their elbows in the appearance of pages or esquires.

At length I was obliged to stand upon a stool to get above the heads of the listeners, leaning against the jamb of the door so that I might not fall off. The room was lit with a thousand candles, or so it seemed, and a painted cloth hung in the hind part of the stage showed a house of columns and a portico of steps in stone with beyond a prospect of the sea and shore and a painted ship asail on the waters. I had never seen the sea yet I knew what was represented to my gaze and might almost hear the distant waves of the prospective.

Their majesties had entered with the court and taken their places. There was a murmur of voices, then a fanfare from an unseen trumpet. Music began to sound and the players came up on the stage before the painted columns, attired in such rich silken clothes they vied with the court that watched them. The noblest of them began to speak and I leant forward to hear. He spoke of love and music.

O spirit of love, how quick and fresh.

His words pierced into my breast and I felt as if a cord binding up my heart had snapped, letting the blood flow through my veins up into my bursting brain. From where I leant on the door jamb I could see the countess dressed in all her finery, the noblest lady of the court as it seemed to me.

The lord said that he would go hunt the object of his love.

O when mine eyes did see Olivia first,
Methought she purged the air of pestilence.
That instant was I turned into a hart,
And my desires like fell and cruel hounds
E'er since pursue me.

Then there entered a messenger come from his lady who said she would see no one, being in deepest mourning for her dead brother. I saw my lady start at this so close it seemed to her own affections that I wondered if he who writ it had knowledge of her grief. The noble and his attendants retired and now came on new players, one of whom I recognised through his maid's clothes as he who had accosted me when I first entered their barn. Yet he acted the maid so truly that after few words only I no longer saw the boy from the barn. The captain told her and us too that they were in Illyria which seemed to me with its fair prospect that it must lie close to Elysium. She too was mourning for a brother drowned. She would seek service with the duke's lady Olivia but the captain who had rescued her advised otherwise, saying the lady would see no one. Then she said she would personate a youth and seek service with the duke. 'Thou shalt present me as a eunuch to him.'

Next came two clownish knights whom I had also seen in the barn in undress but now they too were dressed in the finest silks and velvets with feathered bonnets on their heads. I marvelled at the rude words from their lips yet the king and queen laughed heartily, though my countess was silent, and then again was the duke returned, this time with the maid in boy's attire to be sent on a mission to woo his lady for him.

And now for the first time came on the lady Olivia herself as finely arrayed as my countess at her richest so that it was as if we spied upon ourselves and eavesdropped on our own words. First was the sour steward of her company with a licensed fool who tried to bring the lady out of her grief for her brother. Then entered one of the foolish knights deep in his cups although it was not yet noon. I thought that she was surrounded by fools, apart from her waiting woman who had more sense than the rest together, yet their clowning seemed to please the watchers.

At last the messenger from the duke who had stood at the gate all this time, was admitted and it was again as if he who writ it knew my case. 'I am not that I play.' Yet for me the tables were turned for I loved my lady and she I feared only played with me while I could see that the lady Olivia might love the false Cesario, but he only feigned a passion in behalf of another. So at one and the same time I watched the play played out before me, and yet watched my lady in the front rank among the court and myself where I stood upon my stool in the darkest part of the hall.

The scene came to an end. All clapped and refreshments were brought on for those of the court. Taking a salver from one of the servants I went forward and knelt before my countess.

'Well, well, my little Cesario,' she said low so that others might not hear, 'have you brought me one of your famous potions? I would not sleep through the rest of the play.'

'It is only wine my lady, unless you bid me otherwise.'

'These men make fine maids do they not master physician? And maids may make fine men to strut and peacock but not upon the stage. And if you should take a motto Amyntas I think I know what it might be.'

'*Non sum quod gero.*'

'You are a clever child. Now I remember I have seen this played before in the late earl his day before his last illness. At the behest of the young gentlemen of the Inns of Court but I had forgot much of it, even the Lady Olivia grieving for her brother. These toys are well enough for the public stage, the multitude, not keeping to the classic mould as my brother wrote, and as I did in my translation of the French *Antonius* which I will give you to read. Or better we will read it aloud together as I have done before with Mr Daniel. But see, they are to begin again.'

So I watched as the action unfolded, sometimes entranced with the words of love from the Lady Olivia for the young Cesario, sometimes cast down at the impossibility of his loving her, and instead setting his affections on the duke. Between came the tediousness of the clowns and fools though once when the poet seemed to call in doubt that the devil may deal in witchcraft I remembered my father his belief that witchcraft was but delusion as the words seemed to hint at. I thought a shadow passed across the king's face and he did not laugh at these antics as he did before. Then I remembered his own *Demonologie* and that the Scots are said to be more credulous in these matters under the influence of their mists and mountains.

I thought that plays were witchcraft enough in themselves for what we supposed we saw or believed for a little time under the spell of the words was all imaginings, the stuff of dreams. Those persons who seemed to move so solidly before us were not that they seemed but the actors I had seen in the barn, and the one who played the rude sea captain, Antonio, was he who had gently urged me in jest to join their troupe as player and travelling physician.

At last in the resolution of the action I saw all my hopes and fancies expire when Cesario was revealed as Viola and the Lady Olivia was married to her brother Sebastian as if one might substitute for the other with no loss but only gain. And I understood that all my hope might be to conjure up my dead brother from the grave and assume his shape by that alchemy I did not believe in, not even if I should take up my father's quest again for the philosopher's stone which had the power to transmute all things, and should find the secret where he and all others had failed. For indeed it could not engraft upon another stem to improve the fruit, and without I was thus pricked out, as my lady said, there was no remedy for my love but only the chaste pain of virtuous devotion. Yet even had I been so endowed by nature what mistaken pride made me think, apart from the actor's simulated passion of the Lady Olivia, that her gaze would fall on me who had not even Cesario's pretence to be a gentleman?

'Make love to me,' she'd said but did she really mean it or just 'fuck me', 'screw me' or whatever the in-term is for what can carry all or nothing of tenderness or lust. The dreary shoals of spam with their pathetic peddled porn are more and more

depressing. Yet someone out there must love them, sitting alone
in front of a screen clicking down on penile enlargement, tossing
off among the titties, crawling the 'mega adult sites', the stickers
of the prossies in the old phone boxes replaced by cyber soft-
wares. At least they promised flesh and blood pleasures. Now
I'm left with that old lament of Yeats: 'tell how love fled and
hid his face among a crowd of stars'.

Forget it, Jade. That was in another country and the wench
is dead, to you anyway. Time to get on your bike and mingle
with the natives of Wessex. Let's see if your smart card will get
you in. Soon they'll be asking for a DNA sample before you're
allowed to buy a discouraged substance, not just drugs, booze
or smokes but a packet of full-fat crisps leading to the obesity
of nations and a drain on the medical resources of the state.

Full summer's abloom now and because I'm not in a hurry I
can take my time, idling almost, and arrive at the gates with
my heart thumping but not from doing a ton on the motorway,
just the natural excitement of the chase, the adrenaline of fight
or flight we share with all our mammal kin though whether I'm
hunter or prey I'm never sure when I fetch up against the Wessex
security system. I take off my helmet, get out the plastic pass
card and wheel the Crusader up to the metal fence. I swipe the
card and wait. Hey presto, Aladdin's cave is opening before me.
I push the bike inside. The gates must be operated by sensors;
they begin to close silently, purposefully, behind me. What
would happen if I stepped back between them? An alarm?
Crushed bones? It's something I might badly need to know
sometime: how to get out if things go pear-shaped or my card
doesn't work and I'm trapped inside.

But this time all's well. I'm through. Students are sitting
around on academe's innocent lawns or strolling to classrooms.
I catch a flutter of black gown as I head for the bike shed,
feeling an old hand now, strip off my gear to blend in with the
crowd, take my briefcase holding my mobile and fleshed-out

synopsis from the pannier under the camera's unblinking eye and saunter towards the main building. I'm going to drop the synopsis in on Davidson, push it under the door if that's the only way, sit in the library for a bit pretending to do some research and wander about getting more of the feel of the place. Somewhere there must be a dining room or caff where the students can sustain themselves. Somehow I don't feel Wessex runs to a bar. It might lead to bacchanals or punch-ups.

Following the tangled line of what I remember from that first visit I track down Davidson's room and knock. There's no answer but a notice on the door tells me he's available for consultation from 12–1.0. The door fits too tightly for me to be able to push my envelope under it. I'll have to come back. OK. On to the library where I sign up for a place in the round room in the afternoon then join the other students in the modern extension where one part is set aside by a rank of gleaming desktop PCs.

At other tables fingers are flickering over the keyboards of a dozen laptops while eyes strain at the small screen. Though it's called a library books don't seem to come into it much. I bag a place with my notebook and briefcase, and go to the reference shelves to take down *A Dictionary of Shakespeare's Contemporaries*. Now I can look up Amyntas' countess: Mary Herbert, née Sidney, Countess of Pembroke. It's strange to see her as an actual biographical entry in a book. It makes her both more and less real, without Amyntas' intervening interpreter's gaze. It says John Donne called her her brother's phoenix, rising from his ashes borne up by their psalms. There's a list of her works, her children, her houses and interests, yet all the time she seems to be receding into the distance.

Distracted by a flicker of movement at the edge of my field of vision, I look up from the page to see a dark-haired student has come in and is standing by the door searching for an empty place. His hair has the blackbird's wing sheen of Asia. He turns his face towards me. With a shock I see, or think I do, that it's the Gao nephew, Charlie. Hastily I duck my head. Now I'm not sure. Ashamed of my 'they all look alike' knee jerk, I risk another quick glance. Now I'm sure.

What shall I do? Pretend I haven't seen him? Maybe he won't recognise me. 'The round eyes all look alike.' But it's too risky. I could bump into him at any time in the corridors. Or he could spot me now when I get up to leave and think I'm avoiding him. No, I'll have to sit tight till he goes and follow him out. What a coincidence. But then they happen all the time. It's an effect of randomness. Something like that. Chance. The numbers game. I can't imagine he's following me. Why should he? Even normal paranoia can't make me think that. I remember Mary telling me about his carefully counted hours of study that make his stay in the country legitimate.

I put my head down and try to concentrate on Amyntas' countess but the moment has gone. I mustn't miss Charlie leaving. He goes over to speak to the librarian on duty at the information desk. She consults her screen; says something to him. He turns away, picks up the pad he's left on the table and heads for the door again. I get up, put the dictionary quickly back on the shelf and follow him out, snatching up my briefcase.

'Charlie, Charlie Gao. It is you, isn't it?'

He turns, puzzled. Then smiles. 'Miss Green. What are you doing here?'

'I was going to ask you the same.'

'This is where I do my studies. My uncle in Chicago he pays for me to go to an American college. Then I can get a job in America. And you?'

'Same sort of thing. I'm topping up my qualifications. Maybe take an American master's to give me more options. You didn't stay long in the library.'

'I was hoping for one of the computers but there's nothing free until one o'clock. So I shall go to the gym, and practise my martial arts. Perhaps we can meet later.'

'I hope to see my tutor.' I bend the truth a little. 'But another day. Is there somewhere we could have a cup of coffee?'

'Sure. There's the campus coffee bar on the other side of the quad.'

'I'll ask Mary to let me know when we could get together.' Why don't I want to give him my mobile number, which she will certainly do? Does he really want to meet or is he just being polite? He wears the uniform jeans and long-sleeved T-shirt, black with a yellow and green dragon, and his face is smooth and clear, his hair glossy clean. I've never really looked at him before, going in and out of the shop with deliveries and leaving when I took over.

'I would like to thank you, Miss Green. Mary told me you had offered to help if I was in any difficulty with the immigration authority or the police.'

'It's just that I've had some legal training that might be useful. Please call me Jade since we're students together.'

He laughs, an embarrassed giggle. 'Still I do thank you, Miss Jade. My aunt and uncle are very kind but they are not rich. Lawyers are expensive. I hope I won't need to trouble you but I do thank you very much. I am worried for them. The shop is their only income and now the big takeaway has opened next door perhaps they will need your help too. Meanwhile I practise the martial arts in case there is trouble.'

'Maybe we can do a swap and help each other.' I'm warming to Charlie Gao.

'I would be proud if I could help you, Miss Jade.' He bows a little. 'See you around. Now I go to the gym.'

I have a sudden vision of him in Bruce Lee stance, kickboxing and karateing his way out of trouble as we fight for our lives with the rest of the Gao family clinging to each other behind us. Only I can't see the faces or make out the distinct shapes of the enemy.

At first Charlie's presence on Wessex campus made me

nervous. Now I'm comforted by it. I feel I'm not alone. Batman has a Robin.

In my meanderings away from the library I find I'm near the chapel. I'll just stroll past the door nonchalantly under the eye of the CCTV. On the off chance I pause and try the door handle. It turns. The door opens; I almost fall inside. Hastily I pull the door to behind me but without quite shutting it in case it should lock me in or set off some alarm. Nothing happens. I go forward into St Walburgha's old haunt, the saint who became the patron of Walpurgisnacht. Today the chairs are set out in rows in a semicircle leaving a space in front of the pulpit.

Molders had said the chapel was always open for meditation but this is the first time I've found it unlocked. There's a waiting feel about it, as if the place itself is expectant. Maybe it's just me, unconsciously building on the unstacked chairs. I sit down in one and stare up at the frescoed saints as if they might bend down and tell me everything they know.

A sound behind at the door alerts me that someone has come in. I bend my head as if in prayer. I hear feet, the scrape of a spindly chair, more sounds from the doorway. Several people must be entering the chapel but I daren't look round. I keep my head devoutly bowed. What's the custom here? Do people kneel or sit? A figure passes me to take a place further into the crescent of chairs, and then another. The whole chapel seems to be filling up. Nobody speaks. There's none of the gossipy pre-service chatter you might expect from people who share an institution. Maybe these are the elite, theological students and they've taken a vow of silence.

Suddenly everyone is standing up and there's the sound of an organ. I stand up too so as not to be conspicuous, the spare prick at the wedding. A group, a double crocodile in black gowns, files past me with the Revd Bishop bringing up the rear. They station themselves in front of the pulpit facing us in a line. The dean climbs up into the pulpit. The organ music swells to fill the chapel and the choir joins in, followed by the congregation. It's a hymn I know from way back, from my nan's tales of her days at the Band of Hope when she was a child and sent to church on Sunday morning along with her four nearest siblings to give their mother peace to knock up a Sunday dinner while their father was at the pub or at the allotment.

> Joy, joy, joy, with joy my heart is ringing,
> Joy, joy, joy, his love to me is known.
> My sins are all forgiven;
> I'm on my way to heaven.
> My heart is bubbling over
> With its joy, joy, joy.

The congregation is clapping in time to the joys and I hear a few cries of 'Yes, Lord' or 'Come, Lord'. I sing and clap along with the rest, grateful to dear dead Nana that I know the words well enough to keep up my disguise. Then it's over and the dean is saying 'Brothers and sisters, be seated under the eye of the Lord and in his presence.' I sit down and duck my head again, hoping he doesn't know his flock so intimately that he'll spot the black sheep in the middle.

'Brethren, you know we are living on the fringes of eternity at the latter end of time, and that we here at Wessex have been called to be the children of the last days as Noah was called in his time when God sent the flood to swallow up the wicked and their world. Then again in the last days of the Roman Empire he sent our forerunners, the people of the covenant, to live together in the desert according to the rule in expectation of the Lord who came among them to be baptised by John the harbinger. And after when the Lord's time was accomplished and he returned to his father, God destroyed the evil empire of Rome and scattered the people of the covenant throughout the world to be the seed corn from which a new harvest should arise.

'We are that harvest of the centuries, ready for Our Lord the reaper, ready to be cut down and gathered into his barn, into his arms. "Come, Lord," we say, "and take your children to you." And he answers: "Wait patiently upon me. I will come and not be slow."'

Some of the Gathering, as I remember Mary-Ann Molders told me they were called, are beginning to punctuate his sermon with little moans and barely articulate cries.

'But we must be ready for him, for none knows the hour or the day of his coming. What we do know is that only the redeemed will be saved and that redemption comes by following the rule of the children of the desert and the covenant, miraculously brought to light again in the discovery of the Dead Sea Scrolls. God brought them out from the tombs where they had lain for nearly two thousand years so that those who had ears to hear and eyes to see should be given the means of salvation and each one should be a temple of the latent Christ.'

I recognise a lot of this as a rehash of their website, the words of the Apostle Joachim. I have to admit that the Revd Bishop is quite a goer himself, almost up to his boss in the mixture of carrot and stick.

'Yet there is no sure redemption in simply following a rule. We are a pentecostal church and we know that the spirit must descend on each one of us and possess our hearts, minds and bodies, expelling all evil thoughts so that we may be pure vessels, scrubbed clean for the Lord to enter. So I ask you, which among you is moved today? Let them come forward as we sing together, for singing together is itself a great spiritual experience. We shall sing "Tomorrow shall be my dancing day" with its chorus of "O my love", for we shall all be lovers of Christ when he comes into our hearts.'

The organ strikes up, everyone stands and the choir begins to sing the verse of the old carol, to be joined by the whole Gathering in the chorus.

> Sing o my love, my love, my love
> This have I done for my true love.

It's sung as I've never heard it before, not the usual rather embarrassed rendering but a full keening with closed eyes, bodies swaying to the rhythm. By the time we reach the third verse people are falling to their knees and crying out in an ecstasy that's more like anguish than joy. I begin to wonder what they're putting in the students' coffee.

'Any who are moved to give themselves to the Lord come forward,' the dean calls out, opening his arms. He has come down from his eyrie, the pulpit, and is standing in the space in front of the choir. A young woman begins to sway towards him. Two of the choir step forward to support her on either side. 'Come, my daughter, come. The Lord, your lover, is waiting for you.'

She cries out and almost falls but the two choir members hold her up. 'Yes, Lord, yes. Come into me. Come, come.' I think of the ecstasies of St Teresa of Avila and St Francis of Assisi, the Cloud of Unknowing of St John of the Cross, all with their erotic and s/m overtones of orgasm and abnegation. Her eyes are closed and she begins to sink, her legs buckle under her and the minders lower her to a chair where she moans and cries a bit before lapsing into an exhausted, stunned silence. The organ rolls and choir and congregation break into a chorus of 'Saved by grace', another golden oldie remembered from my nana.

The girl is waking out of her state of trance. She looks around as if still asleep. The Gathering begins to clap. The dean steps forward and raises her up. 'Welcome, daughter. Your body is now the temple of the latent Christ. Go and sin no more.'

I see him nod to the helpers who lead her back to her seat. 'Let us praise him for his goodness to our sister today.'

There are fervent cries of 'We thank you, Lord.'

'Go in love.'

The organ strikes up. The Revd Bishop, not a ginger hair out of place, leads the choir out while we stand in silence and then begin to fall in behind. My turn comes. I follow on in line towards the door. Suddenly I see Mary-Ann Molders is standing where there would usually be someone with a plate or bag for the collection.

'Ms Cowell, what are you doing here? Wait for me outside please.'

It's like being summoned to the head at school. Dutifully I stand in the corridor until the last student has left and she comes out, shutting the door firmly behind her.

I've had time to consider how to play this.

'Well?'

No, she's more like a prison warder than the head. I expect her to be swinging a heavy bunch of keys.

'I found the chapel open as you said it was and went in for some private meditation. Suddenly people began to come in and it seemed too late for me to get up and leave without causing a disturbance. It seemed best just to wait to the end of the service.' I open my innocent eyes as wide as I can and look directly at her.

'I thought I had explained that Gatherings are restricted to accredited theological students.'

'Yes, you did. And it wasn't my intention to gate-crash. It was just that I was caught inside and thought it best not to distract everyone. I would have had to push my way out against the flow, especially when the choir started to come in. At first I didn't realise there was about to be a service and then it was too late. I'm very sorry if I've broken any rule. It certainly wasn't my intention to do so.'

I wonder if she might remind me that the way to hell is paved with good intentions. Instead she says: 'And what was your impression of our Gathering?'

'I found it very moving.' And that was true in a way, that is I could see how people could be moved by it: how the singing and swaying could lead to those altered states of consciousness induced by repeating a mantra or short prayer, the name of God, that the mystics of all faiths practise. 'It made me wonder if I should change my course of study, whether there was something missing in my life.'

'I'm afraid it isn't that simple, Ms Cowell. There's a long period of initiation, of probation, before anyone is admitted to membership, full membership.'

Does she mean of the Temple or the theological faculty? It would seem too knowing to ask so I simply try to look disappointed. 'I see.'

'If you're really interested in knowing more about our beliefs and way of life I can provide you with some introductory literature. Perhaps when you've studied that you will want to ask me some questions. I'm always happy to help genuine seekers after the truth.'

'Thank you,' I murmur as meekly as I can, eyes cast down, hands clasped in front of me. 'I would certainly study anything you could give me most carefully.' I hope I'm succeeding in giving a passable imitation of Jane Eyre before Mr Brocklehurst.

All this time of the plague my lady had been concerned for redress in the matter of the murder of her steward Hugh Davys, yet without any success in her petition, even though her sons stood so high in his majesty's liking, and the court lay still at Wilton or rather had returned there after removing for November to Winchester where Sir Walter Raleigh was tried for his life on the charge of treason, for men said he had favoured a Spanish plot to put the Lady Arabella Stuart on the throne before King James.

'Which is a thing so unlikely,' my lady said, 'as I wonder that any should credit it, Sir Walter having fought the Spaniard at Cadiz and the Azores and even been an enemy to them such as they might not forgive. Dr Adrian Gilbert his brother has petitioned me to do something for him with his majesty. I know there is nothing I can do of myself for I am now a powerless old woman as my failure in my own affairs testifies. Nevertheless I have entreated my youngest son, Sir Philip, on his behalf, he being in his majesty's graces and gone with him to Winchester.'

Two weeks later Dr Adrian Gilbert brought the news to the countess that, in spite of all, Sir Walter had been convicted and was condemned to die and his majesty was returning to Wilton. Then we made ready to receive the court again. It was now at this time of his majesty's second visit as I remember that the actors came to us as I have recounted, every effort being made to divert his majesty. Whether it was this diversion and others provided by my lady and her sons or the petition of them on his behalf, no one could say but the date set for Sir Walter's execution being the 13th of December came and went, the court all making ready to return to London where the pestilence was at last much abated, so many having died or fled and those that lived seemingly insensible to it or, as the clergy said, spared by God's grace, that there were no more for the disease to fasten on.

'Good news my lady.' Dr Gilbert was clasping and unclasping his plump hands before him. 'His majesty of his goodness has seen fit to exercise his royal mercy and spare my brother's life. He is taken to London, to the Tower, but allowed to live.'

'I am glad to hear of so happy an outcome. Perhaps the Sidney fortunes are turning at last, for my brother, Lord Robert, has been made surveyor general of all her majesty's possessions and we must speedily go with her court to Whitehall. Come with us Dr Gilbert and you shall chance to see your brother bestowed in the Tower like a gentleman rather than a reprieved felon.'

I was not to accompany the countess to London but to retire again to Ramsbury. The great house was shut up and there were no festivities kept this year nor any coming and going of the local gentry. Content though I was with my lady's pleasure that Sir Walter had been reprieved yet I foresaw that all this concern would raise Dr Gilbert in her esteem again and that as he rose so I would sink.

Since his first harsh questioning of me when I was new arrived in my lady's favour he had been much away and on those occasions when he had been present he had paid me little attention. Yet I felt a malice towards me as a dog may sniff at the air tasting the scent of someone or thing unseen of human eyes. And now he would go with my lady to London and have every opportunity to gain her favour.

They set out in the middle of December, his majesty with young Sir Philip going on before. After the noise and turmoil of the last weeks the house seemed to echo still with laughter and music, the footsteps and press of several hundreds of people, until a great silence descended upon us and dust began to settle over all. I was glad to be returning to Ramsbury where I had at least some occupation and a daily rule to follow. Yet before I left there came a letter addressed to me in an unknown hand which upon opening gave me news that increased my melancholy.

When I had last written to Dr Gilbard of my experiments with electrics I had pretended to be writing on my father's behalf because of an infection of the eyes that kept him from doing so himself. This I did that any reply might reach me and not be turned away as for someone unknown. Breaking open the package I found a letter in the same yet strange hand as the superscription informing me that Dr Gilbard had died at his home in Colchester where he had retired to escape the late pestilence but that before he fell sick he had written the enclosed letter to my father which his assistant had been kind enough to forward.

Esteemed Doctor, for I think you have deserved the title more than most who lay claim to it. I have received your last account of your experiments with the electricals with much admiration that in the midst of so busy a life you are still able to devote some hours to this study, and add so much to my own, making such accurate observations that all men must admire the precision of your work and the usefulness of the instruments you have devised. I truly believe this is the path which the natural philosopher must pursue towards the truth and I remember that in your own former experiments in search of the philosopher's stone you did apply those same principles, unlike the mere alchemist who throws ingredients into a limbec without the labour of weighing and measuring and keeping accurate account thereof.

Tell me dear sir whether you still pursue your quest for the one principle which, understanding, shall make that man as a god, a Prometheus able to fashion men from stones, or whether what you now follow with the electricals has overtaken that work. Perhaps in this discovery we have stumbled upon the true philosopher's stone and this indwelling force if harnessed, as we have tamed the lodestone to the compass, will prove even more useful to mankind. I am an old man now in failing health and it would give me ease of mind to think that such a philosopher as you would continue with my work and publish our experiments, preserving them in a book for others to follow after as I have done with my *De Magnete*.

I trust that by now your eyes are mended enough to read this and continue your studies. I find the juice of eyebright distilled and dropped in the eyes for several days together helps all infirmities of the eyes, even dimness of sight decayed by age.

I no longer have the hours to pass in my laboratory since the court is so enhanced that all his majesty's physicians are kept in constant business. Also as president of the College of Physicians I am called upon to resolve many matters, and the disputes that arise between learned men often over simple affairs. Forgive me therefore that I do not write at greater length or more often but believe me, dear sir, even in absence and silence that I count you an esteemed helper and friend.

Yours in haste,
W. Gilbard

When I had read this and understood that the excellent doctor, my father's friend, was dead I felt a new pang pass through me as at my own father's death even though the doctor and I had never met. Also I felt a sadness for myself that there was no longer anyone to whom I could communicate those experiments with which I had passed any idle moments I could seize and occupy my thoughts while away from my countess. Nor had I any reason to continue with the work since the conduit for communicating it to others who might value it was stopped up by death.

Now again indeed I was made sensible of my place alone in the world except for what crumbs might come to me from my lady's table. I turned my thoughts to God and my father to see if they would comfort me and taking horse rode down into Salisbury to St Edmund's where my father lay buried. The day was raw and dull. People hurried along wrapped in every rag they could put on and there seemed no touch of Christmas joy to come in any face that I passed.

Reaching my old home I found it and the house of our neighbour Dame Milburn, who had preserved Dr Gilbard's first letter and his book sent to my father, both shut up. I dismounted at the lych gate of our old church and going up the path pushed open the door. Inside I could not see at first for the short winter day was nearly done. When my eyes became accustomed to the gloom I made my way forward up the aisle. Ahead I could see a glow of light coming from a side door which must lead to the vestry.

I reached the spot where my father lay and was surprised to see a black slab had been placed over it with his name upon it and the date of 1601. Below were engraved the words: 'Doctor of Physick who ministered to the poor of this parish,' and the likeness of a skull. I remembered that it was just a year since I had come here before. A twelvemonth had passed and yet I still could not pray. The black stone seemed to press down on his bones and put him further beyond my reach. I knelt in the nearest box and rested my head upon my joined hands but my mind remained void of any comforting idea. Then I glimpsed a light between my fingers coming towards me and heard feet and the swish of a gown approaching. I stood up.

'Do not cease your prayers young man. I do not wish to disturb you.'

'I have done sir. I came only to visit my father's grave but I find there is a stone set upon it and I wonder by whose hands since they were not mine.'

'What is your name young man?'

'Amyntas Boston sir.'

'And this was your father who is now with Christ?'

'Yes sir.' And at this I felt the tears begin to start that had not flowed all this while. Yet I struggled to keep them back. 'Tell me sir who has placed this memorial to him.'

'I am newly come here myself and there are many things as yet unknown to me. Perhaps some of the better sort of the parish have wished to preserve his memory because of his charity to the poor as is engraved there. Had he lived a year longer they had need of him for this parish was sorely visited by the pestilence, especially among the poorest. The priest himself perished for that he would not leave his parishioners to suffer without comfort and your father had he been living and exercising his practice of physick, must surely have been struck down too. At least he was spared the sight of so many perishing around him.

'And Dame Milburn who lived near the lych gate? Her house is shut up.'

'Then she is most likely dead.' The priest paused for a moment and looked hard at me as he would read my thoughts or my face or give his coming words more weight. 'I have heard some say since I came here that for all his godly charity your father did also look into those mysteries that God in his wisdom has hidden from us. Indeed one doubted whether he should lie in holy ground as a known necromancer.'

'My father was no necromancer sir. He tried only to understand nature by reason and experiment.'

'Not by spells and divination as cunning men, and women too, do often? As casting of horoscopes, finding lost goods, conjuring spirits contrary to holy scripture. "There shall not be found among you an enchanter or a witch. Or a charmer or a consulter with familiar spirits or a wizard or a necromancer." Deuteronomy.'

I looked up at him then and saw that his eyes were sparkling in the flame of the candle and indeed one might have taken him for some demon decked out in priest's clothes, his hair standing up like stubble above his ears around a bald dome.

'My father sir despised all such as mere illusion.'

'He had better have seen them as the temptations of the devil.'

'Perhaps he did sir. We did not speak of it together so I cannot tell you his thoughts upon the matter, only such as I have conveyed to you already and that I received while assisting him in his labours.'

'Such labours as involved the furnace and mercury, I have heard.'

'Indeed sir a furnace is necessary for the preparation of many healing substances, especially those that use metals or minerals, among which may be found red lead which some mistake for mercury, quicksilver itself, gold and iron, many precious stones which must be ground or subdued by fire if their properties are to be brought to drive out or soothe gross humours as lapis, topaz, emerald, amethyst, jasper and many others.'

'I see you would be thought a natural philosopher yourself Master Boston. Perhaps there are things you could teach me if they are not of the devil.'

'I assure you sir anything I might impart to you is to be done only in the name of God and for the relief of suffering mankind. As our Lord himself gave ensample many times in healing the sick. And now I must wish you goodnight sir for I have to ride to Wilton and it grows dark.'

'Where do you lie in Wilton?'

'At the great house. I am in the service of the Countess of Pembroke.'

'And what is your trade?'

'I am one of her physicians sir. Like my father, and like him also I assist her in attending upon the poor and sick.' With this I made an inclination of my head and moved towards the door, seeing that the countess, her name, had caused him to fall back.

'Goodbye Master Boston. We shall meet again for sure. God go with you.'

'And with you sir.'

I was eager to be out of his clutches for I saw that he was a kind of rude priest, of little learning, but envious of that of others, who would do me harm if he could and even dig up my father's bones and not permit him so much as to lie quiet in the churchyard.

The next day I set out for Ramsbury fearing that he might indeed come in search of me and finding my protector elsewhere might try to do me some mischief. Riding hard all day

I reached what I understood to be my best haven at night, having ridden fast but not so as to put my poor horse in danger of her life as some do, not seeing them as creatures made by God for us and our use, as the Bible says, with the power of life and death over them, but not thereby to be abused. For my father had taught me that if we are indeed lower than the angels but higher than the beasts yet we all stand upon the one ladder of creation.

In the dear house where I had been most happy and secure I found only the duenna and a few servants, as a groom to tend the horses and keep a fire in the hall, a boy in the yard, a maid to clean and her mother to cook. After all the bustle of the court I wondered how I should pass the hours. Praise be however that all were in health and had no immediate need of my ministrations.

'You will soon find folk come flocking when they know you are returned Master Boston,' the duenna said. 'I hear Dr Adrian has gone to London with my lady to see his brother Sir Walter in the Tower.'

I wondered how she had heard so far away in Ramsbury but they say bad news travels fast.

'So my lady has kept him from a traitor's death. She was ever fond of him and it is hard to tell if she acts out of remembrance of an old flame or in defence of the Protestant cause so dear to her father and brother, as she may need to do now we have a queen of the old religion. Shall we make peace with the Spaniard Master Boston? How is the word at court?'

'I believe his majesty is for peace. And perhaps the Spaniard too is weary of war. If they will let us alone then all may be quiet.'

'They say Queen Anne is already fallen from her first esteem and that the court is likely to be a place of idleness and foolishness where masques are more often seen than sermons heard, to the emptying of the royal purse.'

I did not answer. Her mind and tongue were as sharp as ever and still toyed with thoughts that if they were not quite treason came very close.

She went on, 'Now all my lady's family is of the king's or the queen's court they will be much abroad. You should look to yourself among these new diversions.'

'And you?' I could not help asking.

'I am old and if I am turned away tomorrow I have a little put by and an almshouse I can return to in my own country near Thaxted in Essex but I do not think my lady will put me out, for there is no one to provoke her to it since I am not worth their malice. But your case is otherwise since you are young and have been my lady's favourite which some would see as excuse enough to pull you down. And where would you go if such a thing were to come to pass?'

I answered her as if I had given the matter thought already although my mind had always shied away from the question as too awful to contemplate: a life without my mistress and never perhaps to see her again. 'I should go to London and set up as a physician for there are many there who if they could not pay me in coin might pay me for my medicines in kind so that at least I should not starve.'

'You are brave Master Boston or very foolish. Sometimes I wish I had had more courage to seek my fortune either singly or in marriage rather than spend my days safely under the Sidney pheon away from the cares of the world. But then when I was young, girls were their parents' property until they were their husband's and I had not that chance you had of a philosopher and physician for a father who would let me learn from him. Neither were we set to any schooling. My tutor was my mother who could teach me only those distaff arts she knew herself.'

I realised from this that she did indeed know my secret but that she must be prevented from revealing as much to me openly or it would become a kind of conspiracy between us that would put me in her power, and although I did not think she had any evil intent towards me, yet the chance to use that power and show off her knowledge might become too strong, especially with the countess who might then be forced to reject me.

'Had my father lived I would have wished to proceed to the university and become doctor but without friends and money such is impossible.'

'As you wish Master Boston. I am sure none could have surpassed you in learning whatever else might be in their favour.' To my relief she seemed amused by this game and gave a short laugh that was half a cough and half a bark. And so I left her.

Now the thought that had leapt to my tongue that if matters fell out ill I would go to London and seek my fortune there like Dick Whittington, began to take real shape in my mind and I partly wished I had dared my disguise and presented myself to Dr Gilbard as an assistant and pupil. How I envied the one who had written to me, or rather to my father, his assistant that had had the chance to study with so great a man. I took up the copy of *De Magnete* itself and wrote upon the flyleaf where the doctor had already inscribed it with the words *ex dono auctoris*: *ad Thomasi Bostoni, medici Sarumensis*.

My sense of loss was sharpened when I looked again at the letter which had accompanied the doctor's and saw that in my first grief I had neglected to turn the page. Doing so now I read:

My master has left an unpublished work of natural philosophy even greater in length than his *De Magnete* which treats of our sublunary world, and which he entrusted to me when he knew he was dying to bring before the public. It sets out his new theory based upon the old that the moon too is a magnet that draws up the tides and keeps her face ever turned to the earth.

Therefore sir if you see any occasion of this please
inform me. I would not wish, as I am assured you
would not, that any work from so esteemed a hand and
brain should perish with him. It has as title *De Mundo
Nostro Sublunai Philosophia Nova.*

It was his custom during his life in London to hold
meetings every month of like-minded men grounded in
all branches of natural philosophy and mathematic, as
astronomy, medicine, optics and other intellectual
pursuits, at his house in Knightrider Street beside the
College of Physicians for the exchange of information
on their experiments and ideas. I shall endeavour to
maintain this custom if I can and invite you to be part
of our discussions if you should be in these parts on the
first Friday of the month, such was the doctor's esteem
of your work especially on the electrics and anelectrics.

Now I resolved that if I should be cast off on the world I
would seek out this assistant to the doctor and offer my services to him or else I should try some other, as Master Simon
Forman from my native Salisbury who has made his fortune
treating those with the plague in London while all other physicians fled. And so I might maintain myself and my disguise.
Yet for all my brave thoughts my heart broke again at losing
my mistress and our once happy life together.

'Do you know what they call you Master Boston?' the duenna
said, one day when she had brought me a cup of wine to the
laboratory. 'They call you the young wizard, for they believe you
cure so many that it must be by magic since nature herself could
never do as much.'

At first such an idea made me smile but then I thought it
might do me harm, even if said in jest, and I was glad the new
priest of St Edmund's was far enough away for it not to come
to his ears. From then on I was very careful with all that I

treated that I should use no speech to them that might be thought any kind of spell or incantation and when one old woman who had come to me with hands crabbed in pain asked if there was not some hour of day or night that would serve best for the taking of the potion or rubbing on of the unguent I had given her with some words that she might use for greater efficacy, I answered that the virtue was all in the medicines and that nothing further was needed, they would work as well by day or night and in silence.

'The cunning woman of Savernake who lives in the forest gives us a little bag to hang round our necks with something of power in it.'

'Most likely something to disgust as a dried toad's leg or owl pellet, such as can do no good but may do harm by holding some rottenness against the body until it decays entirely.'

Here in my cell with me lives a mouse I feed with crumbs from my plate since it is the only living creature that does not mock or abuse me or search out my secrets. I am careful never to let it be seen for I know that my gaoler would cry out that I have a familiar to do my evil will and that is where my power comes from, for so the ignorant insist with their belief in magic as the treatment for men's ills and not in natural philosophy to understand diseases and their cure by the light of reason which must come from God as being good. And here lies the danger of that very idea of a white witch or wizard for if there are white then there must, by the law of opposites, be black, evil and of Satan. Then the earth as the psalmist says is not the Lord's but divided equally, and poor mankind the ground where the battle is played out which I take to be that heresy promulgated by the sect of the Manichees to the confusion of religion and men's minds.

I feel my experience in the chapel and meeting with Charlie

Gao are enough excitement for one day so I head off to the bike shed and start for home, trying to make sense of it all. Do the Apostle Joachim and his henchman the Revd Bishop, not to mention Apple-pie Molders, actually believe all that apocalyptic stuff about the fringes of eternity? Are they really trying to save souls, and maybe bodies, by a combination of mass hysteria and self-hypnosis, the favourite tools of both religious fanatics and political dictators? Or is there some hidden agenda? Somewhere I read about a cult that was after its members' money. Maybe it's like signing up to be a monk or nun and having to make over your worldly goods to the order. That would be a scam of sorts but unless you could prove a cynical intent to deceive for gain where's the difference from donations to charity, a political party or the established church? And anyway how does all that fit in with what happened to Galton? Which is meant to be what you're working on, Jade, what you're paid to suss out. The question should be: what do I have to prove to show wrongful dismissal? That's what it boils down to.

There's very light traffic today because I've left early so I've time to think, a part of my brain making all the biking decisions while another part busies itself with the Galton enquiry. I have to be able to prove the grounds for his dismissal were inadequate but that's hard when he's such a weirdo and arrogant with it. Or else I have to prove the setup at Wessex is even weirder than him. He could have stumbled on something that made them want him out. But that would mean there's some sinister plot I haven't uncovered yet. Maybe I can't. Maybe there isn't one. You'll have to do better than that, Jade.

There's a light flashing on the answering machine when I reach home but no message. I dial 1471 and get Galton's number. I don't press it to ring him back. I need to think but like Yeats' long-legged dragonfly my mind moves in silence and nothing comes, no flash of brilliant intuition or deduction, my dear Watson. I don't want to admit to Galton that I'm no further forward as I flounder around trying to make sense of something that may not be susceptible to logical thinking, that may be irrational itself or worse still non-existent.

Most of a bottle of special offer La Chasse du Pape later, I decide to sleep on it and fall into bed. I'm dreaming, as I often do since I got sucked into this case, of somewhere small and dark which I know is Amyntas' prison cell but I can't see her. I grope my way forward with one hand on a cold stone wall and the other stretched out in front of me feeling for something, someone. Then suddenly I'm half awake still in the dream. There's a phone ringing and the logical bit of my mind says that can't be in Amyntas' prison. I switch on my bedside light and catch the phone just before the answering machine can cut in but it's gone dead. I check the number and look at the clock which shows ten past two. It isn't Galton's number. Maybe it's some drunk misdialling. The ringing begins again. I'm wide awake now. This could go on all night if I don't stop it. After three rings I pick up the handset.

'Yes?'

'I need your help.' It's Galton's voice.

'It's two o'clock in the morning.'

'Yes. I'm sorry. I wouldn't have troubled you at such an hour of course but...'

'Where are you?'

'I'm in Wellover police station. They said I could make one call to my solicitor. They said if you came and bailed me I could perhaps be released.'

'What have they got you for?'

'I'd rather explain in person. Please, Ms Green.'

He's never begged before. There's none of the snide arrogance in his voice now. 'Oh Christ! How do I get there?'

'Your motorcycle?'

'I'm probably not sober enough yet. Too much red plonk. Can't you hang on till morning? I'll come and spring you then.'

'Please, Ms Green. I'm not used to such an experience. I can't say much. This may be being recorded. They told me it might. Take a taxi. I'll pay.'

'Don't you have a friend who could get you out?'

'No, there's no one. They're saying I must end the call. Please come.' The line goes dead.

He'd sounded frightened, a real lost cause now. I get out of bed and go into the bathroom to pee and wash my face. I pinch the lobes of my ears to see if they're still numb. I can't tell whether my body has neutralised enough of the booze yet. I drink a glass of water. Why are we so uncivilised that most of our trains stop at twelve? I try national rail enquiries, and get a jaunty Scot in some distant call centre who cheerfully confirms that the next train from Waterloo leaves at 7.10 and gets to Wellover just over an hour later. I start trying to find a taxi.

A quarter of an hour later I'm bowling down the M3 with Lester, a father of two whose parents came over on the *Windrush*. He still has the Bob Marley lilt as he tells me he prefers to drive at night when the roads are empty. His wife is a nurse and so she's sometimes on nights too while he stays home and has to drive in the day.

'You don't see much of each other then.'

'We try to get a couple of hours a day together and our days off when we're lucky.'

We hit the curtained suburbs of Wellover just after three o'clock and look for a friendly native sober enough to point the way to the police station. Lester drops me outside under the blue lamp and goes in search of coffee, promising to come back in half an hour to see if I need him.

I go up the steps to the station with the usual fluttering in my gut I always get entering such institutions. There's a weary looking constable, female, behind the desk typing something on to a screen.

'Yes?'

'You have a Dr Alastair Galton here, my client. I should like to see him, please.'

'And you are?'

I hand over my card, not the Lost Causes one I keep for clients but a more formal version (that doesn't name Lost Causes. A sense of humour doesn't come easy to officialdom) I keep for such occasions. She looks at it and presses an unseen buzzer.

'Could I ask what the charge is?'

'Indecent exposure.' Her sour expression shows her distaste at having to spit out the two words.

Shit. What has the silly bugger been up to? I hope I'm keeping the alarm out of my face.

A Sergeant, male, appears. 'Can you take three to the interview room. His solicitor is here. And could you get number two to shut up.' I'm aware of the sound of muffled singing and the thud of a door or wall being thumped. The sergeant goes off through a solid door. The constable, female, gets out from behind her desk. 'I'll show you where to go.' She leads me through a passage into a room, bare except for a table and chairs and a monitor screen flicking from point to point of the station, including the steps outside. For a second I see Galton being escorted along a corridor. 'We've cautioned him as to his charge and his rights.' I feel as if I've stumbled into a cop soap, and at any moment a hand will feel my collar and I'll be banged up too. Civil practice doesn't prepare you for bars and locks.

The door opens and Galton is ushered in. His usual precise clothing is somehow rumpled and his tie askew. His thinning hair is mussed up. Nobody has lent him a comb or a mirror. We stand about awkwardly.

'I should like to see my client alone.' They exchange looks. Then the woman says: 'Buzz when you want us.'

They leave in silence and I see them for a moment on the monitor. Their body language shows they are talking but I can't hear the words they're saying. I wave Galton to one of the chairs and sink on to another myself.

'Now what the fuck have you been up to? And remember I warned you about lying to your solicitor and, for the moment, that's me.'

'I am so grateful to you for coming, Ms Green.' He puts his head in his hands. This is a very chastened Galton.

'Right. The taxi will be back soon. Let's have your story. They've charged you with indecent exposure. Who did you expose yourself to?' I'm silently praying it wasn't a child.

'No one. At least only to those who were similarly exposed, as they call it.'

'Come again?'

'My interest in white witchcraft isn't merely academic, Ms Green. I practise what I teach.'

'You're a witch?' I fight back an urge to laugh.

'I am the high priest of a group of people who meet together at certain festivals to practise their beliefs and try to live according to them. You will not be aware of it I expect, but last night was a coincidence of the full moon with a traditional sabbat.'

'And what do you do on such occasions? Do they take place often?'

'There are eight in a year plus the main festivals – the solstices, Beltane, Samhain and so on. Some groups choose to meet more often. Once a week, I believe. As to what we do, that depends.'

'Depends on what?'

'On the nature of the occasion.'

'Alright. Another time. Just tell me about tonight.'

'We had found what we thought was a secluded place in woods near Wellover. We all arrived just before midnight and undressed. Then the high priestess cast the circle and we lit our fire. We had begun our ritual when suddenly there were torches and voices away among the trees. I told the rest to get away as quickly as possible while I banished the circle and put out the fire. Above all it was important that there should be no harm to the high priestess.'

'Why was that?'

'She represents the great goddess in her own person.'

'And you? What did you represent?' I knew we had no time for all this but I couldn't resist.

'As high priest I represent Cernunnos, the horned god.'

'And is this group really a coven?'

'That's what we call it, yes.'

'And the rest of the public. Were you still naked when they arrested you?'

'I was about to dress. You see I was the only one not naked for the meeting. I wear a red robe as high priest. I had banished the circle, thrown water on the fire, taken off my robe and was starting to dress.'

'This is very important.' I was taking quick notes. 'How far had you got?'

He bows his head. 'My socks.'

Again I want to laugh. 'But we can claim that you were clothed throughout except for the moments of changing, like someone before and after swimming. OK we deny the charge and ask for bail. You'll probably have to appear in court if they press charges but we'll face that when we come to it.'

I ping the buzzer. 'My client denies the charge and requests bail on his own surety.' I know they have no real grounds for holding him unless he's got a record for this sort of thing. I just hope not and curse myself for not remembering to ask him.

'You will be responsible for his appearing at the magistrates' court at the proper time.'

'My client has no intention of not answering the charge at any proper time and place.'

They produce the bail forms and charge sheet. We sign and pay. Outside Lester is waiting. I murmur to Galton that we won't discuss it in the car and climb in beside the driver.

'They let you out then,' Lester says when we're safely inside. 'Where to?'

'You'll have to give the driver your address,' I say. 'I don't know it.'

Galton leans forward from the back seat and directs him to Kempstoke.

'Now if you'd been black,' Lester says as he sets off expertly up the motorway, 'they'd have kept you for sure until you come up before the beak. I can't tell you man how often I was stop and search as a kid but they never found nothing because I was clean. Me mammy would have skinned me herself if I'd been caught with anything. I was always frightened they'd plant something on me, not because of them but cos of what she'd do to me.'

It didn't take long to the outskirts of Kempstoke where Galton began directions to his home. It turned out to be a semi-detached brick house on an estate of many similar, not council but eighties ticky tacky, anonymous as the next one in its web of little roads and crescents, called executive no doubt in the developer's brochure.

'I can't express my gratitude enough, Ms Green.'

'We're not out of the wood yet. I'll speak to you tomorrow but not too early. I need to get some sleep if I can.'

But I wake at seven anyway and search the literature for similar cases as I eat my breakfast. Surely there must be something in Halsbury. Then I try the internet. Out of curiosity I enter Amyntas Boston after Witchcraft and then Mary Sidney/ Herbert, Countess of Pembroke but both are blank. I ring the Law Library and ask them to put aside anything they have on the subject that's on the shelves. Suddenly I get a sense of how big the interest might be among my fellow library browsers and members. Maybe there are several Galtons among them or even a high priestess or two. I might have passed one on the stairs. How would you know? Presumably they don't walk around naked except for meetings. There's obviously a market for the occult and the alternative, judging by the sections in bookshops, and even respectable broadsheets have their resident astrologer.

Galton rings me at ten o'clock. 'I think you'd better come in and talk,' I say. 'There's a car park on the South Bank where you ought to find a space or you can get a train to Waterloo. Come as soon as you can.'

'I'll be there in an hour.'

'How do you feel?' I ask as I let him in.

'A little shaky, I must confess.'

'I'll make us some coffee.'

'That would be most kind.'

Can I deal with this new, humble Galton? Maybe I would prefer my old sparring partner back. I settle us down with our mugs of coffee and open up his case on screen so I can take notes directly.

'OK. Let's assume they will prosecute and will want to make it as black as they can. First question: how do you set up your meetings?'

'By email. Just because ours is a very old craft, Ms Green, you mustn't assume we are technologically illiterate.'

The old Galton is showing signs of revival. 'I didn't, don't. But email is easily hacked into. Whereas the various forms of snailmail are more secure. You need a warrant to tap somebody's phone or open their post. How did the police know to come looking? Was it just a happy accident for them? Or were they tipped off?' I make a note to ask them. 'They'll probably say a member of the public observed some suspicious late-night activity where none should be: cars or lights.'

'That's perfectly possible of course.'

'But unlikely. You'd made a careful choice. You're used to looking for secluded places. Have you ever been caught before?'

'Never. We are indeed most careful.'

'The possibility is a chance sighting by police or public. If so we would have to ask what they were doing out there at that time. A tip-off by some member of your own group. Have you any enemies? Anyone who's jealous of your position as leader for instance.'

'Unthinkable. Utterly against all we believe.'

'Has anyone else access to your email address?'

'Only the people at Wessex.'

I can't believe what I'm hearing. How can anyone be so naïve? 'There's our answer then. It fits perfectly.'

Galton almost hangs his head. 'It never occurred to me. I should have changed it all when I was suspended. Could they, could they have access to the other members of the group?'

'Probably. But I doubt if they're interested in them. I think this is directed at you, a pre-emptive strike to stop you taking any action against them. But we're unlikely to be able to prove Wessex had any involvement. We shall have to fight this on other grounds. Insufficient evidence for example. Of course there were several policemen who saw you with only your socks on but no independent witnesses. How did they treat you? Were you allowed to continue dressing?'

'Yes. Some of them were satirical but one was aggressive, pushing me and calling me a dirty pervert.'

'The public thinks of such goings-on as Satanism. They're lead to believe perversion and even sacrifice are part of your rituals. At the very least they're envious of what they believe is all that free sex al fresco. The sort of jinks they might like to get up to round the barbecue. So they imagine all kinds of goings on they can condemn, especially with children.'

'Such things never cross our minds. Our craft, Wicca, is entirely benign. We are dedicated to the development of our inner selves. Only when that is done can you attain the advanced skills of healing, clairvoyance and, the ultimate, astral projection.'

'Astral projection?'

'We all have an astral body as well as a physical one, Ms Green, which we inhabit in dreams. The trained adept can enter the dreams of others and learn from them, or advise and often heal.'

'And how do you train?'

'You train yourself by persistence, working and working until you get a breakthrough.'

'But that doesn't tell me how.'

'There are several ways. They all require concentration. One is to sit in an upright chair with arms in the Egyptian position you see in statues and pictures of the pharaohs and their gods. Then, taking a part of the body at a time, often over many months, you concentrate on its astral counterpart until you can project it and control it. Eventually it will become possible for you to make your astral body stand up and move about, leaving the physical body behind, seemingly asleep or in a trance. When witches flew to their sabbats in accounts of their trials it was their astral bodies that travelled while they were sleeping.'

'And Amyntas could do this?'

'Amyntas wasn't a witch. A physician, an alchemist perhaps like her father but not a witch.'

'How can you be sure?'

'You've read the memorial, Ms Green. There's no evidence of any attempt to develop spiritual powers. It's all depressingly physical: herbs and minerals for the earthly body.'

'How do your beliefs differ from the eastern mysticism of, say, Aurobindo, the sort of thing the Beatles went for, ashrams and Hare Krishna?'

'Wicca is our native British tradition for spiritual development through the exercise of ritual and imagination.'

'Imagination?'

'Of course. It is a vital faculty too often neglected in these times which focus on physical consumption, on goods and chattels. Ours is a pre-Christian belief which goes back at least to the Celts.'

'The gods you mentioned. What are they?'

'They are essentially the fertility gods of the Celts. Cernunnos, the horned god, appears in carvings and on the Gundestrup cauldron. The goddess you will find everywhere in Irish and Welsh literature. She has many names and manifestations but she is essentially the fertile earth. She is also Eostre, the Celtic Venus Anodyamene. They put us in touch with the ancient powers of the earth and all elemental things: the seasons, the moon and stars. The Christians of course turned her into the black witch and him into the devil.'

'You don't like Christianity very much.'

'People must believe what they can. Christianity as we see it in modern times is very physical, descended from a belief in the god of a small desert nation with which he had a special relationship. It can't substitute for the principle of the spiritual fertility of all things and the earth itself. And in the Bible, they did say or write, "Thou shalt not suffer a witch to live."'

'And Christ?'

'His teaching is that of a politician, a socialist or even a social worker: prison visiting, hospitality for the homeless, charity, feeding the poor. It has almost nothing to do with developing the spiritual talents of the individual although the Gnostics and some of the saints achieved a degree of clairvoyance through asceticism and mysticism. Wicca of course rejects ascetism.'

I wanted to ask him how Wicca differed from what I'd seen in the chapel at Wessex. To me it seemed only another way of inducing hypnosis. Not necessarily bad in itself. It depended on how it was exploited. After all humans have always used drugs and ritual to tap into altered states of consciousness, all sorts of booze, tobacco, coca leaves, and art, and sex, riding away like the witch on her broomstick in a really great orgasm.

'I think that's probably all we can do today. I'll get on with the paperwork and contact the police to see if they're going ahead with charges.'

'And the other matter?'

'The matter of Wessex?'

'You won't let that drop because of this?'

'The two are intertwined. At least that's what I think. So no. I won't let it drop.'

My lady herself sent for me to London at the beginning of March for there was again great sickness abroad of rheums and fluxes brought on by the harsh months of winter. Yet because the pestilence itself had abated his majesty would proceed to his entry to the city of London which had not yet taken place. So my lady required that all her servants should be physicked, as she herself, to be fit for so great an occasion.

Again then I found myself in the city whither it seemed all mankind was hurrying, for the streets were ever more stinking and crowded, and men and women and even little children ran about their business as if the devil was at their heels. Baynard's Castle itself was crowded with the servants of two noble households, my lady and her younger son, for there was still a coldness between my lady and the young earl who kept himself at court and in his majesty's eye. The Lady Anne attended on the queen at Whitehall or we should have been yet more.

I was able to lie alone and near my lady for there was a closet that had once housed a guard to the bedchamber where my lady gave me leave to put a pallet. And although it was as dark and stifling as this cell it made me private and close to her I loved and served, and perhaps hardened me for what has now come upon me.

I had brought many medicines from Ramsbury on a pack-horse for I always preferred to prescribe my own, knowing how the ingredients had been gathered and prepared for the greatest purity and efficacy. So I assisted in the laboratory where I was obliged to work alongside and at the command of Dr Adrian Gilbert, he claiming the seniority of a licence from the archbishop, that he had been at the university, was of long acquaintance with my lady and a gentleman. So I was forced to hold my tongue and become for a time his apprentice.

When I found fault with his methods of working in the preparation of such medicines as we needed I would silently take the work upon myself, and likewise the diagnostic of patients' sicknesses for I saw that I was more accustomed to treat with these as they presented themselves whereas his interests lay elsewhere in the production of fantastical theories from his own head. I saw also that he was glad to be freed of such base work and therefore would not envy me for it.

One cold morning when I was busy at the small furnace in distilling of cordials he came into the laboratory and picking up my book of receipts, where I was accustomed to write down all new medicines as I devised and tried them, as well as many old and proved, he began to read, turning the pages carefully one by one.

'You have a great many receipts entered in here for one so young. Did you read them in other men's books and make these fair copies?'

'No sir. Some of them are of my father. Others of my devising.'

'I shall make copies of them for my own use. Since you may not be long with us to give us all the benefit of them.' And he left the laboratory with my book.

One morning my lady called to me from her bedchamber where she lay propped upon her bed breaking her fast.

'Amyntas I shall ride in a chariot in their majesties' procession to the city and I wish you to ride behind me as my page as being younger and more handsome than Evan.'

Truly I thought I was older than Evan, a boy she had brought out of her castle of Cardiff to learn the ways of a groom or postilion and indeed I had been a little troubled for that he had a beautiful voice to sing in the Welsh tongue and my lady would send for him in the evenings and make much of him, for she said of all tongues it was the sweetest for singing. He was at an age when in boys the face often flares into a multitude of red pimples and although I had prescribed camphire dissolved in vinegar mixed with celandine water to cleanse them with, and verbena ointment to cover them, I feared they would remain until nature herself chose their cure, for though some believe they proceed from filthy vapours ascending from the stomach and therefore apply purges, in the very young, especially boys, such methods have little effect but only time will clear the skin.

So early in the morning I was dressed in a livery of white satin sewn with pearls and got up before my lady who most resembled Venus in her gilded chariot with white feathers about the sides as if it was indeed drawn by swans as the goddess her own, and we set off to join the procession at the Tower. By eleven o'clock all were assembled and the company set forward. First came the king's household and his ministers, then his majesty himself riding under a white canopy borne by the gentlemen of the privy chamber.

Next was the queen's procession. First her household with the Lady Anne, then her majesty, followed by ladies according to their degree, the countess coming fourteenth. We passed by the seats of the city guilds where were hung ensigns, streamers and banners with the blazons of their crafts. Behind a rail the multitude were held back and cheered as we passed until we were stopped at Fenchurch before the first ceremonial arch signifying Londinium. It showed the city itself adorned with houses, towers and steeples, set off in prospective. Upon the battlements were writ in Latin the city's titles and then a tableau of personages, foremost among them Britannia richly attired in cloth of gold and tissue, holding a sceptre in her hand, and at her feet Divine Wisdom in white. Then came the Genius of the City, an ancient with white hair all in purple, the river of Thames in a skin coat made like flesh, naked and blue, his mantle of sea green, leaning upon an earthen pot out of which water with live fishes was seen to run forth and play about him. He pointed to the six daughters of Genius, all fair ladies descending the arch, among them Euphrosyne or Gladness and Agape: Loving Affection. Then came speeches of gratulation from Genius and Thames, which done and all cheering the procession moved on to Temple Bar.

After Temple Bar which was dressed as a temple to peace filled with personages representing peace, plenty and liberty and their opposites, as tumult, danger and misery, we continued to the Strand where we were stopped by two pyramids over ten times a tall man in height and binding them a rainbow with sun, moon and stars, and among them Electra, hanging in the air in figure of a comet, with a speech promising to be an augury of peace and justice and splendour to his majesty. So we left the city passing under the arch of the rainbow and entered in to Westminster city, the seat of kings.

All along the way music played and banners streamed in the wind. Among the musicians at the first arch of Londinium was Signor Ferrabosco who had been in my lady's employ when first I came to her and had since removed to London where he was engaged in composing for masques and other entertainments, sometimes sending a fair copy of a new song for the countess her pleasure.

The court and nobility proceeded to a banquet in Whitehall for it was now five o'clock of the afternoon and although the speeches were cut short, as we saw later by the printed version not to weary his majesty, yet all were tired and eager to dine. And this ceremony was first devised for his majesty's coronation but could not then take place on account of the plague when the multitude were forbidden to assemble for fear of spreading the sickness.

I returned with the chariot to Baynard's Castle. My lady told me after on her coming home, that there had been masking, dancing and making merry at the banquet and many had gone drunk to bed. She was driven back in her coach a little tipsy herself and when her ladies had undressed her, fell into bed saying she had no need of a sleeping draught for she was so weary, and contented with all, that she should sleep with ease. From this I understood that she had received that respect that was her due as one of the noblest in all the realm. Indeed as I watched by her bedside until she slept I heard her murmur: 'The name of Sidney is still potent in the land.'

The next day all others slept late. Myself was restless and rose early. It was in my mind that Knightrider Street was but a step from the dark bulk of Baynard's which lay like a vast ship wrecked upon the shore of Thames and that I could walk up from the castle towards Paul's by Godliman Street and be at the College of Physicians in but a few moments. This I determined to do. So after a breakfast of bread, stew from the pot and small beer, I left the household sleeping, apart from the cooks who had served me in the kitchen. I knew I must be back before the countess woke and called for me. And was this expedition in itself not a little betrayal for what was I about but looking to secure my future if my present employment should fail? Therefore I slunk through the gate as one guilty but when I stood upon the road outside and saw it rising up towards Paul's with a little mist coming off the river, for although it was but March yet the sun shone and the many boats at anchor at Queenhithe Wharf bobbed on the smiling water as symbols of freedom and adventure, I felt my heart lift and set off uphill accompanied by the mist that was like a benediction from another world although I knew it was but a common vapour.

Turning into Knightrider Street itself I soon stood before the College of Physicians where so lately Dr Gilbard had lived when busy with his duties as secretary in London but it was all shut up, perhaps on account of the holiday. I stood before it wondering what I should have done had it been open. Would I have been brave enough to enter and look for the doctor's assistant? But that was foolishness. He would be still in Colchester at the doctor's house there or already removed in pursuit of his own business. Now there must be a new secretary to the College who would know nothing of my father or the experiments with electrics, so quickly do a man's concerns fade from sight after his death. My dream of freedom and a way to earn my bread if cast away was only that, a fantasy from a head heated with wine, risen like the vapour that accompanied me here, now dissolving as the morning advanced. Had I indeed been what I seemed I could have looked for an apprenticeship to a practising physician but such a course was too dangerous for that, inhabiting the same house as I should, it would be hard if not impossible to prevent discovery. In this only my lady could protect me.

And now I longed again for my father in whose house I could have worked and learnt without deception and yet it was in that same house that my confusion had begun if not in my mother's womb itself. Again I could not see how to make my way in the world except to abandon my nature and future happiness which I knew lay among my experiments and in the laboratory, for only great ladies can mix such pursuit with marriage, unless I could find one with like interests whose helper I could remain. Yet even such a one must mean a subjection to the desires of another for which I was all unready.

As I cast around in my mind for some passage through my difficulties it came to me that if I could make a book of some of my receipts and experiments and find one to publish it I might by this means earn my bread. I determined to have again and soon my book which Dr Adrian Gilbert had taken away and to try to make acquaintance through my lady with a printer who might issue such a book and pay me for it. Then I thought that she might be suspicious of such a desire and that I must be careful to find some way to present it that would not offend or alarm her and bring about the very thing I feared most, to be put away from her presence.

Looking up at the College I made a vow that when I had my book printed I would return again with a copy so that at least my name should be known among the learned. I made my way quickly downhill towards the river and found the castle beginning to stir although I had been away but a little while. My lady was calling for me and taking a silver tray I loaded it with a cup of wine and fine white bread thinking that after the surfeit excitements of the day and night before she would need some sustenance easy of digestion and a draught of liverwort bruised and boiled in small beer to calm and cleanse her stomach.

She declined the draught saying she felt exceeding well. 'We are bidden to a play in her majesty's private apartments given by the king's servants. It does not please his majesty to be present but to make ready for the progress that he intends. And indeed I observe that he thinks such toys are principally to amuse women and young courtiers and therefore he leaves such presentations to the queen while seeing their use in the entertaining of foreigners as ambassadors and the like. It may be that the coldness of Scotland both of their clime and their religion makes men less susceptible to poetry than is the custom among the nobility of England. It might be expected that the Danes being on the same cold sea would be of the like temper but they say the queen's brother keeps musicians always around him, as indeed some from England who could not stomach our religion being that of her late majesty and could get no preferment under her. And our actors went there in the reign of Queen Anne's father to the palace at Elsinore during a time of plague before the Spanish invasion. So her majesty delights in plays, masques and all manner of entertainment and has taken a poet, my son's old tutor Master Daniel, to be groom of her Privy Chamber. You will attend me again as my page Amyntas. The Lady Anne is still asleep and will not be present. I must excuse her to the queen.'

That afternoon we rode to Whitehall again but this time through no cheering crowds. Already the seven arches began to appear the things of paint, cloth and wood that was their nature stripped of illusion. On our entry to the queen's apartments we found new magic however. A stage had been set up as before at Wilton but with more lifelike scenes painted in prospective on flat screens so that we looked into a little world within our world as if we had passed through the hill of the fairies as some old wives tell, or the old song of True Thomas, and could perceive their realm with our mortal eyes.

The ladies and Prince Henry took their seats while I placed myself behind the countess her chair. This time I was prepared for the players' illusion and was not to be deceived by their rich silks and air of command to think them other than they were. I looked about me at the courtiers lounging at ease, gossiping among themselves. My Lady Bedford leant to whisper in the queen's ear, she sitting close as the favourite since she brought her majesty out of Scotland.

The play began and all were hushed. There entered four personages all in black. A lady and her son, an old man and a maid. The lady was parting from her son, a ward of court as the young earl had been, and chafing at it as he had. The old man spoke some words in praise of the king to which the lady replied asking for news of the king's condition. The old lord answered that his majesty had abandoned his physicians and resigned himself to death.

The lady spoke again and at her words in spite of my resolution that it was but a sham, I felt tears prick my eyes for it seemed she spoke of me.

'This young gentlewoman had a father – O, that had,
how sad a passage his – whose skill was almost as great
as his honesty; had it stretched so far, would have made
nature immortal, and death should have play for lack of
work. Would for the king's sake he were living! I think
it would be the death of the king's disease.'

The he/she that played the physician's daughter began to
weep and I felt to my shame my own tears, until then pent
behind my eyes, begin to fall at which my lady reached up a
hand and touched mine where I held to the back of the chair
behind her so that a drop fell on it shining in the light of the
torches.

As to the rest of the play I remember little of it. The maid
applied her father's prescription to the king and cured his fistula
but there all resemblance to my case ended for she acted out of
love for a young count whose mother had befriended her as
Naomi did for Ruth. The count was a cruel boy that she could
win only by a bed trick. The lady his mother seemed nobler to
my eyes and ears and I was all the more ready to say with the
maid who cheated him into his wife's bed, 'Marry who will, I'll
live and die a maid.'

My lady called me to her when we had returned to Baynard's.
'Well my young physician, what did you think of the play? Did
it not bring home to you that maids must marry and it is time
to leave this game? Your tears for your father, as I took them,
should have perhaps been for you that like Helen have none to
provide a dowry for you that would help you to a husband worthy
of you. You know that when my son shall marry I shall lose these
houses that have sheltered you. You must think of your future.'

I felt the tears come again and went down on my knees before
her. 'I will never be a charge upon you my lady whatever falls
out. Only do not turn me away until you must. When the time
is ready let me go of my own will.'

Then she lifted me up and kissed me on the mouth. 'We shall play our game of Arcadia a little longer child until the world and time decide otherwise.'

As I'd expected when I confronted the police I was 'informed', you're never just told, that a member of the public had reported lights and vehicles where none should be. There was a question about whether the owners, some kind of environmental trust, would want to bring a private prosecution. It sounded as if the police themselves were wondering about pressing charges. What after all would they get: a fine, community service? Was it really worth the time and expense? I pointed out that my client was of good standing, without a previous record. I suggested there were no independent witnesses and that the whole affair could smack a bit of farce if it came to open court before the local press. I also queried the public order implications if the media went over the top and whipped up local anger. I tried a cool, measured, faintly amused tone and waited. They said they would let me know. He could be served with a summons to appear in due course.

'What isn't clear, Ms Green, is what your client was doing there. Maybe the public could feel safer if he was on the sex offenders' register.'

A red light was flashing in my head. For that they would need a conviction. It would make Galton unemployable anywhere around young people or children at least. I would have to risk the truth or some of it.

'I can assure you that there was nothing of a sexual nature involved. Any more than there is in people gathering at Stonehenge for the midsummer sunrise. Like the Druids. The right to practise one's religion is a fundamental human right.'

'The Druids have their clothes on, Ms Green, long robes and hats like the Archbishop of Canterbury. If they were stark naked we should have to arrest them.'

'My client was changing out of his robe.'

'Can you produce this robe?'

'It was among his clothes when he was arrested.'

'Everything was returned to him when he was bailed.'

Mentally, I crossed my fingers and took a deep breath.

'Exactly. So we can produce it.'

'Is this it on the list? Red nightshirt or dressing gown.'

'That's it.' I hoped it was, and that Galton hadn't felt the robe had been contaminated by the experience and thrown it away.

'You or your client need to bring us this garment so that we can verify its existence and its purpose.'

'We'll get it to you as soon as possible.'

'Today, if you want to avoid a charge of withholding evidence as well.'

So that's my day fucked. I ring Galton and arrange to meet him at the station.

'Do I have to go in, Ms Green? That place, those officers, terrify me.'

'That's what they're supposed to do. The public likes it like that until they're subject to it themselves of course. If you'll pay for it I can meet you at the train station and go there by taxi. Then you can sit in the cab, in case they insist on seeing you and taking a further statement.'

'I do hope not.'

He's his usual neat self when we meet at the station. He hands me a brown paper parcel in a plastic carrier bag and we join the taxi queue. 'If they want you to make a statement I'll come out and get you. All you need to say is you were there for the purpose of practising your religion.'

'Do I have to mention anyone else?'

'God, no. Then it could become a conspiracy. You'd have to give names. They'd be dragged in as witnesses. Keep it simple.'

'I wouldn't want anyone else to be involved. I was trying to protect them by being the last to leave.'

'Try not to lie. Just be a bit selective with the truth, that's all.'

I leave him sitting in the cab and go in with my parcel. If I can I want to keep Galton out of it. In his present jumpy state he might say far too much or too little. I ask to see Sergeant Parry who had dealt with us before and sit meekly waiting while he's fetched. This time the monitor doesn't show him coming. Suddenly he's emerging from the bowels of the station with an expression on his face as if I've got him out of bed. 'Ms Green? Come this way, please.'

We traverse the corridors again. Today there's no flutter in my gut, just a numbness that's probably lack of sleep, or else familiarity already breeding contempt.

'Have you brought the garment?'

I proffer the carrier bag. Perry takes it, wrestles with the Sellotape bindings and finally bursts it open. I see a piece of red cloth with some gold embroidered edging. Perry opens it out and holds it up distastefully.

'What was he doing, rehearsing for Father Christmas?'

'I believe it's part of a ritual.'

'And were there other persons involved in this ritual? The officers reported the remains of a fire still warm though an obvious attempt had been made to put it out and conceal the evidence. The caller reported lights and vehicles present.'

'An easy mistake to make in woods at night. There would have been lights from my client's car, a torch, a fire. Possibly, even a lantern.'

'What was the nature of the ritual, Ms Green?'

'As I understand it, it was, is in honour of a mother goddess.' Always mention mothers if you can squeeze them in. 'As I'm sure you know, sergeant, many ancient religions have worshipped a mother goddess.' I don't add – and very nasty some of them were too – thinking of Cybele and Kali, Medusa and even Diana on an off day. Not to mention that old sourpuss Juno. 'Getting in touch with nature, like ramblers and the Green Party.' I must be careful not to ramble on too much myself.

Perry is looking tight-lipped and sceptical. 'But what do they do? What exactly was going on, Ms Green?'

'I believe you light a fire and cast a magic circle around it. And then you say a few prayers.'

'And what do you make of all this?'

'Well, between ourselves, sergeant, I think it's all a bit theatrical, for my taste. But I can't see any harm in it for others or really that it breaks any laws, except perhaps trespass and that's a civil offence. From the point of view of the owners I think they would be ill-advised to follow it up publicly. All sorts of people might get the idea that their woods were a suitable place for goings-on of a less innocent nature.'

'We haven't established yet that it was innocent.'

'I can assure you it was.' And I believed it too. Foolish and naïve perhaps and potentially harmful for those who might rely on it for emotional or physical healing, but then thousands of people were now into alternative therapies. It was only that Galton's lot called themselves witches, that raised centuries old superstitions and alarms. And, who could say that if you believed enough, you couldn't, in some cases, alter the body's chemistry, stimulate the immune system or set the serotonin flowing?

'We'll keep this a bit longer until we decide how to proceed. Sign for it, please.' Perry pushed the robe to one side and produced a daybook. I signed and gave my address.

'You aren't local?'

'No, as you can see I have a practice in London.'

'How come you're his solicitor then?'

'I'm acting for him in another matter.' I risk a question of my own. 'The member of the public who reported the incident that led you to investigate, can you give me any more information on that? What time was it reported for instance?'

Perry consults his records. 'It was an anonymous call at 11.41 p.m.'

'Did anyone follow up where the call was made from?'

'It was a mobile. Number unknown.'

'A pity. You could have asked them what they were doing out there themselves.'

'I expect it was what we used to call a courting couple though these days it's most likely to be with someone else's husband or wife.'

Suddenly he's weary of it all. This wasn't the world he signed up to police. I sense a nostalgia for the old law and order that never was except in the tabloid imagination.

'Too true,' I say.

Perry closes the book. 'You'll hear from us, Ms Green.'

I'm being dismissed. I've kept Galton out of it and if it's cost him an arm and a leg in taxi fares, that's money well spent.

'Just one thing: my client's car?'

'It's in the police pound. He can collect it on payment of the removal fee.'

Galton is waiting nervously in the cab. I shake my head at him to stop him from asking questions and tell the driver to take us back to the station. Galton pays up without a murmur, adding a substantial tip.

'Let's have a cup of coffee in the station buffet where we can talk.' The cafeteria has Mediterranean pretensions in its name and décor but inside it smells of stale dishwashers, and the coffee tastes of them too.

'You haven't got the robe.'

'No. They kept it. I signed for it. They should let you have it back in due course as the police might say. I think there's a strong chance they won't prosecute. I've shown that we'll fight it if they do and I hope I've done enough to persuade them to close the book on the whole incident. One thing worries me though. Can you remember exactly what time you all got there?'

Galton looks coy. 'Midnight is, of course, the witching hour. We need about five minutes to get our clothes off. We don't like to hang about too long without some activity. It can be rather chilly until the actual ritual takes over. Then of course you forget the demands of the flesh. So we try to arrive as close to midnight as possible; ideally about ten minutes before.'

'Is it necessary to be naked?'

'Oh, you can't really exchange the fivefold kiss without it.'

I decide to think about this later.

'And that night?'

'As usual, as far as I can remember. When I looked at my watch it was five to. Everyone was ready. The high priestess led them in the dance to the site. Then we performed a ring dance joining hands and the high priestess cast the circle. I had just lit the bonfire when we heard the noise of cars and saw lights. Fortunately they were still some way off. We didn't know it was the police of course but I told everyone to get away as quickly as possible while I covered their retreat. I doubt if everyone got all their clothes on. They were only just able to get to their cars in time. Fortunately the site was between two roads and we had parked in a picnic parking spot on the opposite side from where the police were approaching. Otherwise we would all have been caught. I'd doused the fire, we always keep water to hand in case, and banished the circle. The police were crashing about in some bushes: I hoped they didn't have dogs with them. I miscalculated. I thought I had just time to dress but they suddenly burst through and found me.'

'So you would say you were there no more than fifteen minutes before twelve when the circle was cast? And you saw no evidence of anyone who could have called the police at 11.41?'

'They would have had to be in a car like us and if we'd seen any such thing we would have aborted the rite. That happens sometimes. The goddess won't manifest herself if there are strangers about.'

'The police say you can pick up your car from the pound. Apart from that I would advise you to keep a very low profile. Keep your head down. I'll let you know as soon as I hear anything.

You might try a prayer or two or crossing your fingers. Whatever turns you on.'

'I am grateful to you, Ms Green.'

'Just try to stay out of any more trouble.'

He's at least ten years older than me but I hoped he'd if not recognise at least respect the Marlowe voice of authority.

It's a relief to get home, make myself coffee and sit down to think. Galton had, inadvertently, told me a lot more about what went on at their meetings almost as a kind of boast or a claim for the authenticity of their cult or belief or craft, whatever they called it. Yet there was something both creepy and hilarious in middle-aged men and women dancing about naked in the woods, no doubt blue and goose-pimpled and the dangly bits, male and female, shrivelling up with cold. There was probably a lot more he wasn't telling me and that I didn't need or want to know. It wasn't relevant either for the Wessex case or this one since they'd been surprised before they could do anything much except get their kit off.

After all, a bit of open-air sex has a long and respectable history of hey nonny no, long before D.H. Lawrence turned it into an erotic version of the Chelsea Flower Show. There's something liberating about it which is maybe why so many of the boys head for Hampstead Heath or Brompton Cemetery.

That day out with Helen clinging on to me as we zoomed into Sussex down the motorway was a kind of apotheosis that caught us up into rose-coloured clouds after which there was no other way but down though I didn't know it at the time. But maybe she did. When we got back she wouldn't come into the flat except to change and then asked for a cab right away.

'All that fresh air is exhausting!' It was a conspiratorial smile she gave and then a peck on the cheek when what I needed was to hold her hard against me and drown in her scent. 'See you back at the firm. We're out to dinner tonight with clients. I hope I can stay awake!'

I didn't bump into her in the corridor next day by accident on purpose. And she didn't ring down. That night I went home and played *Rosenkavalier* all the way through, burying my face in the gear she had worn the day before to see if I could detect any lingering scent of her and breathe it in but the smell of the leathers overpowered any there might have been. It was as if yesterday had never happened and perhaps for her it hadn't. Perhaps I'd dreamt it all. And then the other Marlowe kept going through my head. 'Sweet Helen, make me immortal with a kiss. Thy lips suck up my soul . . .'

Mine was no Faustian contract with a myth though. What I wanted was flesh and blood, a cheek to touch, lips to cling to, a presence not an illusion or a dream. Obsessively, I played a dialogue over in my head in which I asked her what we were going to do. I wanted her to leave James and come to me, but when I looked round at my flat and considered their glossy way of life and position as partners in Settle and Fixit my fantasy collapsed in a heap on the floor as reality let go of the puppet's strings. I cast round for ways to set it up on its feet dancing again but it refused to be raised. Pinocchio would be tossed into a corner for firewood as the caravan rumbled on its way.

> A ship there is and she sails the sea,
> She's loaded deep as deep can be,
> But not so deep as the love I'm in,
> I care not if I sink or swim.

Every love song of loss haunted me with the impossibility of what I yearned after. Could I make myself play it cool, enjoy what was on offer without hankering after more? I'd try. I had to. I wouldn't ring. Let her ring me.

But after another day of silence I was desperate, arguing, pleading in my head, unable to concentrate on the brief I'd been asked to prepare for James, unwilling to go down for a long session with a witness in one of our underground client rooms for work on their rambling statement in case I missed a call from Helen. And as I begged and pleaded like a convicted prisoner given a chance to speak in mitigation, I was also the judge pointing out that at no time had Helen led me to suppose what she was doing was any more than an experiment, something perhaps she'd always wanted to try or read about but it wasn't going to change her lifestyle. And I stood accused by my own ethos since I didn't see anything morally wrong in fun sex, just that it didn't really work for me. Besides I'd fallen in love but that couldn't be helped either. Those whom the gods wish to destroy they first make mad or something.

Then there was Rosalind: 'Men have died and worms have eaten them but not for love.' Was she really that cynical or just expressing a typical view of the times that men were the romantics while women had their eye on the main chance? But Olivia was in love though it was only with a dream 'poor lady'. The whole country was a merry-go-round of thwarted desires set against the social need to marry, like the ordered landscapes of Austen's England. Illyria is Arcadia, itself a dreamscape of perpetual summer and pursuit as if we were in sunlit Greece instead of our sodden island. I was running round my own hamster wheel of unjustified recrimination and need and I didn't know how to get off.

Drew came over to my desk next morning and perched himself on the edge. 'I think I ought to tell you. I've found a new job.'

I'd been expecting it but I was still shaken. 'Oh, man, what will I do without you?'

'The humiliating thing is they didn't even try to make me stay or talk me out of it. Chalmers suggested I take my full holiday even though I'm only entitled to half. They've even waived me working out my notice.

'"I don't think we should require that of you, Drewpad. I

always think once one has made up one's mind one should go for it."'

'The shits!'

'That's bosses for you.'

'So where are you going?'

He grinned. 'Geneva.'

'Geneva!'

'I've got a job with an international organisation, well it's a sort of charity really that provides cheap legal advice and assistance for musicians in Third World countries or whatever they're called at the moment, who feel they're being suckered by the big media boys.'

'That'll make you very popular.'

'I know, it should be fun. Somehow I'll feel I'm getting my own back over the post-colonial rip-off merchants. My only worry is my mum but she says it's my big chance and I've got to take it.'

'Maybe you'll find a Swiss maid who wants somewhere to keep her cuckoo clock.'

We had to toast his new life at the end of the week.

'I'll keep in touch,' Drew said as we got steadily and sentimentally pissed, but we both knew the time and place that had called up and supported our workaday friendship would fade, driven out by new faces and demands. He was excited by the chance of such a big change with all it might bring while I felt even more apprehensive and lost. James Chalmers had summoned me to appear that afternoon.

'I expect you've heard that we're losing Drewpad, that he's going on to higher things. That means you'll be in charge of that office and take over his briefs. More money of course and we've got an assistant for you in view. I'd like you to get them up and running as soon as possible so that you're still here to help me out in court. Helen said she had a fantastic day out with you. She's gone to stay with friends for a few days. I'll go down and join her for the weekend. You seem to have given her a taste for the country.'

I didn't know what to make of all this. It explained Helen's silence but why hadn't she told me she was going away? She must have known all the time we were together. And Chalmers? Was he just laughing at me or playing some little game of his or their own? Perhaps they really were an ageing wolf couple, swapping partners and stories to turn each other on as other pairs watch porn movies together. I felt repelled and angry and yet I didn't want to let her go, to simply walk away.

On Tuesday I was due in court with James. 'I'm sure you could handle this on your own but the beak and the clients like to see a man in charge. It's different in the States, of course. Even big media corporations there are used to a woman up front but we're still more traditional here, even in the field of media law. After all Butler-Sloss is only allowed the Family Division. A woman's place is still in the home even on the bench. Those women who try to go beyond that get a very bad press, I'm afraid. It'll be worse if they do away with the wig and gown and turn the court into a catwalk. We'll start to get comments from the tabloids on what the judge was wearing instead of any attempt at serious reporting.'

What had begun as a seeming compliment was sourly putting me in my place in the guise of a rational justification for the glass ceiling. Before I'd been jealous, envious of James Chalmers. Now I began to actively dislike him and yet I'd already seen enough to know he wasn't alone in his way of thinking, of prejudice disguised as the very British pragmatism of let well alone, don't rock the boat.

We won the case and went back in a taxi together to Settle and Fixit. 'Short and sweet,' Chalmers said in the gloom of the cab.

'Is Helen back yet?' I tried to sound as if it was just a polite enquiry.

'Yes. We drove back on Monday morning to avoid the Sunday night rush. Delightful weekend. Handsome house in Berkshire with a launch on the river, just a little runabout. The weather wasn't bad either for once. Did you stay in town?'

It'd been Sunday lunch in Acton again but I wasn't going to admit it. Mam had worried that I was looking tired and Roger had joked about too many late nights and the fast pace of a city lawyer. My niece and nephew had been fractious and demanding, stealing each other's toys and pushing each other over to get attention from the grown-ups, finally but then only briefly pacified with *Dumbo* on DVD. I'd felt estranged from them all, unable to take part, and the ache in the pit of my stomach and feeling of queasiness made me unable to appreciate the food that had taken Linda all morning to prepare – a summer echo of our Christmas dinner – roast chicken, new potatoes with mint from the garden, beans and carrots and a fresh fruit salad with cream to follow. We were alone at the table, the children had eaten their fish fingers, potato waffles and peas and were now watching *The Jungle Book* in the front room. In spite of his usual complaints about our parents' unsophisticated food, this time Roger was making a better job of tucking in than I was while Jenny played the dutiful daughter-in-law. I could imagine the exchange that would take place in the car on the way home.

'It's free range, Jade. Do have a bit more. You've hardly eaten a thing. Just picking at it like when you were little. I thought you'd got over being a fussy eater.'

'I've had a stomach bug this week, Mam,' I lied.

I got away as soon as I could. 'I'll ring you in a day or so,' Linda said as I was leaving, 'to know if you're feeling better. I don't like to think of you all on your own up there.'

'Anyone would think I was in Scotland, Mam. It's only half a dozen stops on the tube.'

'It always seems like a different world to me.'

Sometimes we would all meet for a pizza at the big open-plan pizza parlour they'd taken me and Roger to as kids for a family outing but I knew they weren't really comfortable there. As the area had been gentrified it had gone upmarket. Joel and I would go there occasionally so that he could admire the waiters, slim dark boys in bumtight black trousers and bumfreezer black waistcoats over green silk shirts. You expected them to carry a rose in their teeth or behind an ear to present to the customer, male or female, with a flourish and a flash of so perfect teeth you'd imagine they'd all been capped.

'Don't worry about me, Mam. I'm used to the big city. I can handle it.'

But my flat seemed cold and empty without even a welcome sigh from the answering machine that someone was dying to talk to me. I couldn't wait to get in to work on Monday morning. But without Drew my office seemed cold and empty too and no call came from Helen. Perhaps she wasn't back. Then I passed James Chalmers on his way out to lunch. 'See you in court tomorrow,' he joked.

It was meant to be a friendly reminder but it fell across me like the shadow of a sword. Well, if the way to Helen's heart was carrying her husband's files and finding the right place for him in ring-binder 'X' I would do it. And I wouldn't call her. She would have to call me.

Before our return to Wilton from Baynard's Castle I determined to have my book of receipts again from Dr Adrian Gilbert who went almost daily to wait upon his brother Sir Walter in the Tower where had made a little garden for growing herbs and had set up a laboratory with the Wizard Earl of Northumberland where they conducted experiments together in which Dr Gilbert as he informed us also bore a part.

Therefore when I knew that we were shortly to leave I sought him out early in that part of the castle where he was lodged.

'Sir,' I said, 'it seems that we are soon to return to the country and I would have that my book of receipts again if it please you, so that I may be the readier in my lady's service.'

'It might indeed please me but I do not have your little book to hand having ordered a clerk to make copies of those of its entries that seemed to me to have possible merit though I would try them on the dog before entrusting a human to their kindness.'

'My receipts are for the most part of my father's devising sir and so of proven efficacy as many still living in Salisbury can testify.'

'Country people of a coarser humour perhaps but of far different effect upon those more nobly and delicately bred.'

'These such then can be of little use to you sir. And therefore if you would be good enough to return it before we must leave I should be greatly obliged.'

Some days passed and my book was not returned. I did not know what to do to have it again. At last I determined to speak to the countess.

'My lady,' I said, 'there is a matter in which I must beg help of your great kindness.'

'Why Amyntas, what could it be? You have asked me for nothing before in all the time of your service here.'

'Madam, it is my little book of receipts which Dr Adrian Gilbert borrowed of me and now I would have again before we leave, for we may have need of them if a sudden sickness should come upon us at Wilton or Ramsbury. I have asked Dr Gilbert for its return but he is often at the Tower with his brother, Sir Walter, these last days and comes little to the laboratory here where I might have spoken with him again of it.'

'You shall have your book. I will send for him and say I have need of it myself.'

The next day my lady came into the laboratory, where I was packing my case with those instruments and medicines I would take back with me. 'Here is your little book, Amyntas, returned at my command.'

I thanked her for her aid in the matter not thinking in that moment that I had only increased Dr Gilbert's displeasure towards me. But when I took the book from her, I saw that it must have passed either through many hands or else careless ones for it was stained with beer and wine in places and broken-backed, so that the leaves were many of them coming loose and indeed I did not know at first glance but that some of them might be altogether missing.

'As recompense for my help you shall make me a fair copy in a book which I shall give you, for your own seems in danger of dissolution through much use. It will be a fitting occupation for you in my absence and to keep me always in mind.'

'My lady knows she is ever in my thoughts, sleeping or waking.'

'Do you indeed see me in your dreams, Amyntas, even though I am growing old and "forty winters besiege my brow" as I read in my son's commonplace book?' She meant her younger son, Sir Philip, for she was still estranged from the young earl, even though she had played hostess for him for his majesty during the recent sweat, as the common people call it.

As soon as we were installed again in Ramsbury, I began on the new copy, with more care in the writing, since it was to be put into my lady's hands, but at the same time I took pains to restore my little book, finding indeed that some pages had been altogether removed as I remembered, which I supplied from some papers of my father's, glad that I had not thrown them away after entering the receipts in my own book. In special I saw that a cordial water of my father's which is good in all diseases and harmful to no one, had been lost from its place among Spirit of Mints, Treacle Water, Spirit of Saffron and of Roses. This I replaced but with a new title in honour of my lady: *Tragea Comitesse Pembrokia* which the poets would often style her in their dedications as I had read among the books in the library at the great house. This cordial requires much care and the finest ingredients in its composition if it is to have that full efficacy it is capable of. You must begin with a distillation of roses, cinnamon, gilly flowers, scallions, cloves and peaches with other herbs, in which must be dissolved if it can anyways be come at, powdered horn of unicorn which merchants bring from Africa, and all combined with civet, musk and aubergines in a linen bag. The dose is a good spoonful or in great extremity two. And to these well-tried remedies I added new ones of my own devising sometimes with the help of my lady before all the comings and goings with the new court filled up her time.

Suddenly the air was full of talk of marriage, first of my lady's niece to a hunting companion of his majesty. The countess called me to her in her bedchamber.

'My Lady Anne and I are summoned to my sister Sidney's at Penshurst for help in preparation of her daughter's wedding. If I have need of you I will send for you from Ramsbury.'

So I was left alone again. Even the duenna had gone to see her old place where she had first been nurse to my lady in her uncle's mansion of Penshurst and to make herself useful in all manner of sewing and embroidery for the bride's chest. It seemed that my lady's brother, Earl Robert as he now was, was hard put to it to find a sufficient dowry for his daughter or the marriage had been sooner. Before she left, the duenna told me that the young earl himself, my lady's son, had agreed to lend a large sum to his uncle for the honour of the family and to procure so desirable a match to one high in the king's favour and perhaps this might reconcile him and his mother. A thousand pounds she said.

Earl Robert's daughter gave me some cause for jealousy knowing that my lady valued her highly for that she too had learning above what was usual for her sex, and followed my lady in her delight in books and in writing herself, going under the name of Urania, though as yet she being but eighteen years, and

not as I am without the protection of parents to spur her genius
with necessity has only wrote some verses which nevertheless
the countess highly approved. Yet whether her new husband
will take kindly to a poet wife is to be seen, for many men
believe that the world of books should be theirs alone and that
too much learning may distract a woman from her duties. In
this my lady was fortunate in that the late earl her husband was
much away as President of the Council in Wales at his castles
of Cardiff and Ludlow of which the administration now falls
so heavily upon my lady.

All summer I lingered alone at Ramsbury going sometimes
to that garden and mansion all shut up where my lady had
bathed in the fountain among the stone nymphs, and in the
overgrown and desolate gardens I began to write some verses
myself, the words coming into my head as I gathered those
herbs and plants that I saw growing among the useless weeds
and long grasses, for some I found when I parted the stems had
survived their long neglect and yet others had been blown there
by nature and thrived among the stones of the many winding
paths and in the hedges. In special in a piece of lawn turned
again to meadow I found many orchis of which those roots
which are round are to be dried and ground for medicines or if
bruised and applied to the place may heal the king's evil. Some
say they are of Venus and as a potion provoke to lust and they
are therefore much prized by physicians who supply the wants
of those whose loins are cold or who would arouse lust in others.

As I dug for them these words came to me which I wrote
down in the tablet I carry always to keep note of herbs I find,
the time of their blooming and coming to seed and where they
may be found again.

> The orchis with its plume of fire
> Inspires to lust which feeds desire
> Yet no philtre need I who have seen

My lady bathe in Diane's stream.
Hear when she comes the birds sing out
And all the woods return their shout,
But when she's absent then how drear
The very summer flowers appear.

The mansion itself seemed to sink more into decay each time
I visited it. The second time I found myself there again I
ventured to search for the key where my lady had bid me replace
it under the flagstone in the little brick cistern and finding it a
little dirtier and spotted with bright rust I made to try it in the
lock of the front door itself under the portico. It turned, I
pushed and the door groaned open. As my lady had bidden me
before, I opened a shutter to see better. Perhaps I hoped that
my imagination would conjure up the shape of my absent mistress
out of the gloom and she would come towards me holding out
her hands and smiling as she sometimes did in dreams. But the
place seemed danker and more umbrous even than before.

Nevertheless I determined now I was inside to explore further
and began to go from chamber to chamber, climbing the broad
oak stair till I could look down into the hall. And now I went
from bedchamber to bedchamber opening a shutter here and
there the further to see and then up a narrow stair to the attics
where I found many stools stacked, a broken chair, a bed beneath
which little mounds of sawdust gave evidence that the worms
had got in.

In a closet at the very corner of the house I came upon a
jumble of ancient clothing from which flew out a cloud of
silvery moths when I stirred them with my foot. Then I saw
that leaning against the back of the closet was a lance such as
men use for the tilt, with a helmet as it were placed upon a
head. As I drew it out into the light it struck against something
in the pile of moth-eaten clothes and, on my reaching in, I came
upon a cuirass that had once been of polished steel and dama-

scened in some precious metal but now pitted and with a bloom of mildew over it. Behind this again was a shield of which the impresa was quite lost. I brushed the dust and cobwebs from the cuirass. In size it seemed fitted for a youth rather than a fully grown man. I put it on over my tunic. Although it pressed a little over my breasts it was otherwise as if made for me. Likewise with the helmet when I put it upon my head.

It had once been adorned with a plume of feathers of which only the stumps remained. Now I felt myself indeed to be the amazon, Zelmane of that *Arcadia* her brother had written for my lady in his exile or that Forsaken Knight worsted by Amphialus. I therefore determined that I should return again to the mansion with all necessary ingredients and tools to restore the armour's brightness. Yet I wondered about its first owner and what had been his fate that it should be left behind in that manner when the house was shut up.

So I now had more reasons to return there often as the summer weeks passed. And soon when I had finished the cuirass and helmet to my liking I set up a ring on a pole that I might prac-tise riding at it with the lance and found that my horse that I was accustomed always to take, showed some remembrance of what was expected of him and of the exercise, for instead of rearing up in fright at the pole he carried me bravely on and would repeat the pass until I grew quite skilful in winning the ring with the point of my lance. Then I wished there might be dragons to slay or that I could rescue my countess from a giant's castle as in the old romances. Yet now the jousts are only in sport, in imitation of those of former times and instead of the chivalry in single combat of the lance, for warfare there is the thunder of the musket and the cannon.

With the coming of autumn when harvest was over my lady sent to tell me that the wedding would be soon and she would be returning. I was to go to the great house and help to make all ready there. So I packed my chests of instruments and medicines and rode back to Wilton, not stopping to lie anywhere on the way but sleeping one night under the stars beside my horse who had become my familiar in our long weeks together and seemed to understand my humour whether it was light or dark. But before I left I fetched my armour, for now I believed it was indeed my own, from Sir Harry Stilman his old house and hid it in another chest under a cloak to be sent down with my other things in a wagon.

The maids and men had already received warning of my lady's return, brought by Dr Adrian Gilbert on his way to his friends in Devon with news of how Sir Walter his brother did in the Tower and with what equanimity he took his imprisonment, not railing at his ill fortune but determined to win his majesty's favour when the opportunity should arise.

As soon as my chests arrived, I restocked the laboratory and began again to treat those sick who hearing I was returned presented themselves at the house. One day when I was busy washing the wound of an old man who had gashed his leg chopping wood, a deep cut which had festered and become quite rotten before he had come into my hands, Dr Gilbert entered the barn where I was working.

Coming up behind me he peered at the wound. 'No good may be done for that. You must take off his leg if that is not beyond your skill.'

'Oh sir,' the old man said, 'leave me my leg. I will live with the badness and aid myself to walk with this stick but leave me my leg.'

'Do not distress yourself,' I said. 'We have not come to such yet. And see the wound is already less inflamed in the two days I have treated it.'

'We shall have you cried for a miracle worker Master Boston if you can save this. What magic have you been using or have you had the help of demons?'

'No sir. I use only nature herself to drain out infection. This wound being of an axe is nothing supernatural and therefore needs treating by natural means and remedies.'

'And what then may they be? If it is no secret from the world?'

'I wash it daily in a distillation of cinquefoil.'

'Cinquefoil?'

'It is a small creeping herb, very common by the roadside and therefore may be overlooked by some. It grows like a strawberry in strings with little yellow flowers. The root boiled in vinegar I have used distilled to wash this man's wound, thereafter leaving it to dry. He will testify that the inflammation is abating.'

'And is this also in your little book of receipts which my lady commanded me to bring to her?'

'No sir. It is only in my head as yet being a simple remedy, but I shall include it in the fair copy she bade me make for her use. And in that which I will one day hope to place before the world.'

'You must buy yourself an accreditation first before the world will accept your homespun scribblings as of value to it. Perhaps this silly old man will testify to your skill before the bishop.'

'Indeed sirs I will. If the young master do save my leg from the saw he shall have my prayers and my wife's as long as we live. And see she has sent some fresh eggs from her hens being all we have to pay you with.' And he drew a kerchief from his hat which he had nursed carefully while I was washing of his wound, which I knew must sting mightily from the vinegar, and showed the four speckled eggs nested in it.

'These old rogues always cry poverty. He will have a nest egg of another kind under his straw pallet.'

'No sir, for all our money has gone to buy books and pens and paper for our son who is learning to be a clerk in Salisbury so that he may keep accounts and one day if God wills be the steward in a great house as this.'

'You will find that he has learnt only to despise his parents and that station in which God has placed him.' And he left us.

'Keep your eggs old man for they will do good for you and your wife and strengthen you against the winter. We must have your leg healed fully before then or the cold and wet will inflame it again. I will take just one of your eggs to bind up a poultice for a boil that must be brought to a head.'

When the old man was gone and I thought on what had been said I blamed myself for boasting of my design to Dr Gilbert for I saw that it could only feed the envy he nursed towards me, and had since our first meeting, fearing perhaps that I would supplant him in the countess's favour in spite of his advantage of birth and schooling, and her love for his brother Sir Walter.

The next day with the clattering of many horses and the groaning of cartwheels my lady returned. With joy I went to greet her and hand her from her carriage, for the Lady Anne was sick again and her mother had travelled with her from London where commonly she was accustomed to ride horseback like her late majesty.

'Perhaps country air and your attentions can do her some good Amyntas. Certain the stink of the city, now that the people begin to burn coals against the winter, has made her worse since the wedding was over and we left Penshurst. God grant this marriage go well for my brother writes that his new son is discontented already. It is very soon for an unkindness to begin but she must endure as women must or be shut out from a household of her own and live dependent on others.'

I heard this as a reflection of my own state but my lady's thoughts were elsewhere. She went on: 'And how have you occupied yourself in my absence Amyntas? I hope you have not allowed your skills to decline through idleness. My daughter has need of every attention and I myself am worn down with the cares of this marriage and her sickness. Attend on her as soon as you may and for me I would have a draught for ease of this black melancholy that has settled on me when I hoped that the sight of my own home would raise my spirits. Also it will soon be mine no more for the earl my son has it in hand to be married to the daughter of the Earl of Shrewsbury. As yet no contract is agreed and all may still founder on the terms of it. Still I feel in my heart that this time matters will go forward and his majesty himself shows a great liking for the match which must promise well. Then all will be change and confusion. You will go to the Lady Anne.'

'Madam I will go as soon as she is rested from the jolting of the carriage over so long a way. Now I will attend you so that you may be rested and refreshed too.'

For both of them I prepared a light sleeping potion that would give them rest without heaviness, bringing hers for my lady with my own hands, and sending for her daughter as well a dish of coddled eggs and creamed white breast of chicken. When I judged that the Lady Anne would be rested, I went to her chamber where she was used to lie when visiting her home, taking with me the duenna who was returned with her mistress and, in spite of her age, in better health than either the countess or her daughter.

The Lady Anne was sitting up in her bedgown, a little lawn cap upon her head. Her face bore two red spots of fever in its whiteness. She was very thin as one who had been these last weeks at a fast not a feast, and when she coughed she spat green phlegm into her kerchief. I took her pulse which was shallow but fast. I conceived that the immediate cause of her fever was a pleurisy for which I could prescribe a soothing linctus, for I noticed she held her hand to her side when she coughed. But I feared more from her general appearance, and particularly from that wasting I observed, that underlying it was a consumption of the lungs, phthisis, for which I would prescribe her an electuary of plantain which I kept in a pot, to be taken at night three hours after supper and because the base of it is honey then it soothes and is easy and pleasant to swallow.

'She will never make old bones,' the duenna said. 'Can you make her well enough Master Boston, to be married before she dies?'

'If as I fear she has indeed a phthisis then I can only try, for this disease apart from canker is the hardest of cure, especially when it appears in one so young and takes such hold as I see in her sunken cheeks which should be in full bloom of youth. And indeed no physician can truly cure it but only drive it underground for a time where it ferments in the body until, like a mine engineers tunnel to lay a charge under a city wall, it suddenly explodes and brings all down with it.'

'You must keep your fears from the countess, and pretend to that confidence of care you do not have, for I have seen these past weeks that her own health falters from some woman's complaint that makes her think her own youth and even life are gone. In her old home of Penshurst she was most sad, remembering those days before her marriage when she and her younger brothers and sisters played and learnt together after Sir Philip was sent away to school. Both her sisters died young and she must see the same danger for the Lady Anne although she conceals it perhaps in the hope that what is unspoken may not happen.'

I thought that my lady would not take refuge in such a superstition but I kept this for myself. Two days later she called me over to her again together with the rest of the household.

'All is concluded,' she said, addressing us in the hall. 'My son the Earl of Pembroke is to be married for the Lady Mary Talbot, daughter to the honourable Earl of Shrewsbury, the match to take place here on the 4th of November. Their majesties themselves will graciously attend and it will be a most splendid occasion for which there is little time to prepare. There will be presented a masque and a tilt for the nobles and gentlemen on the meadows beyond the river. We must begin at once and all must bear their share.'

The countess her household broke out clapping and cheering, each vowing to do their best but my heart was heavy with dismay at the news and what it might portend, and when I looked upon my mistress her face I saw that same unease written there although she was forced to try to disguise it before her family.

It's a long time since I've been to the Gaos or maybe it's just that so much has happened, it feels like for ever so I get on my bike and ride over. It's Saturday night, their busiest time. Mary seems pleased to see me. She blushes a bit and looks down at her order book not to catch my eye. Packing the carrier with an order and riding the darkening streets is somehow soothing as if life could be this simple but I have to tell them tonight that I can't go on with it. Whether it's by some kind of osmosis from the Galton affair, or more people needing a cheap lawyer, or our increasingly litigious society I read about in the press when I've got time to read a paper at all, but suddenly all sorts of clients with their sad or corny stories are beating a way to my door. Maybe it's because I've set up my own website for Lost Causes and they like the spiel I put out there. Anyway it leaves me no time or energy for delivering takeaways especially since these things seem to have an exponential growth rate, the demands multiplying by some mysterious X-factor so that if this goes on I'll be looking for an assistant to make the tea.

So after I've done my stint and Mary is packing up my supper in the little silver lidded boxes and Mr Gao comes through from the kitchen to smoke a joint, I begin to apologise and explain.

'We wonder that we don't see you so much,' Mr Gao says. 'Charlie he say he see you in college. Then we wonder why you need for go there.'

'You can't have too many qualifications,' I say.

He nods. 'Charlie agree with you. He very clever, very fit. Martial arts. He long time in America with my brother.'

'I thought Charlie was from Hong Kong.'

'He first from Hong Kong. His mother my sister there. Then he is in San Francisco and American college.'

'I wondered about his English being so perfect. Will he stay here now?'

'A little maybe. I don't know. Chinese people all over the world, make businesses, where can work. Now make business in China, Quanjiao, Shanghai, good business for all over the world.'

I thought it was a pity Mary and Charlie were cousins and wondered if she was a little in love with him. I hoped Charlie would stay and look out for them but not break her heart.

'How are the friends next door behaving themselves?'

Mr Gao looks round nervously, as if the room might be bugged: 'At first they try to give trouble. Let down Charlie's tyres. Break a window, stop customers coming in. Say "our food better – you come to us". But they don't come. My customers stay with me. Call me up to order food and now email. Charlie fix that up. Next week I take on new boy for delivery, so many orders. Charlie writes a letter to say we will sue them for harassment. Now all quiet. Maybe they thinking they buy me out, is better. Maybe I think so too.'

'Well, my offer is still open. If you need me, I'll always come and do what I can.'

'Thank you, Miss Jade. Your business do good now?' It was an imperative Mr Gao understood.

'It's doing better, Mr Gao. How long for, we shall see.'

'Business up, business down,' he shrugs. 'All the same in the end.'

I feel a part of my life is over as I head back towards Waterloo, and I'm sad about that and a bit frightened too. Working for the Gaos gave my life some sort of structure, was less lonely for the snail out of the shell it had retired into so that it could stretch out its horns, put out feelers into the world before recoiling back in to hide. Now it's time to move on if I can free myself at last from Settle and Fixit and Helen.

She had finally rung me to flirt a little while letting me know she was busy elsewhere. I texted Joel and spent an evening getting pissed, trashing the government and the world generally.

'You OK?' he asked halfway through the session.

'Don't I seem it?' It wasn't like him to ask.

'You seem a bit tense, look a bit tired.'

'Thanks. I've been in love but I may be falling out of it.'

'Oh love. That old merry-go-round.'

'Roller coaster is more like. Nothing "merry" about it.'

'Well I wouldn't know. Since the big A I've been virtually celibate. Virtual sex. Maybe that's the thing to go for. Trouble is it's served up by some grubby sleaze merchants thousands of miles away and nobody even gets to touch.'

'All breathing human passion far above . . .'

'Something like that.'

We'd moved away from my danger ground. I'd lied to Joel, except that it was just a bit of self-defence not grey enough to be a real lie. And he probably knew that anyway.

James Chalmers called me in to talk about a case we were involved in, a squabble over merchandising rights in a toy that was itself a spin-off from a tele advert. The company that had made the original short claimed they'd been cheated out of a share of profit on the toy. The toymakers who'd enjoyed a Christmas killing said it was all theirs. The advert had come from a small indie production company making films on a shoe-string. The toy boys were a branch of a conglomerate marketing around the world. Now the makers of the original product being advertised were asking for their share too.

'This is counsel's opinion.' James pushed it across his desk at me. 'It gives us the backing we need.'

We were representing the puppet masters whose product would delight the hearts and bring smiles to the little faces of children throughout the globe, of every hue and feature. It stood on James's desk, a hairy blob of jelly in green bendable plastic with no neck and a toothy grin. The makers had given it a name, the Whirly-gon, which was part of their case. It had started life as a germ to be driven out by a new cleaning fluid. They hoped it was the next ET.

'I don't think this is right.'

'Jade, you can't just dismiss counsel's opinion. It cost enough. And well, he is rather more experienced than you. One of the most prestigious in the field, in fact.'

'I know his reputation. It's just that in this case I think he's too optimistic. After all there was a contract, though not a very well drawn one.'

'That's his point. Hardly worth the paper it was written on. Back of the envelope stuff.'

'But a contract. I think the judge could take the view that given the inequality of the parties the weight must lie with the original creator. Saltire versus Ableson for instance.'

'That isn't how counsel interprets it. We must go with his advice or rather advise the client to.'

'I think I'd like my doubts on record,' I said carefully, 'and I think the clients should be warned. If they were prepared to come to some arrangement...'

'You seem to be keen on settlements, Jade. We don't get money or prestige out of settlements. Winning damages and costs – that's what counts.'

'But losing counts even more. Against us.'

Chalmers sighed. 'I wish I could carry you with me, Jade, but in view of your opinion, I think I'd better handle this on my own. I can understand that women don't have the same stomach for a fight, that you tend to avoid confrontation, but there are times when you have to stand up and be counted, even take a risk.'

So I was off the case as Chandler would say. S and F didn't stand for Settle and Fixit as Drew and I had always joked, but rather Subtle and Floggit, two unsavoury characters from a comedy of bad manners.

'You've blown it, Jade,' Helen said when at last we met in the corridor. 'Why did you have to disagree with counsel's opinion? You know men don't like to be crossed, especially senior partners.'

I'd forgotten that QCs, counsel, were like old-style hospital consultants for us, the ones matron had to follow, from ward to ward with: 'Yes sir, no sir, three bags full sir.' But if they got it wrong it was the nursing staff who somehow took the blame or at least the patient's disappointment and pain.

Then I had to wonder whether my judgement had been infected by my own predisposition to be on the side of the underdog. Carefully I went through the whole brief again, looking for flaws in my argument. Well, maybe I'd overstated the case. Maybe there was room for doubt. But if there was then the law itself was an ass, braying in favour of the letter rather than what was fair and right. OK, Sir Galahad, get back in the kitchen.

Drew's replacement turned up the following week. I'd caught sight of him sitting nervously in reception when I went down to collect some documents and wondered if he was a client. He'd been waiting to be interviewed: short, lank fair hair and built like a rugby fullback even in his dark pinstripe.

'This is Sebastian, Jade, who's taking over Drew's job. Be nice to him. He rowed for his college.'

'Only in the second boat.'

'I'll see you later, no doubt.' Helen smiled up at him and was gone.

She had let me know, quite deliberately, that whatever there had been was over. Thinking I might throw up I shut myself in the loo, raging and weeping by turns. I had been her little experiment that hadn't delivered the expected result. And it was my own fault. 'You blew it, Jade.' Or would it have happened anyway? In traditional style that evening I fell to pieces playing *Der Rosenkavalier* over and over; the last scene, but now the roles were reversed. The countess was going off with Sophie and it was Octavian who got to sing her heart out alone on stage.

The next day I called in sick but it was only postponing the moment when I had to go back. Suddenly it was clear to me not only that I had no future with Helen, never had except in my dreams, but that I had none with S & F either. And what the firm was doing seemed increasingly unrelated to why I had switched my degree to law in what now seemed a lifetime ago. I'd seen myself as a kind of Robin Hood, defending the defenceless, the poor and the underdog against the powerful whether that was political or corporate power. Now I seemed increasingly asked to use my talent such as it was to support the strong and knock down the weak who couldn't afford the superior advice of a Settle and Fixit. Our old name was seemingly embedded in my brain now and I couldn't think of them in any other way.

I would play it cool when I went into chambers, let no one see my hurt. Be bright and efficient. Above all Helen should never know although in that hiccuping cry of Sir Thomas Wyatt, the last word on changed love:

> . . . all is turned through my gentleness,
> Into a strange, fashion of forsaking;
> And I have leave to go, of her goodness;
> And she also to use new-fangleness;
> But since that I so unkindly am served
> I fain would know what she hath deserved.

When we lost the case in spite of counsel's opinion, or perhaps even because of it making us too sure of ourselves, I hid my glee and murmured words of sympathy to James Chalmers when we met beside the water-cooler. Stony-faced he merely ducked his head in acknowledgement and walked stiffly away. I had committed the unforgivable sin of being right as I realised as soon as I read the full judgement.

Helen was still just as distant. I wondered if she had tried out the new boy, Sebastian, but what could he bring that was fresh for her to experience unless, I thought bitterly, a touch of SM? Obviously my own days at S & F were numbered. I began to study the alternatives. I could try for some teaching. Media departments and studies were burgeoning in the universities. I signed up to a society of lawyers, experts in the field who met once a month to discuss the legislation and theory underpinning what we did from day to day at S & F. A lot of the members combined practice with academia. I sensed there was an integrity to their discussions though they would have seemed unbearably dry to an outsider. I began to get back a sense of what it was all meant to be about. I found myself speaking out and was asked to contribute to a study of recent cases. It gave me something to do in the evenings, now that I no longer expected to spend time with Helen. But it was also my little hand grenade. Publication would pull out the pin and I would lob it into the glossy offices of S & F. The explosive was my analysis of the Whirly-gon case and why we had lost it.

'Great stuff,' Jack Silver, the distinguished editor, said after I had delivered my chapter. 'You'll probably be blackballed.'

By now I'd decided I wanted to be on my own anyway, where I didn't have to be patronised or watch my back all the time. If I could hang on at S & F for a few more months I'd have clocked up enough experience for the wide world. So I ran around as a smiling dogsbody who was never asked to comment on a case any more, but spent my time on witness statements and organising the stacks of files that would accompany the real movers and shakers into court. Then my time bomb went off. The doorstop of a book on media law dropped on to James Chalmers' desk.

It was the latest thing and everyone in our field had to have a copy as I'd known they would. When he summoned me to his office I was ready. The volume sat fatly in front of him.

'I imagine you know why I asked you to come in. I regard your analysis of the Whirly-gon case as a serious breach of confidence.'

'I was careful to use only the accounts in the public domain; the very full report of the judgement and the transcript of the proceedings. I don't think I can be said to have breached confidence.'

'You've made us look complete idiots. And as for counsel . . . He's livid. I saw him at the Groucho yesterday evening. He'd had an advance copy. We won't be able to use him again.'

'I'm sorry he's taking it like that. It wasn't meant to be a personal criticism.'

'Of course it's personal. Everything is.'

'If you'd like me to resign . . .'

'In the circumstances I think that would be for the best.'

'I have been here for quite some time . . .'

'How much do you want?'

'Perhaps we should discuss it another day. I imagine you'd like to consult first.'

I knew exactly how much the law entitled me to as severance pay, of course. It was a calculated part of my set-up costs if I was to have a hope of going it on my own. I didn't rush to clear my desk but I stayed out of James Chalmers' way while the negotiations about my settlement dragged on. Then suddenly it seemed one Monday morning my days with S&F were nearly over. I was leaving on Friday.

That evening I was settling down to fill in the required forms that would give me the Law Society's go-ahead for putting on my own show, when the phone rang. It was Helen.

'Can I come and see you before you leave, Jay?'

'When were you thinking of?'

'James is at a dinner tomorrow. He'll be late back.'

The rest of the evening and the next day was spent in the old ferment as I ran through the different scenarios of how our last meeting, for I sensed that's what it was, would play. My flat had declined into bachelor squalor in the last few weeks so I had to get up early to clean it and change the sheets. On my way back from the office I bought a decent bottle of wine and the cheese that Helen liked. I was just in time. She was buzzing the entry phone ten minutes early.

'I left just after James. I must be back before he is.'

'Did you bring your car?'

'I thought I might be offered a drink so I came by cab.'

'G and T or wine?'

'G and T, then wine.'

I mixed her drink, poured myself a glass of Gamay and brought them over.

'James doesn't know I'm here. He's more or less forbidden me to see you. Not in so many words but the meaning is quite clear. It's not just everything else. The book is the last straw because he's never been asked to contribute to anything like that. He says your analysis is very good and he can't bear it. He thinks you'll go to a rival firm and be in competition with S & F.'

'Settle and Fixit.'

'Is that what you call us?'

'Drew and I used to have a joke about it.' I was playing it cool just as I'd rehearsed to myself. Helen put her glass down and came towards me.

'Aren't you even going to kiss me? Are you so angry?' The scent and warmth of her so close were too much.

'Make love to me, Jay,' she said as she had all those months ago. And it was Thomas Wyatt again but this time:

> Thanked be fortune; it hath been otherwise,
> Twenty times better, but once in special,
> In thin array, after a pleasant guise,
> When her loose gown from her shoulders did fall,
> And she caught me in her arms long and small,
> Therewith all sweetly did me kiss,
> And softly said, 'Dear heart how like you this?'

After, when we were lying finishing off the bottle of wine, she sat up and looked at her watch.

'I must go soon.'

'How's Sebastian?'

'Plodding. No imagination. I call him Bash. He doesn't know why. You're much better. The best, in fact.'

'Then why can't we go on?'

'Because you're a romantic, Jay. You want too much; more than I can give. I realised that very soon. You're dangerous or you could be if I let you and I like my comforts. I'm not brave. "All for love and the world well lost." That sort of thing. Being a senior partner is important to me. Not many women make it. I took a short cut by marrying James. After all those years of exams and slog I wanted some fun, to be at the top without having to struggle for it. I like a lot about my life and the rest I take care of in my own way.'

'James needn't worry that I'll go to a competitor of S & F. I've decided to try and go it alone. Set up by myself. If that doesn't work then we'll have to see. Meanwhile let's say I'm having a sort of gap year though I won't be going round the world. I'll be holed up in a dingy office touting for the briefs nobody else wants.'

My lady was right that there was too little time to prepare for the young earl's wedding that was to be of an unsurpassed splendour though some wondered why the bride had it not at her father's house as the custom was. Once again we made ready to entertain their majesties. Whole trees were felled for firing, bushels of wheat were taken to the mill to be ground for making of bread, vats steamed with the brewing of gallons of beer. The forests were hunted of game of every kind of bird and beast until nothing more stirred and the river was emptied of fish which now swam round and round in the ponds until called for. Maids churned butter and made cheese. The royal beds where their majesties were used to lie at Wilton were aired, sprinkled with herbs and rose petals and made up with silken sheets.

Meanwhile I pounded, distilled and mixed against a possible multitude of distempers and broken heads. As the day approached the house filled until it seemed its walls would burst. Not only the barns but many houses in the town, the Pembroke Arms and other inns as far as Salisbury were all taken up until there was nowhere for any to lie in that country. At the last came the court, together with the bride her family, which my lady greeted as if no shadow of doubt for her own future troubled her.

On the day, the bride was led to the church by Prince Henry and his majesty himself gave her away. The queen followed in her train as the whole party returned to the house for the bride cake and the usual sops in wine. Rich gifts of gloves and garters were exchanged, his majesty making a gift of plate, and other nobles too to the tune of three thousand pounds. Then it was time for feasting and drinking of wine until bedtime when the young earl and his bride were carried to bed and with much laughter she was stripped of her clothes, her lace hose thrown for who should catch them and, as I heard, twenty other like pretty games before they were left together with the sheets sewn up.

In the morning came his majesty and lay in or upon the bed

in his shirt and nightgown to quiz them on the night's sport and how they found each other, and to inspect the sheets for her blood. Many came to me for potions to ease their aching heads and queasy stomachs. Only my lady seemed calm and unmoved. She had asked me for a draught to render her quiet and cheerful for, said she, 'The name and title of Mary, Countess of Pembroke will now belong to another from this day and I must submit to God's will.'

The time of the tilt approached and all made their way over the bridge to a meadow bounded on one side by the river Nadder. Banks of seats had been set up for royalty and the nobility, especially the ladies, to watch in comfort and safety. When I saw the countess seated with the duenna and her steward to attend her I slipped away before she could call for me. I had determined that I would have a hand in these sports as Zelmane in the guise of an Amazon had done in the *Arcadia* and fight on my lady's behalf as I had practised in Sir Henry Stilman his garden.

To this end I retired to the stillroom and exchanged my satin doublet for a peasant's rough tunic and over it put on my cuirass which I had hidden in a closet there, together with the helmet for my head which helmet I had graced with three plumes. Then I girded my sword and went down to seek out a lance, taking up my shield with its impresa of my own devising which showed a double A, one inverted within the other, with two arrows piercing it in imitation of my lady's Sidney pheon and cupid's dart.

I went out to the stables and got upon my horse who knew me in spite of my disguise, and rode around by the backside of the house for the Salisbury road as if I might be coming from the city, and so to the field where the heralds were commanding knights to draw near and prove their valour in defence of their mistresses' beauty. As I looked out through the visor of my helmet I heard a buzz of voices for none knew me except that my mistress leant forward and whispered in the duenna's ear. But I kept on to where the shield hung that the knights must strike to be admitted to the tourney.

'What is your name, Sir Knight?' the herald demanded. 'And what lady do you serve?'

'My name is Anonimous and I serve the most beautiful lady Anonima.' I dared not say my lady's name for fear I might disgrace it. At this there was a new buzz of voices.

The other knights had pasteboard shields like mine but prettily painted with ingenious designs as a sinking ship or a house on fire to wittily signify marriage and I heard after that many had been made by the king's servants for the players' company was well skilled in the painting of scenes, shields and such toys for the stage.

First we were to run at the ring, which pleased me as a trial I was much practised in. And indeed when my turn came I easily bore it away to the cheers of the crowd. I rode up to where the countess sat and placed it at her feet with the tip of my lance. Then I bowed to her from the saddle and returned to the contest.

Now we were to fight in earnest. At first I was lucky for I was paired with a knight who bore a shield with a she bear on it and he being stout and wearing a heavy breastplate I was able to run under his guard, prick him and then away before he could bring down his sword. At which the people laughed mightily and he cried out that he was stung by a gnat and would have his revenge but the judge who was his majesty's chamberlain would not permit it.

So I had borne myself well and luckily in two of the trials but this time was to be with staves. I was drawn against a tall strong knight upon a big roan horse, his impresa showing a tower under siege. We took our choice of weapons and rode apart to the ends of the field. A trumpet sounded. The herald raised his staff and let it fall. I spurred towards the knight of the tower but his horse being stronger than mine he met me three-quarters of the way and from his greater height struck hard down upon my head. Even so I believe in pity of what he esteemed my youth he did not strike with that force he might have. Yet the strength of it, as well as thrusting my helmet down upon my collarbone, broke the girths of my saddle, which tumbled from the horse with me still upon it, my foot caught in the stirrup on one side. Luckily I was able to cry for my horse to stand, which he was accustomed to do on command or else he had bolted dragging me along with my head thumping on the ground to crack my skull and addle my brains.

Even so as I fell I put out a hand to save myself and felt my wrist bone break and my dagger ride up in its hanger to pierce my body where the cuirass ended. So I hung upside down and bleeding. The knight of the tower being nearest to me got down from his horse to come to my aid. Untangling my foot from the stirrup he lowered me gently to the ground and began to unfasten my helmet.

By this time the duenna came panting up, as I learned, sent by the countess. The knight took off my helmet.

'Why, it is but a boy.'

'Yes, sir, a foolish boy, page to my lady who has sent me to see him safely bestowed.' And indeed two were coming with a hurdle to carry me off the field.

'Should we not remove the cuirass and search his wound to staunch the bleeding?'

'It is better for me to take him back to the house to his pallet and as he is something of a physician he will no doubt tend himself when he wakes.' For from my wounds and the pain and the fear of discovery bringing shame on my lady and her wrath upon me, I had swooned away.

When I awoke it was on my pallet in the laboratory where I had been forced to lie because of the press of people. I found the duenna's ancient face peering down at me.

'So you wake at last Master Boston,' she said as one who knew otherwise. 'I have staunched your wound which is indeed only slight though it bled a deal. But I think your wrist is broke. Now I must go to my lady and tell her you will live. It was she sent me to make certain no one else should attend you.'

'Who undressed me?'

'I did.'

'Is my lady angry with me?'

'You have put her honour in danger but by good fortune no one knows. However the knight who laid you low is also eager to know how you do and I think will insist on coming to see for himself. He thought you a most pretty youth and admired your courage. Such likings are all the fashion now, following the pattern of his majesty. And indeed kings have always had their favourites of both sexes, even her late majesty as my own Lord of Leicester and the Earl of Essex. Power ever attracts beauty as moth to candle flame which often has its wings singed there.'

'Madam, before you leave me I would ask you kindly to fetch me certain things as I direct. I do not wish to rise and set my wound bleeding again which you have so skilfully staunched.'

'Well, I have tended many wounds in my time, especially from this most dangerous game of the tilt that the noblemen will play, and noblewomen encourage them. And for what: to act out an old play of the romances as Sir Gawain and La Belle Iseult, as if they were Arthur and his knights risen from the dead who were long dust before my grandfather was born if they ever in truth walked the earth except in story books and broadsheet ballads.'

So grumbling still she brought me the things I asked for that I might strap my wrist with a poultice, soaked in tincture of oil of Solomon's seal, under a leather wristband stiffened with smooth fillets of wood and the same to be applied on a cloth for my wound. I asked also for a draught of poppy to quell the pain and with a double purpose drown me in Lethe for I could bear neither the sting of my wounds nor of my thoughts.

When I woke again it was to find the knight of the tower, as I judged for I had never before seen his face without his helmet, sitting beside me on a stool and leaning his hands on his sword, his chin on his hands.

'They say you are something of a physician Sir Boy. Will you live? I would not be the cause of such a spark put out.'

'I thank you for your asking sir. Are you that knight that worsted me? If so I thank you that you did not strike harder as I believe you might have done, and that as I remember you came to my aid.'

'It is no part of courage to strike harder than is necessary to gain the end or to be the oppressor of the weaker party.'

'Then sir you have an unfashionable idea of chivalry for these harsh days.'

'So young and so out of sorts with the times. You would be a philosopher as well as a pasteboard soldier. What is your name Sir Boy?'

'Amyntas Boston, sir. And yours? By your manner of speaking you should be a Scotsman.'

'Aye. For I came south with his majesty looking for some preferment in England since in Scotland I am only the youngest son of Sir Hector McQueen, a landless laird who left my mother nothing but debts, and a crumbling tower besieged by the bailiffs. Hence my impresa. My given name is Duncan, after the kings of Scotland. His majesty was gracious enough to knight me for my attendance on him as a page but now I must make my own fortune by my sword. That is not easy in time of peace. So I think to go abroad where there are still wars and booty to be had by taking and ransoming of prisoners or in defence of new colonies in lands still to be explored by the Northwest Passage if that may be found, where a landless man may gain something of his own. What is your lineage?'

'My father was a physician sir in Salisbury and I follow his calling.'

'Then you could be most useful for my enterprise for I mean to settle in the New World either in the north where there are many animals as beaver and silver fox that may be trapped for their fur and a fortune made that way or in the south where gold is to be found among the idols of the heathens who live there. You are a lad of courage. Come with me.'

'I am honoured sir that you should wish to make me of your company but I am servant to the Countess of Pembroke and cannot leave at will.'

'Fortune changes. Now that her son the earl has a wife your countess must move over. Who knows where she will go or what she will do? She may no longer have need of a page physician.'

'Then I shall follow my fortunes elsewhere sir but for now I remain in her service.'

'If you should change your mind Sir Boy you may find me until I sail at the Unicorn in Southwark.' And he left me.

I was glad to see him go for the truth of his words pained me and the strength of his will in my weakened state might have prevailed on me to go with him though it would have been hard to keep my secret for many months on board ship. If I were discovered I might suffer all kinds of indignity as indeed I feared might also be the case if I were not. Sir Duncan McQueen had stared at me too hard with a look of lechery and I remembered my night-time visitor when first I came to the great house.

Later after I had slept again a servant was sent to me with bread and broth and a hot posset to which I added more poppy and so slept pretty well, except it seemed to me that my lady came and leant above me so that her naked breast nearly rested on my lips and her hand on my brow. In the morning I remembered some words of a poet: 'It was no dream I lay broad waking' but could not tell if this was true or false.

Within two days treating of my wound I was well enough
to rise and make my way, though shakily, to my lady's chamber.
The house was quiet and empty, the court having gone away
for Windsor carrying with them the bride and groom. I found
her seated in her chair and saw at once the settled melancholy
on her face.

'Well Amyntas, you have not killed yourself with your foolishness.'

I fell on my knees and kissed the folds of her skirt. 'My lady
is rightly angry with me.'

'At least no one knew your folly except myself. I saw to that
or I had been shamed to have been deceived as men would have
thought it. Were you mad Amyntas to play such a trick? And
where did you get your antique armour that caused all to laugh
that saw you?'

'I found it in Sir Henry Stilman his house.'

'It must have been his son's. A boy of great promise struck
down by the smallpox. And where did you learn your skills?'

'By practice my lady.'

'Why did you expose yourself and me to discovery rash child?'

'I thought to do as Zelmane in your brother's *Arcadia*.'

'But Zelmane was a youth, a prince in disguise.'

'Then I could be Parthenia when she fought as the Knight
of the Temple.'

'And was worsted. The *Arcadia* of my dear brother is to be
understood like one of Our Saviour's parables as showing forth
an inner meaning, not to be followed slavishly word for word.
Again I say Amyntas you must give thought to your future.
When my son returns after the Christmas festival I must leave
this place, as well Ramsbury and my Ivychurch and I do not
know where I shall go except to lodge a while at Baynard's. I
shall be poor, Amyntas, and must cut my coat according to my
cloth. You must shift for yourself though I will give you what
help I may but I shall be myself a vagrant. You must consider

whether it is time to give up your disguise and look for a husband, some merchant or physician or servant to a noble household as a steward.'

My heart sank at these words. She went on: 'I would provide you with something towards your marriage portion.'

'My lady, it was not the lack of a dowry that brought me here at your command.' And here I felt the tears begin to start in my eyes.

'There child, do not distress yourself. Only think of what I have said and we will speak of it again when you are more recovered from your wound.'

Then I said that I would go to London. 'Not to be a charge on your ladyship but to make my own way; never to bring you any discomfort but only to be allowed to come to you sometimes and to be always ready if you should need me.' And here I could no longer stay my tears but wept openly.

My lady reached down and drew me up and into her bosom. 'Come now be calm. Do not drown us both in your tears. You shall come with me when I go and we will see what the future will bring and what God intends for us both in his own good time. Perhaps the course of nature will settle all. Who knows but we shall both find husbands.'

I decide not to do any more paperwork after signing off with the Gaos. Instead I switch on the tele and zap in on the ten o'clock news. There's the usual political shenanigans going on of how the minister lied. Cries of 'resign, resign'. Smiling ripostes and animal howls and groans in reply from the Commons bear garden. Public service workers are threatening to strike. The dead will be unburied; the living uncared for; fires will rage; refuse pile up in the streets for rats and foxes to rummage through. The spectre of ancient anarchy is invoked to keep us in line.

'Symptomatic of a lawless age,' the newscaster is saying against a background panorama of clenched fists, stones being thrown. The sound cuts in above his voice: men's shouting and women's screamed abuse. 'This normally quiet street of respectable citizens . . .' The camera focuses on the street name and then pans to the house number. It swings to the words on a couple of placards: 'Satanist; Pervert; We don't want you in our town.' The address is Galton's.

The camera sashays from face to face contorted with self-righteous rage and then to the back of the small crowd to capture the arrival of the police. As it zooms in on the police cars (Z cars, jam sandwiches? What are they called now that they're fruity coloured as ice lollies?) for a couple of seconds it picks up a silent figure at the back, a little apart. I think I recognise Ms Apple-pie Molders.

I switch channels to see if I can find another version of the news, with perhaps a second shot of her in confirmation. This time I get the beginning of the story. The protesters were alerted by a piece in the local paper. But how did the rag get hold of it? I dial directory enquiries for its number. Will there be anyone there as late as this? Perhaps I should ring Galton to see if he's inside the house and OK. I try his number.

'Yes. Who is it?'

'It's Jade Green, Dr Galton. Are you OK?'

'How did you know?'

'It's on the television news. The police have just arrived. I expect they'll want to come in. You should let them. Be nice to them. You're an innocent citizen who hasn't been charged with anything, besieged in your own home. They have to protect you. Do you want me to come down? Is there anywhere you can go? They should put a guard on the house.'

'There's nowhere I can go, except perhaps to one of our coven but I don't want to involve them. If they'll send these people away and leave someone on duty here I'd rather stay in my own home. It's good of you to offer to come down but by the time you could get here I hope they'd all be gone.'

While he's speaking I'm watching the Molders moving away from the back of the crowd. Mission accomplished. I decide not to tell Galton what I think I've seen. After all I'm not absolutely sure and he might spill it to the cops as a fact or do something silly with the information.

'There's someone at the door, Ms Green. I expect as you say it'll be the police. Thank you for calling. I'll ring you in the morning.'

'Earlier if you need me. I'll try to find out how all this started.' Is he frightened or just excited? I can't tell from his voice. I decide it's too late now to ring the paper. Sleep on it, Jade.

When I ask for the editor in the morning I can just imagine the set up. 'Trisha speaking. Can I help? I'll see if Mr Hanks is available. Who shall I say is calling?'

Hanks comes on the line with a triple note 'Hal-lo-ah. Ms Green, is it? What can I do for you?'

'I represent Dr Alastair Galton, Mr Hanks. The man whose house was besieged last night as a result of a piece in your paper. I'd like a copy of that article and to know where you got your information.'

'We never reveal our sources, Ms Green.'

'Don't make it hard for me, Mr Hanks, or I could make it hard for you. I don't imagine your paper could stand an action for libel, let alone the damages Dr Galton would undoubtedly be awarded.'

'We merely reported the facts.'

'There are no facts except that Dr Galton has not been charged with anything and is therefore entitled to his privacy and to not being libelled by your publication. Are you a lawyer, Mr Hanks? If not I suggest that you consider carefully what I have said.'

'The local library has a copy.'

'I haven't time for that, Mr Hanks. I need one now. I suggest you fax one to me as soon as we finish this conversation. Now for my second point. Did your information come from the police?'

'Alright.' He's suddenly understood the seriousness of what I am suggesting. 'It was an anonymous tip-off. A phone call.'

'Did you get the number?'

'I told you it was anonymous.'

'And you didn't use 1471 to find out?'

'No.'

'Did you attempt to verify the allegation?'

'I checked the name and address on the electoral roll. I rang the college and asked to speak to Dr Galton. They said he no longer worked there. So I knew I'd got the right guy. Look, I don't want any trouble. We run on a shoestring. I can't tell you any more than I have, and what's in the piece.'

'Fax me a copy then, Mr Hanks. You do have a fax machine? What was the voice of your informant like? Male or female?'

'It was muffled. It could have been deep female or light male. I thought they'd put something over the mouthpiece. People often do if they're giving information anonymously. Or else these days they text or email.'

'I need to see the whole piece to decide how libellous it might be.'

'Look, we didn't mean any harm. I wasn't to know they'd besiege the guy's house. I can't be held responsible for people getting worked up about something they read in the paper. Christ knows it's hard enough to get them to buy one, unless it's got their kid's birthday in it. OK, I'll fax it to you. What's the number?'

When I tell him he says: 'That's a London number.'

'Yes indeed. My office is in London.' Just in case he thinks he's dealing with some little local firm.

When the fax comes through I see why Hanks suddenly decided to cooperate. It's all there: the arrest, Galton's name and address, the fact that he was naked, his dismissal from Wessex. The only thing that isn't in the piece is why he was sacked. But the implication of 'not safe with young people' is enough to damn him as a paedophile, and bring out the self-appointed guardians of public morality baying for blood. If it weren't all true, Galton could demand a printed apology at least. But anyway that isn't what I'm after. I'm trying to figure out why the Wessex people should pursue him in this way. Is it just spite or their own version of self-righteousness?

By getting himself arrested he gave them the opportunity to hit back at him, even if someone (Molders?) was behind that too. But it doesn't tell me why. I could ask Galton point-blank but somehow I don't think I'd get an answer, not the real one anyway. An evasion if not a full-blown lie.

I ring Galton. 'How are you this morning, Dr Galton? Did you talk to the police? Did you get some sleep?'

'I did as you suggested and asked for their help. They were quite correct and polite. I realise of course that our beliefs seem strange to them. One of them I thought would have been less sympathetic if he had been on his own and in charge. Fortunately his superior realised his responsibilities in keeping the peace and protecting an innocent member of the public.'

He's sounding smug again and I can feel myself getting tetchy. 'If anyone tries to interview you from the press don't talk to them. Have you still got police protection?'

'They went off about midnight after all the people had gone away. They said I should telephone if there was any more trouble.'

'And the TV cameras?'

'They left soon after the police turned up and dispersed the crowd. I watched it all from my bedroom.'

'Can you see if there's anyone there now?'

'There is someone, I think. On the other side of the road, looking up at the house from time to time. Unless he's a burglar I can't think why else he would be there.'

'He'll pounce on you if you go out, and try to get an interview. Be very careful. Remember what I've said. Don't talk to anyone, except me or the police. I think I'm going to be paying a visit to Wessex. I might need to talk to you. If you're going out call me on my mobile.'

'Ms Green, I have to say when I asked you to help me out with my little problem I had no idea things would escalate in this way. I am so grateful for your support.'

'Don't worry Dr Galton, my bill will soon fix that.' I ring off angry with myself at my own sharp tongue. It's when the guy gets yucky I find myself lashing out. I wonder why he hasn't tried to recruit me for his coven. I should have warned him above all to lie low and not go dancing about in the woods at night.

There's no pleasure in a run on the Crusader today. For one it's raining and two it's Friday. Everyone's already heading out of town in the spray from the car in front. Pile-up time on the motorway. I steer well clear of both the plodders and the racers. I can't wait to get out of my wet gear when I get to the Wessex bike shed. Are you getting old, Jade? You used to find bombing along in the rain, using all your skills, exhilarating. Or is it just that for so long post-Helen you didn't care if you lived or died and now, suddenly you have a stake in being alive; though I couldn't pin down what if anything it's based on and it may not last, may be just a delusory false dawn. There goes Rosalind again in my head cocking a sharp eye, sticking out her sharp tongue. 'Men have died and worms have eaten them, but not for love.'

Maybe I should just come clean. March into the dean's office and say: 'I'm representing Dr Galton, the lecturer you sacked and we're going to sue you for unfair dismissal and harassment.' But I still haven't any proof. I'd be thrown out of Wessex at once with no chance to gather any evidence ever again. How can I prove it was an anonymous tip-off from here that set the mob on Galton?

I head for my tutor's room and knock on the door, not expecting any result. To my surprise the door opens and Dr Davidson is peering out at me. 'Yes?'

'Lucy Cowell, Dr Davidson. I wonder if you could spare a few minutes.'

He smiles in recognition. 'Ah yes, of course. How are you getting on, Ms Cowell? Do come in. As a matter of fact I have an envelope for you here. Ms Molders, the dean's secretary, asked me to pass it on to you if you should be in touch. Now where did I put it? Do sit down.'

I take the chair on the opposite side of his desk, while he opens drawers and fumbles about in them. There's a newspaper upside down on his desk that he must have been reading when I knocked. I see it's the same page of the local rag that I'm carrying among my own papers. He looks up shutting the drawer and pushes a manila A4 envelope across the desktop towards me. I point towards the piece of newsprint.

'A nasty business,' I say. 'I understand he was sacked from Wessex.'

'How do you know?'

'I read it in the same local paper. And there was something about him on the news last night. Did you know him, Dr Davidson? Perhaps you didn't overlap here. That was a strange thing: for the crowd to attack his house. I mean it was a very extreme response to just a paragraph of newsprint.'

'"Though shalt not suffer a witch to live." Isaiah.'

'A witch? I thought they died out long ago apart from children's fiction.'

'Children's fiction deals in wizards, I believe. Think of *The Wizard of Oz* among others. A witch is a quite different matter. They don't wear pointed hats and jet about on broomsticks of course. The witch is a very real figure.'

'But the accounts of witch trials . . .'

'Can be read either way. You can take Reginald Scott's view

that they were deluded and mostly old, women. Or you can read the accounts of the trials as very often showing malevolent intentions to harm, even kill, their victims and of evil familiars who did their bidding or pacts with the forces of darkness. After all many of them confessed to all these things. And if you believe there is a force for good operating in the world then you must also envisage a force for evil. Otherwise how can you account for all the violence and immorality in the world?'

'Human folly?' I know from our last meeting that it's no good putting forward the view that, being just very clever apes, *Homo habilis*, not very *sapiens* and not genetically far removed from *Pan troglodytes*, our cousin, who also commits rape and murder on occasion, so-called evil is only what's to be expected of us.

'Led into temptation by someone or something.'

Again I want to say: by territorialism and competition for status and the food supply, and the chance to pass on your genes through the best combination for survival, beauty and brains.

'Good and evil: a constant struggle but in the end good must prevail and we must make sure we are there among the elect.'

I realise now that Dr Davidson isn't just a lecturer at Wessex. He's one of the chosen, the inner elite. It isn't only the theology students who are the Temple of the Latent Christ. There must be others like Davidson scattered through the faculty. And there's nothing to stop them spreading their nutty beliefs except common sense. Just sometimes a judge will rule that a child must be given a blood transfusion against the parents' wishes and beliefs or parents be forced to send their children to school, but on the whole we don't interfere. A child's body is found half burnt with strange signs cut into the soft skin or another is beaten to drive out the evil spirits, and then the social services are blamed for not doing a proper job, a job we make sometimes impossible with our tolerance of individuality to the point of negligence. You mustn't interfere. Live and let live. Freedom of expression. The fifth amendment or is it the first? You're wandering, Jade. Davidson is looking at me curiously.

'I'm sorry, Dr Davidson. What you were saying was so interesting, even inspiring, that my mind was carried away. Would you say those ideas are close to the beliefs of the Manichaeans?'

'The Manichaeans were called heretics, Ms Cowell. I don't know how much church history you've studied. I find that students these days rather wish to concentrate on the twentieth century to the neglect of the more distant past, the origins of our faith. What interests them is the rise of fascism. That sort of thing. But in the history of the last two thousand years that's just a blip.'

Suddenly I have a vision of our sorry human past where two world wars and the Holocaust are just a hiccup in the depressing vertical panorama of malfeasance with only an occasional upland lit by hope. I dig around for something to say that will keep this insane, yet illuminating, conversation going.

'I seem to remember the Albigenses were Manichaeans too. Didn't they come to a bad end?'

'They were wiped out by a crusade against them by the Christian church: that is the institution that managed to gain power over The Word at the end of the first century of Our Lord and that has decreed ever since what is God's Word, the true way of life and how he should be worshipped. But there have always been those who resisted, often in secret, and who kept the temple of their bodies and hearts. The first were the Essenes into whose embrace the Lord came when he was baptised by John in the desert and fought the spirit of darkness, fasting on the mountain top.'

I recognise the cadences of this speech from the internet sermon by Apostle Joachim. 'After our discussion, Dr Davidson, my thesis seems irrelevant.'

'Who can say, Ms Cowell, where any piece of research will

lead? It may be you will be guided to some revelation for yourself or others that will change your view of the world for ever.'

I can't quite see Tudor stage cross-dressing fitting into this scenario but then, as the man says, who can tell? I stand up.

'I'm sorry; I've taken up far more than I should of your time. It has been most enlightening.'

'Study the material Ms Molders has given you, Ms Cowell, and then we can talk again.' He stretches out a hand to shake mine and I realise that the flesh I had thought dry and papery before is now hot and moist. Davidson is really hooked on all this stuff and he thinks he has a chance of making a convert.

I'm outside his door clutching my notes for my supposed thesis which we haven't even discussed, and the manila envelope that I guess is meant to show me the way, set me on the path for enlightenment or whatever word they use. I wander off into the quadrangle. The rain has stopped. The sun comes out and the grass smells fresh and damp with spangles of diamond light catching on every blade. O brave new world that can be renewed by this fall of natural spray. I need to think. A pity I hadn't got a mini recorder wired up in my pocket so that I could run the interview by again and tease out its implications. Instead I shall have to remember all I can, hoping that not too much has slipped my mind.

I wander on through the arch at the other side of the quadrangle and realise I'm on the edge of a part of the grounds I haven't visited before. Away beyond a stretch of grass with a path running through there's a modern red-brick building partly sunk below a sloping mound that's like the defence for a medieval castle. The red brick will be a cosmetic skin over steel and concrete. The lower windows and doors look out into a grassy well. A way of having another storey without going too high, typical of late twentieth-century public buildings, uni campuses and hospitals.

Following the path I'm led down to a glass door. No one

seems to be about. The windows are blankly shut with no sound of music or voices coming through them. There are no trees nearby so no birdsong, and no insects zooming busily over the grass that looks tired because it's been shaved too close. Scorch marks show through the greenish bristle that the rain hasn't refreshed. There's a nameplate on the door. The Temple of John. John who? Baptist or Evangelist?

'This building is protected. Back off or an alarm will sound!' I reel back a couple of steps, out of range as I hope of a security system that sounds more like the most extreme of car alarms with its aggressive transatlantic vocals. I can see an entry phone like the one on the main gate. I get out my pass card and approach the door quickly hoping to beat what must be an outer beam and stick my card in the slot.

'This card is not valid for these premises. Insert the right card or return to the main building.'

I extract my card and hastily back away. I don't want to be caught seeming a snoop. People might begin to wonder why Lucy Cowell is so often in the wrong place at the right time. As directed by the disembodied voice I head back for the central block. Passing the chapel I hear singing and rhythmic clapping and scurry away to the bike shed before the elect come out and find me there again where I shouldn't be.

Is it fear that is so enervating that when I get home I can hardly climb the stairs and fall asleep on my bed without bothering to check my messages? When I wake it's dark and I'm hungry. I think with nostalgia of Mary Gao's takeaway suppers steaming in their little foil dishes. Opening the fridge I settle for some Camembert from the French cheese stall in the market. The bread in the bin has spots of leprous mould. I find an unopened packet of water biscuits that might not be quite stale, ignore the use-by date, and pour myself a glass of wine. Then I set the computer to search for Manichaeans and Albigenses.

My take on them both was rusty but as it turns out when

the machine finishes its search, quite close to the facts, given that I hadn't considered either of them since my student days when I'd briefly had to think about how other value systems might affect a society's laws.

'What is the possible effect on the perception of crime and its treatment in legislation of a belief system that sees the world and society as an eternal battleground between darkness and light? Discuss.'

Manichaeans: system based on old Babylonian religion modified by Christian and Persian influences. Founded by Mani circa 200 AD who taught that Christ had come into the world to restore light and banish darkness but that his apostles had prevented his doctrine and Mani was sent as the Paraclete to put it right.

Albigenses: Manichaean sect twelfth to fourteenth century in southern France and northern Italy. Called after the city of Albi in Languedoc where they were first persecuted. Finally exterminated by church and inquisition at the end of the fourteenth century. Also called Cathars and Bulgarians. Many of the aristocratic troubadours were members of the sect.

Were they accused of buggery, 'unnatural' practices? Is that where The Word comes from?

Paraclete: the Holy Ghost, the Comforter. See *Abelard* and *Heloise*.

There's no end to this but I don't follow up on the two starcrossed lovers. Their story is still poignant, an open wound that searched, leads to too much related pain, a wound that you hoped had scarred over. And how much suffering lies behind that phrase 'finally exterminated'; one of the constantly recurring genocides only, like the Bosnians and Croats, ethnically the same people divided by history and religion.

So the Manichaeans and the Albigenses all perished, did they? Well, I have news for the encyclopedists: they are alive and well, and living in modern Wessex, as well as the many other parts of the world wherever the internet spreads its mesh. Old beliefs die hard or perhaps they never do. Maybe they're embedded deep in the human psyche just waiting for the right button to be pushed to pop out again with all their bizarre compulsion.

What does it all mean for Galton? You might think his lot and all the Latent Christ lot would have lots and lots in common. Except that the latter-day Albigenses would probably think witches are Satanists, worshipping darkness, just like the popular image of them in the tabloids. Abusing children with unspeakable obscenities. And now the internet itself has become a trawling ground for real paedophiles and their porno pics that somewhere must involve the abuse of real children. You can see why the Manichaeans might have had something going for them with their doctrine of the perversion of Christianity and setting themselves against the triumph of darkness, when the established church was at its most repressive and venal. They were the pre-Reformation Puritans. All those religious taking backhanders for pardons to support their lovers just as Chaucer tells it.

But that's history as they say. Here and now it's the televangelists conning people, going on their knees on screen for their sins while salting away the dosh. Then there's the leaflets that come through the letter box with the rest of the junk mail. Madame Sosostris, Eliot's clairvoyant, had nothing on the palm, crystal ball and tarot readers preying on mostly migrant people, uprooted, disenfranchised of their own language and culture.

Ever since I started on this case I've been making a collection of them, instead of binning the mostly A3 leaflets with their seductive offerings of problem-solving and hope.

'Do you feel your life is being controlled by evil spirits and darkness? Are you a victim of witchcraft or black magic?' Sister Sabera has the answer. 'My work is powerful and accurate. Suffer no more for I will cure you and set you free.'

Then there's the Rasta guy in the market who gives out advice off the cuff. His clients must pay him something but I've never actually seen money change hands. I wonder if they go home and follow the advice, comforted. 'Do you need your home blessed, Aura cleansed, Spirit Enlightened? Mrs Telrala is the one for you.' Kala, Jaada, Obeah, Ju-Ju curses.

How contemptuous Galton must be of this lot and yet his is only the upmarket version of what they're offering. Peace, hope, the longed-for love. Suddenly I'm remembering a part of my conversation with Davidson. He knew Galton was a witch, and if he does then so do other people at Wessex. The likelihood that he was set up with the police by them or some of them is almost irresistible.

It wasn't enough to sack him. He has to be destroyed because his beliefs contradict theirs or rather he is the enemy, darkness, the evil one, the great beast, and his high priestess, no doubt, the whore of Babylon.

My lady called me to her. 'My brother's secretary Mr Roland Whyte, writes at his command to tell me my younger son is secretly contracted to Lady Susan de Vere for love, neither his friends or hers knowing of it, except my son, the earl, who was it seems acquainted with his brother's intention even before his own wedding. It appears that at first her uncle, her guardian, was very troubled at it, my younger son not standing to inherit his father's lands and title, but his majesty has given them his blessing and makes all friends. The marriage will be at court on St John's Day so I must go to London again and the Lady Anne also for she is to take part in a masque to be presented on Twelfth Night. Therefore you must come with me to oversee her physick.'

I was glad to be part of all this. It would give me the chance to make further provision for my future, for my lady went on,

'While I am there I must seek out some convenient lodging to lie in for all now must be ceded to my son, the earl, once this second match is concluded. So I shall make close enquiry among my friends and those of my sons. God grant I have enough remaining for me to pay for my decent lodging but his will be done.'

So again I prepared myself, my instruments and medicines, for London but this time not knowing whether I should ever return to my home country. And again I rode under the gloomy walls of Baynard's but not to lie there, for the castle was filled to overflowing with many come as well for the marriage as for Christmas and although some lay at Whitehall at the court, as my lady's brother Robert, Baron of Penshurst, now chamberlain to her majesty Queen Anne, yet his family lay at the castle for his daughter was also to bear a part in the masque for Twelfth Night. Therefore I found myself lodging at the house of a good woman nearby, rather than be forced to lie in the stable or under the stairs. She was the readier to take me on hearing I was physician to the countess, begging me to prescribe something to relieve her husband's gout, which affected his humour to anger so that he would often strike her in his pain, and when I was able to do this and gave him back his accustomed kindness, she let me lie without payment.

From her house I was the more able to go about without notice when not expressly sent for by the countess. I began to make myself acquainted with all the branches of my profession, as apothecaries, physicians, barber surgeons, their halls and favoured taverns so that I might rub shoulders with them. I found that there were many that had been in like case with myself, unlicensed practitioners who had no degree of learning from either university nor any licence of a bishop but had set themselves up, sometimes beyond the city walls or across the river where the Barber Surgeons Company could not reach them. Yet I feared to be on my own in the world with none to turn to, still considering how I might become assistant or apprenticed to some master, and how that in those days which the duenna remembers, sometimes lamenting their passing, I might have found refuge in a nunnery where I could practise my cunning.

On the day before the eve of Christmas I made my way to Bread Street Hill close to the College of Physicians in Knightriders Street and therefore but a short distance from Baynard's and the house where I lodged, to the sign of the Star where the printer Peter Short, who had put out that book of *De Magnete* by Dr Gilbard, had his shop. In the pocket of my slops lay a fair copy of my book of receipts. Master Short's apprentice, as I thought him, received me, asking if I would buy or sell and if the former I must go to the bookseller's in Paul's churchyard or Paternoster Row.

'Had there been one here for sale I would have bought a copy of *De Magnete* even though I have come here principally to sell. And if you will fetch your master I will show him my wares.'

'You may show me first,' said the lad who was about my age or younger. 'I will tell you if what you have is worth anything which I doubt if it is a work of your own.'

'It is a work principally of my father's and therefore far above your understanding. If your master is not to be spoken with I will take the book elsewhere. There are many printers in London so I am told,' then I made as if to turn away.

'Please sir be seated,' the boy said hastily knowing that he had gone too far in his arrogance, and retired to the back of the shop returning with an old man who pulled himself along with difficulty by clutching at the table and leaning heavily on a stick.

'Well young master what do you have that I must see?'

My heart sank at the sight of him for I had hoped that he might oversee my future but I saw instead that he had not long in this world.

'It is a book of receipts of my father's devising that was a noted physician and philosopher in his own country of Wiltshire, and a friend to Dr William Gilbard of Colchester, physician to his majesty.'

'Lately deceased, whither I shall soon follow him. A man of great wisdom and learning whom the world will one day justly recognise as a prince among natural philosophers.'

Drawing the book from my pocket I put it into his shaking hands.

He opened the cover and read aloud: 'A Dispensatory of the choicest and most efficacious receipts for use in the household, Robert Bostoni Sarumensis; augmento AB.' And are you AB?'

'I am sir, Amyntas Boston, physician to the Countess of Pembroke.'

'Among many, young man, in such a great household.'

'Indeed sir.'

'I shall need time to consider this. Can you return tomorrow?'

So I left my book in his hands and went back to my lodging where I found a boy waiting on me come from the countess. It seemed the Lady Anne was sick and in need of my help, for the marriage of her brother was in only a matter of days at which she must play her part, to be closely followed by the masque in which she was among those ladies who principally attended upon her majesty.

It was clear when I came into her bedchamber that she was indeed very sick. I would have had her rest in her bed but she cried out that she must rise and not be left out of the ceremonies and that if I could not give her something to restore her vital spirits her mother should send for someone who could. Thus I was driven to prescribe a pectoral syrup of *Marrubium album*, or horehound, which is hot and dry, to cut and bring away the concentrated blood of ulcerated lungs and conglutinate them. And after, she vomited much black blood and phlegm, then lay back on her pillows exhausted. Next I prescribed a cordial of powdered gold to strengthen her heart, vital and animal spirits, a remedy only to be applied *in extremis* as being too costly for everyday use.

The next day I prevailed with her to rest in expectation that she would be well enough to rise for her brother's wedding, continuing the medicines as before until her breath came more easily and she voided no more blood, a sign that the ulcers were conglutinating indeed. So I passed the feast of Christ's nativity in watching over her sick bed. In the afternoon of Boxing Day she rose for the first time and by the next day, which was set for the wedding, she appeared perfectly well and attended the ceremony in the chapel and after at the masque, but did not dance and I did prevail upon her mother to bid her leave the company at a reasonable hour, for the revels continued long into the night with all the usual jesting as at the young earl's wedding.

As the time of the great masque for Twelfth Night drew near I made sure she was fed well on broth, blancmanger of chicken breast, and eggs beaten in milk, so that by the 5th of January she appeared in the bloom of her youth. All this consumed so much of my time that I had not returned to Mr Short the printer his shop to hear the verdict on my book whether he would print it or not. Until on the eleventh day of Christmas leaving the Lady Anne in good spirits I was at last able to make my way there, only to find it all shuttered for the holiday, as I hoped, and not through any mischance of Mr Short.

We rose in the dark next morning for the household had three masquing ladies to dress. After all had broken fast I persuaded the Lady Anne to take a draught of the gold cordial to sustain her throughout the long day's festivities and then went to my lady.

'You shall attend me as my page Amyntas so that you are at hand if the Lady Anne should begin to fail. I hope she will take no harm from the thin attire and the staining of her skin for personating Ethiopians. My brother says it is the queen's own fancy to dress as a Negro she having the whitest skin in the world. My brother has a new suit for the occasion of ash-coloured satin, trimmed with peach taffeta and silver lace.'

We set out in several coaches for Whitehall where the ladies were to be painted and put on their attire while the rest of us took up our places. At last his majesty being sat, by the light of what seemed a thousand sconces we saw a landscape of woods where hunters roamed until an artificial sea shot forth with waves and billows which seemed to break on the shore. In front of this sea were six Tritons, their upper parts human and their hind parts fish, with their tails above their heads of blue hair, blowing music on seashells. Behind them were two mermaids singing, then, mounted on the backs of seahorses, Oceanus and Niger came forward to introduce the masquers seated in a mother of pearl shell that rose and fell on the waters and was lit by a garland of lights that showed off the masquers' attire, all alike in azure and silver, laced with ropes of pearl, their arms bare to the elbows and painted black like their faces with strings of pearl to set off their dark skins. Twelve torch-bearers were carried on the backs of the sea monsters illuming the whole scene, which was in motion and prospective as if the ocean were come into the hall under a cloudy moon.

There followed a song and speeches by Oceanus and Niger. This last, who according to the poet was the father of the Ethiop masquers, explained that his daughters were to seek a land whose name ended in Tania where their black skins would be whitened in the temperate climate. The moon herself appeared all in white on a silver throne that seemed to float in the upper part of the hall. She proclaimed that the land they had reached was formerly Albion but now restored to its ancient dignity and style of Britannia. The masquers descended from their shell and chose everyone a man to dance with, her majesty leading out the Spanish ambassador for several meas-ures and corantoes. My lady whispered to me that the music was by Mr Ferrabosco who was now in the queen's service.

After all the dancing two boys of the Chapel Royal sang in treble to call the masquers back to the sea which song was iterated in its chorus by a double echo from several parts of the land. So the ladies danced their way back to their shell, returning to the sea with these verses:

> Now Dian with her burning face
> Declines apace:
> By which our waters know
> To ebb, that late did flow.
>
> Back seas, back nymphs; but with a forward grace
> Keep still your reverence to the place
> And shout with joy of favour you have won
> In sight of Albion, Neptune's son.

His majesty led the applause which echoed round the hall. The music struck up again and the queen and ladies returned to refresh themselves and dance some more. A gentleman standing close behind her caught my lady's eye. 'Well Mr Carleton,' she said, 'was that not a pretty conceit of the poet to find cause to bring Ethiop ladies to Albion and also restore the old kingdom of Britannia as it was known to Caesar and Tacitus?'

'You will forgive me madam that I must disagree. As one who has been part of his majesty's embassy in Paris I am sorry that strangers should see our court so strangely disguised. The ladies' apparel was rich I grant but too light and courtesan-like and their black faces and hands a very loathsome sight.'

The Lady Anne came running to her mother with her new sister Lady Susan, and her cousin Lady Mary, still with their black arms and faces.

'Were we not beautiful Negroes madam? The queen was so

delighted with it she says we shall be blackamoors again next year.'

Her face was very pale under its blackness, her eyes burning too brightly, and I knew that were her cheeks washed the red flush of fever would appear. She coughed a little and put her hand to her mouth. When she brought it away I saw a fleck of blood on her palm.

'Madam, the Lady Anne should rest now.'

'Oh your page is such a spoiler madam. I am here to dance. Give me some more of your cordial Master Boston to keep my vital spirits tuned to the music.'

'I would rather give you something madam to make you sleep.'

'You lean too much on the skills of a mere boy madam my mother. If he cannot give me the strength to play my part among my peers you must find me one who can.'

I knew that it was the disease that spoke, for often with phthisis it is the case that it affects the humour making the person of an impatient that is to say a choleric temper by raising the heat of the blood even in those who are by nature phlegmatic, cold and moist.

I fetched a box of remedies and drew out a flask of the gold cordial which I now kept always at hand, but as I was measuring it into a cup I was able to slip in a little powdered poppy for I feared to see her vomit blood from her lungs before her mother and the whole court. She took some wine after and some marchpane sweetmeats while I watched to see the poppy work on her, and after a little while she yawned and said: 'Perhaps I will go to the ladies' tiring room where is a soft pallet to rest on, and afterwards I will dance.'

One of the maids led her away, and returned saying she had fallen at once into a deep slumber as soon as she lay down.

'Is this your doing Amyntas?'

'Yes madam. The Lady Anne was so lately sick almost to

death, that she must not put her body to exertions it is yet incapable of if she is to recover her full strength.' Yet I knew that when she woke she would be angry and would look for some way to punish me or rid herself of my care.

And so it proved. 'The Lady Anne is no longer willing that you should physick her. She has obliged me to send for Dr Adrian Gilbert to be her physician, for in talking to him on several occasions he has assured her of a cure and cast up her horoscope to prove it, as she believes. She says you have never attempted to make any such prediction or to call on the influence of the heavenly bodies that direct our fates.'

'Madam this I confess, for my father . . .'

'Your father also refused to help me when I almost begged him to come into my household.'

I understood the danger I was in, yet I thought that I must speak for the Lady Anne her sake as well as my own.

'My father did not believe that our fate is within the stars for he was of the opinion that they were not fixed and that the planets moved as the earth does about the sun and so could not determine the future; that Venus and Mars their influence were conceits of the poets. Madam be careful of false hopes raised in a sick person, especially one so young who desires above all to live and thrive.'

'What are you saying Amyntas? Why do you threaten me? I cannot lose my only daughter.'

'My lady, God knows I do not threaten, only warn that the Lady Anne must be treated with great delicacy and not weakened with purging or letting of blood.'

'Some believe that such courses are necessary to drive out ill humours and diseases as a cat or dog will eat grass for physick, vomit up some foulness it has taken and then be well again.'

I saw that this dispute was hardening her against me by the tapping of her foot, and her hand upon the arm of the chair she sat in. 'You will be always disputing and yet you are yourself only a child, a child who thinks she knows better than men of learning. I will send for you if I need you. I am to rent a house of the Earl of Southampton, friend to my sons, at Crosby Place. I shall have much to do to furnish it to my liking. Perhaps you can be useful in this in some way.'

'Madam you know I am only at your service in all things.' So I bowed and left her, making my way to the little attic room in the goodwife's house where I slept among rows of apples stored there and the scent of their sweet decay. The next day I went out into the city and resumed my search for employment with some master. When I returned to my lodging the woman stopped me as I was about to climb first the stairs and then the ladder for my attic, where I could sit upon a little stool beside the window under the eaves and look out on roofs and clouds and sometimes a bird beating its way against the wind or riding the air light as one of its own feathers.

'Here is my neighbour Master Boston, who has a withered hand and begs your help. I have told him of the ease you brought about in my good man, so that now he is able to go about his business again.'

I made the man, who was thin and stooped, with wire-framed spectacles on his nose, sit down at her table and stretch out his hand which he was not able to do easily it being turned in upon itself like a bird's claw. 'What was your occupation sir? It would seem that you suffer from scrivener's palsy in an extreme state.'

'I am indeed a scrivener but now I have lost my employ, and my customers, for I cannot hold a quill with this hand and however much I try with the other the letters are so crabbed that no one can be pleased by them, least of all I who have always prided myself on the neatness of my copying hand and the fineness of my penmanship.'

'It will need patience on your part if there is to be an improvement. I cannot promise that it will be so but if you will do as I say you may be able to hold a quill again.' I took his hand in my two and began to press upon it and to flex the crooked fingers while kneading in oil of Exeter. 'Do you have a wife sir?'

'No. But I have a daughter who helps me in my work as well as keeping house. Have while she is mine before a husband takes her from me.'

'You must have your daughter do as I do now, morning and night, with this same oil warmed and her hands also. Now try if you can move your fingers of yourself.'

I let go of his hand and placing it upon the table he found that he could move the fingers a little from the second joint of each. 'As soon as there is more flexing in the sinews you must practise each day in spite of the pain and stiffness and continue your daughter's rubbing the parts twice daily with the oil. That you can move your fingers now must give you hope and patience to persevere.'

'How can I reward you young master? Here are two gold crowns and you shall have more if I can hold a quill again.'

'If that should happen you may make me a fair copy of a little book I have which will be payment enough.' For I feared that my dealings with the printer had been short indeed and stopped by infirmity or death itself so that now, apart from that I gave my lady, I had but one remaining copy and my own life was so in doubt that I could not foresee when I should have the liberty to make another.

Now alone in my attic I felt the bitterness of being cast upon the world where no one knew me. From the bustle and constant movement of court and castle I was forced to pass my hours in solitude or in converse with my landlady or her good man.

At last came a message from the countess to attend on her at Baynard's but if I had hoped to be received alone and given some commission to do her service it was not to be for when I was shown to her chamber I found she was accompanied by her steward, a lady of her bedchamber and Dr Adrian Gilbert.

It was he who spoke to me as soon as I entered while my lady remained silent and grave.

'The Lady Anne is very sick and wasting daily. I believe you have poisoned her with your pretended medicines, either through envy or lack of that skill that comes only from learning and the accreditation of the learned men of the profession, I mean the Royal College of Physicians or some such. Your meddling has put her life in danger and I do not know if all my efforts can save her, in spite of the favourable prognostication given by her horoscope. I will not be blamed for the mistakes of another. The constable has been sent for to arrest you for practising as a physician without a licence like your countryman, the rogue and necromancer, Forman.'

Then a servant entered. 'Madam the constable is here and asks admittance.' I fell on my knees before my lady.

'Madam I cannot go to the common gaol. I would rather die.'

'The information has been laid by the Lady Anne and Dr Gilbert and I cannot gainsay it. My sons and other friends are angry too and believe that I have been cozened too long. I cannot help you Amyntas. You must shift for yourself.' And my lady signalled for the servant and turned away from me.

Last night I felt I'd been neglecting Amyntas Boston's memoir through the pressure of the day and especially the developments in Galton's life, if you can call it that. So I eschewed TV and settled down with my bottle of D'Oc (was that the Languedoc of the Albigenses?) to catch up on Amyntas' story. After all that was what had set everything going. Or was it? Was the memoir just a blind on the part of Wessex to get rid of Galton or was it just a blind on his part to get me hooked on his case? But then how did he know it was the kind of story that would get to me? Because I called my firm Lost Causes and hers is such a lost cause. Maybe he waited to decide until he saw me or maybe some weird ritual of his own picked me out from the Yellow Pages. Eenie, meenie, minie, mo.

A couple of glasses later I put down the neatly typed pages in horror. Once again I'm gripped. I want to reach back across four centuries and offer her help, comfort. She's been arrested. The countess has turned her back on her. There's not much more to go. The pages are thinning out. I could easily read on to the end. But I have to stop. It's too painful and too late at night. I don't want to know. I don't want it to be over.

Now it's morning and other problems need my attention. You've got bread to earn, Jade. I've been asked to write another article on the difference between common law and civil law systems and how the twain can meet. I find myself actually enjoying it like chewing on a stale crust. I'm beginning to wonder whether I'm really an academic manqué, not cut out for the harsh reality of commercial practice, when the phone rings.

'Miss Jade?'

'Charlie?'

'Miss Jade, I am so sorry to trouble you but something has happened.'

'To your aunt and uncle, to the shop?'

'No, Miss Jade.'

'Where are you, Charlie?'

'I'm at Wessex at the uni. Miss Jade, someone has died. I think we must talk. I don't know anyone else.'

'Meet me at the bike shed in an hour. You know where it is?'

'Yes, Miss Jade. I will wait for you there.' It looks like I'm not destined to be a don after all.

Charlie's face is even graver than usual when I wheel the Crusader into the shed nearly an hour later. I take off my helmet and gloves.

'Thank you for coming, Miss Jade.'

'Tell me what's happened.'

'One of the students has been found dead.'

'How do you know? Why aren't the police here?'

'They are trying to keep it quiet as long as possible.'

'They?'

'The dean and others.'

'What others?'

'The owners. The Temple people.'

'Then how do you know?'

'I have a friend here. One of the theology students. He is very worried, frightened.'

'Which of the students has died, Charlie?'

'She was in theology too. She was from Africa. Ghana, I think. Her name was Hester Ado.'

At once I have a picture of the girl in the chapel, in a state of trance, falling down and being lifted into a chair and, after, led away stumbling.

'And your friend. Is he from Africa?'

'He is from Goa.'

'Why is he frightened?'

'He thinks she has collapsed and died because of pressure that was put on her that her heart wasn't strong enough to deal with or even that she has been persuaded to kill herself.'

'What kind of pressure?'

'My friend says that she was recently made one of the elect because she can easily go into a trance. They call it receiving the spirit. But afterwards she was very sick and depressed.'

'Like coming down from a high. Well, they won't be able to conceal it for long. It's a serious offence not to notify a death. Someone will find out.'

'Perhaps they have a doctor who will say she was ill.'

'Provide a death certificate you mean?'

'Then she will be flown back to her family for burial.'

'Who else knows about this?'

'My friend says the theologs all know and some of the staff. No one is talking about it.'

'Aren't they all frightened like your friend?'

'He says they are brainwashed. That they believe the world is coming to an end soon anyway so it doesn't matter when they die.'

'Why doesn't he think like that too?'

'He came here because he wanted to be a missionary. He is from a Christian family but after he had been here a few months he began to have doubts. Then when we met it all came together for him.' Charlie is looking at me very straight. 'You see they are taught not to have friends, not to love except God. They must be celibate, even in their thoughts.'

'"God make me chaste but not yet."'

'I don't understand, Miss Jade.'

'St Augustine, I think. There was a lot of celibacy about among the early Christians. St Paul's fault. And others. The question now is: do we inform the police? We've got no evidence. Maybe they've spirited her away already. Poor girl.'

'A letter will be sent with a copy of the doctor's certificate. She's probably on her way to the chapel of rest at Heathrow already. What can her parents do or even know so far away? They thought their daughter was just getting a good education. These people must be stopped, Miss Jade.'

'Did you know her, Charlie? Was she a friend of yours?'

'No. I never met her. It's that . . . I haven't been quite honest with you, Miss Jade, not told you the whole truth.'

'I don't think I believe in a whole truth. But go on.'

'I didn't come here only for study. I think I told you I was being paid for by my uncle in America. There was a reason for him to do this. His only daughter, my cousin, came here to study. They got to her. At least that's what my family believes.'

'And the Gaos? Do they know all this?'

'No. They are ordinary people with their own problems. There's no need for them to be concerned with all this.'

'So how did your cousin die? I'm presuming that is what happened.'

'They said she had anorexia. She caught flu and it turned to pneumonia because of her weak condition. That was what the dean wrote and the doctor backed him up.'

'Who was the doctor?

'The name didn't mean anything to us. But he isn't here now. Now they have a Dr Hedley who attends to the students.'

'And what were you hoping to do here?'

'I suppose to try and find out some more that would help my uncle understand how Cecile died. And if anyone was to blame. You're a lawyer, Miss Jade. You could help me, advise me. If I can find out something, what should I do? You say you don't believe in "the truth" . . .'

'I've seen it distorted too often by clever lawyers to win a case. I've probably done it myself in the excitement of going after something. The chase, and then the kill. The law isn't a way of looking for the truth, Charlie. At its best it's a way of maintaining the checks and balances so that society can more or less hang together. Only at Wessex it seems to be being badly distorted, the scales weighted in favour of someone or something.'

'There's another thing, Miss Jade. My uncle is a wealthy man and my cousin had money from a trust set up by her grandmother which became hers when she was twenty-one. She left it all to the Temple. She was twenty-one and three months when she died. My friend says they all have to make everything over to the Temple when they become the elect. Some students haven't got much but others are from rich families.'

'And your friend. Where does he fit in?'

'His father is a kind of prince, I think. So far my friend hasn't been made one of the elect.'

'No aptitude for trances? We need evidence, Charlie. That's a kind of truth if you like. Facts.'

'What should I do?'

'Stay here. Keep your head down. Don't let them suspect you. They could turn nasty. What would I tell your aunt and uncle if you were found floating down the river? Keep in touch. What's your mobile number? Find out as much as you can. I have to tell you I haven't been completely open with you, either. Like you I'm not here to study. It's too long to explain but let's just say I believe your interest in Wessex and mine are linked and maybe even the same. How did you get here?'

'I came on the shop bike. It's rather slow. Not like yours but I look after it and it's very reliable. Now I must go back. I am on duty with the takeaways tonight. What will you do, Miss Jade?'

'I think for a start you should drop the handle, Charlie.'

'The handle, Miss Jade?'

He's far too young to know and from another cosmopolitan culture. He doesn't have Linda, Rob and Nana looking over his shoulder and thickening his tongue from the days when English wasn't a homogenised Lingua Americana. 'It means title, form of address. Just call me, Jade.'

'OK. Cheers, Jade. I'll be in touch.' He goes to where his own bike is propped and locked and begins to put on his helmet.

What shall I do now? As I'm here I might as well take a walk through campus and see if I can pick up anything, even if it's only from the faces of students. I go through the grounds towards the main building and take a diagonal path across the quadrangle to enter by a corner door I haven't used before. I've come into a new stretch of corridor with classrooms and labelled doors on one side and the long windows on to the quad on the other. This part of the building is quieter than others I've been to though not as deathly as the theologs' hall of residence. As I'm passing along this corridor a name on a door catches my eye. Dr R. Raval. On an impulse I knock.

'Come in.'

Now what are you letting yourself in for, Jade. 'Hallo,' I say. 'Dr Raval, I'm Lucy Cowell.'

'I'm very sorry. I can't place you. You're not a student of mine, are you?'

'Well, I nearly was. For my thesis. I couldn't decide whether I should have an overseer from English literature or history. I discussed it with the dean and in the end I went for Dr Davidson and history. But I'm not sure it wouldn't have gone better in the English department.'

'What was the topic?'

'Cross-gender in Tudor and Stuart theatre.'

'I see. Yes, you could have fitted it into either department. But it's hardly original, is it? You'll find it quite difficult to come up with a new angle. There's been a lot of published work, whole studies, that's apart from papers and theses. You'd probably find more under gender studies than literature or history.'

'So I'm discovering. I may have to reconsider the whole thing. I don't think any external examiner is going to be impressed with a rehash of Spinks. I'll have to start it from scratch and perhaps sign up with you this time.'

'I'm afraid I shan't be here much longer. I'm going to a new job in the autumn where I've got a chance to set up my own creative writing department. Just exams and grades to get through and I'm off.'

I take a chance. 'That sounds as if you'll be glad to go.'

'I don't know how long you've been here Ms . . .'

'Cowell, Lucy.'

'But my advice, in confidence, of course, would be to take your thesis elsewhere. Shall we say that Wessex isn't really geared up for postgrad research.'

I risk another throw. 'Well, I was surprised when Dr Davidson turned out to be a creationist.'

'He isn't the only one.'

Now I really go out on a limb and start sawing through the

branch behind me. 'I hear one of the students was found dead last night. Or was it this morning?'

'Who told you that?'

'I have a friend in theology.'

'No one is supposed to know.'

'You can't keep something like that quiet.'

'She was one of my students for a time. She came here to perfect her English and to study the work of African writers in the language. She was a devout Christian and joined the SCU.'

'SCU?'

'Students Christian Union. After a bit she said she wanted to change courses to theology. I tried to dissuade her. Said her work on African literature could be valuable in itself. But I lost the argument. Now she's dead. I feel I failed her. It makes me even more sure I'm doing the right thing by leaving here.'

'Do you know how she died?'

'Do you?'

'No. I do know she wasn't the first.'

'But that was different. That happened just after I came here and the student was severely anorexic. That was a very sad case.'

'Girls often find the pressure of being away from home for the first time, with so much that's new and unknown, very disturbing.'

'Oh it's not just girls. A male student hanged himself but that was in the holidays. Nothing immediately to do with Wessex.'

'Even so, you'll be glad to get away.'

'I find the atmosphere here oppressive. It's too . . .' she hesitates, 'too small. I shouldn't be saying that, of course, but since I'm leaving anyway and have another post waiting for me I have nothing to lose. But I do seriously advise you to take your thesis elsewhere. Not that you look impressionable material.' Dr Raval smiles.

Now I remember her first name: Ranee. Ranee of the raven-wing hair. I think we could have got on just fine.

'What did you want to see me about, Ms Cowell?'

'Oh, I'm sorry. I've rather wandered off the point. It was really just to apologise. I should have come to see you when I first came, in fact before I made my choice. Now I think I made the wrong decision and it's too late.'

'Let's hope it's never too late Ms Cowell, for anything. Look, if you're worried, I'm not going to the ends of the earth. I'll give you my email address. You can contact me if you want to talk about any of this further.' She scribbles it down on a sheet of paper. It's just a number and a server. Nothing to give her whereabouts away.

'Thank you. That's very kind. I'll definitely be in touch. Where are all the students today? The place seems very quiet.'

'Exams start next week. They're all at home revising, those that is that don't live on campus.'

'Like the theologs?'

'Exactly.'

Outside her door my head seems to be singing and my heart's threatening to choke me stuck somewhere in my windpipe like that same old piece of cold potato that won't go down. Before I set off I call up Galton on my mobile.

'Dr Galton. It's Jade Green. I'm at Wessex, just leaving. I thought I'd call on you. There are some things we should talk about.'

'I'll be glad to talk, Ms Green. Do you have my address?'

'Oh yes. I know your address.' I can see it in my mind's eye: the name of the road and the outside of the house as it appeared on the screen, fronted by howling faces and raised fists.

Galton opens the door for me. I've never seen him not smartly togged up in a suit before. I should have suspected that at home he wears a sandy cardigan and soft slippery moccasins. As he leads me to his sitting room I glimpse a blue silk robe, either a dressing gown à la Noel Coward or witch's mufti hanging behind a door. The furniture is almost antique. Sixty-year-old Tudor repro in dark oak, I remember from Nana's old home. The house has a musty, dusty smell as if the windows haven't been opened for a long time.

'Do sit down. Can I get you some tea or coffee? I'm afraid the chairs aren't very comfortable. This was my mother's house and I've changed very little except for my study. That's a bit more high tech. These days people seem to expect you to answer an email instantly.'

This is a new facet of Galton: the eager technobuff. Then I remember that the coven keeps in touch by email and no doubt they also contact like-minded people all over the world faster than by broomstick. I don't think I'll be offered a tour of the study. There might be a big picture of the Great Beast himself, Aleister Crowley, or some other giveaway decoration, a magician's wand, a steeple hat, eye of toad and ear of bat.

'Coffee would be great, thank you.'

While he's gone I suss the room as best I can without leaving my chair. For all I know he's got some way of observing visitors or he might come back suddenly and find me snooping. And indeed when he returns with a neat tray, laid out with cups and saucers, coffee in a pot, milk and sugar in matching china I don't hear him approach but fortunately I'm sitting sedate in my chair. He pours out the coffee with a feline delicacy. I think of *Psycho*. I wonder if Mum's still sitting skeletally upstairs somewhere.

'What do you think we should discuss, Ms Green?'

'One of the students has died but they don't seem to be informing the police. Something is going on there beyond the ordinary or even, shall we say, beyond arcane studies. I think you were set up, your dismissal that is, to get rid of you. Now I wonder whether they thought you knew what was going on and might blow the whistle on them.'

'That's a lot of questions, Ms Green, a lot of supposition. But then I've been waiting for you to reach this point. To realise

there was something more than academic spite.' He's back to
the old Galton of an almost smiling smugness that so pisses me
off. I want to get up and leave now.

'Why didn't you tell me? We might have saved a lot of time.'

'I'm afraid it was a kind of test, to see whether you were up
to the task.'

'What task?' The arrogance of the guy is breathtaking.

'Of finding out what I couldn't because they sacked me first.
There is something evil there.'

'Just because a student kills herself? Come on, Dr Galton,
we both know these things happen. Young people get depressed.
Some of them try to kill themselves with not eating, drugs or
booze, others with an overdose. I suspect if you looked into the
statistics there's at least one a term in every institute of higher
education, let alone those that go unnoticed or are covered up
by the students themselves or their families. This may be no
more than that.'

'Or much more. Those people thought I was evil. They found
a way, through my own foolishness I admit, to get rid of me,
but I believe the evil is with them. That they take vulnerable,
impressionable minds and turn them for their own purposes.'

'But what purposes?'

'I hoped you would find that out in the course of looking
into my case. And you're getting there, Ms Green. I of course
have been doing all I can in the background. I don't suppose
you believe in special powers or the influence of thought ener-
gies but I assure you it can work. After all, look at the progress
you've made already.'

'Well if the stars are on our side it's taking them a long time.'
I couldn't begin to imagine what he might be doing; what mumbo
jumbo might be going on on my, our behalf. Involving who for
fuck's sake: the goddess, the horned god?

'I must urge you to be careful, Dr Galton. No more rituals
al fresco or we could be completely discredited and then the

whole investigation would go out the window. Whatever they're up to at Wessex they would have got away with it and you would be personally no better off.' I've never told him I think he will never get another job in education. Let him find that out for himself.

'Then you do believe there's something going on there?'

'Perhaps. But if there is I don't intend to alert them by showing my hand too soon. Do you know Ranee Raval?'

'The Indian woman?'

'The girl who died was in her class for a time until she switched to theology and became one of the elect. Apparently she had the gift, if you can call it that, of being easily induced to go into a trance.'

'An ancient technique for getting in touch with other forces, part gift or aptitude but often part training. We use it ourselves, of course.'

'Anyway Dr Raval is leaving. I think she may know something or at least be sufficiently disturbed by the atmosphere to want to get away.'

'Strange, I hadn't put her down as particularly empathetic.'

'Is there anything further you haven't told me? Any scrap of information that might conceivably be useful?'

'If I think of anything after you've left I'll telephone. But at the moment I believe I've been as much help as I can.' In other words I won't get any more out of him. I'm being dismissed.

Well, perhaps there's something he knows that he doesn't know he knows, I'm thinking as I ride back. Or it may be just an aspect of his arrogance to always seem to be withholding some vital bit of the jigsaw that would bring the whole picture into focus.

Why did he give the students extracts from Amyntas Boston's memoir to read? To show how seriously other times treated witches or how old the craft is? He said he wanted to stretch their minds, to shock them a bit, to suggest even that what we see as hard drugs were just truly for medicinal purposes at one time, that even the demon tobacco was thought to have a curative use. It was all another aspect of that arrogance. He thought he was fireproof, that he could say anything he liked and get away with it. And he probably did under the old dispensation, until the Temple took over Wessex and turned it into a fake uni so they could attract young people and work on them, like Charlie's cousin, and Hester Ado, and the nameless young guy who killed himself in the holidays but under the influence of Wessex I'm sure.

Galton doesn't see it in terms of young lives lost or blighted. He sees it as some kind of personal crusade, him against them, or simply as revenge for what they did to him. He wants me to find out what's going on just to destroy them and when he talks of evil it's almost an abstraction. He believes in its separate existence as a force as they do or pretend to do. Whereas I see it as 'the evil that men do' out of stupidity or genetics, upbringing, a culture of greed, a lust for power not because of what you can do with it but to massage your own depleted ego.

I stow the Crusader downstairs and climb up to my eyrie. The office life of phone messages, faxes, emails all busily humming away has been going on in my absence and now demands my attention like clamorous mouths asking to be fed. But not tonight. I'm knackered and low. How do you keep going without love in a world turned upside down? 'With how sad steps O moon thou climb'st the skies! Is constant love deemed there but want of wit? Are lovers there as false as here they be?'

No, that's not quite right but I'm too tired to look it up. It was what he meant, my lady's 'dear brother' who died a hero, passing down a legend of gentlemanly compassion. 'Thy need is greater than mine.'

The phone rings but I don't answer. I hear my own voice saying 'Hallo. You have reached Lost Causes. There's nobody

here at the moment to take your call . . .' Then the line goes
dead.

'Of what is he accused?'

'That he did go about to poison the Lady Anne Herbert,
sister to the Earl of Pembroke by feigning to be a physician.'

'How came he to physick her?'

'By insinuating himself into the favour of Mary, Dowager
Countess of Pembroke, her mother, on a pretence of knowledge
of diseases and their treatment, he being unlicensed of any
authority. As a result the lady is sick near to death.'

'But not dead sir?'

'Nevertheless poisoned by this arrogant boy who thinks himself
equal to the finest doctors in the land.'

'Since the lady is not dead her body cannot be opened to
prove whether she is poisoned or not. What is your name young
master?'

'Amyntas Boston sir.'

'And what do you say to the charge laid against you?'

'That I am innocent of any evil intention sir. It is true the
Lady Anne is very sick but she is so by natural causes of a
consumption. I have only tried to give her strength and treat
her lungs which have every symptom of the ulcers which the
disease causes.'

'And where did you learn such skills?'

'From my father sir, who was a physician in Salisbury. One
that the countess would have had in her service for the esteem
in which he was held but he preferred to remain in his own
house.'

'He was a noted necromancer, an alchemist whose chief pursuit
was to find the philosopher's stone. This boy is known himself
among the people, my lady's servants, as the young wizard.'

'Then he treats others than the Lady Anne?'

'I help the countess with her works of charity among the sick and needy, such as have little money to pay a physician.'

'And how do you treat them?'

'By bathing their wounds and dressing them sir, and administering such medicines as are fit for the case.'

'And where do you procure these medicines?'

'My lady has a laboratory in all her mansions where we make up our receipts from herbs and minerals.'

'And such you gave the Lady Anne, her mother consenting, perhaps even assisting?'

'He has wormed his way into the countess' affections by his pretended innocence and skill.'

'You are too choleric sir. Give me leave to conduct the inquisition without interruption. So far I do not find cause to charge Master Boston. It is true he practises without authority but not in public, only in the household of a noble lady who may be allowed to employ whom she will.'

'The lady's friends believe she is cozened, even perhaps bewitched.'

'Then the accusation is now not poisoning which could it be shown, as it cannot for the reason I have given, would have caused him to be hanged. As for practising without authority in this town you would have to arrest half the inhabitants of Alsatia who are a commonwealth to themselves of thieves, quacks and mountebanks beyond the city jurisdiction. Therefore a thing impossible to the law to meddle in. Now you would accuse him of witchcraft since you cannot succeed with your first charges. Does he look like a witch, who are mostly old ill-favoured women? Are you a witch Master Boston? Remember you can be put to the trial.'

'Sir many times when I have been treating the common people of the village on my lady's behalf they have asked me for charms and spells, incantations that they believe will make the medicine cure faster. Always I said no: that the disease is of Nature and so must the cure be too.'

'You are of the new school of thought then. Take care that you do not find you have thrown out God and the devil with the trappings of superstition that still linger from the old ways. Have you read Mr Bacon his *Advancement of Learning*?'

'Yes sir. And found in it much of my father's way of thinking.'

'Then you would be a natural philosopher? Take care of hubris that cometh before a fall as scripture tells us. If nothing else it will make you more enemies. I find nothing in this young man why I should charge him. Let him be bound over to keep the peace and keep him from the Lady Anne. You are free to go young sir but do not come before me again.'

So I escaped my first trial and made my way back to my lodging. Yet as I was leaving Dr Gilbert came up to me and with great menace said: 'I will have you still. Do not attempt to throw yourself on the countess her mercy. That gate is stopped for you.'

Now all had fallen out according to my worst fears for I was alone in the world with no way to make my bread. Remembering the words of the magistrate I left my lodging and set out to find that Alsatia he had spoken of. But first I asked my landlady where it might be.

'Goodness, it is no place for a young gentleman.'

'Nevertheless madam I must find it. I have business there.'

'Well sir from here you must go towards the city of Westminster and along the Fleet until you come to Whitefriars gate where you turn down towards the Thames. Do have a care Master Boston for there are some thereabouts that would murder you for your hanger let alone your sword which although as my good man says is not of the first fashion, is no doubt serviceable enough to be worth the stealing and you are but slight and easily to be overcome if several rogues should set upon you together.'

As soon as I left the main highway I saw only too clearly what she might mean for here there were nothing but stews where the largest dwellings were the many taverns and those between little bigger than stalls for cattle. Yet some had signs that suggested the physician or astrologer within as the symbols of the zodiac or of the cabbala. Among the throng in the streets were also some that suggested their trades by their antique caps and cloaks and their chests of God knows what bottles and jars. One had his wares displayed at a little booth by the pavement and was hawking a cure-all for love and lost goods that was also, he cried, sovereign against the pestilence.

I saw many signs hung out of fencing masters who when they were not teaching might be hired for more deadly work so my landlady's husband had told me, especially by gentlemen who had a score to settle with someone not worthy to risk their lives against in a duel. There were also cook shops selling meats and sweetmeats and pawn shops where anything might be bought or sold, especially anything unlawfully come by as I understood from their signs, for the law had no jurisdiction here.

But that which most troubled me were the many women in the streets, some in doorways, some passing through the throng their faces painted as if for the theatre that showed harshly in the light of day, their silks as if slept in, and they just risen from their straw pallets, stained with the mire of the stews, and with wine and the grease of many days.

I knew they must stink yet they laughed and called out to passing men with a cheap easefulness, as if they had not a care in the world. They were also of all ages from ripe matrons, as they seemed, to green girls. Those who stood in the doorways beckoned men in, some of whom I saw entered but did not linger to see them come out again for my purpose might have been mistaken. As it was, here and there a woman called to me in passing offering the young master a clean girl fresh from the country with no touch of the pox upon her. Then I understood another way to make my living and shuddered that I might be forced to assume woman's dress and the customs of Alsatia.

So I turned back again towards the Fleet but losing my way among the alleys and stinking courts I found myself to come out at last further to the west among the fair buildings of the Temple where men could safely breathe again without benefit of a nosegay and where indeed the lawyers strolled in their gardens conversing, their gowns flapping like so many crows. Continuing north I found myself in a lane called Mitre Court where there were many shops that waited upon the members of the Inns of Court, including those of scriveners for making fair copies of all manner of bills, and at last among them the name of that friend to my landlady who had brought me his gnarled hand.

Then upon my knocking the door was opened by a servant. 'My master is not at home,' he said, 'but my mistress is here. Please to wait in the shop until I fetch her.'

When he returned he brought with him a girl who I judged to be but little older than me, dressed neatly but not finely and of a fair countenance. 'My father has gone to buy paper and ink sir but I will help you if I can.'

'I came to enquire how his hand does and if he continues with that cure I taught him.'

'You are the physician who lodges at Mistress Elder her house? If so we are indeed grateful to you for he is now able to hold a knife to cut up his meat and we have hopes that in time he may be able to copy again.'

'I am indeed glad of your good news. You will need more of the oil of Exeter to continue the cure. If you or your father will come to my lodging I will give you another bottle but I fear it must be soon for I may be suddenly called away.'

'I will come tomorrow sir or send our man Harry who opened the door for you.'

'Your father said that if he regained his skill he would make me a copy of a book of receipts of mine in payment. I have it with me and would leave it with you in case any misfortune should befall me. Here I will know there is a copy safe and another in the making.'

'Indeed sir it will be safe here for we are used to handle and keep such originals as part of our trade. I will begin to copy it myself and not wait for my father's hand to be fully healed for already the benefit to us both from the oil is great. That my father can feed himself and begin to perform other tasks is such a joy for him that makes him kinder to all the world beside. Tell me sir the nature of your book.'

'It is a book of receipts for use in common households, such as Dr Turner his herbal of many years ago or newer Mr Gerard, but with more of the physician to it than the herbalist. Therefore because the receipts may lead to life or death it must be most carefully transcribed. Are you trained in the scrivener's skill mistress?'

'Yes sir and used to take pains in the work. No one must know how much I help my father or they might wish to pay less for a maid's work. Yet if they cannot tell between my hand and his where is the harm?'

'None that I can see. I intend that my book shall be ready for a printer . . '

'Have no care Master Boston it shall be so neat you will think it already set. John Davies of Hereford himself once praised my father's calligraphy and mine is the child of his.'

'You have the advantage of me. You know my name but I do not know yours.'

'I am called Katherine Palmer. Kate among my friends.'

'Then may I call you Mistress Kate?'

She dropped me a curtsy of assent and I longed to linger in the shop where I felt strangely safe and content with our conversation as one dreaming with all my cares laid aside or as if I walked in Eden before man's fall or in that Arcadia of my lady's brother. Yet I knew that I could not stay there longer but must return to my lodging and my quest for a way of life to support me.

I could not believe, in spite of Dr Gilbert's words, that the countess had turned her back on me for ever and abandoned me after so many months in her service and close to her person. But I remembered the words of the duenna so long ago of the fickleness of great ones. Some lines of Sir Philip her brother found an echo in my thoughts: 'Are beauties there as proud as here they be?' And though they did not exactly mirror my state yet they were near enough to resound in my head again and again like an often repeated prayer. There came to me too the lines of another poet:

> And wilt thou leave me thus
> Say nay, say nay for shame . . .

Yet no poet could rehearse my case exactly for where was the shame to my lady? The shame was mine that had endangered her repute among her friends. Unjustly as I believed for I did not accept that I had encompassed or even endangered the Lady Anne's life and so I thought any impartial judge must decide as indeed he had. Nevertheless I felt no safety in his opinion. I knew that Dr Gilbert was determined to drive me from my lady's service or do me a worse injury if he could.

When I reached my lodging again my landlady had news for me. 'Here was one enquiring for you Master Boston. He asked me if you practised as a physician from this house. I said not; only that you treated such friends of mine as come here but the wonder was that you would take no payment. And that for us you might lodge here as long as it liked you. And so I would say to all Master Boston. But if he was a friend to you I am sorry, for to speak truth I did not like the fellow and think you should have a care of trusting any such.'

'How was the look of this fellow?'

'Like one scraped out of the Marshalsea, a brawling rogue I would not like to meet in a dark alley.'

Her words suggested no one to me that I knew. They were unsuited to Dr Gilbert who in spite of his choler was of the gentry as befitted the brother of Sir Walter Raleigh. His stoutness and greying hair in no manner suggested a brawling rogue. Perhaps he had hired someone to seek me out and murder me or at least gather such damning evidence as my landlady had in part supplied out of the kindness she had for me. Had there been anywhere for me to go I would have fled further but what I had witnessed in Alsatia did not dispose me to return there where I had no friends, even if I could hang out my sign for a physician without prosecution. That night I ate a supper of bread and broth with the landlady and her husband.

The next day I set out for Mr Short his printer's shop at the Star in Bread Street hoping to have back the copy of my book I had left with him but again the shutters were closed against me. As I stood there hesitating before the door a woman came out of the opposing house and sharply enquired of my business and what I did there.

'I have come to see Mr Short who has in the press a book in which I have an interest.'

'Then your interest is sunk and your capital too as much as if it had been in the hold of a ship lost at sea. Mr Short has been dead these two weeks and all his goods taken to pay his debts, type and press, paper and ink, even the thread to stitch the pages. Swept clean as if a hurricane has borne all away before it. The shop is to be let if you should have a mind to set up in business.'

My fears for Mr Short his health had been all too true. Now I was doubly glad of the copy at the scrivener's. I did not even know whether Mr Short had printed any copies before he died or into whose hands it might have fallen and whether they might consider it worth the selling for their own profit. Had Mr Short even had time to register it at Stationers' Hall or was it gone for ever without trace? I returned to my lodging saddened at Mr Short his death and the loss of my hopes.

Again my landlady had news but this time of another colour. 'Here was young Mistress Palmer, Master Boston, who says that you promised her some more of that oil that has done such marvels with her father's hand. I thought her very sad not to find you.'

'I will take her some myself.'

'Perhaps you will catch her on the way for she is not long parted from here.'

Suddenly I felt my life given a new purpose. I climbed upstairs to my attic for the remaining bottle of oil in my chest and set off after Mistress Kate. I found my thoughts running ahead of me as when I should catch up with her what I might say. Of what sweet friends we might be and how I should find employment as a calligrapher and then perhaps as a printer of my own book or issue it to friends in manuscript. With all these ideas shaping themselves in my head into an illusion of hope I hurried along Fleet Street to avoid the way through Alsatia and turned into Bride Lane leaving the press of people, horses, carts and coaches going towards Westminster.

The lane was narrow with the upper storeys on either side overhanging the street and cutting out the light of sun and sky. Yet this was nothing to the darkness that fell upon me when one from behind threw a cloak or sack over my head choking me in its folds, at the same time pinioning my arms. I felt he had the barrel of a pistol pressing into my ribs and heard a voice I did not know warning me not to cry out as I was hurried stumbling along, with my feet hardly dragging on the cobbles.

At length I felt myself being bumped down a stairway and smelt the river stink even through the folds of the cloth covering my head. Then I prepared to try to swim for my life, though I had no skill in it, thinking my captors intended to drown me in the Thames. Instead I was thrown into the bottom of a boat that rose and fell with the waves from other passing boats. I lay there face down with a great weight pressing on my back which I understood from the reek of piss and ordure was one of my captors sitting on me. At length the boat drew in to the shore again. I was lifted to my feet and hurried up more steps. At the top we paused. Suddenly I felt a blow on the back of my head. Darkness overcame me and I fell down in a swoon.

When I came to my senses again all was still dark. Now my arms and ankles were bound and I seemed to be completely shrouded in a sack from head to foot. I thanked God that it smelled of straw and nothing worse and was of a loose weave or I might have stifled unable to catch my breath.

Even so I swooned from time to time and the bumping of the cart or coach in which I lay gave me a great pain in my head from the blow it had suffered. Sometimes I felt a sneezing fit threaten me from the dust in the sacking but I knew that I must be very quiet and pretend still to a swoon or one might silence me for ever with a cold blade. Many hours as I believed passed while the carriage rumbled on jolting my every limb as I lay there.

Sometimes I despaired at the thought that I was being taken to some lonely spot to be murdered. At others that I would simply die of pain and thirst so that I was grateful for those times when I lost all sense of the world and blackness closed in on me again. At last after one such fit, I woke to find the cart had stopped.

A voice said: 'We should let him drink. We were charged not to let him die on the way before he can be brought before the justice.' I recognised in it the speech of my native country.

'What has he done?' another voice asked.

'I was not told, only that the doctor could get nothing from the law in London where they are all rogues and atheists and would have him brought home to be judged by our own magistrate, and where witnesses can be summoned to speak against him. I will take off the sack and give him some water.'

I felt one to jump down beside me where I lay and continued to feign dead as the cover was taken from me and I could smell night air. 'Wake up young master,' the first voice said and I suffered a stinging blow to my cheek that made me open my eyes. 'That's better. We would not have you die on us. Drink some of this.'

My head was lifted up and a leather bottle of water put to my lips which I sucked on greedily. 'You have hit him too hard Master Avery. See, his head still bleeds.'

'It is but a little blood.'

'There is more on his shirt. How came that there?'

'How should I know? It is none of my doing. Something in the bottom of the boat or the cart.'

'Nevertheless we should search it for fear he should bleed to death and we have laboured for nothing.'

I heard the first man curse and then he laid hands on my shirt and tore at the fastenings. I turned my head away.

'What have we here? Look, Woodman, a woman's teats.'

'Not so Master Avery. They be too small.'

'Small I grant you but a maid's. See the nipples on there. A boy's lie small and flat no bigger than half a young pea. Remember your own as you was coming to manhood.' He here slapped my cheek again. 'Tell us, are you man or a maid?'

'Perhaps it is a eunuch. As I have heard they have the breasts of a woman.'

'There's one way for the truth of this. Off with his slops.' They began to drag the rest of me from the sack.

'Stay, stay.'

'Ah, it speaks at last. Tell us what you are.'

'I am my father's daughter, and his only son.'

'Do not jest with us or try to trip us with fine words.'

'I am the survivor of twins and therefore may be carrying both within me.'

'This is scholar's talk. Answer us plain.'

'My brother died when our mother bore us.'

'So in place of a pretty boy we have a pretty maid.'

'But she is in man's attire Master Avery and such are either rogues, whores or witches.'

'Have we here a thieving Moll Cutpurse or Joan, the French witch, you mean? We could throw her in the pond nearby to see if she floats. What do you say mistress? Or I could make trial of her myself. If the rest is as pretty as what we see it would be no great penance.'

'Have a care Master Avery. They do say that if a man lie with a witch his prick will blacken and shrivel for he goes where the devil has been before. And it may be that as the devil gives witches the power to change shape, then this that we thought a man at first is indeed so, only now changed to deceive us into kindness. Then had you lain with a man in likeness of a maid who might perhaps change back even in the midst of the act.'

'God defend us, you are right Woodman. I will not meddle with her. Let us close her up in the sack again lest she cry out against us, for she has a nimble wit and tongue and might accuse us of a felony against her. By her manner of speech she may have powerful friends. Let us be on our way and rid of her as soon as may be.'

I hadn't opened the envelope Davidson had passed on from Mary-Ann Molders since he had given it to me. I'd put it in the drawer of my desk and forgotten about it. Now I'm wondering if it might hold any clues to what's really going on at Wessex. I spread the contents out to give them the onceover, as Marlowe might have put it, or maybe that was Damon Runyon.

There's a glossy brochure with stuff I recognise from the Temple website including Apostle Joachim's address. This is public stuff and doesn't add anything to what I already know. Then there's a couple of sheets stapled together, marked strictly confidential: Guidance for the Elect. Introduction. Aspirants for Election. Submission to The Word and the Covenant. There's a lot about 'purity', by which they seem to mean abstinence from sex, and having all things in common. Then there's a section headed: 'Resurrection People'. It's Joachim's old theme of living in the last days, on the fringe of eternity.

'And in the last days the children of light shall gather together to wait upon the coming. And they shall all take oath together to be lifted up, leaving the darkness below, and they shall rise into the light and stand before the lord of the covenant forsaking Belial and the snares of this world. And those who have gone before shall welcome them into the resurrection.'

Where does this rigmarole come from or is it Joachim's own confection, whipped up with bits of religious texts from here and there and put through the Temple blender? Even more bizarre is why anyone should go along with it. Except of course those deep in depression or who can't cope with all the stuff just living throws at you. The unsure, the vulnerable. It's a clever mix made up of the security that can come from belonging to a community and of the simple life away from the messiness of being in the world. And they all lived and died happy ever after.

I still can't see what the Joachims and Bishops get out of it apart from an exercise of power, of being able to manipulate other people. But then I'm forgetting Charlie's cousin and the will she made in favour of the Temple. All the soaring high-mindedness may boil down to simple greed. Except that greed is never that simple.

The phone rings. It's Charlie.

'Where are you, Charlie?'

'I'm at my uncle's. My friend says there is great excitement among the elect. Something is going on but he doesn't know what it is. Yesterday evening all the theology students were called to a special service in the chapel. The dean told them that Hester Ado had gone to prepare a place for them. That she was tired of this world and wanted to go home. Then the rest were asked to leave and only the elect stayed behind. It was when they came back to hall that he noticed the excitement but no one would talk about it.'

'How do you know all this?'

'My friend rings me on his mobile. He says he's sure something will happen soon. All the other students are away revising. What can it be, Jade?'

'Is your friend frightened?'

'Not for himself. He thinks whatever it is only concerns the elect. But he says they were all told to wait for the coming of the Paraclete at Pentecost. I don't understand what that means, Jade.'

'You're not a Christian, Charlie?'

He laughs. 'Confucius he say . . .'

'Well if I remember rightly the Paraclete is the Holy Ghost, the Comforter in Christian terms and he or it came down as tongues of fire and settled on the heads of the followers of Jesus and they were able to prophesy but in different tongues from their own. A sort of mass takeover by a spiritual power with a divine translation service.'

When Charlie rings off promising to keep me up to speed on anything more his friend learns, I worry about the timing of this event the elect are being prepared for: Pentecost. The happening itself could be just another of those 'Gatherings' where somebody goes into a trance, the next Hester Ado. In which case he or more likely she could be in danger of some kind especially since, according to Charlie's friend, everyone's pretty hyped up already.

I log on to Google and search for Pentecost. Alias Whitsun in the Western Church. The date was last Sunday and nowadays it doesn't even merit a Bank Holiday to follow. I seem to remember having at least a day off school when I was at primary. Was that the day Hester killed herself? If that's indeed what she did, and does the date have some symbolic meaning? There's more to the entry. In the Eastern Orthodox Church I see Pentecost is a week later. Everything is: Christmas, Easter. So it's still to come. Maybe the elect get two goes at Pentecost. I dig out the Bible I keep in the bottom drawer of the filing cabinet in case anyone wants to swear on it. According to the internet entry Pentecost is described in the Acts of the Apostles. I turn the pages and read: 'When the day of Pentecost was fully come, they were all with one accord in one place. And suddenly there came a sound from heaven, as of a rushing mighty wind and it filled all the house where they were sitting. And there appeared unto them cloven tongues like as of fire . . .'

The theology students were all told to wait for the coming of the Paraclete at Pentecost. So whatever happened to Hester Ado wasn't the big number, even if it happened at the Western Whitsun. The real happening will be next Sunday to coincide with the Eastern date. That's what the elect are being whipped up for. But what do they expect? Tongues of fire. The gift of prophecy. To be transformed.

On an impulse I go downstairs to the Crusader and set off for Wessex. I'm too hyped up myself to sit still and I've chewed over what we know until there's nothing more to be got out of it like a lump of overworked gum. I wonder if my security card will let me through the gate or if the CCTV cameras will set off an alarm somewhere deep in the building. But the theologs who live in can't be locked up for ever. Presumably they're allowed to go out into the town to buy toothpaste. Even so it's a relief of sorts to be through the gates and wheeling the Crusader along the tarmac path without, as far as I can tell, all hell breaking loose around me.

I decide to play it cool, knowing I'll be watched, and head for the library. Almost I expect to find the door locked but it swings open with a push. There's no one sitting at the desks. I'm alone. I browse along the shelves pretending to search for a book, take down a couple, check the contents pages, linger over the index and put them back. Finally I settle on *Who's Who on the Elizabethan Stage* and try to look engrossed. As the minutes run by, time doesn't tick any more, it goes with a digital flow, I'm sucked in by the ghostly procession of actors in that old history play that was the backdrop to Amyntas' life. After half an hour in which no one else has come into the library, I feel I've established my bona fides and return the book to the shelf with a show of reluctance that's only half feigned.

Everything about the place seems normal, apart from the absence of students. Then I think I hear a voice from the direction of the chapel and head off there framing my alibi as I go. Just popping in for a quiet word. As I get closer the sounds get louder and more varied: voices and knocking. I turn the corner, stop and backtrack quickly. It's a regular hive of activity out there with unidentifiable equipment being carried in under the supervision of the Molders.

I decide not to confront her but to try to get round the back of the chapel and see if I can find another way in. There's a little door in the corridor that might lead outside, a door that Alice might have squeezed through to another world. I turn the handle and slip out. Presto! I'm where I want to be alongside the chapel walk. There's a fringe of tall nettles growing out of the gravel giving off their unmistakable acid smell under a hot sun rare for early June. I make my way round two sides with the long windows high above stretching towards the cupola. I try to visualise the inside of the chapel as I saw it before but I find I have only an impression of elongated saints and columns in dried blood, purple and gold.

Round the next angle I see the nettles have been hacked away at the foot of an iron stairway that must have been an emergency exit put in by the Victorian builders. There's a small door underneath the bottom spiral, another halfway up the building and a final one at the top. Perhaps it wasn't an emergency exit but for access to the roof for maintenance. The top of the cupola has a lightning conductor. Maybe that's it. Or perhaps there was a bell up in the roof for summoning the girls to matins when it was St Walburgha's. The nettles have been cleared right up to the first little door under the curving fretted iron treads. There's a big iron ring I grasp and turn. The latch lifts. The pointed Gothic door gives. With a quick look round and hoping there's no one already in there I step inside. I want to close the door behind me but it's too dark to see apart from a thin rectangle of light that must be outlining a door on the other side. I can hear noises from beyond it: the same noises I heard in the corridor. I run my hand down the damp stone door frame and find a switch but daren't put on the light. If only I had a torch.

Gradually my eyes begin to pick a shape out of the gloom: a big fuse box that looks as if it dates back to the original Victorian Gothic building. Beside it gleaming in white plastic is a new installation. I cross the coldly sweating brick floor and pull carefully on the front corner. Suddenly it drops forward on a hinge at the bottom. There's a main fuse and two switches in the off position. I close the cover. Time to get out of here. At the door I peer quickly round the frame. There's still no one about. I step through, pull the door to behind me and drop the iron latch, expecting every second to hear a voice demanding to know what I'm doing.

My legs are watery with fear and tension but I have to go on. With another quick look round I start up the iron stairs hoping they're not going to collapse in a heap of rust under my feet or the old brackets fixing to the brickwork be wrenched out with my weight, letting the whole spiral cascade in slow motion down the side of the chapel, with me clinging on, like in a Tom and Jerry cartoon.

The two higher doors are duplicates of the one at the bottom with the same big iron ring latches. I open the lower one and step through. The floor is stone not brick and there's the same outline of a door opposite. I need to know what's out there. Surely you can't just walk out on air with a sheer drop to the chapel floor. Splat! I can't hear the noises up here. Is it because I'm too high? Or have they really stopped? I must find out if that door will open and what happens on the other side. I cross the floor and feel for some kind of handle.

It's the same ring as the others. I turn it as silently as I can and edge the door open a crack. I put my right ear to it and listen. Silence. I risk opening the crack up a couple of inches and put my right eye to it. I can see that the door opens on to a gallery with a twisted barley sugar railing only a few feet away. I crouch down and open the door enough to get my head through so that I can turn it to look in both directions and across at the far side of the chapel. The gallery runs all the way round. There's not a sound from below. I crawl out on hands and knees and look down through the twisted fretwork of rails. The chapel is empty. The big doors are shut but I don't risk standing up.

Craning my neck to look up I see there's another smaller gallery running round the inside of the cupola. That must be what the top door opens on to. Looking down again I see a giant screen has been fixed to where the altar would have been. Then I notice at equidistant points along the railings what looks like some kind of spotlight. There's one not far from the door. It seems to have a strange bulb. Halogen perhaps. But I daren't go out on to the gallery to examine it properly. Instead I crawl backwards through the doorway. Stand up. Close the door and go out on to the iron staircase into a sunlight that hurts my eyes.

At first I can't see at all and feel naked, exposed up there against the wall like a fly waiting to be swallowed. Again I'm lucky and there's no shout of command to come down. When my eyes have adjusted I begin to climb the last bit of staircase.

By now I'm an expert with these doors. It occurs to me that the locks and hinges must have been used or even oiled recently for them to work so smoothly. I step off the emergency stairs into the last little darkened room. This time I cross boldly and open the door a whole inch. The second gallery, railed like the first, is in front of me but above it are the panes of the cupola letting in a strong white light. I glance down and my head swims a bit with vertigo. Not for the first time I decide abseiling, skydiving and all the dangly sports aren't for me. I cling on to the door frame for support.

Looking along and across this gallery I see there seem to be small round cylinders like tins of beans, positioned like the spotlights below but I can't make out what they are and vertigo stops me going out to examine them. I feel as if I've been climbing up the chapel wall for hours. I know my luck is about to run out and I'll be spotted at the last minute. The way down seems more perilous than the climb up and my legs are decidedly shaky by the time I reach the bottom. For a minute I lean against the wall risking discovery, vulnerable on the ground now, in the open.

The campus is deserted again.

I reach the bike shed without challenge and feel a surge of relief when I'm back on the Crusader heading towards London. No stopping for a cosy chat with Galton today. I put it all out of my mind and concentrate on the traffic. As I weave in and out my confidence is gradually restored by the sense of being in control again, exercising a skill I enjoy.

As soon as the office door shuts of course the questions start. What's really going on at Wessex? Is some holy floor show planned for Sunday? That must be what the screen's for. An inspirational video to encourage the troops. If I could get in there I might find out. But it's clear their security is going to be tight with Molders on the door vetting everyone who tries to get in. Only the elect allowed. Not even the ordinary theologs.

The only way to find out would be to hide in one of the upper rooms off the staircase. You'd be trapped. Unless you had some other way down into the chapel. Wait until the Gathering was all over and hope one at least of the doors wasn't locked. You might have to wait a long time in the dark. You'd need a torch and a rope at least. Today has shown me I've no head for heights but I might have to face it.

There are safety ladders I've seen advertised that can hook on to a windowsill in case of fire. You could do it in stages from one gallery to the next. Don't be wet, Jade. Each climb wouldn't be so far. You wouldn't need a very long ladder. Just something light and strong like mountaineers have. I'm mad even to think of it but how else can I find out what's going on? A pity there wasn't a key for any of the doors. There were locks as well as the ring handles and latches. Probably Molders keeps them hanging from her belt like a wardress. You might be able to stuff up the locks with chewing gum or putty so that the keys wouldn't go in. I'm going round and round on this hamster wheel. I have to get off and try to sleep.

But the phone rings. It's Joel. 'You OK? Long time no see.' His familiar voice stops the wheel.

'Let's have a drink one evening next week. I'm sorry I've been so out of touch. I'll explain everything when I see you.'

'Lust or work?'

'Work. Look I have to do something on Sunday that could be dangerous. I need you to know where I am so that if something goes wrong you can tell the police. I can't explain it all now. There isn't time and anyway I couldn't do it on the phone. I'll ring you on Monday. If I don't, ring the fuzz and tell them to go to Wessex University. I'll send you an email with a complete address.'

'Hey, Jade, do you have to do this whatever it is?'

'I do, Joel. I really think I do.'

'Take care.'

'I will, I promise.'

I pour myself a drink, whiz off the email to Joel and settle down to watch a TV cop solve an improbable murder. The other channels are all offering hospital dramas or sport. For a moment I consider playing a little *Rosenkavalier*. But that was another country and besides the wench is dead. Just as I'm yawning over the convoluted improbability of the sleuth's intuitions the phone rings again.

'Jade?'

'Charlie!'

'My friend says that something will happen on Sunday.'

'I know, Charlie. That's the Eastern Pentecost they were told to expect.'

'He says the elect are even more hyped up. They're called to the chapel at eight o'clock in the evening.'

'I'm going to find a way to be there.'

'Where?'

'In the chapel, to see what's going on.'

'How will you do that, Jade?'

'There's a back way in to the galleries up an outside iron ladder like a sort of fire escape.'

'Suppose you're seen.'

'I'll take care not to be.'

'I don't think you should do this alone. It's too dangerous. My friend and I will come with you.'

I'm both nervous that three people are harder to conceal than one but relieved to have backup. 'We'll need a torch and some sort of rope ladder in case we have to climb down into the chapel because the doors to the staircase have been locked behind us.' I don't mention the chewing gum. That seems too much like the boy detectives. But this is little old England where traditionally we prefer to murder by stealth according to the rules of fair play.

After many hours the jolting of the cart stopped again. I was lifted out in the sack and as I judged thrown over a shoulder as if I were a bag of corn, carried inside and put down on a cold floor that smelt of earth. I cried out for them to untie the sack so that I could breathe more easily.

'This is some witch's stratagem to work upon us to free her so that she may charm us with a spell and make her escape.'

'I desire only to breathe and for a drink of water.'

'It were a pity if she should suffocate before we have the money Master Avery.'

'True Woodman.' Twere a pity indeed. I will undo the mouth of the sack so that she may put out her head.'

I felt him pulling at the cord above my head and in a moment it was freed and I could breathe again yet still lay on my side doubled up as I had been forced by the shortness of the sack so that now all my limbs were numb and I could not stand up of my own will even if I had dared to attempt it.

'There, see our kindness to the witch,' the one I judged to be Avery said. 'She shall have some water to drink lest she curse us.' And he put a bottle to my lips for me to suck on. 'Now we must to the doctor for our pay.' He picked up the torch he had lodged in a jar by the door whose flame threw the men's shadows hugely on the walls of the round shed where I lay. I could see no window by its light but only the thatch of the roof above. I judged it some kind of store place. They opened a low door and taking the torch went outside. I heard a bolt being shot and I was alone in a blackness so complete I seemed to have lost the sense of sight.

As soon as they were gone I rolled in the sack until I fetched up against a wall and was at last able to sit up, wriggling the upper part of my body free of the folds of cloth that restrained me. By pressing my back against the wall I was able to raise myself to stand but when I tried to walk my bound feet made me fall down so that I was forced to begin again. Nevertheless

I persevered to get against the wall. Sitting there in the darkness I began to work on the bonds that tied my hands before me and after much twisting I felt one hand loosen a little and working at it harder although it chafed my wrist, I finally got it free. Then feeling in the dark I was able to free my feet to stand and walk about until the numbness had gone from my legs.

Next I felt round the rough walls until I came to the door. I pushed against it but it was bolted fast from the outside and although it gave a little in its frame I knew I did not have the strength to push it open. A dozen plans for escape went through my head but I had no means to put them into execution. I had gained freedom from my bonds but was still a fast prisoner. I sat down again beside the door and a strange drowsiness compounded of fear and exhaustion overcame me. I fell into a kind of slumber under the blanket of darkness that enshrouded me.

Voices from beyond the door aroused me. The bolt was being drawn back and the light of a torch was so bright that my eyes that had been so long in the dark were dazzled.

'If you have snatched the wrong one your pay is forfeit,' a voice said, the voice of Dr Adrian Gilbert. 'You were to take a man not a girl.'

'And indeed sir we thought we had. But see the witch has loosed her bonds, by witchcraft, no doubt with the help of the devil for we had her tied tight.'

'Hold up the torch. This is Master Boston certainly.'

'Yet see sir.' One of them stepped into the hut, reached forward before I could move away, and tore open my shirt. 'See a witch's teats.'

'You are right. She or he whichever must be brought at once before the justice, not to escape with honeyed words. Perhaps this is a shapechanger. This time the charge will not be practising without a licence but seeking the life of the Lady Anne by witchcraft. And others too perhaps. By what name will you be charged?'

'That I shall tell only to the justice.'

'Tie her hands again and bring her out.'

Now indeed I saw that I was in danger of my life for all know that bringing about a death by witchcraft carries death for the witch in turn. My hope was that the Lady Anne still lived however sick and might yet recover if only for a time enough to save my life, for however desperate my condition I did not want to die.

Again I was pushed stumbling along, this time weakened by want of food and sleep. I saw that we were passing under the garden wall of a house. A stinking hand was put over my mouth to stop me from crying for help and I was hurried towards a cart, picked up bodily by the two men and thrown down on the floor which was dirty and smelling of stable litter. At once the cart moved off with one of the men up on the driving board while the other walked behind. Dr Gilbert rode beside me on a horse I had myself often ridden accompanying my lady. The change in my state brought salty drops of weakness to my eyes yet I resolved they should not see me weep to give them greater power over me and so I swallowed hard to keep back those tears that threatened to unman me quite.

Through the slats in the cart I saw that we had passed beyond Wilton and were now in the country between that town and Salisbury which we reached all too soon although our pace was slower until the cart began to go faster down the hill into the city so that the man beside it was forced to run along holding on to the cart tail. Now I was jostled and bruised over cobbles as we approached the city.

'Where to doctor?'

'The house of Justice Ludlow where he lodges beside the gaol in Fisherton Street.'

So we were not to go into the city proper but stop short

before the bridge and St Thomas' church, where I had sometimes gone with my father in another life. I was lifted out and
stood upon my feet while one of the men knocked and bellowed
at the door of a house whose lineaments I could not discern in
the dark.

At length someone came, the door was opened and Dr Gilbert
stepped forward to speak to a servant. Then there was silence
apart from the blowing and stamping of the horses and the
jingling of their bridles. Once again there were low voices. Then
Dr Gilbert nodded at the men who held me and I was pushed
forward into what I saw at once was a panelled hall whose
ceiling was lost in the gloom above. A gentleman all in black
sat in an armchair by the stone fireplace. Dr Gilbert took off
his hat and bowed.

'We are sorry to disturb you sir at such a late hour but I
judged the matter could not wait.'

'Not even until the morning?'

'I feared she might contrive an escape sir.'

'You say "she" yet I see a young man. What charge do you
lay that is so urgent?'

'Witchcraft sir.'

'You must go further than that.'

'The bewitching of the Lady Anne Herbert who lies close
to death.'

'Your evidence?'

'In the witch herself who has gone about in male attire
pretending to be a physician and cure the sick by her potions,
so that she is known as the young wizard.'

'What gossips say is not evidence.'

'You have only to consider sir that first she has denied her
sex and assumed man's clothing. Second that as she is not a
man she cannot be a physician for they must be licensed, as you
know, and therefore she is a cunning woman such as the common
people resort to which is a kind of witch. Yet she has deceived

persons of quality into accepting her into their houses with her feigning to treat them in the guise of a man. As the Dowager Countess of Pembroke.'

'I see the drift of your argument. Is the noble lady herself prepared to be called to give evidence?'

'That I cannot say sir. She has been so cozened by this impostor. But there are others who can be called to testify who have worked and lived under the same roof. As well as the Lady Anne if she be fit.'

'Has exorcism been tried upon her to counter the curse?'

'No sir.'

'Sir there is no cure,' I said, 'only a phthisis which the lady suffers.'

'You are not asked to speak. There will be a time for you to defend yourself. Let this person be remanded to the gaol. And the midwives be summoned to search whether it be a he or a she. And if it be indeed a she, given female attire against her trial. You have witnesses, you say. Let them stand ready to testify.'

'Sir I can surely produce witnesses.'

'And you the alleged witch. What do you say? Are you man or maid?'

Then I saw that I was trapped whichever way I answered for if a maid as they would soon discover I was a witch. So I said only: 'I am my father's child sir who was a physician of this city.'

'A saucy answer. You must do better than that.'

'I must tell you sir,' the doctor said, 'that he was a noted alchemist and necromancer. These things often run in families. Where there is a witch mother often there is a witch son or daughter.'

'Was your father an alchemist or necromancer?'

'He was no necromancer sir. Some might call him alchemist for that he sought for the truth at the root of all things.'

'To turn base metal into gold for gain.'

'No sir, to understand the mystery at the heart of creation.'

'To search out God's ways and know good and evil as our first mother did, for which we all suffer. Such matters are best left to priests but now any man who can measure quantity, presume to read the leaves and blow the bellows thinks to unpick creation. Did you assist him in this?'

'I was too young sir. He did not permit it.'

'And did he not invoke the demons of Satan or Satan himself to assist him?'

'No sir. He said that he tried only to understand Nature and natural causes.'

'There can be no natural cause for a divine creation.'

'Do you not think sir the creator may use whatever means he wills to achieve his design and that if he use natural means because he has given us dominion over the earth and the apprehension to understand nature's workings then nothing is forbidden to us to seek out the truth of?'

'You speak like an atheist which may be worse than a witch and too saucily for a maid if such you are. Summon the constable and take this philosopher to the gaol until the midwives can make their search. Then let the he-she be brought before me again. Prepare your witnesses sir but with care for this is a cunning tongue that would argue with the lord justice or the archbishop himself.'

Then my captors took me away out of that house leaving the doctor and Justice Ludlow together and through an arch, across a yard and knocked at a low postern. When their knocking had no result they looked about for a bell pull and we heard the note from it jangling away inside a high wall.

'Justice Ludlow orders that the constable take this person in charge and lodge them in the gaol until summoned.'

The constable lifted up a lantern so that the light fell on my face. 'A pretty boy. What's the charge? Some wench got with child?'

'Witchcraft. And none knows if it be a he or a she. You are to employ the midwives to search.'

'Witchcraft? But if it be a he we had best have a doctor on hand. It is not proper for midwives to search a man.'

'That is your business. We have discharged the witch into your care to keep safe against the trial.'

'If it be a witch, it must be lodged separately for fear it should bewitch the other felons to assist an escape.'

'Keep it bound until you have turned the key. It has a tongue of honey whatever it be. Perhaps a eunuch of nature or by the knife for I have heard of such among the Egyptians and the Turk. Goodnight to you constable.'

They left us then and the warder pushed me inside and locked the postern. 'Now will you be quiet witch or must I bind you more?'

'I will be quiet sir if you will lodge me apart from the other felons for I have done no wrong.'

'None comes here that has done no wrong, for we are all sinners. But you do not have the mien of someone troublesome and if you will promise to be quiet you shall lodge apart, but if you give me any disquiet I shall throw you among them as young Daniel was thrown among the lions and then we shall see if you sink or swim.'

So he led me deeper into the building, passing a barred cell from where came groans and cries. One looked through the bars and pointed a crooked finger at me. 'There goes a gentleman to lie soft while we sleep here without straw.' Then he began to sing some street ballad and I saw that he was drunk.

At last the gaoler turned a key and opened a door into a narrow room. 'Here is the royal quarters with a mattress and even a pisspot.'

'Sir how may I use it with my hands tied? I have a little money in my pocket. If you will untie me and bring me something to eat and drink I will pay you.'

'You will get nothing without, except water. That I am obliged by the law to give you.'

'On my oath I will be quiet and make no attempt to escape. If I can come at my money I will pay you what you ask.'

He stared at me hard for a moment weighing the matter. 'What would you? White bread and wine? Stand still while I cut your bonds. Remember I have the knife in my hand and will use it.'

'I will give you no cause sir.'

'Nor no cursing to bewitch me neither.'

'I curse no one sir.'

He took a knife from his belt and advanced upon me with it. It would be easy for him to murder me now and take my money, alleging I had tried to escape. I held my breath and myself quite still as the knife sawed at the cords. When they fell away we both stepped back quickly, he with his knife pointing at my throat.

'Show me the colour of your money.'

I felt in the pocket of my slaps and produced a penny. 'If you bring me withall to eat and drink I will give you sixpence.' I saw that he trembled between greed and fear. 'But if you harm me there are those that will avenge me.'

'I will trust you for the sixpence. You must sit over in the corner with your back to the wall so that I may see you at once when I return.'

'Of your kindness sir bring me a lantern too when you return that I may see to eat.'

And so it was. When he returned with my requests I sweetened him with the sixpence and another penny. My stock of money was small and I understood that I must lay it out carefully for when it was all gone I should be no more than a beast. Sinking down on my pallet I began to eat a little bread and drink some wine to keep out the cold of this place, and to consider my situation. In vain my thoughts explored every passage out of my imprisonment and trial. Each was blocked as surely by the freezing air of reason which coated every vista with ice as thick as any that barred the mariners seeking the Northwest Passage to hope and the spice lands.

I could not ask my lady for help without bringing shame upon her or her denial of me which would break my heart. And yet I understood that my very life was in jeopardy and that if the Lady Anne should die I would be hanged. Dr Gilbert's word would stand against mine. Here was no malicious village neighbour accusing a poor old woman to whom he had refused a cup of milk or piece of bread, but a man of learning and the brother of a noble knight although he lay in prison, sometime favoured of a queen.

Then I began to wonder how I might contrive to die rather than suffer the pillory or being drawn through the streets to be hanged before the multitude. With this I fell into a kind of ecstasy in contemplating my death and how I would die rather than any evil repute should fall upon my lady and she should know somehow of my sacrifice that whatever they might inflict upon me or threaten me with, my lips would be sealed. So keeping the lantern still lit that I should not be surprised in the dark I fell into a kind of stupor rather than sleep, only waking to piss and then to sink into my stupor once more.

When I woke again I saw that it was day for there was a little window high up which I had not observed in the night, where a grey light entered my cell. I was glad that the night was over, for in my dreams I had ridden the nightmare of nameless fears and hopeless flight through streets and then woods where hands clutched at me.

Suddenly there was a noise of the turning of a key in the lock, the door was flung open and the gaoler entered with three others, two women and a man.

'We have come to search you to see whether you be man or maid or witch. Or all three. Will you lie quiet or must you be constrained?'

'I will be quiet if you will do me no hurt.'

'Take off your clothes.'

I undid my shirt and laid it aside and the band about my breasts. Then I dropped my slops to my boots.

'It be a maid,' one of the women said at once.

'You must lie down for us to search for the devil's marks. Upon your face first.'

I lay upon my pallet, face down, hiding my shame. I felt their hands upon me parting my buttocks to search, rough hands pulling them apart and a finger thrust between.

'Her back is clean. Now the front.' They turned me over and while I tried to look away for shame probed my navel and my armpits, fingered my breasts and came at last to my secrets. Parting my legs one began to dally there.

'Is this not a witch's teat?'

'Nay sir. All women have those, some greater, some lesser. Ask your wife if you have not seen for yourself.' And I heard one I supposed to be a midwife laugh, at which the other joined in.

'The justice has ordered that she be brought a gown to be dressed more seemly now that her sex is known.'

'I will do that sir. A woollen gown instead of her fine lawn shirt and silken slops that might become any true gentleman. And if you live mistress, and are not hanged for a witch, perhaps you will be glad to earn your bread in our calling instead of pretending to physician.'

'I must make my report for Justice Ludlow that we found no evident mark of the devil or witch's teat but that she is woman born and then her going in male clothing may be enough to convict her.'

They all withdrew, the midwives still laughing together and I was locked in again. I put on my shirt and pulled up my slops and because my legs trembled I lay down on the pallet. Yet the memory of the last time I lay there caused me to sit up again and drink some of the wine I had saved to try to restore my courage for I understood this was only the beginning of my trials.

Once more I heard the door being unlocked and one of the women returned with a russet grey gown which she would not give into my hands but threw upon the pallet.

'You must pay me for that. I will take your old clothes in exchange.'

'I will give you tuppence for it,' I said for I saw it was neither new nor clean. 'But my old clothes I must keep to wear under it against the chill of this place and the chafing of the wool.' And I took two pennies from my pocket.

'Your skin is softer than others then. The lice will feed well on you.' And she turned about and left. When she had gone I settled down with the gown and began to search it for lice which I cracked between my thumbnails wondering whose blood was smearing them as I worked.

After some time the gaoler returned. I had heard him approach and threw the gown over my head and was again sat upon the pallet as he opened the door.

'Where are your old clothes? You were best have given them to my wife in exchange for her gown. Now give them to me.'

'I gave her tuppence for it. It is worth no more. I need my clothes to keep my money in, for the gown has no pocket and I no other purse. Beside if I am here for long I may need to sell them for their true worth or at least nearer than a tuppenny gown.'

'What would you have for your dinner then, mistress, for such it seems I must call you now. Or else witch.'

'I am no witch.'

'That shall be seen. It is true my wife says they found no marks on you yet you go about in man's attire like Joan the French witch who was burnt.'

'Perhaps I am rather a Moll Cutpurse who will call upon my roaring boys to break down the doors and rescue me.'

'Thieves can be hanged as well as witches.'

'No one has come forward to swear I have stolen anything. Master constable or gaoler, whichever you are, let us not wrangle but come to an understanding. If you do what I ask I will pay you and if you help me to more money I will pay you more.'

'I am both constable by election because no one else will suffer it, and gaoler for my livelihood. What would you have me do, so it is lawful and does not put my living in danger?'

'First fetch me pen and paper. I will give you money to buy them,' for he had opened his mouth to protest. 'I wish to write a letter which you must have carried for me.'

'And will you also write a spell to curse me then?'

'I shall curse you if you do not fetch them,' and I forced myself to laugh in lightness for I knew that if he should turn against me in truth, as now he wavered, he might testify against me that I had said or done this or that devilish thing. 'But you must bring me as many sheets of paper as the money will buy for I have letters to write to such of my friends who can help me but who do not know where I may be found since I was snatched in the dark.'

'Snatched you say.'

'Yes, by those who wished me harm. And there will be those even now enquiring for me.'

'I had no hand in this. I only do my duty as ordered by the justice who committed you to my charge.'

'And so I shall testify when my friends find me as they surely will.'

'I will do what you ask mistress, in case you are a witch or have powerful friends, either of which might destroy a poor man like me.'

'Here is a shilling. Get me what I ask, as much paper as may be had, a capon for my dinner, and some small beer.'

'Even in my wife's old gown you speak like a young master.

This may be a kind of witchcraft itself.' And he left still grumbling.

This time I awaited his return without fear, comforted and emboldened by the feel of the silk against my skin under the gown. My secret was out yet I was not broken. And I had set myself a task to write an account of all that had happened so that, whatever my fate, some word of my presence on the earth might be preserved. But first I would write to my lady.

It's taken me some sleuthing on my computer and in the Yellow Pages to track down a couple of rope ladders. Torches were easy. Now they're packed in the Crusader's carrier and I'm spinning down the M3 feeling like a real prick or anorak out to foil I don't know what with my pathetic amateur seamus equipment. A call to Charlie's mobile has set up a rendezvous in the bike shed at seven. And now I'm wondering why I bothered with torches. It's June and we're rushing towards the longest day. It'll be broad daylight most, if not all, of the time we're at the chapel. Not very bright, Jade. Cockup time.

In fact the madness of the scheme looms larger and larger as I turn on to the road for the college and head towards the gates. I must have a story ready in case I'm challenged but my skull is suddenly full of loose sand where a brain ought to be. If only I knew enough, had enough evidence to go to the police and dump it on them. I see myself trying to explain.

'A conspiracy, you say? To hold a religious service? I'm afraid there's not much we can do about that in a free country. We're all entitled to our views no matter now strange they may seem to others. Unless they promote racism or terrorism of course.'

The adrenaline's racking up my pulse rate as I dismount and push the bike up to the gate. But my pass card works. No alarms go off. I'm inside with the bars swinging to behind me. I make for the bike shed. Charlie is there already with a slim brown young man I can imagine gliding skilfully between the tables of an Indian restaurant. Willowy rather than robust. I hope that it doesn't come to a punch up.

'This is my friend Omi.' We shake hands. 'Some of the elect have already left St John's Hall. The others, not the elect, have been warned that they must stay in until after the Gathering is over. Then a bell will sound and the doors will be unlocked automatically. Omi came out with some of the elect.'

'They don't all know each other then?'

'They aren't encouraged to get together or get too friendly except during their services,' Omi says.

'That's some help for us. But Molders will know who everyone is and I bet she'll be keeping a lookout. If only I knew a way to the outside of the chapel at the back without getting so close to the main door.'

'I do, Jade,' says Charlie. 'I tried it out earlier. You see I didn't go home last night. I hid and slept here in the bike shed. It means a bit of climbing, I'm afraid.'

'Let's have it.'

'There's a window above the wall bars in the gym. It leads on to a flat roof above the kitchens. From there you can get down into the grounds on the far side and go through a shrubbery to the outside of the chapel. I've seen your iron staircase and the three doors.'

'The most dangerous part will be getting to the gym. You go first, Omi, as the least suspicious. Then you can signal Charlie and I'll come along last. We have to pass the dean's door. Let's hope he's psyching himself up for the big number, whatever that is. What's for sure is if we're caught on the way all hell will break loose. We'll just have to risk it.'

We leave the bike shed after Omi has sussed outside to see all's clear. He trots off towards the main campus building and disappears inside. Then he reappears, nods for Charlie and vanishes again. Charlie follows. At the door he stops, disappears, comes back and nods for me. I'm hurrying after, not wanting to be left behind. Once inside I can spot him ahead at the next turn in the corridor. I see his head bent forward, peering round. He looks back, waves a hand and is gone. Round this bend I know is Dean Bishop's room, halfway along the corridor. As I pass the door I can hear voices but I hurry on, thankful to reach the next corner and see round it Charlie beckoning from the entrance to the gym. Gratefully I duck inside and Charlie closes the door behind me with just a little click.

The gym reeks with the memory of rubber mats, ropes, varnished wood and old sweat. Charlie leads the way across to a set of wall bars. Too late I remember I was hopeless at gym, could never vault over the box or horse, dangled useless at the end of a rope, unable to haul myself up hand over hand like a jolly Jack Tar, took half an hour to climb the rungs of the wall bars, reverse and hang proudly like a crucified Christ.

No good thinking about it, Jade. Already Charlie and Omi are shinning up, nimble as meerkats. At the top Charlie opens a narrow slit of window and props it up with the bag of equipment before slithering through. I start on my painful way up. I just hope my bum doesn't get stuck in that narrow gap. It would be so shaming if the boys had to push and pull me through. Omi has followed Charlie, and is looking down at me anxiously. He must be standing on the flat roof.

Somehow that, and the fear of failure before his concerned eyes, gives me a boost. I've reached the top. The boys have taken the bag away and are holding the window open for me, giving me the maximum space. I start to feed my head and shoulders through the gap, levering myself forward on my arms. The bitumen surface of the roof is only half a metre below. My nostrils are filled with its tarry, friar's balsam fumes drawn out by the hot sun. I bring my arms up and through the window. The danger now that I'm not holding on is of falling back into the gym. I try to squirm through but the waistband of my jeans is caught on the windowsill. Fighting down panic I reach down to my hips and flatten it over the metal bar, wriggle again and I'm going through, falling forward with my face in the tar, drawing up my knees, turning on my back and pulling my legs and feet further into the foetal position and I'm there. What a dog's breakfast. I vow to take up kick boxing, yoga, acrobatics.

'Well done, Jade,' Charlie says solemnly just like an old PE teacher, cheering on the slobs when they'd managed not to fall off the horse.

'What next?' I ask, still catching my breath. My diaphragm feels as if I've been socked in the guts.

'Now we go down to the ground. With the rope ladder. I will go first. You next, Jade. Then Omi last, bringing the ladder. We can hide behind the bushes.'

Stupidly I go to the edge and look over. It seems a long way down even though the kitchen block is only a single-storey extension. 'Ready?' I nod. Charlie comes across to the edge and hooks one of the ladders over the low parapet around the roof. He crouches down and begins to lower himself on to the first rung over the side. I see his body disappearing as if sinking in mud or quicksand until there's only his face. Then that's gone too.

I go forward at a crouch and try to imitate him as closely as possible. My feet fumble around before they make contact with a rung. Then I begin to lower myself, my hands grazed by the stone coping, my legs weak with fright. It seems to take for ever going down because all I can see is the brick wall in front of my nose. My feet are reaching blindly for another rung when they touch ground with a hard jar to my spine. I'm down. I let go. Turn, look round and head for the cover of the nearest institutional azalea.

Omi is down in a flash, jerks the hooks off the parapet and catches the ladder as it comes hurtling down before it can hit the ground with a clang. He must be invaluable on a cricket pitch as the traditional safe pair of hands. The top of Charlie's head comes out from behind a nearby bush and then a hand waving us on. We set off, dodging from shrub to shrub and then suddenly I see one of the side walls of the chapel. We're there. Time for me to resume charge of this operation. I head for the iron ladder. No time to check whether the bottom door is locked. Mentally I cross my fingers that the other two aren't.

I can hear Charlie and Omi, panting a bit now, behind me on the ladder. I pull on the ring door handle. It turns. I'm inside the little room. Now I remember the reason for the torches. It's pitch black as Charlie blocks out the light from the door. I take the bag from him, grope around for a torch and switch on. Omi joins me. I gesture for them to shut the door. Then we all stand still and listen. No sound comes up from below.

Taking a tin of putty out of the bag I force some into the keyhole until it's completely blocked. Any attempt to put a key in from the other side would, I hope, force putty deeper into the lock, jamming the mechanism. I move over to the little door opposite and begin to prise it gently open, switching off the torch at the same time.

A muted hum rises from the body of the chapel, not of voices but an amalgam of breathing and shuffling with an occasional cough that tells us there are people there, people who aren't speaking to each other even in whispers, who're just waiting. You can almost feel the throb of expectancy in the air, steaming up from where they must be sitting. I have to risk being seen and take a look. After all that's what you're there for, Jade.

Crouching down I inch forward as I did before until I can just see down through the gallery railing. There are indeed people in the chapel, some on their knees, others sitting quietly with closed eyes. I switch my view to the main door. It's open and in the corridor outside I can see Mary-Ann Molders vetting the students as they approach. She seems to be asking their names and ticking them off on a list before letting them in to join the rest.

The big video screen I saw being carried in is glowing faintly. Someone begins to doodle fragments of mood-enhancing music on the organ. The show, whatever it is, must be about to get on the road. The organ swells, as Dean Bishop comes through the door which shuts behind him. Decked out in green and white silk like an old ship in full sail, mitred and croziered, he makes his way to the pulpit, the Molders slipping into an empty front chair. I'm wondering what authority he has to be in full fig as an ordained cleric, whether you have to get permission, and whether there's an offence of impersonating a minister like that of assuming police or military uniforms, of if anyone can play. I'm still turning this over and deciding that he could probably be done for fraud at least, when he begins to speak.

The little stock of money I had carried with me when I set out from my lodging was nearly gone. I had hidden the rest in a bag under my mattress but that was a hundred miles away in London. I supposed that if I did not return my landlady would find it. I wondered if she would send it to me if I writ to her for it but this seemed a burden on her honesty and in any case I did not know if she could read what I might write to her.

My best hope was in the duenna that she would carry a message to my lady or that the countess herself would return to the great house to oversee her removal to London for I could not imagine that she would leave that to servants.

Now that Mr Davys, her steward whom she had trusted in all things, was dead there was none I believed, apart from myself, that she would put such faith in. Therefore I writ to my lady with the superscription that the letter should be opened and read by the duenna in the countess her absence. I prayed that it would not fall into the hands of Dr Adrian Gilbert or I were as good as dead, for I believed that if he could not accomplish his design by lawful means that he would have no compunction in having me smothered in my cell as the hunchback king did for the two princes in the Tower.

When I had my letter done and the gaoler came to bring me clean water and empty the pisspot, I gave him a penny, promising him more if he would see it safely delivered to my lady or the duenna and I bade him by no means to let it fall into the hands of another if he wished for more money.

'Then indeed you have friends in high places and can read and write like one bred to the university. But there is something more I would have of you if indeed you are a witch and have the power from the devil to kill or cure.'

'I am not a witch master constable and I have no truck with the devil except like all men in respect that he goeth where he listeth like the wind about the world. But for all that I may be able to help you if your ailment has a natural cause.'

'It is not natural for it is natural for a man to be able to do his duty and pleasure his lawful wife. But my man will not stand and therefore I believe I am bewitched and would have you perform a counter-magic of your devising and skill to take off this spell that is upon me.'

Now I saw that I was like a coney in a snare, that pulling against the noose would only tighten it about me for if I did nothing for him he would cease to serve me and if I pretended to be what I was not he might speak against me before the justice, especially if his state did not improve.

'I will think upon what you say and see if I can find a way to help you. But first you must carry my letter and report on your success or that of anyone you may appoint to do it if you cannot leave your post.'

'My wife shall take it herself. As midwife she has entry to many places closed to others.'

'Now tell me how you came by this spell if spell it is.'

'There was an old woman, ill formed and bent like a hoop, that my wife had helped once, but would not again when she came begging, that cursed me through her and said she should have no child of her own out of my body.'

'And why did you not accuse her as a witch?'

'I would not have the world mock me.'

'If you succeed in bringing me help from the countess then I will set about a cure. But I must have the means to practise my art or I can do nothing. But what I do will be with the help of nature not the devil. Your humour is moist and black and therein lies your problem. You are too under the influence of Sagittarius and inclined to melancholy.'

'My wife says I often have the black dog it is true. I will take her your letter and she will go with it immediately.'

After he was gone I grieved that I had had to speak in those terms used by physicians who hold that the stars influenced our fate from our birth and that our humours came from their ascendancy for I believe that a man may suffer melancholy or choler of his own nature without help from the heavenly bodies. And that our fate is in ourselves from our mother's womb. Yet I do observe that a certain humour as cold and moist may seem to be master over the others in each of us and that we suffer in body and mind according to our composition and that the physician is most likely to bring about a cure by fitting his remedy to the prevailing humour, either by its opposite to drive it out or by its companion to soothe and calm it as sometimes we prescribe heat for those in a fever and at other times an opiate to bring sleep in which the body may heal itself. Yet I knew that if I did not use the language and the tricks of those physicians that pretended to knowledge of the stars that the gaoler would not believe me, would not follow my instructions and would therefore not be cured and be turned against me.

To compose myself I began to write my memorials on the

paper that he had brought me. I had begged him for a knife to sharpen the quill when it became blunted.

'If I should give you a knife you might use it to harm yourself and cheat justice.'

'I have no wish to die but only to write those matters that might enable me to live.' So he brought me a little knife with the pen and ink and a stool to sit on which I set as close under the window as I could to catch the feeble light as long as it lasted. And as long as I held myself to my tale the hours passed quickly enough.

Sometimes I wondered if I should pray that God would make plain my innocence to the world and deliver me from this place but no words would come and no priest visited me to help me in my devotions. I tried to remember some words from my lady's psalms but only those the household had sung on our first visit to Wilton would come to me. Then I asked myself whether the devil had indeed taken hold of me that my thoughts were unable to turn to prayer when I stood so in need of any help.

At last when my eyes were beginning to weep from writing so long in the little light I heard a sound at the door as of the bolt being drawn back. The door was pulled open and my lady stood there with the duenna behind her and the gaoler holding up a lantern. I fell on my knees before her.

'Leave us,' I heard her say. 'My woman shall attend me outside the door. Leave me the lantern.'

'Suppose the witch should escape . . .' he began but she cut him off.

'How dare you! Leave us.' And then when he had gone she said to the duenna, 'Wait at the door and warn me if any approach. Stand up Amyntas.' But I could not for shame. 'What have they done to you? What is this filthy gown?'

I raised my eyes then and saw her looking down on me.

'My lady should not have come to this place.'

'You wrote to me.'

'I asked only for your help, not that you should come to see me like this. Let me take off this gown madam, for I find it hard to speak to you as I would in this attire.' I stood up then and pulled its dark folds over my head. When I was revealed in my own clothes again I went on one knee.

'Now tell me what has become of you, for I thought you still in London although when I sent to your lodgings they said you had not returned. The woman feared you had come to some harm for you had spoken of going into Alsatia.'

'I was taken by two men madam who brought me here in a cart and carried me before the justice to be examined since the magistrate in London found no fault in me. But the men who snatched me discovered my true sex when they laid hands upon me, and set me up for a witch.'

'Your true sex?'

She glanced towards the door where the duenna waited. I saw then the game we were to play which was our old game and that however it fell out with me I must protect her from any shame or insult.

'That what I had pretended to all this while was false, a dream merely that I might serve you in disguise.'

'But how should this set you up for a witch? Do not the players assume such disguises commonly on the public stage and even at court by royal command?'

'There are those that would destroy me madam out of envy because they believed you favoured me.'

'Who has brought the charge of witchcraft?'

'Dr Gilbert madam, it is who still pursues me. That I was your servant protected me before when they did not know my true nature. The magistrate held that as I did not practise publicly as a physician there was no charge to answer. Then I was snatched and brought here because it was believed a country justice would see matters differently but now with this new knowledge they can bring the greater charge that since I went about in male dress pretending to heal I was as much a witch as French Joan.'

'What would you have from me? I cannot speak on oath against the truth. I could not defend you from that charge.'

'How does the Lady Anne?'

'She lives.'

'Then none can say I have brought about her death and this will save my life.'

'She lives but only just. I intend to take her to Cambridge to a notable physician there, Dr Mathew Lister, to see what he can do. He is young but well spoken of. Certainly she grows worse in the smoke and stink of London. When will they bring you to your trial?'

'No one has told me.'

'What is the worst they can do?'

'If I am convicted they may stand me in the pillory, fine me, keep me in gaol.'

'You will need money if you are not to die in such a place.'

'I never needed before since your service provided all my wants but what small sum I had was left behind when I was taken, except for a few shillings in my pocket and most of them are gone.'

'There is little I can do for you Amyntas, as I still must think of you, but this I can.'

She called to the duenna to bring her purse. 'There, this will keep you for a little.'

'Madam I am ashamed to take it and do so only out of my great need. To be thrown among the common felons would be my death.'

'I paid you nothing while you were in my service except my love. I do not believe you went about to kill my child. My fault was to trust too much to your skill and to let her have too much her own way. Therefore I must share some of the blame.'

Her speaking of her love to me and taking blame upon

herself brought the tears into my eyes. 'Do not weep child. Tears will not help you. Use some of the money to buy a new gown for your trial that you may put the best face on matters. You are young and supposed witches are usually old. The justice may acquit you or at least make your imprisonment short. Do not fall into despair. Lift up your eyes to the hills. God does not let the innocent suffer and I believe you are innocent of any malice. I shall return to the house I have taken in London when I have finished here and then for Cambridge. If my daughter grows well enough to be married I mean to travel as soon as she is settled. There is nothing to keep me here. Even those poets who once wrote me their fawning dedications have lines only for my sons. 'They flee from me that sometime did me seek!' I must learn to be an old woman and powerless. I have commanded fair copies of my psalms from John Davies, the master calligrapher, and will send you one for your comfort in this place.'

She gave me her hand to kiss, still fine and white. I could not keep a tear from falling on it for I understood that I might never see her again. 'The Tears of Amyntas. The poet Fraunce dedicated that to me so long ago in the third part of his poem on my mansion of Ivychurch, gone from me now with the rest. It is strange that I have never thought of it before.'

There's been nothing new to start with about the dean's opening speech. Nothing I mean that I haven't heard before on their propaganda website and in the Molders printed material. My mind switches off until I realise that he's coming to some kind of climax when he turns towards the screen holding out his hands as if ushering in a real presence but it's the virtual Apostle Joachim who comes on next. Bishop was only the warm-up act.

The students, some of them anyway, greet his appearance with little cries and moans. Obviously he's the big cheese served up on special occasions. At first he too says nothing more revealing than on the Temple website. We live on the fringes of eternity, soon to stand in the presence of God if we have made our hearts open for Him only. The time has been long promised. Now it is here.

The organ, but it may be just piped sound, begins to play the *Veni creator* as Joachim speaks the words and the text appears on the screen. 'Come, Holy Ghost, our souls inspire, And lighten with celestial fire . . .' One of the students calls out. 'Yes, Lord, yes. Come.' I risk a look further into the chapel through the railing. A girl seems to have sunk down crying as Hester Ado did but this time no one's hurrying to pick her up. All eyes are on the screen, except for those shut tight.

'Yes, the spirit is coming to you the elect, as he came to the apostles, to catch you up into the heavenly arms,' Joachim thunders out, spreading his own arms.

'This is the fullness of time my children. You have waited too long crying in the wilderness. How long, O Lord? How long? He descends to each of you in tongues of cleansing flame and on the wings of the wind.' There's a rushing sound as if the domed roof has blown off or been snatched away and a gale is howling round inside the chapel. There are more cries from the students. Some are standing with their arms outstretched, others kneeling.

Suddenly what seem like points of flame appear to dance about the building, settling on the students' heads. Lighting by Pentecost, Son et Lumière plc. Plc? Per Latent Christ, I think. Concentrate, Jade. My mind seems to be wandering off. I look at Charlie and Omi. They're transfixed staring down at the show below. There's a smell of incense. Perhaps it's from the strange canisters on the railing of the gallery above.

But there's another smell too that it's only partly masking. I wonder if I'm feeling a bit sick. I look at Charlie again. He shakes his head and begins to cough. On the big screen Joachim is exhorting us all to come to him, to leave our sinful flesh and rise through death. Death?

Watching him seems to have cleared my head a bit. The smell behind the incense I suddenly realise is that of burning. Something is on fire. Now I see real flames springing up here and there. 'Charlie, open the door. We need some fresh air. I can't think properly.'

We all stumble through the little room towards the door. Charlie wrenches it open and we step quickly outside to hang on to the iron staircase, gasping and retching. It's such a relief to be out of that sickly atmosphere in the real world again. But I know I have to go back in there to see what's going on. Something is horribly wrong but I still don't get what's happening. I have to find out.

'Right,' I say. 'I'm going back in. Stay here and if I don't come out in a few minutes come in and get me because I'll have passed out, or fallen over the rail. At least one or two of us has to stay fit to do something.'

'OK, Jade. We'll wait here for you. But not for long. I'll also do some deep breathing and teach Omi how to do it. It gives you more oxygen like swimming under water. You can stay down longer.'

Charlie's clearly in much better shape than I am with his martial arts practice, but it's my job to go back in. I'm supposed to be the professional after all and I'm being paid to risk my life, even though I didn't know that'd be called for when I signed up for the job. I take a couple of deep but, I fear, inefficient breaths and propel myself through the room on to the gallery. This time with the boys holding the fort behind I go right up to the rail and, still standing up, take a good look down into the chapel.

It's like *Towering Inferno* or a scene from Dante down there. Fires are burning fiercely in several parts of the building. Some students seem to have been overcome by the fumes. Some are struggling at the door with Daniel Davidson trying to pull them away. He's shouting but I can't make out the words or those of Joachim still pontificating from the screen. There's no sign of the Molders or Dean Bishop. Some of the students get to the door past Davidson and are trying to open it. They seem to be locked in. I feel the fumes starting to get to me again. Time to go. Before I duck back through the little door I glance up towards the dome. The saints in their window niches seem to glimmer and waver through the smoke as if they're bending forward to watch the scene of poor struggling humanity below.

'Charlie, dial 999 on your mobile. We need fire, police, ambulance, the lot. Omi, you'll be quicker than me. Go down the stairs through that little door, turn left round the corner of the corridor. The entrance to the chapel is just there. See if you can open it. If you can't, come back.'

His slim figure is running down the iron treads and whisking through the door while Charlie is still trying to raise the emergency services. In a couple of minutes Omi reappears, he shakes his head and runs up the stairs. 'No good, Jade. It won't move.'

What can we do? The lower door was locked too and there's nothing to break it down, no convenient scaffolding pole or plank forgotten by workmen. Then I remember the rope ladders. Will they reach to the floor of the chapel? We'll have to find out the hard way. 'Come on. We'll try the ladders I brought for us to use.'

We go back in again. The smoke and fumes are denser now. I can hear the roar and crackle of the fires below. Flame is licking up the walls. The chairs are burning like bundles of kindling. I take the ladders out of the bag and give one to Omi. With half my mind I hear Charlie talking on his mobile. Omi and I go out on to the balcony and drop the ladders over the rail. 'I'll go down, Jade, and show them the way up. Some of them know me. They might trust me more than a stranger. Hold the ladder at the top in case it slips off the rail.'

I can't see the bottom of the ladder or what exactly he might be going down into like some lower circle of hell. 'Be careful,' I say uselessly. As if he had any choice.

He goes nimbly over the side. Charlie moves to the other ladder, waves to me through the smoke and follows him down like a couple of acrobats on parallel trapezes. I dash through the room, take a few quick breaths of clean air and go back to the railing. The first ladder is stretched tight. I hold on to its hooks. Someone is coming up.

It's one of the students. I help her over the rail and push her towards the door hoping she's got enough of a clear head left to see the daylight coming in from the outside. Because another head is appearing on the first ladder and another now on the second, I have to position myself between the two, shoving them towards the door before the next arrives. It's a human conveyor belt. I'm not sure how strong the gallery is, how many it can support before it breaks away from the wall and falls into the furnace below that's now climbing up to where I'm standing and threatening the escape route. How can I signal to Omi and Charlie that they must come up before the ladders catch fire and they're cut off? I've lost count of how many students have come over the rail. But then I didn't know how many there were anyway.

I'm trying to peer down through the smoke. No more heads are appearing. I look across to the big screen and see it beginning to melt into a toxic gel that folds and crumples even as the face of the Apostle Joachim is snuffed out.

Charlie appears at the top of his ladder. 'Charlie, where's Omi? Have you seen him?'

'He's coming up. We agreed there was nothing more we could do. There are still one or two students down there passed out. But we can't carry them.'

'Davidson.'

'He won't come. He says we're frustrating God's will. He wants to die. He thinks he'll go straight to heaven.'

'Molders and the dean?'

'No sign of them. They must have had a way out of their own.'

'So must we now. We'll leave the ladders in case Davidson changes his mind.' The reverse of the road to Damascus, I think in my almost hallucinogenic state that's taking on all the sensations of a bad trip. 'The whole building will be gone if the fire brigade doesn't get here soon.'

One of the lower windows suddenly bursts into a shower of deadly coloured shards. 'Let's go. Now!' We scramble through the door, and on to the stairs and down. Some of the students have collapsed on the grass, others sit and sob. I hear sirens and then a crash. We run round to the front door of the chapel but the heat coming through the walls and the stench of burning drive us out of the corridor and through the campus to the courtyard entrance.

A fireman has just smashed the lock with his axe and the gates are being folded back. We wave them on. I run up to one of the control cars. 'It's the chapel at the back. There were still people in there we think. You'll have to break the door down. There are some other people round the back too who may need treatment for smoke and burns.'

'You don't look too good yourself.'

After my lady had left me I wept again. Then it was first that a little mouse crept out looking for the crumbs from the bread I had eaten and I, believing that I was now quite alone in the world and at the worst facing death by hanging, took off a little piece of what remained, in gratitude that a living creature should visit me. Watching it nibble upon that bread and seeing its will to survive even in this dismal place and that it had the wit to seek out one that might help it do so, my spirits became a little lighter. I began to turn my mind to my own survival.

First I remembered my lady's words and that I should present myself as cleanly and decently as possible. Then I thought that I should prepare something in my own defence. And all this must be done soon for at any moment I might be called to appear and give account of myself. My lady's generosity meant that I could at least take steps to follow that advice.

After an hour or so, for I had no means of knowing how time passed except as the little light came and went in the high window, the gaoler returned with the prison ration of bread and water.

'I see that you indeed have friends in high places. Remember that you must pay me for your lodging here.'

'I shall not forget master constable and now that I am better provided for I shall ask you of your kindness to get me certain necessaries more. First, for your wife's loan of her gown there shall be payment if she will buy me another to appear decently before those who will examine me further, and she shall be paid for her trouble as you for your pains in providing food, drink and candles. Then I must ask you what next is to happen to me or how long I am to be in your charge.'

'They do not tell me such things, only when I am to bring you somewhere. Nevertheless there is a servant in Justice Ludlow's employ who may be persuaded to listen for news, for a price.'

'Then ask him and he shall be paid when you bring me news but make sure it is the truth at least as he understands it. I am not to be cozened. As for the gown let your wife set about it. Say to her that it must be neat and as becomes my rank and age but not gaudy. She knows from her searching of me the bigness of it.'

When he was gone I fell to my writing again, first of some arguments I might use and then of my memorials to make the time pass, for when I thought to set out my case I rested much on the knowledge of my innocence in every matter I might be charged with, except of going in man's attire and that was not a hanging offence as Moll Cutpurse her continuing survival after several prosecutions testifies.

I considered how I should plead and wished that I might not answer at all but then I could be taken back to prison, a board and heavy weights laid upon me until either I agreed to speak or was pressed to death which I did not believe I could endure. Then I thought that the nature of the charge would determine my answer. If Dr Gilbert was determined to press witchcraft upon me I must answer 'not guilty'. Yet for a lesser thing if I judged I might escape with a fine I might plead the contrary. I was helped in these considerations by thinking how the countess might advise me in her wisdom and knowledge of the world and its ways.

When next the gaoler opened the door his wife stood behind him.

'Now mistress, no tricks.' And to his wife he said: 'Knock when you are ready to come out. But beware the witch's cunning.' Then he locked us in together.

'I have brought you a gown that I trust will suit your purpose better than my old one, which was all that I could spare.'

'And indeed I am grateful for your kindness and will pay you for the loan of it,' I said while she was opening the bag she carried. This gown too was grey of a stuff that was good but not fine as satin would be and with points of lace at the throat and wrists.

'In this you should appear like an honest wench even if you bain't. And for that end I have also brought you a cap for your head and a kerchief for your neck. My husband believes you may be a witch and you can give us a remedy to work on him. Yet we found no marks on you and it may be you deceive him to gain his favour. I clearly long for a child of our own. They blame me that I do not conceive yet if the man cannot stand then the woman is not to blame. But I must hold my tongue for I would not shame him.'

'He believes he is bewitched which is easier for him than a failure in nature. I will do what I can but you must follow my instructions exactly and even if his state is no better he must swear to tell no one that I tried to help him. I will need some things that you must bring me. But soon, for I may be taken from here any day. I will set them down on a paper which you must show to the apothecary in Eastgate.'

'You will not ask our souls for the devil or fill my belly with a changeling?'

'I have no power to do such things. What I can do is only to assist nature and try to take off that impediment in the mind that hinders him.'

I told her then what I should need to set about his cure and paid her for the gown. She had brought a piece of glass so that I could see a little of myself and promised an old comb on her next visit. Then she knocked upon the door and was let out.

It was beginning to grow dark before the gaoler came again and although I had candles I had no tinder box for lighting them so I was forced to sit in the twilight, hearing sometimes the scamper and rustle of my little friend the mouse, but otherwise no sound from outside and only my own breathing and heartbeat from within. I had heard that in watching for witches to betray themselves when they were imprisoned their keepers had sometimes a spyhole through which to see when their familiars might visit them to suck their blood before doing their bidding. And such even a spider, fly or creeping thing might be thought, so I was wary of the mouse and had searched the door and the wall it stood in carefully for any crack that might serve such a purpose but found none. Yet I was glad that the mouse had whisked away at the first sound of the bolt being drawn.

'My wife sends you these.' The gaoler set down a rush basket. 'And I have news from my friend in Justice Ludlow's service. He is to examine you again with the intent to put your case before the Grand Jury which will meet on Friday to consider what should be tried at the assizes.'

'And when will Justice Ludlow examine me?'

'Tomorrow forenoon.'

'And after what will happen to me?'

'You will be brought back here until the Grand Jury decides, which will be on Friday, as I say.'

'And what is today?' For I had lost all account of time and understood now why prisoners scratched marks on their prison walls to signify the passing of the days.

'Today is the first of the week. You are fortunate mistress to have friends for the friendless are often kept without meat, drink or sleep to force them to confess. I am glad that not many such come my way. For all my employment hardens me to suffering I do not like to be the instrument of it. But if it is my orders I must do it or lose my place. I see my wife has chosen you a fine gown to appear in so perhaps they will have pity on you if none comes forward to speak against you.'

'I am indeed pleased with your wife's choice of attire. Tell her that she should attend on me after tomorrow. What I have to say is for her ears.'

'Yet it is my body that ails.'

'Nevertheless you must do and suffer her to do what I will tell you but above all be secret or I cannot help you.'

When he was gone for the night I took off the gown to keep it clean and neat and set to work on the things she had brought me in the rush basket.

The next morning I ate some bread and drank some small beer and when the gaoler returned to empty the pisspot I begged him for a basin to wash my hands and face in and said that the water must be heated for I needed some to dissolve the powdered herbs his wife had brought me of satyrion and nasturtium, both of a hot moist temper to provoke lust and increase men's seed.

When he came again it was to take me out of the gaol to

the justice his house nearby. Once more we passed the dungeon where the common felons waited out their imprisonment, cursing and weeping surrounded by the stench of the pail which served them all as a jakes and must surely breed gaol fever. I was determined to die rather than suffer a similar fate and to this end I had included certain herbs cousin to hemlock in my shopping list for the gaoler's wife as also opiates to dull the senses while they did their work.

Once again I mounted the stairs to where the justice waited with Dr Gilbert.

'You understand that I am to make my deposition for the Grand Jury,' he said when I had given my name and the house where I had lodged in London. 'How do you plead to the charge of witchcraft which has been made against you?'

'Not guilty sir.'

'If you were to plead guilty and save me and the gentlemen of the Grand Jury, the judge and jurors at the assizes, much trouble then it might go easier with you. Come now, confess your sin and make your peace with God and man.'

'Sir, I cannot confess to an untruth, even to escape hanging.'

'If the Lady Anne dies the charge becomes capital murder by witchcraft.'

'But by your leave sir she has not died. She is grievously sick and has been these several years. Her mother takes her to a notable physician in Cambridge yet he is not to be charged with witchcraft if she dies while under his care.'

'What do you say to your going in male attire to the confusion of those around you?'

'Sir when I was left alone and friendless after my father's death it seemed to me best for the preserving of my virtue and earning my bread by honest means.'

'By this counterfeiting sir,' Dr Gilbert said, 'she has procured a noble lady to unlawful love which is one of the ways by which we may know a witch.'

'Sir,' I cried out, 'my lady loved me in all truth as she saw me which was as her page and helper in her laboratory and with the numbers of sick people who flock to her. And if she loved me as noble minds may love those who serve them faithfully who can point the finger and say this is unlawful?'

'A thing may be unlawful even so. Ignorance is no defence in the law. Did you go about to procure her to unlawful love?'

'I do not understand you sir. What could I do to bring this about?'

'Did you not often give her potions of your own making? Were these not love potions?'

'No sir. Only such remedies as physicians use for melancholy or sleeplessness, many of which she assisted in preparing with her own hands.'

'Have you not made a pact with the devil? I have been told by a witness that you were called by many "the young wizard".'

'They called me that when I prescribed for their sickness and they were healed but out of their ignorance not understanding that medicines work upon evil humours to drive them out or calm their effects and that every evil has its counterpart herb as Master Gerard has set out in his *Herball*. This being published some seven or eight years ago is in common use in many houses throughout the land as Dr Gilbert knows.'

'Can you confirm this?'

I saw that Dr Gilbert hesitated but knew he could not deny it or if he did must appear very foolish when the truth was out.

'Even so this does not preclude the practice of witchcraft but may go hand in hand with it like the rogue and necromancer Simon Forman.'

'Sir, I will swear upon the countess her own book of psalms that I intended no mischief for her or her friends but only to find a little corner where I might be protected from the harshness and wickedness of the world.'

'Dr Gilbert,' Justice Ludlow said then, 'I cannot find great evidence of what you allege. Can you not bring the testimony of the countess herself or her daughter to support the case?'

'The countess has already taken her daughter to London with a view to their removal to Cambridge and in any case the Lady Anne is not fit to appear. You must make the best you can sir, with what I have given you, as her counterfeiting and administering physick, and going as a man, and the opinion of her as a wizard among the countess her servants and tenants.'

'Well I will do my best but you must give me your own written testimony to put with what I shall depose. Let her be taken back to the gaol.'

'Sir, let it please be also set down that I have amended my attire as you commanded and endeavour to show myself obedient in all things and heartily sorry for any distress I have caused. But as for the charge of witchcraft I utterly deny it.'

'Enough mistress. You are too saucy with your betters. You should stand in the pillory or be sent to a bridewell as a suspected vagrant, there to be whipped.'

Once again the gaoler took me down to my cell and left me to think upon my fate. Dr Gilbert was determined to pursue me, even though I was no longer a threat to him in my lady's favour. Now I could only wait for the Grand Jury to rule upon whether I should be tried. My mind was inclined first this way then that. Sometimes I thought that they would find there was no case to answer, at others that I must prepare to defend myself before judge and jury.

Now I took the little piece of glass in my hand and studied my own face. If I should appear before them would they think it the face of a confirmed witch? Already I hardly knew myself in my woman's attire with a cap and kerchief. I was becoming estranged from that self I had inhabited since my father's death and did not know if I could ever return. And yet I did not see an Amaryllis in my reflection but rather as a face appears in a pool when the wind ruffles and dissolves it, two images side by side slipping in and out of each other.

I confess that I feared for myself. I knew that I must keep the gaoler as my friend if I could and so I set about a remedy for his ill. The next day his wife presented herself as I had asked.

'My husband tells me the Grand Jury will decide your case whether you shall be tried or not tomorrow. What can you do to help us in that little time?'

'You must carefully mark all I say. Tonight you shall make him drink this instead of ale. Then in the morning when he wakes you must take his prick in your hands and rub it gently with this powder, mixed tonight with a little grease to make an ointment and set by the bedside ready. This will cause him to tingle and as you work on him you say: 'Rise little man and stand. Make the cock crow.' When he begins to swell, as I have no doubt he will, you must slip this ring over his member and tie it firm but not so as to strangle him, and guide him to you, still speaking those words and encouraging him with the ointment.'

'What are these marks on the ring?'

'They are symbols of heat and power.'

'Not marks of the devil? And where did a young girl get such knowledge that married women themselves do not have?'

'From my father's receipts with which he cured many men in this city.'

'And do you have that book with you?'

'I carry it in my head where it is safest. Let me know how you do if I should still be here. And if it does not suffice that first time then go to again, strictly as I have told you, and your belly will swell within the half year. But in everything be gentle as if you stroked a cat and your voice soft so that he shall cry out for more, not push you away.'

The gaoler's wife crossed herself: 'This is indeed magic for I feel the heat rising already in my own privities. It is a pity we women cannot conceive as and when we please, with or without men. Then the world could be better ordered.' She gathered up the things into her apron pocket and went away laughing.

All next day I waited for news of the Grand Jury, sometimes able to write in my memorials, sometimes only to walk about the cell or stare up at the changing square of light. Even the mouse seemed to have left me. At length as the day was fading and I was in need of a light for my candle, I heard the door being unbolted. I stood up in spite of the trembling in my legs. It was the gaoler.

'Your fate is decided mistress, the Grand Jury finds not enough case for a trial in the allegation of witchcraft since there is no evidence from others than the doctor, and the lady lives. Yet your confession of being a counterfeit will keep you here, for they say that you showed no real penitence. Therefore you are remanded to the gaol for a twelvemonth. But for your help to my wife you shall have no harshness from me. Only I could say something if I would that could yet have you tried as a witch. But you are safe with me. Here is the light for your candle and a cake of my wife's baking.'

When he was gone I was torn again between relief and despair: relief that my trial was not to be but despair that I should languish here at the mercy of the doctor. And no matter how grateful the gaoler and his wife were now, if he should fail again and my remedy cease to be efficacious, then he would turn against me, and I knew no more that I could prescribe to his help. Then he might accept a bribe and let in the men who had brought me here. It would be easy for them to smother me and put it about that I had died of gaol fever as indeed I might. So I turned this way and that, seeking a way out and wishing I were indeed what they had alleged and had the power to shrink myself to the size of the mouse that came and went as it pleased or fly away out of that place.

The ambulance man insisted that all three of us, me, Charlie and Omi, should be checked out for smoke inhalation or burns and whisked us off to the nearest A & E department. There we sat about, falling asleep while the real wounded were attended to, getting cups of vile coffee and bars of chocolate from a machine until called, examined and discharged.

'You're not fit enough to drive, however. Where do you live?' the tired young doctor said as I sat on the examination couch with its dried-blood plastic skin.

'London.'

'Take a train.' So we abandoned our bikes which anyway were five miles behind us in the shed at Wessex if they hadn't gone up in flames with the rest of the building. I was too tired to ask or even to care. I slept most of the way to Waterloo, said goodbye to the boys and staggered through the streets where the shapeless, headless bundles of the drunks and the homeless huddled in doorways. I had just enough energy left to shower off the soot and sweat, knock back a glass of wine and fall into bed.

When I woke in the morning I switched on the news while I drank the mug of tea I had taken back to bed. Four people had died in a fire at a private college in Hampshire. The cause of the fire was unknown but an electrical fault was suspected.

I get out of bed and go over to the computer, log into my server and key in the Temple website. There's nothing. It's gone. Pulled. As if it had never been. I'm totally zonked, bone weary and wander about like a zombie making toast and coffee and having a long slow bath. I know I have to go back and find out what's happened and if the Crusader survived. And there are the four dead, one of whom is almost certainly Daniel Davidson. Then the phone rings. It's the police.

'Ms Green? We understand you were involved in last night's events at Wessex University. The officer in charge took your details.'

Just in case I might try to pretend I hadn't been there. Honest, guv, it wasn't me. I'd had just enough sense left to give my own name. Lucy Cowell is dead.

'We'd like you to come in and make a statement as soon as possible. If you're up to it. We understand you were among those taken to hospital. When might you be able to come?'

We fix a time. 'There were three of you, weren't there? We only have contact numbers for the other two, mobiles and an address for Mr Gao. I understand Mr Omi was resident at the college.'

When he's gone I ring Charlie. He hasn't been contacted yet. Perhaps they're going to hear what I have to say first. We agree a story that's a part of the truth. We were curious. We wanted to watch the ceremony. I'm still so tired I fall asleep on the train and then take a taxi to the police station. Eventually I'm shown into an interview room. The man behind the desk stands up and offers a hand.

'Detective Inspector Bradley, and this is Detective Sergeant Beavan.'

The sergeant is an attractive, confident thirty-something, hoping to be the next female commander à la Helen Mirren. Could I fall for a member of the fuzz? Concentrate, Jade.

He switches on the recording machine and goes through the identification ritual. 'Now, Ms Green, could you tell us in your own words what happened? Why were you three there and indeed where were you?'

'Before I go into all that, inspector, could you tell me what happened after we were taken to hospital? The BBC wasn't very informative.'

'The fire brigade managed to break down the door but they were beaten back by the heat and smoke. They did stop the fire spreading to the rest of the building and eventually they got it under control in the part where it started, unfortunately they were unable to save anyone. Four bodies have been recovered but it will need DNA or dental records to identify them. A pity they didn't know about the trapdoor. They could have all got out.'

'Trapdoor?'

'You didn't know about it either? It was in the floor behind some kind of wooden structure. We're still trying to get a picture of the inside of the building. It was completely gutted.'

I see the chapel rising in a great Pentecostal flame, taking Davidson up into his imagined heaven like an image of a burning ship in a sea story by Conrad we did for GCE. 'An immense and lonely flame from whose summit black smoke poured continuously at the sky.' Something like that.

'The building was a chapel. The trapdoor must have been behind the pulpit.'

'So what were you doing there, Ms Green, and where were you? We haven't of course ruled anything out yet. We don't know if we're looking at an accident or arson. But four people are dead and that makes it very serious.'

'We were up in the first gallery. There's an outside staircase at the back that leads to the two galleries.'

'It doesn't any more. The roof seems to have fallen first and then the windows.'

'The roof would have brought down the galleries?' He nods. I see a John Piper stump of a building, silhouetted against flame.

'I understand from some of the students who have recovered enough to be interviewed that someone let down rope ladders from the galleries and helped them escape. Was that you?'

'Yes.'

'So what were you doing there with rope ladders?'

'They, the authorities, didn't like anyone to watch their religious ceremonies, anyone who wasn't a member, that is. We knew this was going to be a big one and we were curious to see it.'

'But why the ladders?'

'We thought we might get locked in and have to climb out of the building somehow. It was a precaution.'

'In fact the doors must have locked automatically when all the electrics shorted out so you would have found yourself down there with everyone else all shut inside a burning building.'

'Well, lucky for us, inspector, the doors leading to the galleries were the old-fashioned kind and weren't on the automatic circuit.'

'Lucky for the rest I'd say or we'd be looking at nearer thirty deaths. There are a lot of things that still aren't clear to me. We may well need to talk to you again so stay where we can reach you. Most of the students we've talked to seem to be foreign.'

'It wasn't a regular English college. More of a private one.'

'The whole building has been sealed off while we and the fire brigade make a more thorough investigation. Nobody seems to be responsible for the place and it's legally owned by some company abroad. Do you have any thoughts on that, Ms Green?'

'I only met the dean and his secretary and a couple of the staff.'

'Names?'

I give them and wait while Sergeant Beavan writes them down. 'Could you give me some sort of authorisation to get into the college? My bike is still in the shed there and I'd rather like it back.'

'Bike?'

'Motorcycle. Cheap, quick way of getting to classes.'

'If I may say so you look a bit older than the average student. I've a daughter in her first year at uni – Leeds.'

'These days you have to keep topping up your skills and qualifications. They call it lifetime learning but it's really just a way of not being left behind in the rat race.'

'Don't we know it. Even in our job.' He smiles conspiratorially at the sergeant. 'I can't see why you shouldn't be allowed to collect your cycle. Just let them have the number and other details at the desk. They'll give you a chit.' I'm being dismissed. He presses a bell and a young constable appears to take me to reception where I sit on a worn pale-blue plastic and tube chair until

summoned. Then at last I'm let out with the paper in my hand
authorising me to take my own bike.

Why haven't I told them everything I know or think I know
instead of just the bits I agreed with Charlie? Because it's
complicated. Because they wouldn't believe me and I would have
to explain endlessly, involving Galton who couldn't be relied on
not to feed them some garbled tale of witchcraft and persecu-
tion. Because they might suspect that Charlie, Omi and I had
something to do with the fire and they haven't ruled out arson.

I take the bus to the gates of Wessex. They're closed with a
policeman on duty in front. I produce my authorisation and he
swings open the gate. Not locked then. He wanted to know
exactly where I was going and cautioned me for my own safety
to stick to the paths. But I have to see the chapel. The smell
of smoke and burning stains the air all over the campus. I take
a chance that the electricity is still off and the CCTV not working
and duck round the back of the bike shed. But I don't get far.
The area leading to the chapel is cordoned off. The corridor
that runs past it has gone too. Smoke is still filtering out of the
blackened stubs of walls and from the piles of debris on the
ground. Men in uniform pick through the charnel heaps. I turn
away, hoping at least the three students had lost consciousness
before they died and that Daniel Davidson's beliefs had somehow
anaesthetised him against a horribly painful death.

Bishop and Molders, if those were their names, must be out
of the country by now. Were they lovers or just partners in
greed? And then there was the Apostle Joachim if he existed
and wasn't just a phantom conjured up by the new alchemy,
virtual reality, part of the trappings of the scam. I am glad of
the throb of the Crusader, its solid metal and leather, and the
rush of air over my helmet. I know I have to make contact with
Galton but as I near the point where I could turn off for his
road I notch up the engine and roar on.

There is a message from Charlie waiting for me. The police

have merely told him to keep himself available but haven't called him in. Omi is staying with him at the Gaos. He has rung some of his Wessex friends on their mobile phones. They had seen the chapel burning from the hall windows but couldn't break the locking circuit until suddenly it went, presumably with the rest of the electrical system. They'd been evacuated by the police to a church hall in the town. Now they were making arrangements to go home.

Some of those who'd been in the chapel are still in hospital. Their families have been notified. The staff are being interviewed in turn but since they all live away from the college they know nothing, except that they no longer have an employer or a job. Wessex University has simply melted in the flames, dissolved into an airy nothingness.

I feel I should be doing something but I don't know what. Presumably the police will get round to setting Interpol on to the supposed owners of Wessex, to trying to trace Bishop and Molders. Unfinished business. To pass the time and deal with my own restlessness and frustration, I decide to read the last few pages of Amyntas' memorial though what reference it has to recent events I can't really see. Still it's something to do and it may give me the impetus to ring Galton.

Thus I contemplated my fate and the remedies I had in my hands which could offer me only the comfort of death. And so the night came and I fell into a sleep with the help of a little of the poppy the gaoler's wife had procured for me. Then in the morning when I was ready to despair at the emptiness, except of fear, of the days ahead, for I had brought my memorials up to the present and no more was likely to befall me in that place except that I should not live to record, I heard the gaoler at the door of my cell.

'You have a visitor mistress.'

I could not descry the figure that stood behind him in the darkness of the passage but terror seized me that it might already have the face of death. Great was my relief then when the duenna came forward into the poor light of my cell. 'I will leave you,' the gaoler said. 'Knock when you are ready to go.'

'Our lady hearing of the decision against you has sent me. I am sorry to see you in such a place for all you have put her in some jeopardy.'

'How could she hear in so short a time since she is gone to London?'

'She removed only to Ivychurch but let it be thought that she had gone away. She was brought word of the Grand Jury its judgement that you were not to be tried but also of Justice Ludlow's confining you at Dr Gilbert's insistence.'

'I cannot endure this place for so many months together. I would rather die.'

'Do not be so passionate child. The countess knows this well enough. She sends you this letter and purse and your own little chest from the laboratory at the great house. She has made provision for your safety. You must leave here as soon as it is dark. Ask no more and speak to no one of it. Now I must go. No one must know that I have been here, except the gaoler. But you must not speak even to him of it.'

Then she knocked upon the door. It was opened, she passed through and I heard it bolted behind. I went to stand beneath the window and opened the letter from my lady.

'Child, I know your distress and will not abandon you. Yet my hands are tied. Do as you have been bid and God go with you. Think of me sometimes with kindness.'

It was signed MH with the Sidney pheon as was her custom. I opened the purse and discovered more than sufficient money to effect my escape and sustain me for a while. In my own little chest I found as well as several of the things necessary to a physician, a little ivory-handled dagger, with her symbol engraved on it, to cut up meat, sharpen my quill and defend myself. Yet I wept, half in gratitude but most because this was a last farewell. I knew I must vanish from her presence and never attempt to be near her again.

I have waited out the day in fear that some harm should come to me before the night. When the gaoler came to bring me meat and drink he would not look into my face. At the last when he returned with a taper to light my candle he looked back at the door and said: 'A good night to you mistress from me and my wife.' Then he left. I heard the latch fall but no bolt being shot. Now I am dressed in my clothes as Amyntas with my other few possessions bundled into my gown. I must put out my candle before I see if the door will open. Then I must make my way feeling along the wall, silently past the cell where the felons lie, trusting that the door at the end and the postern beyond are open and unguarded. I have put down a crust of bread for the mouse and am ready to take my leave.

I close the page. I hope she made it but I'll never know. I feel as if someone has gone out of my own life. Time to ring Galton.

'Ah, Ms Green. I thought I might have a call from you soon.'

'I'm not sure how much you've heard. It's all been rather hairy.'

'I saw the reports of the fire but they didn't give a great deal of information. Can you tell me any more?'

'I was there.'

'Where?'

'In the chapel when it caught fire. Up in one of the galleries.'

'Indeed. I believe they found four bodies.'

'Yes. There would have been more killed but most of them managed to climb out.'

'So what is happening now?'

'Wessex has ceased to exist. As far as anyone knows Bishop and Molders have left the country. That's my guess anyway.'

'Almost a kind of justice. Retribution.'

'Except that four relatively innocent people died.'

'Yes, yes, of course. What do we do now, Ms Green?'

'We do nothing. There's nothing to be done. You can't take a chimera to an employment tribunal.'

'The Temple of the Latent Christ? The putative owners?'

'Vanished. If they ever existed. How much did you really know, Dr Galton? I believe it was all set up to get gullible young people to make over their money to the organisers. That it was meant to look like a mass suicide. If you suspected this and you could have told me right in the beginning we might have prevented even those four deaths.'

'I didn't know the details. I only knew something was wrong. I'd felt it, a miasma of evil from the time they took over. I came to you because I hoped that in looking into my dismissal you would find out. If I'd tried to tell you, or anyone else for that matter, that I felt that something was wrong you would have said, quite rightly, "where's your evidence?"'

'Why me?'

'I needed someone independent. The name attracted me of course. I hoped you would be young. Willing to delve more deeply into rather strange waters than a conventional firm.'

'Why exactly did they sack you? How did the Amyntas memorial come into it?'

'I used it to teach the students about alternative philosophies, ways of looking at things, ways of being. And about the evolution of knowledge; how we've stumbled down the centuries looking for answers. I handed out extracts from some of Amyntas' recipes; prescriptions I suppose we would call them now. I took in some of the ingredients and one of those little gas stoves campers have and that we sometimes use in our rituals so that we could try the recipes out.'

'Were they ones that included opiates?'

'Just a mild sedative. The garden poppy. Such a handsome

flower, *Papaver somniferum*, double frilled lilac petals and silvery leaves. They pop up everywhere in my vegetable garden. A gentle calming herb. But some of the students thought they were hallucinating. Word got to the dean. It was all the excuse they needed to get rid of me.'

'Did they think you knew something about what was really going on? Is that why they wanted to get you out of Wessex?'

'Perhaps. But more I think they were afraid I would undermine their influence with the students. I see now that would have spoilt their plans. At the time I thought it was just jealousy and fear of any alternative system of belief.

'There's one thing I have to tell you, Ms Green, one thing I embroidered a little. I said my copy was stolen. That was a little fiction, a white lie to make my story more convincing. No one apart from you has ever seen the whole thing.'

'I warned you not to lie to your lawyer. What else have you been keeping from me? How was I supposed to do my job on such flawed information? How much did you know about the Temple setup?'

'I know it encouraged people to join their absurd sect. I didn't know why.'

'Absurd?'

'Manufactured from quasi-scriptural bits and pieces with no real foundation.'

'Couldn't the same be said of your beliefs?'

'We have a distinct ancestry, an historical basis. Ours is a belief system that encourages the personal development of the individual. That's why we appeal to many people today.'

I realise I'm getting nowhere in this conversation. It's time to go. 'What will you do now? I think you might find it difficult to get another educational post.' Maybe it's a mean thing to say but I'm trying to inject a little reality into his thinking.

'I've decided to realise some of the equity in my house. The high priestess and I would like to travel. So I suppose this is goodbye, Ms Green. You'll send me your final bill. After all you're not responsible for how things turned out.'

'And the manuscript?'

'Keep it. I don't need it any more. I'm not at all sure it isn't a complete forgery anyway. But it's served its purpose.'

The line's gone dead. I feel completely defeated but I'm not sure why. Galton and his high priestess are going off to dance naked hand in hand around the world. He's even cast doubt on Amyntas, someone I feel I've been living with all these weeks but who he says might never have existed. I look at the pile of mail on my desk. The computer is showing thirty-two emails demanding to be opened.

The future seems empty. Helen's gone and fading even from my dreams. Is that what the countess is saying in her last aria or what Donne meant with his 'I am every dead thing'? This absence, nothingness we fall into and that we try to climb out of on the silken ladder of love or the gossamer of faith, the old transforming alchemies that are still as potent as ever.

The phone is ringing. I pick it up.

'Yes?'

'Lost Causes?'

'Yes.'

'I asylum seeker. Please help.'

AFTERWORD

This is fiction. The known facts about the life of Mary Sidney Herbert, Countess of Pembroke, can be found in *Philip's Phoenix* by Margaret P. Hannay, to whom this romance is indebted.

After her son's marriage, before building herself a handsome mansion in Buckinghamshire, courtesy of James I, Mary was reported to be enjoying her retirement in the continental town of Spa where she could be seen in company with the Countess of Barlemont taking tobacco and shooting on a pistol range, both being 'very merry' and their lodging 'the court of the English for play, dancing and all entertainment'. She lived until 1621 and died at the age of 62.

p.s.

Ideas,
interviews
& features . . .

From Accident to Experience

Louise Tucker talks to Maureen Duffy

Tell me about your background.
The family, my mother's family – because I know nothing about my father's family at all – are East Enders, from Stratford, but I was born, by accident, on the south coast. My mother and father weren't married; my father was a wandering Irish labourer and in the IRA, he said. They lived together for a couple of years, partly in London, but when she was pregnant he had a job on the south coast and they went down to Worthing. I was born in hiding down there. Two months after he left, and that was the end of that.

In my mother's family there was a lot of tuberculosis among the girls; it was a family of ten and I think there were six girls, four of whom died of TB and another would have died of it if she hadn't died in the war. My mother was diagnosed at fifteen so when I was a child she was whisked off to various sanatoria, for several months at a time, and I was either put into care, sent to a children's home or looked after by relatives. After her first bout, which happened when I was about three and a half, we went back to London. Then at the beginning of the war we returned to Worthing because we were offered a very cheap house to rent, on condition that my mother would take her slightly older sister out of the sanatorium and look after her. We were bombed in September 1940 and my aunt was killed, which is how she managed not to die of TB. Having lost everything, the house, the furniture, our clothes, my mother decided that she would evacuate us to her brother in Trowbridge, and we stayed there throughout the rest of the war. But she became increasingly ill and, realizing she was dying, she sent me back to London in 1948 to live with her remaining sister's family. She was very worried that my stepfather would make me leave school and go out to work and she was determined that I would go to 'college', as it was called, if possible.

So I came back to London, went to the local grammar school and then eventually on to King's College, London. I was the first in the family to go to university though my cousin did go to teacher training college. I tried to get into Oxford, inspired by one of my teachers, but I was only 17 and at the interview they said go back and have another year in the sixth form. Of course I couldn't – I was in the care of the council at that point and my grant from them was finishing. So I thought, To hell with this, I've got enough A-levels anyway for King's, so I went. I think I would have been out of my depth at Oxford – I might have been very seduced by academic life instead of writing, and I'd always wanted to be a writer.

When did you decide you wanted to be a writer?
I was 12 when I decided. I was absolutely made up in my own mind, but with the sort of background I came from obviously nobody had ever been a writer. It was a great ▶

6 I was 12 when I decided to be a writer. I was absolutely made up in my own mind, but with the sort of background I came from obviously nobody had ever been a writer. 9

3

From Accident to Experience *(continued)*

◄ aspiration to become a teacher, so I had to conceal this decision I had made and pretend I was going to teach like everybody else. Even up to when she died in the eighties my auntie was still saying, 'I know you're doing very well dear but I do wish you had a proper job'!

What was the inspiration for your first novel, and how did you start writing it?
I didn't want to be a novelist, I wanted to be a playwright but it was virtually impossible. I wrote my first full-length play in my third year of university and I sent it in for a competition which was the brainchild of Kenneth Tynan, run by the *Observer*, to find new playwrights. It didn't win but they asked me to become a member of the Royal Court Writers' Group so I joined and I was in it with Edward Bond, John Arden and Arnold Wesker. Arnold always says that he did some reading for the competition and he was the one who picked out my play. So I wrote several plays, but meanwhile I'd met a publisher. He was starting a list called New Authors at Hutchinson and said, 'Stop wasting your time writing plays that nobody will put on. Write a novel and I will publish it.' This was a pure con trick since he had no idea, and nor had I, whether I could write a publishable novel. But I was tired of not having an audience since it was incredibly difficult for a woman in those days to be a playwright. The only female contemporaries were Sheila Delaney and Ann Jellicoe and in effect they both had to give up, even though they were the most successful.

This editor's request coincided with me

6 Once you've finished writing a book you feel completely bereft, totally lost, miserable and hellish, and you think, "I'll never write another!" 9

trying to make sense of my rather unusual childhood – the drowning man looks at past life routine – so eventually I wrote my first autobiographical novel, which is still in print. That was how I got into novels.

Alchemy is full of historical detail. How and where did you do your research, and how long did it take?
I had the Culpeper so that was to hand, and Sidney's _Arcadia_ and Margaret Hannay's scholarly biography of the Countess, but I use the London Library extensively, intensively, and I like to be able to carry things away from there. I used to do a lot of work in the Public Records Office and the British Library, but as I said I like to carry things away and surround myself with them. I go on researching – I don't research and stop – so the book took a couple of years. There's usually six months' gestation before I start to write – I'm thinking, reading books, making notes – but the whole thing never takes less than eighteen months. Once you've finished you feel completely bereft, totally lost, miserable and hellish, and you think, 'I'll never write another book!' I felt quite drained after _Alchemy_, particularly because it's a big book and quite dense. I'm only now ruminating on the next one.

Both characters encounter gender prejudice. Do you think much has changed? Do women like Jade still come up against such prejudice?
At the moment, yes. One always hopes it will change, really change, but I saw an article just recently about how few top lawyers ▶

> 6 I love doing plays – they're much faster to write and you're also working with people. There's a wonderful moment when you go to the read-through and it works! It's so good to witness your work coming alive. 9

◄ are women. The police and publishing are better; they've changed a lot. From time to time I do a head count in the pages of the *Guardian Review*, and of course the number of men who are reviewed, and are reviewed by men, still enormously outweighs the number of women. Women are reviewed by women, ethnics are reviewed by ethnics . . . it drives me mad. I feel very equivocal about the Orange Prize; it shouldn't be necessary, but unfortunately it is, because again and again the lists and judges are male-dominated. When I was much younger I would have imagined that by now the genders would be level-pegging, and they're not.

> 6 Our lives are pretty regimented and dull in many ways. It's all very nice and comfortable but there is a loss of imaginative food, a loss of contact with the real and the concrete. So people need a sort of compensation, to be transported into something which is not immediately familiar but can feed the imagination. 9

Many of your novels and plays deal with sexuality, particularly homosexuality, and yet you are not known as a gay writer. Do you think such distinctions and names are helpful or a hindrance, and are they necessary any more?
I don't think they're necessary and I don't think they're helpful. I'd much rather people just came to you as a writer. Sometimes you're exploring the experience of gay characters and sometimes you're exploring the experience of straight characters. It was necessary when I wrote my third novel, *The Microcosm,* in the sixties because since *The Well of Loneliness* there hadn't been a full-blown treatment of female homosexuality but, having done what I thought was an exploration then, I feel that such distinctions shouldn't be necessary in 2005. You write about what you

want to write about; sometimes it's one thing and sometimes it's another.

Historical fiction is very in vogue. Why do you think that is?
Our lives are pretty regimented and dull in many ways. It's all very nice and comfortable – the dishwasher does the dirty work – but there is a loss of imaginative food, a loss of contact with the real and the concrete. So people need a sort of compensation, to be transported into something which is not immediately familiar but can feed the imagination.

What has been the most satisfying part of your career?
I love doing plays – they're much faster to write and you're also working with people. There's a wonderful moment when you go to the read-through and it works! It's so good to witness your work coming alive. A real high was having my play *Rites* produced at the National Theatre – which was still at the Old Vic at the time – to go in there and see my play, that was great.

Who are your influences as a writer?
Oh, there are masses. Lots of poets – John Donne, Gerard Manley Hopkins, Milton, John Keats – he was my childhood hero – I was going to be John Keats! James Joyce and Joyce Cary – who is brilliant at interior monologue but is rather out of fashion now – then there was a whole clutch of American writers, especially Steinbeck when I was younger. Sartre, de Beauvoir, Genet and ▶

LIFE AT A GLANCE

BORN
1933, the year Hitler came to power and the Loch Ness monster was seen.

EDUCATED
State schools – Trowbridge High School for Girls, the Sarah Bonnell School, Stratford, and King's College, London

CAREER
Poet, playwright, novelist and screenwriter. Works for various societies including the Copyright Licensing Agency and the Authors' Licensing and Collection Society. President of the European Writers' Congress and the British Copyright Council.

LIVES
London

From Accident to Experience *(continued)*

◀ Violette LeDuc were all extremely important too. But you begin to forget who was important to you because you move on.

Are there any books that you wish you had written?
The whole of Shakespeare!

What do you do when you're not writing?
I do copyright work for the British Copyright Council, the Authors' Licensing and Collecting Society and the Copyright Licensing Agency, among others. If you can improve conditions for writers, for example by encouraging the government of Hungary to set up a public lending right scheme, it is very satisfying. And I like to garden when I can. I find that very therapeutic. ■

A Writing Life

When do you write?
In the morning.

Where do you write?
Sitting in an armchair.

Why do you write?
Because I must.

Pen or computer?
Pen and notebooks.

Silence or music?
Silence.

How do you start a book?
An idea comes.

And finish?
Last sentence.

Do you have any writing rituals or superstitions?
The biro and the notebook are a ritual. I have to have the connection down through the hand, so it's all longhand. And I can't write at a desk; I have to be in a comfortable chair. Someone else types it up: I thought if I learnt to type someone would say you must go and work in an office. I hate typing.

What or who inspires you?
I don't know where it comes from, it just sort of comes. I have an image of something suddenly, then that accretes. ▶

A Writing Life *(continued)*

◄ **If you weren't a writer what job would you do?**
I would probably be an archaeologist. I love digging and delving and reconstructing the past.

What's your guilty reading pleasure? Favourite trashy read?
I read the papers and watch telly, especially *Time Team*.

The Alchemy of Words

By Maureen Duffy

Like most writers, I'm often asked how I get my ideas for books; how do they come to me? Mostly they begin with an image of someone in a setting that's a bit blurry round the edges. I carry this about in my head for weeks, sometimes for months, like a faded photograph that, in the opposite of the usual direction from life, gradually becomes stronger, the image more coloured, more solid. The person gets a name, a present, some past, the beginning of a future which is a plot. I begin to write a note or two in a new spiral notebook, opaque notes that sound like nothing to anyone but me, a notebook that I am suddenly obsessively attached to and carry around with me everywhere. The journey, the process has begun, somewhere in a part of the brain Freud called the unconscious, bubbling away on its own like magma under the earth's crust, a process that can't be hurried by merely conscious thought.

So what was the image that came to me as the start of *Alchemy*? It was of a young woman in black leathers on a motorbike. I thought it was based on the niece of one of my closest friends, but he says it wasn't, that she never rode a motorbike. Did I make it up then? Anyway there she was, a lawyer, like my friend's niece, but further into her career, independent, with her own struggling law firm, Lost Causes. And her name, suddenly, was Jade Green, an echo of her own wry sense of humour and of a girl skilled in the martial arts, Jade from China.

And Amyntas? Because images can be sparked by literature as well as life, and ▶

The Alchemy of Words *(continued)*

◄ behind every book stands a line of other books like the ghosts that haunted Macbeth, s/he sidestepped out of *All's Well That Ends Well*, via Sir Philip Sidney's romance *Arcadia*, with its jousting ladies in armour, bringing her Sidney connections with her, and the charge of witchcraft, in an age when alchemy was transmuting into science.

Witchcraft in its various manifestations as part of the body of English folklore has interested me ever since my dancing and singing years in the heyday of the post-war revival of English traditional music in my teens. Twenty years later I combined this interest with a largely Freudian interpretation of the supernatural in literature, beginning with the remnants of Celtic paganism and ending, for the time being at least (pre *Dr Who* and *Star Trek*), with the science fiction creations of Isaac Asimov, bottling up this collection of genies in my first non-fiction book, *The Erotic World of Faery* (1972), published in one of those recurring periods when critics and publishers announce that the novel is dead.

As so often in writing, the tap root for *Alchemy* goes back a very long way and even deeper into childhood stories like *Puck of Pook's Hill*, or films like *The Thief of Baghdad*, or deeper still to a nightmare about a witch standing on one side of a blackly gleaming coalfield while I watched paralysed as she laughingly pointed her wand at the edge and shrank the whole mass to one small knob. Those were the years of coal rationing.

I knew that in *Alchemy* I wanted to write about the bigotry and fanaticism which seem

❛ Mostly my ideas for books begin with an image of someone in a setting that's a bit blurry round the edges. I carry this about in my head for weeks, sometimes for months, like a faded photograph that, in the opposite of the usual direction from life, gradually becomes stronger. ❜

to be on the increase at this cusp of the twentieth and twenty-first centuries. Both Amyntas and Jade come up against the glass ceiling for women of their time. Today, a century after the struggles of the Suffragettes, there are still very few women in the top echelons of the legal profession, and in the early seventeenth century it was hard for any woman, unless she was a queen, to pursue any profession, let alone as a physician. Those who did were usually midwives or 'cunning women' who ran the risk of being labelled witches.

Fiction, especially historical fiction, requires a lot of research to make it convincing to the reader. For the kind of medicine that would have been available to Amyntas to practise I used Nicholas Culpeper's *Complete Herbal*, published in 1653, which includes many earlier prescriptions, some from the Sidney household itself. Please don't try them at home. For Jade's legal expertise I drew on my own experiences in pursuit of authors' rights. I had to create two distinctive voices as well so that the reader would know at once whether it was 1603 or 2003.

My two protagonists are both brought up against the fundamentalisms of their time, whether Christian or other, either as a clinging to tablets of stone or the pursuit of strange cults and sects, a resurgence of flat-earthism, a refusal to accept rational and scientific explanations of the universe and our place in it, and the evocation of mass hysteria or self-hypnosis, often these days induced by unscrupulous preachers, ▶

❝ In *Alchemy* I wanted to write about the bigotry and fanaticism which seem to be on the increase at this cusp of the twentieth and twenty-first centuries. ❞

13

The Alchemy of Words *(continued)*

◄ through the media of television and the internet.

Against these forces they both oppose the equally irrational alchemy of love in all its transmutations, the creative force of nature necessary for renewal and for life to go on, the only power that can put out death if only for a time. And when love fails, as Amyntas and Jade learn, there's always work, the 'old toad', to 'help us down cemetery road'. ■

Have You Read?

Other books by Maureen Duffy include:

That's How It Was

Maureen Duffy's first novel, originally
published in the sixties, is the story of Paddy, a
young working-class girl growing up in
wartime England. Abandoned by her father,
Paddy is brought up by her mother, and their
relationship is at the heart of the story.

The Microcosm

A collection of different voices, characters
and time periods cross the threshold of a
lesbian bar in London, providing a candid
and lively depiction of what it means to be a
gay woman.

Restitution

Betony Falk, a young woman in her late
twenties, was brought up by her grandmother
after the death of her parents. Between jobs
she decides to find out more about her father
and thus herself. However, she soon realizes
that the more she finds out the less she knows.

The Passionate Shepherdess: The Life of
Aphra Behn 1640–89

A biography of the Restoration dramatist,
now considered one of the greatest and first
female artists.

If You Loved This,
You Might Like . . .

Fingersmith
Sarah Waters

The French Lieutenant's Woman
John Fowles

The Countess of Pembroke's Arcadia
Sir Philip Sidney

The Chymical Wedding
Lindsay Clarke

The Daughter of Time
Josephine Tey

Waterland
Graham Swift

A Place of Greater Safety
Hilary Mantel

Possession
A.S. Byatt

The Red Queen
Margaret Drabble

Slammerkin
Emma Donoghue